The Doom of Odin

ALSO BY SCOTT ODEN

Twilight of the Gods
A Gathering of Ravens
Men of Bronze
Memnon
The Lion of Cairo

The Doom of Odin

SCOTT ODEN

ST. MARTIN'S PRESS
NEW YORK

This is a work of fiction. All of the characters, organizations, and events portrayed in this novel are either products of the author's imagination or are used fictitiously.

First published in the United States by St. Martin's Press, an imprint of St. Martin's Publishing Group

THE DOOM OF ODIN. Copyright © 2023 by Scott Oden. All rights reserved. Printed in the United States of America. For information, address St. Martin's Publishing Group, 120 Broadway, New York, NY 10271.

www.stmartins.com

Map of Rome by Mario Cartaro

Library of Congress Cataloging-in-Publication Data

Names: Oden, Scott, author.
Title: The doom of Odin / Scott Oden.
Description: First edition. | New York : St. Martin's Press, 2023. |
  Series: Grimnir series ; 3
Identifiers: LCCN 2023031037 | ISBN 9780312372965 (hardcover) |
  ISBN 9781250022905 (ebook)
Subjects: LCSH: Mythology, Norse—Fiction. | LCGFT: Fantasy fiction. | Novels.
Classification: LCC PS3615.D465 D66 2023 | DDC 813/.6—dc23/eng/20230703
LC record available at https://lccn.loc.gov/2023031037

Our books may be purchased in bulk for promotional, educational, or business use. Please contact your local bookseller or the Macmillan Corporate and Premium Sales Department at 1-800-221-7945, extension 5442, or by email at MacmillanSpecialMarkets@macmillan.com.

First Edition: 2023

10 9 8 7 6 5 4 3 2 1

For my sister, Sara Lee, and for her son, Cody:
Gæð a wyrd swa hio scel.

It was so long ago and far away
I have forgotten the very name men called me.
The axe and flint-tipped spear are like a dream,
And hunts and wars are like shadows. I recall
Only the stillness of that sombre land;
The clouds that piled forever on the hills,
The dimness of the everlasting woods.

—Robert E. Howard, "Cimmeria"

And so the Shaper of Men has laid this middle-earth to waste
until the ancient work of giants stood empty,
devoid of the revelry of their citizens.

—"The Wanderer" (Hostetter translation)

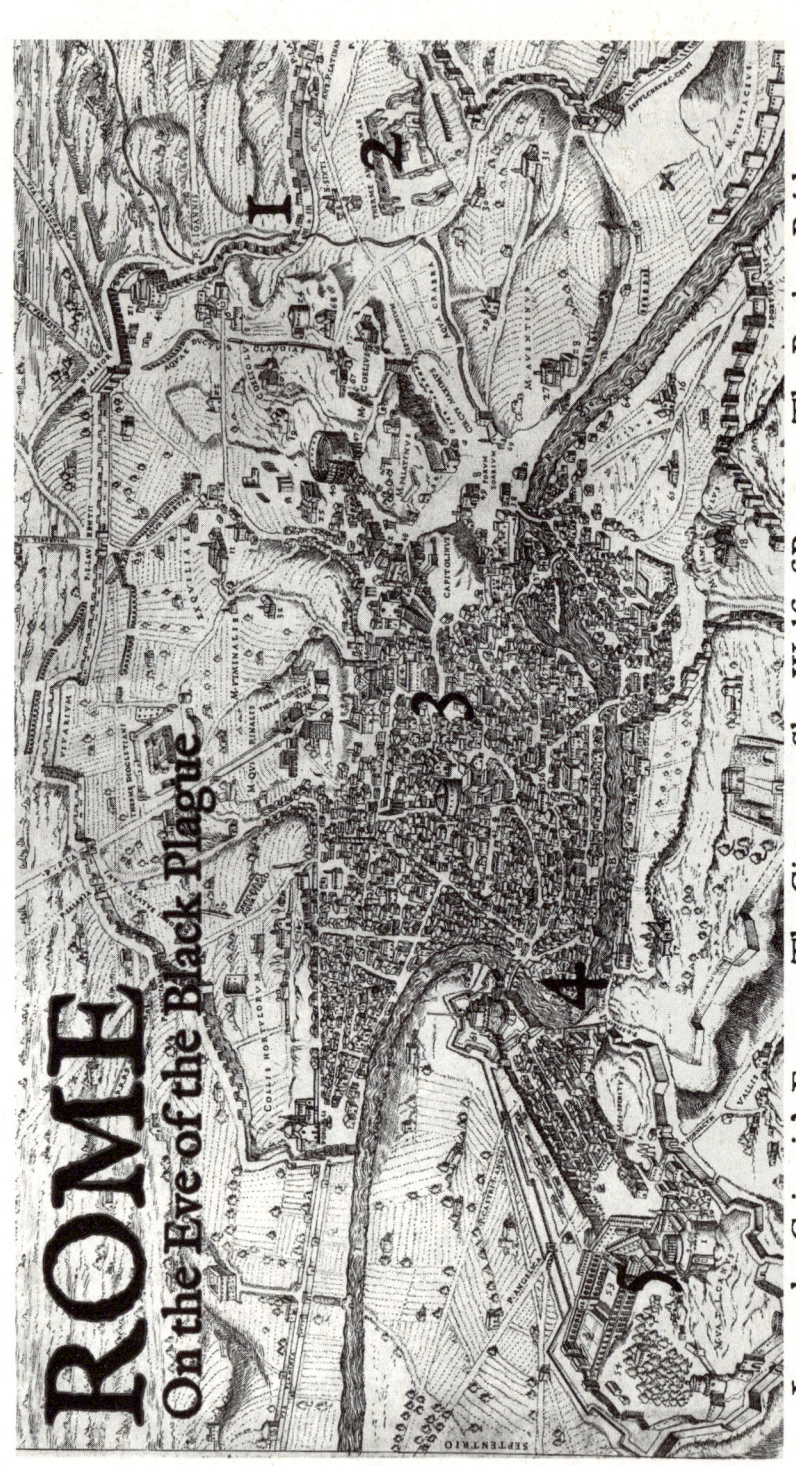

Legend: 1 Grimnir's Entry; 2 The Cistern; 3 She-Wolf of Rome; 4 The Broken Bridge; 5 Old Saint Peter's Basilica.

NÁSTROND
On the Eve of Ragnarök

- Kaunheimr
- The Undired
- Skrælingsalr
- Jardvegur
- Gjöll's Inlet
- Snaga's Beach
- The Bone Ferry
- Lokaean Witches
- Úlfsstadir

The Doom of Odin

I
NÁSTROND

The figure struggled against the water's embrace; he thrashed as the cold undertow sucked him deeper into darkness. He tasted bitter salts and ash, as though from burned driftwood. His tattered mail, his heavy boots, his leather weapons belt ... these things did nothing to help him against the grasping fingers of the *sjóvættir* who pulled at his legs. He could see them, these spirits of freshet and fjord, like smudges of corpse-pale flesh in the depths below; their eyes were black sockets, and hair floated like lake grass around skeletal faces. He could hear their whispered songs:

> *"Child of Angrboða's folly,*
> *Filth-born skrælingr,*
> *Why do you fight*
> *Dark Gjöll's embrace?*

> *"Or is Christ-haunted Miðgarðr*
> *So dear to your black heart?*

> *"Keep from the surface,*
> *Sweet son of Bálegyr,*

*And let our thralls ride you
Like Svaðilfari!"*

Their mockery, their laughter—like the burbles of air escaping the lips of drowning men—kindled something hot and raw in the figure's breast. He bared jagged yellow teeth, jaws clenched against the water; his single red eye flared in the gloom. Legs knotted with muscle kicked against the undertow. They thought they knew hate, these *sjóvættir*? They thought they knew fury? *Nár!* He would show these filthy spirits what such words meant! He clawed for the surface.

Skrælingr, they called him. *Son of Bálegyr.* Yes, he was these things. He remembered, now. He was these things and much more, besides. In his veins ran the hot blood of Angrboða and the cold ichor of Father Loki, but Ymir—the Lord of Frosts—was his people's sire. He was *kaunr*. He was Grimnir.

Grimnir.

Like the meeting of flint and steel over a cold bed of embers, the names clashed and sparked, igniting the edges of the darkness muffling his mind.

Grimnir.

Son of Bálegyr.

Skrælingr.

Kaunr.

And through that smoldering cerecloth came the ghosts of memory . . .

An ancient ruin in the heart of a marsh, blackened and rotting. Domes of old marble cover shrines to heretic gods and forgotten nymphs. He sidles up the crumbling road—a road verged by sedge grass and gnarled cypress; he keeps to the shadows, the gloom thickening as the sun sinks into the west. Hobnailed boots crunch old Roman stone.

Ahead, he spots those who defend his quarry: a dozen thin and wasted figures—mailed mercenaries leaning on heavy spears; arbalesters with their crossbows shouldered. The Company of the Sickle, they are called. Weak-minded fools! They are the wyrm's thralls, and they stand between him and his foe, the dragon Níðhöggr, the cursed Malice-Striker. For that they must die.

They guard a strange conveyance: a pageant wagon with a broken axle, a gaudy ship on wheels meant for the court of the Nailed God's earthly chieftain, the so-called Pope. The beast's hiding place.

THE DOOM OF ODIN

"Spread your men out," a voice says. A eunuch's voice, thin and reedy—the priest from Messina, black-cassocked and filthy. "That devil is still out there."

The man who answers is a giant, his frame shrouded in a mail haubergeon and a coat-of-plates; he has a patrician nose and eyes that have seen death. "Devil?" he replies, scoffing. "I'll bugger your devil, priest! He is nothing! Do you hear me? Nothing! A milk-livered whore's son!"

Grimnir hisses at the challenge, his single eye alight with rage. He draws his long-seax with a mirthless smile . . .

Grimnir kicked and struggled; without warning, his foot touched solid ground, rocky and thick with silt. He thrust himself forward until his head broke the surface. He coughed; spluttering, he took in great lungfuls of acrid air.

He strikes with the onset of twilight, as the sun slips over the rim of the world. He strikes even as a fire is kindled in the weed-choked plaza, whose stones were laid in the time of the Caesars. Old wood crackles; embers drift up into the cold November air.

His first victim turns away from watching the dancing motes of cinder. He is young, barely beyond the cusp of manhood, with jaundiced, pox-scarred features and watery blue eyes. His last vision this side of the grave is of a burning eye wrapped in shadow; he opens his mouth to shout . . . and dies with Grimnir's long-seax wedged in his gullet. He crumples, choking on bloody froth.

Screams erupt. Cries of warning.

And the shadow that is Grimnir moves among them, reaping a red harvest. Their mail is useless; their spears and their crossbows only hamper them, their muscles wasted from the disease the wyrm's jaws exude—the same disease that burned through Messina a fortnight ago. They move too slow. Their shrieks and cries spark laughter in him; steel rasps on steel; iron punches through flesh, and the half a dozen mercenaries who remain standing scatter.

Their giant leader comes for him, but Grimnir gives him no respite. The blade of his long-seax flickers out, quick as a striking serpent. Only a sharp sideways lunge saves the man from a split skull; nevertheless, he roars in pain as the edge of Grimnir's blade shears through the gristle of his ear. Laughing, Grimnir rams his shoulder up and into the man's belly, driving him off his feet and pitching him back to snarl the legs of the squawking priest.

The way forward is open; the wyrm, Níðhöggr, is in his grasp. He reaches out with one black-nailed claw and rips the door at the rear of the pageant wagon off its hinges . . .

Grimnir dragged himself across knife-edged rocks, slippery with muck. He gagged and spat, retching up a stomachful of acidic water. Around him, reeds rustled in a warm wind—a wind that reeked of smoke and ash, charred meat and scorched metal, like the breeze off a killing field.

The blow that kills him . . .

"Am I dead?" His voice profaned the silence.

The blow that kills him comes from inside the wagon. From a sickly arbalester, too riddled with weeping sores and buboes to walk; his eyes go wide with terror at the sight of this blood-drenched ogre, murder dancing in its one gleaming eye. The dying mercenary's sweat-slick hand grips too tight the carved oak stock of his weapon. He screams, eyes screwing shut against the coming of oblivion. Two fingers convulse around the triggering mechanism. The flat crack of the crossbow is only barely heard. Grimnir feels it as a fist to his sternum. He reels away. The bolt enters his chest at an upward angle, its diamond-shaped iron head punching through mail and leather and splitting the bone beneath. He staggers from the wagon, incredulous.

The first bolt is a fluke, yes. But the second is sent flying by some bastard opportunist who sees an opening, a chance to make a name for himself. He hears a cry of alarm, hears the thump of release as it, too, tears through mail and muscle and lodges in the meat of Grimnir's heart. For a moment, he feels an icy wind, laden with smoke and blood.

Grimnir, son of Bálegyr—skrælingr; kaunr—teeters. His heels find the mud-slick edge of the canal; he slips and topples back into the marsh . . .

He caught himself on his balled fists before he could fall face-first into the shallows. A faint reflection in the water stared up at him, backlit by a sky the color of banked embers. "Am I dead?" he roared, his hot breath sending ripples across the shadowy visage.

It was a face familiar to him, this reflection: a broad forehead, heavy brow, prominent cheekbones descending to a hard pointed chin; an old scar bisected the left side of his face, running from the bridge of his nose, through his left eye, and into his hairline at the temple. That eye was cold and dead, an orb of carved bone, inlaid with silver. Thin lips curled into a sneer over yellowed fangs.

Through a veil of stringy hair as black as night—woven throughout with worn discs of bone, beads of scrimshaw, silver, and amber, and still-bright cylinders of gold, heavy and ancient—his right eye burned as hot and red as a forge-glede. He tossed his head back and loosed an inarticulate roar. "Answer me, you dunghill rat! Am I dead?" No answer came from his watery reflection. "*Faugh!*"

Grimnir spat; he pushed himself up and sat back on his haunches. Black-nailed fingers searched through sodden cloth and mail for the leather-vaned ends of a pair of crossbow bolts. He found nothing. Grimnir drew breath, exhaled, and felt no pain in the keel bones of his chest. His heart was whole. But was he dead? That was the question. Staggering to his feet, he waded ashore.

Whatever had befallen him, he was certain he was no longer in old Langbarðaland—the place those miserable hymn-singers called Italy; no, the landscape around him was rocky and deserted, like the coast of Lake Vänern in the land of the Swedes. And, it was utterly silent, but for the soft lapping of waves on the rocks and the rustle of the wind. No insects chattered in the marshy verge where the reeds grew thick; no birds arose in calamitous warning at his coming. The place was as silent as the grave.

Under a sky bereft of moon and stars, under thick scudding clouds lit from behind by some half-hinted cosmic conflagration, Grimnir beheld an unbroken rampart of trees before him, thick and primeval, rising up from the edge of the lake. Most were black pine, though he spied the spreading boughs of ancient ash and willow among them. He expected to see ferns in plenty, bracken and ivy; instead, he saw naked thorn and stinging nettle and other plants, as well. Here, wolfsbane grew alongside pale snakeroot; there, deadly nightshade flourished with hellebore, larkspur with yellow oleander, and hemlock in profusion. Enough poisons to kill every cross-kisser in Langbarðaland a dozen times over, and none of it lethal to him.

No, this was not old Italy.

Whipcord-thin, Grimnir prowled along like a starveling wolf who hungered for hot blood and the choicest cuts of flesh. His arms were long, knotty with gristle and sinew; his coarse skin was the color of old shale, veined by scars and tattooed in cinder and woad. He was clad in the same war-rags he'd worn before. His hobnailed boots were soaked through; his trousers and gambeson, too. His mail hauberk, taken off a dead Turk at Caffa, in the Crimea, and cut down to fit, had steel links threaded with silver that gleamed in the twilight. Of silver, too, were the fittings on his weapons belt. A short bearded axe rode his right hip; on his left, the carved bone hilt of his long-seax jutted from its gilt-worked scabbard. The long-seax, called Hátr—Hate—had at its heart the shards of Sárklungr, the Wound-Thorn, forged by the *dvergar* when the world was young.

Grimnir stopped suddenly, brought up short by something more than the absence of noise. He looked down. It took a moment for him to puzzle it out. When he did, though, a wicked half-smile twisted the corners of his thin lips. His bones no longer ached. In Rome—and, indeed, in every quarter of Miðgarðr poisoned by the Nailed God's influence—Grimnir's existence was marred by constant pain. It seeped up from the ground, plaguing his shins before moving into his hips and spine: the sensation of iron nails being dragged across bone, of razor-tipped whips scourging his flesh. It diminished him, sapped his strength, and threatened to sever his last connections to the Elder World and the sorcery of the ancient gods.

And now it was gone, as was the stench he'd come to associate with the lifeless nature of the hymn-singers' god: the smell of iron boiled in brine.

Grimnir flexed the fingers of his blade hand. His muscles and sinews felt reborn, brimming with power. And he could smell blood on the wind, coppery-sweet and freshly spilled. He flared his nostrils and let his head tilt back as he reveled in it . . . all while realizing it did not bode well. This place reminded him of something, some scrap of doggerel old Gífr used to spout. How did it go?

"*I know a hall standing far from the sun . . .*" Grimnir muttered. The rest of the verse fled as sounds intruded upon his reverie—the rattle of a dislodged rock, a soft hiss, and the faintest clash of bone, as though from a bracelet or beads. He leveled his gaze, his good eye sweeping the tree line to his left. Something or someone was trying to get the drop on him; his hand fell to the hilt of Hátr.

"*Nár!* Leave off your sneakery and show yourself, you wretch," Grimnir roared. "And if you mean to try and slice a hank off my hide, then get on with it!"

For a long moment, there was nothing but the echo of Grimnir's challenge. Then: "Don't go and get your innards in a twist," someone answered, in a voice still a few years shy of maturity. "We're just curious, is all."

Grimnir hid his surprise at the sight of a pair of young *kaunar* rising up from behind the trunk of a fallen tree, just inside the eaves of the wood. The one who spoke was a thin scrap of a lad, nearly Grimnir's equal in height but lacking any weight—a mannikin of dark jaundiced skin stretched over sharp bones, decorated with cracked white sigils painted in lime. White, too, was the skull painted across the youth's red-eyed face, which hid a patchwork of old scars; his stringy black hair was pulled into a topknot, tied with leather thongs, and hung with raven feathers. A necklace of finger bones clattered against his hollow chest. Grimnir did not miss the stone-bladed axe that the lad tried to keep out of sight.

"Curious, eh?"

His companion was short and stout, with long arms and spindly legs already bowing outward. This one had a blunt face with a bulbous nose, fleshy lips, and a protruding tongue. The little rat had only half a head of black hair; the left side he kept shaved, revealing crude tattoos in a half-moon over his ear. He was clad in piecemeal rags and scraps of fur, lashed together with sinew and dried gut, with a collection of pouches and tied bags hanging from his makeshift belt. He leaned heavily on a staff of flame-charred ash, reinforced with iron straps and set with rusting nails.

The tall one nodded. "Aye. Been an age since we saw a fish flopping around in the shallows. Thought there might be something in it for us."

Grimnir eyed them. "You know what they say about curiosity." Quick as a snake, he drew Hátr and leveled the long-seax at a third *kaunr* youth who had tried approaching from his blind side. The blade stopped an inch from the nose of the urchin, who recoiled but refused to back away. "It'll get you killed." Grimnir motioned with the tip of the blade. "Get over there with your mates, you dunghill rat."

The head of the third youth—the smallest of the three—came barely up to Grimnir's chest. Barefooted as the youth was, clad in a long and shapeless sack of patched burlap, Grimnir could not discern if it was male or female. Nor did it matter. Lank black hair covered its face, save for its bright-gleaming eyes, and gave it an eerie aspect, like a wraith who meant to bleed him dry with the two thin-bladed knives it clutched in its small hands.

"Move, you!" Grimnir snarled.

Grudgingly, it did as it was told.

"Well, fancy that," Grimnir said, sizing up the trio. Steel rasped on leather as he slid Hátr back into its scabbard. "Three little *skrælingar*, pretty as you please. Thought you'd catch me off guard, eh? Answer me this and there still might be something in it for you: What is this place called?"

The tall one looked at his mates, then back at Grimnir. "You're having a laugh at us, ain't you? Bah! You're where the dead go, friend."

And, like that, the verse Gífr used to sing came back to him. He said:

> "I know a hall standing | far from the sun,
> In Nástrond, under the | shadows of Niðafjoll;
> War-reek rages | and reddening fire:
> The high heat licks | against heaven itself."

"Don't know nothing about all of that," the tall youth replied. "But you and us, we got a different problem."

Grimnir's lip curled into a snarl. "Aye, the problem is, if I'm standing here, that means those sons of whores I hounded up from Sicily got me, after all. *Faugh!* I was this close! *This* close to seeing that blasted wyrm get its comeuppance!" Grimnir's jaw clamped in frustration.

The tall lad frowned, white paint crinkling across his forehead. "That problem ain't ours, either. Listen good, long-tooth. Problem is, this is our beach. And you're trespassing on it."

"Your beach, is it?" Though Grimnir chuckled, the lights of murder danced in the depths of his eye. "What are you going to do? Kick me off? Ha! You cheeky little git! I might take a shine to this beach and make it my own."

The tall youth started forward, axe rising. "Piss off, you shit-heel! This stretch of beach is ours, fair and square! We earned it fighting for Njól's crew, and Dreki's! And if you ain't got our leave to be here, then you're trespassing! Who are you? One of Gangr's boys?" The youth hawked and spat. "That old piss-bucket, he's always trying to get one over on us!"

"I'm no one's *boy,* filth!" Grimnir snarled. "And tell that fat one if he keeps hopping around, I'm going to rip him open and make his guts into sausage!" True enough, the stout lad was shifting his weight from foot to foot, all the while trying to pluck at his mate's elbow, to get his attention without daring to touch him.

"Snaga," he muttered, barely loud enough to be heard. "Snaga!"

The youth rounded on him. "What, Blártunga? Spit it out, you useless bag of suet!"

The fat one, Blártunga, mumbled his apologies, grabbed his mate's narrow shoulder, and dragged him down where he could whisper something in his ear. After a moment, the tall one—whose name Grimnir took to be Snaga, "Snag-axe" in the tongue of their people—straightened. Under the mask of white paint, Snaga's face grew sallow. "Interesting," he said, looking askance at the third member of their little trio, who sat on the fallen log with its legs crossed, creating an annoying susurration by scraping the backs of its knives together. "That's very interesting. Blártunga, here, thinks we might have gotten off on the wrong foot. He says he's heard there's only one of us left in the world out yonder," he gestured haphazardly at the sky, where clouds hid a great burning; bursts of red, orange, yellow, and green radiance sent rippling shadows across the somber landscape of Nástrond. "One who's sworn to hunt down the wyrm, that old Malice-Striker. And that *you* must be him. You're Grimnir."

The little one stopped scraping its knives together; it glanced up. Blártunga stood a ways back, cowering in Snaga's thin shadow. Grimnir reveled in the scent of their fear. To his credit, though, Snaga met his gaze without flinching. His eyes were sharp, calculating. Grimnir bared his yellowed fangs. "And what if I am? What is it about that name that would make you lot change your tune, eh? What have you heard?"

"Oh, we heard he's a good lad," Snaga replied. "A trusty lad. That one we'd give leave to cross our land. Even offer him meat and ale, if he had a mind to sit a spell."

Grimnir looked around. He looked at the bleak shore, the leaden water, the night-dark woods. He was dead, and this was his reward, his afterlife. Until the Gjallarhorn blew the death-note that kindled Ragnarök, the Last War and the Twilight of the Gods, *this* was what he was in for. He had kinfolk out there, somewhere; some of them might even be glad to see him. And he surely did not want to come before them for the first time in centuries looking like a bedraggled tramp fished from the water by a pack of urchins.

"*Nár!* Why not?" Grimnir spat. "You little rats scrounge up a fire, will you? We might as well dry out my war-rags if all we're going to do is wag our chins and swill."

FLAMES CRACKLED. Embers burst forth from the heart of the fire, burning like minuscule stars as they spiraled into the perpetual twilight to dance on drafts and eddies of air until they died in darkness. Grimnir caught one smoldering mote between his fingertips and snuffed the brightness from it. He flicked the dead cinder away.

The meat they'd eaten had been pork, the ale passable; now, with a full belly, the son of Bálegyr turned his attention to his three companions. The runt of the pack, whom the others called Köttr, the Cat, was curled up by the fire, its knives unsheathed and clutched in dirty black-nailed claws. The fat one, Blártunga, was proving himself to be a useful rat, eager and desperate to please. Already, he'd mended a tear in Grimnir's mail with silver wire he'd fished from one of his pouches; now, he whistled tunelessly while he smeared pork fat into the leather of his boots.

Snaga, who seemed in his way older even than Grimnir, watched as the latter spat on the blade of his long-seax, Hátr, and worked a whetstone over its edge. Steel rasped and hissed above the sounds of the fire.

"So, there is no day or night here?" Grimnir said.

Snaga stirred the fire with a stick. "Just this measly half-light. Sometimes the fume and broil from Múspellsheimr thickens the clouds so there is true night for a change. But that's rare as golden arse hairs, as they say."

Grimnir gestured into the sky with his seax. "What is that, then, eh? Is that not the sun, you worm?"

Blártunga chuckled, then fell silent with a guilty glance toward Snaga. The tall lad cracked a rare half-smile. "Ain't no sun down here, long-tooth. That's the light of the Worlds Above, in the branches of the Old Ash."

"Yggðrasil," Grimnir replied.

"Here's another one for you," Snaga said. "Ain't no north or south down here, neither. Nástrond's an island. Sits in the middle of a bleedin' lake; the Well of Hvergelmir feeds the lake, and the lake feeds the River Gjöll. Yonder," the youth pointed with his charred stick at the conflagration that marked ancient Yggðrasil, "we call 'toward the Tree.' The other way is 'toward the Root.' 'Cause there's a root of the Old Ash jutting up like a plateau on that end of the island. There's a line of hills on this side. Other side slopes down to the stinking bog-lands."

Grimnir nodded. "And on that root, that's where the great hall of our people sits, eh?"

Snaga's elusive half-smile returned; beside him, Blártunga snickered. "One of 'em. There's—what is it, now?—four of 'em? And only two are halls, in truth. Lútr's Skrælingsalr, in the hills at the center of the island, and Jarðvegur, the hall of Hrauðnir and his folk, down in the bog-lands. Úlfsstaðir, the Wolves' Abode, is a fortress atop a hill toward the Tree where Bálegyr and Kjallandi rule as equals. The last one, the one that sits atop the Root, is Kaunheimr—now, that's a city, right and proper. Mánavargr rules that one, with the True Sons, those *kaunar* who died fighting the Æsir in the Ironwood. They despise the *skrælingar* who fled that battle and hid away in Miðgarðr. Your old da, most of all."

"Ymir's balls!" Grimnir snarled. "Is nothing that old sot, Gífr, taught me true?"

Snaga shrugged his thin shoulders. "That pretty song you sang, it was written by some poor bastard who never set foot on Nástrond's shore. *That* one ain't never stood on the tip of the island, under the light of the Old Ash, and looked across the water at the cold fences of Helheimr. Or hoofed it up the Thousand Stairs to the top of the Root, the highest point on Nástrond, just to see what goes off toward the Well of Hvergelmir, where the Corpse-River has its head. But, by Ymir, they have now, ain't they?"

Grimnir lapsed into silence. He spat on the blade, and the rasp of steel on stone was renewed. After a moment, he glanced up and said: "Where are your people, eh? Which of these halls do you rats belong to?"

"None of 'em," Snaga replied. "Me and Blártunga, little Köttr, over there, and there's a score or two others . . . we're what you call *scrags*. We're the bottom of the slop heap. Died as brats, we did, and brats we remain. Too small to fight in the line, and none of us want to be thralls, so we're just more useless mouths in their way of thinking. Sometimes, the big lads'll hire us out to kill off a rival, or to bolster their ranks with blade fodder ere they go into battle. Usually, though, we just waylay 'em and take their loot. Or, they hunt us down and kill us like dogs."

Grimnir gave the blade one last pass with the whetstone, then stropped it clean on the thigh of his trousers before sheathing it. He was naked to the waist, his chest a patchwork of scars and tattoos, lean muscle knitting together bone and gnarled gristle. "And when you die, around here? What then?"

Snaga and Blártunga shared a malicious grin. "We're like those *úlfhéðnar*, then, ain't we? Like Odin's little toy warriors, plucked off the battlefield where they died and stuck in that pisshole, Valhǫll! We swill and fight and die, just like them. And just like them, we come back good as new. It ain't no cakewalk, either. You're going to feel the bite of every blade, the kiss of every spearhead and arrow. Being murdered hurts, long-tooth. Don't let those lads in the halls tell you otherwise. You're going to know who did you, and you're going to want to get a little payback when you return, mark my words. But that's our way, ain't it?"

A slow smile spread across Grimnir's lips. He eyed the three of them like a wolf eyes its prey. "Oh, aye, that's our way, little rat. What about food? Who controls the meat and the mead?"

"Listen to you," Snaga said. "You sound like some topside general planning his invasion."

Grimnir leaned forward. "*Faugh!* I like to know where my next meal is coming from, and whose arse I have to kiss to get it! You and your Cat might be savvy enough hunters to rustle a pig or two, but this sad sack," Grimnir jabbed a finger at Blártunga, "doesn't strike me as the ale-making sort. Makes me wonder where you little swine got it, eh?"

Snaga's eyes narrowed. "Sometimes, the big lads will pay us in the sort of vittles we can't catch—especially Lútr's folk at Skrælingsalr. Ale, mead, butter, and cheese. We bring them wild boar and deer, maybe a brace o' rabbits or some bog-chicken, to trade, or else we work it off another way. We *scrags* pick up a lot of chatter and see things we ain't supposed to see, here and there, and we're quick to share it out if it means there's something in it for us."

"*Nár!* Crafty little bastards!" Grimnir took his boots from Blártunga, drew them on, and stood. His gambeson, its once-black quilted cotton rust-stained and still damp in places, hung near the fire. This, too, he donned. "When I get set up in Úlfsstaðir, come find me. I'll have some work for the lot of you, mark my words." The Turkish mail came next. Unlike the hauberks of old, this one Grimnir pulled on like a heavy coat; it had buckles of brass and leather running down its length and plates of enameled bronze reinforcing it in the chest and belly, each one covered in the inscrutable runes of the Saracen East. Over this, he buckled his weapons belt, settling his axe and his long-seax on his hips. "I'll repay your hospitality in kind, by Ymir."

Their first hint that trouble was brewing on the wind came from Köttr, who bolted awake with a hiss. Startled, Blártunga rolled to his feet. Snaga stood, as well. Grimnir eyed Köttr, whose knives glittered in the firelight. The Cat sniffed the air, red eyes blazing. Grimnir caught the scent, too—the sickly-sweet smell of perfume.

"What is it?" Grimnir said.

"He's here, ain't he?" Snaga murmured, glancing Köttr's way. "Skollvaldr?"

The Cat nodded.

And from beyond the fire's light, Grimnir heard a peal of savage laughter …

2
SCRAG-LORD

"Your little pet is good, Snaga," a voice said. "Very good. My father could use a hunter like that. We might be able to come to a price, you and I."

"Köttr's not for sale," Snaga replied. His eyes darted from the Cat to Grimnir and back again.

A figure hove into view. Grimnir saw a tall *kaunr*, as straight-limbed and muscular as a Danish reaver. The newcomer had long black hair, combed and perfumed and held in place with a circlet of hammered iron. He was more sallow than Grimnir, at once haughty and barbaric, and sported a rarity among their people: a short, pointed beard gathered at the ends by a bead of carved bone. He leaned on a heavy spear with a lugged head; mail glittered beneath a rich red cloak.

The newcomer laughed, again. "Everything's for sale, little Snaga." He looked Grimnir up and down, raw disdain curling his lip. "Everything."

"How much for that rag you're wearing, wretch?" Grimnir snarled.

The newcomer made a subtle spitting gesture. "I'll deal with you in a moment, *skrælingr*," he said; to Snaga, he added: "I've come for the gelt, you filthy *scrag*! I told you, my father claims this land. It was given to him by King Mánavargr himself. So, if you and your little band of swine want to live on it, you pay the gelt!"

Though he lacked weight and muscle, Snaga did not lack courage. He drew himself up to his full height and faced the newcomer with a resolute sneer on his lips. "And I told you, Skollvaldr, your precious Mánavargr ain't got no claim on this land, so it ain't his to give! Not to your old da, not to anyone! This stretch is under Lútr's protection! We ain't paying you lot a damned thing!"

Skollvaldr's smile never wavered, Grimnir saw. Even as he moved, his arm launching forward like a spring uncoiling, he had the same condescending smile on his face, framed by that ridiculous beard. His spear lashed out; little Köttr danced aside, but Blártunga—stout Blártunga—was neither as quick nor as lucky. Skollvaldr's broad-headed blade tore through cloth, flesh, and bone; the heavy spear-lug thumped against Blártunga's side, driving him to his knees with a bellow of agony. Before Snaga or Köttr could retaliate, though, Skollvaldr gave the spear a savage twist and drew it back, black blood dripping from its head. He leveled it at the two remaining *scrags*. "Where is that rat Lútr's protection, now? Will he strike me down, as I struck your mate? Ha! Lútr is a worthless *skrælingr*!" Skollvaldr glanced sidelong at Grimnir. "You'd do better to place your trust in a rabid dog."

"How are you called, you blustering ape?" Grimnir said.

Snaga opened his mouth to answer. "This is—"

Grimnir shut him down with a sharp gesture. "I'm not asking you! Name yourself, swine!"

The newcomer squared his shoulders. "You don't deserve my name, *skrælingr*! But I'll play your little game. I am Skollvaldr, son of Gangr of the Three Horns, and I am a prince of Kaunheimr and a captain of the True Sons of Loki!"

Grimnir sniffed. "Is that all?"

"I was on the right flank at Ironwood, you cur! When the Æsir came against us, hot to get their hands on the Tangled God's children, we stood against cursed Thor!"

"And Thor ground you under his boot, did he not? And took our lord's children, anyway?" Grimnir replied, an icy smile twisting his thin lips. "*This* is the source of your pride? You think yourself mighty because you failed the

THE DOOM OF ODIN

charge the Tangled God laid upon you? Because a son of Odin crushed you under heel? *Faugh!*"

Skollvaldr bristled. "Name yourself, then, *skrælingr*, if you think your blood is more pure than mine!"

"*Pure?* Ha!" Grimnir laughed. "Your blood is as black and stinking as any of ours, you oaf! Deeds, not blood, are what sets us apart. As for my names, they are beyond number! Corpse-maker and Life-quencher, I am called; the Bringer of Night, the Son of the Wolf and Brother of the Serpent. The Hooded One, I am, the Tangled God's last immortal herald. The last of Bálegyr's brood to plague Miðgarðr, last to prey on the sons of Adam.

"To the bastards of Langbarðaland, I am *huorco*! Aye, I am *orco* and *ogre*!" Grimnir flung his arms wide. "To the hymn-singers of England, I am *orcnéas*! The cursed Irish would name me *fomoraig*, and to the folk of the North, the Danes and Swedes and the doom-haunted Norse, I am *skrælingr*! To the Kievan Rus and the boyars of Holmgarðr, I am Likho, the Night-Skulker; to the Greeks of Miklagarðr, I am the lord of the *kallikantzaroi*. I am all these things, you milk-blooded swine, and none of them! I am *kaunr*!

"I am the slayer of Hróarr, of Hrothmund of Badon, of Nechtan of the *vestálfar*, of Bjarki Half-Dane, and a thousand more, besides! I walked the branches of Yggðrasil and shook the bones of Ymir! I stood in the shield wall at Chluain Tarbh, outside the walls of Dubhlinn, and on the pitiful ramparts of Hrafnhaugr against the hymn-singers of Konraðr, the Ghost-Wolf of Skara!" Grimnir clenched his black-nailed hand into a fist. "And by this hand was the Malice-Striker—that filth-eating wyrm, Níðhöggr—freed from its prison and loosed upon Miðgarðr! By the hand of Grimnir!"

Slowly, Skollvaldr leaned over; he hawked and spat. "All that, and you're still nothing but a mud-born *skrælingr*! Bah! Who needs the hand of Grimnir? It's the head of Grimnir I'll take to my father! And when we're done with it, we'll wrap a pretty ribbon around it and send it back to your bastard sire!"

Grimnir did not move. He merely chuckled, a humorless sound like rocks scraping together; it echoed across the gray landscape, shadow-striped from the lights of Yggðrasil. "You have to take it first, you whoreson dog. Tread with care, though . . . I'm not some miserable *scrag*!"

Skollvaldr smiled, lips peeling back over jagged teeth. He reached up with his right hand, snatched open the giltwork clasp of his rich red cloak. It fell from his shoulders in a bloody cascade of fabric that drew Grimnir's covetous eye for a single heartbeat. And in that split second, that moment he thought the *skrælingr* distracted, Skollvaldr struck.

His spear swept out in an arc, low and fast, its gory blade whistling; had it connected, it would have severed the muscles and tendons above Grimnir's knees, crippling him from the outset. Skollvaldr could have finished him, then, at his leisure—and sent a message to *scrags* and *skrælingar* alike.

But Grimnir was neither distracted nor some slow-witted brat. He danced back a step, let the spear pass, and drew his blade from its scabbard. He reversed his grip on Hátr, holding the long-seax point down, and dropped to a fighting crouch. His single eye shone with the murder-lights of Hel, alight in the perpetual gloom of Nástrond.

Skollvaldr did not fight like some vile manling. No, he was quick, flashy, full of piss and vinegar. Having missed his mark, he turned the blade's weight and momentum into a spin, bringing the spear shaft up and across his shoulders. Wood scraped mail; by the end of the maneuver, he, too, had sunk into a fighting crouch, with the spear resting across his right shoulder, his right fist clenched around the shaft by his cheek and his left arm extended. He braced the spear loosely between his left thumb and fingers.

His smile never wavered.

Nor did the homicidal glare of Grimnir's gaze.

The *skrælingr* started forward, as though he meant to hurl himself on Skollvaldr's spear. The bearded captain of the True Sons shifted his weight to the right, leaning in to get the best angle for Grimnir's suicidal rush.

Except, there was no rush. Grimnir feinted. Snarling, he reached down, ripped his axe from its moorings on his belt, and threw it underhanded at Skollvaldr's head. The short-hafted bearded axe *thumped* past the bastard's left ear, driving him even more off balance to the right. Skollvaldr's spear dipped; the shaft slipped from the cradle of his left hand. The blade scraped stone . . .

His smile faltered.

And that's when Grimnir struck.

Breath whistling between clenched teeth, he crossed the interval between

THE DOOM OF ODIN

them in two loping strides and launched himself against the taller *kaunr* before he could recover. Grimnir's mailed forearm smashed into the left side of Skollvaldr's head, rocking it even farther to the right. Black blood sprayed from his gashed cheek. The blow exposed the juncture of his neck and shoulder, above the collar of his mail. Sallow flesh gleamed, there, like an invitation, and Grimnir took it.

Grimnir rammed Hátr into the soft hollow formed by the bastard's collarbone. The long-seax bit deep, sawing through the sacks of his lungs to split his black heart in two. In his last moments, ere the undeath of Nástrond claimed him, Skollvaldr, son of Gangr of the Three Horns, felt Grimnir's iron fingers clasp the back of his neck, supporting his weight. He felt Grimnir's hot breath on his lacerated cheek. "Blood doesn't matter, you swine," the *skrælingr* whispered. "Only deeds matter. Remember this when you wake up with a mouth full of dirt, and let it be a lesson." And with that, Grimnir spat in Skollvaldr's eye, ripped Hátr free of his fresh corpse, and let him fall.

The son of Bálegyr stood over his kill. His chest rose and fell; with his good eye, he glanced back at Snaga and Köttr, who knelt beside the dying Blártunga. "Fetch my axe, rat," he growled. "I'm going to send his bastard father a message of my own . . ."

BLÁRTUNGA DIED before Grimnir finished composing his message to Gangr. The lad gave a shudder, mewled around a mouthful of blood, and then was still. Beside him, holding his hand, sat Köttr. Snaga kept to himself by the fire; there was a dark look on the lad's face as he stabbed the glowing heart of the blaze with his charred stick. "He's died more than the rest of us," Snaga said.

Grimnir sat back on his haunches and admired his handiwork. His hands were blood-slimed, black and stinking nearly to the middle of his forearms; sweat dribbled down his nose. He wiped each cheek on the shoulders of his gambeson, the bone and silver fetishes in his hair rustling with the motion. In one hand, the son of Bálegyr cradled his seax. He glanced up from the corpse of Skollvaldr, stripped to the skin, now, and looking pale and pitiful in the perpetual half-light. "You rats should have just sent him on half an hour ago," Grimnir said.

"We got pacts, the lot of us," Snaga replied. The tall *scrag* looked up, frowning at Grimnir. He stood and ambled over to see how the *skrælingr* was getting on. "Swore we ain't going to be the ones who put steel in our mates, not for any reason."

"*Nár!* It's not like he won't be back in a few hours, is it?"

Snaga shook his head. "You ain't going to understand what dying's like here, not till you've been killed a time or two. We're mates, I said, and mates don't shank one of their own."

Grimnir let it drop with a snort of derision.

Snaga looked down at Skollvaldr's head and gave a low whistle of admiration. Grimnir had wrenched the dead *kaunr*'s mouth open and pierced his pallid tongue in two places. Into those lacerations, he'd threaded all of the dead bastard's gold and silver arm rings. That done, he had just finished carving a word into Skollvaldr's brow:

ᚠᚱᚴᚱ

"What's it say?"

Grimnir gave a short bark of laughter. "*Argr*, that is. It can mean lots of things, but old Gangr is going to read it as he sent out a son and got back a daughter. One last bit." Grimnir reached down and took up his bearded axe. He eyed Skollvaldr's neck like a woodsman squaring up a sapling. It took him three swift blows to hew muscle and part sinew, to crunch through vertebrae; the fourth blow separated the head from the body. Grimnir mounted this grisly trophy on Skollvaldr's own spear and handed it to Snaga. "Take him back where he belongs," Grimnir said.

"And if they ask who did this?"

"Tell them." Grimnir snatched up the dead *kaunr*'s tunic and wiped the blood from his hands and forearms. "Tell them it was Grimnir Bálegyr's son who did this! *Faugh!* And tell them to seek me out, if they have a grievance. They can find me at Úlfsstaðir."

Snaga turned his head and looked back at Köttr, who remained by dead Blártunga's side. The tall chief of the *scrags* shifted his gaze, looking up at the severed head before glancing sidelong at Grimnir. There was a glint of malice in the lad's eyes.

THE DOOM OF ODIN

"You want to humble that fool, Skollvaldr, even more?" Snaga said. "Put him in the water, yonder. Ha! Be a sight to see that shit-heel splashing about without a stitch of clothing while all them water-spirits are trying to get a handful of him."

Snaga's suggestion was met first with silence, and then by a howl of laughter. Grimnir nearly doubled over; tears of mirth dampened his eyes. "By Ymir, lad," he said, cuffing his cheeks. "I like the cut of your jib!"

Chuckling to himself, Grimnir wrestled the headless corpse down to the lake's edge. He dragged the body by its feet into the shallows, heedless of the rocks that tore at the flesh of Skollvaldr's back. It floated free, black blood staining the water around the stump of its neck. The languid current of the lake caught it. Already, he could hear the song of the *sjóvættir* as they circled their prey, the lure of flesh and blood proving too great for them to resist.

"Sleep well, you poxy wretch!" Grimnir bid Gangr's son farewell with a rude hand gesture, turned, and waded ashore. Snaga stood under the grisly spear-mounted head of Skollvaldr and watched, an enigmatic smile twisting his white-daubed features. Köttr padded to his side, as silent as its namesake. They watched as Grimnir rinsed blood from his hands, as he dried himself on Skollvaldr's tunic; they watched as he drew on his mail and settled his weapons belt around his lean waist, axe and long-seax in easy reach. And they watched as he swirled the gaudy red cloak around his shoulders and fastened it by its giltwork clasp.

"Split what's left, or leave it for the ravens," Grimnir said, indicating what they'd taken from Skollvaldr's corpse—good mail, an embroidered gambeson, boots, trousers, belts, all with fastenings and fittings of good silver, bone, and heavy gold. He shrugged. "I care not. I'm for Úlfsstaðir."

Snaga nodded in the direction of the Old Ash, its conflagration of lights burning behind the clouds like a world-consuming fire. Shadows striped with green and yellow radiance, with orange and hateful shades of red, swirled before him. "There ain't one single road or trail that will get you there," Snaga said. "But if you head toward the Tree, and keep to the ridgelines and hilltops as much as you can, you'll get there, soon enough. Fair warning, mate: the vales and deeps 'tween here and yonder got a queer air about 'em. Makes my skin crawl, it does. I think we ain't the first or the only folk to call Nástrond home."

Grimnir nodded. He jabbed a thumb at the severed head. "Take that swine home, and I'll see you in Úlfsstaðir." And with that, the son of Bálegyr headed inland, in the direction of that light-wreathed titan, Yggðrasil.

SNAGA SQUATTED on his haunches. He let the air of youthful guile he cultivated around long-toothed swine like *that* one slough away. Behind the white-daubed skull mask, cruel eyes glittered like knife points as he watched Grimnir vanish into the dark forest. "Grimnir the fierce," he muttered, speaking the tongue of his native folk, the *dvergar* of Svartálfaheimr. "Grimnir the bold. Grimnir the fool!"

"You did not tell him what he has done," Köttr said. The Cat spoke in a low, throat-cut hiss—a feminine voice; the voice of a girl still shy of womanhood who had died on a stone altar, under the blade of a *kaunr* witch.

"No," Snaga replied, glancing up at Skollvaldr's severed head. "There'd be nothing in it for us if I'd told him."

"What now? We wait for Blártunga?"

Snaga nodded. "We wait. And then we're going to deliver that fool's message—along with a message of our own."

AWAY FROM the leaden waters of Lake Gjöll, Nástrond became a land of shadowed vales and rocky scarps, where shoals of mist drifted under black pines; gnarled and leafless ash trees strained toward the cloud-veiled lights of their sire, great Yggðrasil. Faint paths threaded through the undergrowth, some fresh, others barely visible even to his keen eye. Grimnir followed the paths that kept him near the crests of ridge-backed hills.

Time had no meaning. An hour? A day? Who could say. Here, at the roots of the Nine Worlds, the faint light of the Old Ash never wavered, never moved. And while Grimnir's loping stride ate up the miles, the landscape never lost its *sameness*. Stone and scree, branch and bole, one identical to another. Shadows flitted around him, and in their shapes and guises he could see suggestions of the world he'd left, of Langbarðaland—old Italy—in the realm of Miðgarðr, of the ancient empire of Rúmaborg—Rome—with its domes and arches, its crumbling monuments and eternal roads. Rome, which had become the heart of the Nailed God's kingdom on earth.

THE DOOM OF ODIN

Grimnir spat.

For nigh upon one hundred and thirty years, he'd chased that shabby sack of scales, Níðhöggr, the thrice-cursed Malice-Striker, from the cold shores of Lake Vänern to the fly-ridden marshes along the Appian Way. There were a thousand places where it could have hidden along that long road. A thousand bolt-holes where it could have lain low for a generation. The bastard needed blood, though. It needed hot, reeking gore to reknit its muscle and its sinews, to restore its ancient scales. And it was canny about it. It took Grimnir ten years, alone, just to find its trail because it wasn't hiding in the wilds, feeding on sheep and cattle as it had in Raðbolg's day. *Nár!* It slipped into villages and towns by the dark of the moon; it slithered under slate-roofed houses and into the undercrofts of the Nailed God's churches. It found men with weak wills and forced them to do its bidding, to bring it sacrifices—their sons and daughters, wives and mothers. The Malice-Striker made these slavish thralls watch while it drained their kin of blood, tore their flesh from their bones, and sucked the marrow from their skulls. Then, it clouded their minds and left them steeping in the broth of its slaughter. And always, it headed east.

Grimnir learned its signs in those years. He learned what to look for, how the air tasted in the lands the wyrm haunted, the stenches that traveled with it—the sulfur and grave-rot. It left disease in its wake. For seventy-five years, he stalked that snake across the Svear-lands and up into the Oster-lands, to the shores of the Baltic Sea. There, he made his way east as best he could; he picked up its spoor again at Lindanisa and hounded it inland, south along the old Varangian trade road.

He could count on one black-nailed hand the number of times he almost had that snake under his blade. Grimnir got a piece of Níðhöggr at Holmgarðr, on the Volkhov River, and again at Caffa on the Black Sea; he nearly had the blasted wyrm in the cisterns beneath Miklagarðr, and again at a monastery in Messina, where it consumed a score of brown-robed hymn-singers and loosed a pestilence on the rest ... but it skinned out, as always, riding old Odin's luck to safety and leaving Grimnir to piece together its next move. And then, the Pontine Marshes along the Appian Way, in the heart of the Nailed God's empire.

"Where some cross-eyed rat with an arbalest cut loose and skewered my heart like a choice piece of tenderloin," Grimnir snarled. And *that* was the rub. He had survived sword cuts and axe blows, tooth and talon; he'd been burned, scourged, pierced, slashed, and beaten. He'd nearly drowned more than a few times, and been shoved off a siege ladder at Caffa. For thirteen hundred and twenty-six years, he'd taken wounds and been dealt grievous injuries; blows that would have killed a milk-blooded manling, he shrugged off like they were nothing. "An idiot from the stews of Messina drops me with a lucky shot? *Faugh!*"

Something about that just didn't sit right with Grimnir. It felt off, somehow. *Sour grapes,* as old Gífr would say. *Bastard killed you, fair and square!* Was it, though? Was it fair and square, or did that one-eyed raven-starver, Odin, figure out another way to cheat?

What difference does it make? He heard Gífr's voice in the back of his mind. *Dead is dead, you lout.* And that was what galled him the most: to know that now he was just one more corpse in a long line of the dead, another victim of the Malice-Striker and its master!

Grimnir screamed his rage at the cloud-girt sky, at the distant conflagrations burning like stars among the unseen boughs of Yggðrasil. He ran full-out along the narrow path, chasing the echoes of his fury; he ran until sweat stung his one good eye, until his heart threatened to burst. He would have run to the very fences of Helheimr had the path he followed not simply . . . ended.

The *skrælingr* caught himself before he went pitching over the weed-choked rim of an escarpment. He skidded to a halt, his mailed chest rising and falling as he gulped great lungfuls of mist-damp air. Grimnir stood at the edge of a broad and jagged valley—like a savage wound hacked into the flanks of the hills by some mad titan's axe. Shadows were thick upon the ground here, and the trees that reached up through the opaque veil of fog were dense with leaves, creepers, and twisted ropes of flowering thorn. Across this valley Grimnir could see the ramparts of a fortress, dim and gray in the distance. This, he was certain, was Úlfsstaðir, the Wolves' Abode.

He had two choices: he could go around—a journey of several hours, even days—or he could go through. *Keep to the ridgelines and hilltops,* Snaga had warned. *The vales and deeps 'tween here and yonder got a queer air about 'em. I think* we ain't the first or the only folk to call Nástrond home. Grimnir, though, was in no mood to court the safe path.

"Nár! I'm already dead," he growled. "What's there left to fear?"

With that, Grimnir went to the edge of the escarpment. He kicked at the weeds and the moss-slick rocks until he found a place that reminded him of some giant's ladder. Here, he took off his cloak, rolled it up, and tied it across his body like a sash. Exhaling, he went over the side. A cascade of dead leaves, loose soil, and scree preceded him as he clambered down, finding precarious toeholds in cracks and crevices, wedging his black-nailed fingertips into fissures in the rock that supported his weight as he hunted for more. Twice, he grasped at the thick creepers around him to save himself from plummeting into the deepening gloom. He hung there a moment, catching his breath. That's when he heard it . . . a sound, faint even to his keen ears, that made his hackles rise. It was a voice, a female voice, and it was raised in song:

"Muninn, hark! | rouse thee, Memory,
Huginn's kin, | shake off thy torpor!
Late is the hour, | and dark is the road
Beneath Niðafjoll."

Grimnir's one eye narrowed. He wondered what sort of folk would call these darksome depths home.

And it *was* dark. Like clambering down into a cavern. Gray light chased him into the valley, but as he passed through the level of the tree canopy, even that paltry light was snuffed out. The swine of Miðgarðr would have found it as black as pitch; to Grimnir's uncanny sight, however, it was as if the light of a small candle illuminated his descent. Down he went, knotted muscle screaming in agony, until his boots struck a surface that was soft and yielding; crouching, Grimnir's rock-torn fingers touched a thick carpet of damp moss, old leaves, and fallen pine needles.

Here, he paused to let his vision adjust. By touch and by sight, he determined he had dropped into a tangle of detritus that had fallen down the sheer wall of the escarpment. He crouched, now, in a hollow wrought by two fallen trees—ancient forest titans uprooted by some unimaginable tempest and cast down into darkness. Close by, Grimnir heard the burble of water. He slithered over root balls and between bare, ivy-clad branches; thorns scraped over mail and skin, or snagged in his rolled-up cloak. Dense cobwebs brushed his face, sending an unaccustomed shudder down his spine. "Piss off, you blasted crawlers!" He spat and swiped a hand across his face, certain he'd dislodged a fat black spider. "*Nár!*"

He heard the voice again; its song came clearer, now:

> "*Huginn, hark! | hear me, Thought,*
> *Muninn's companion, | a lamp have I made!*
> *Forged in gold it is, | and marked by*
> *The Hanged One's runes.*"

Grimnir crept clear of the thicket of fallen rubbish. He grunted; it *was* like being under the earth, at the mouth of an overgrown forest cavern. Giant trunks like stalagmites soared into darkness, upholding an impenetrable canopy of leaves. No grass grew here, on the valley floor. What muffled the hard tread of his hobnailed boots was a matted carpet of curling leaves and twigs. Small bones crunched under his heel.

Not far off, Grimnir spied a light gleaming through the trees, an eerie will-o'-the-wisp that twinkled like candlelight through a pane of dirty green glass. It did not move; but something moved around it, the shadow of a thing too distant to see.

Grimnir's nostrils flared. He caught a fleeting scent; a familiar scent, though he could not place it. As he suspected, too, a spring bubbled up near the foot of the escarpment, feeding a shallow creek that chuckled over lichen-clad rocks and spilled into frothy pools. He knelt, dabbled the fingers of his off hand in the flow. It was cold; he touched his tongue to his fingertips and found it tasted sweet, though with the faint bite of minerals. Shrugging, Grimnir scooped out half a dozen draughts to slake his thirst. Then, like a hunting beast, the *skrælingr* padded downstream, drawn by the twinkle of a ghost-lamp in the impenetrable dark and the echo of a song.

3

THE LOKAEAN WITCHES

Something watched him.

With every step into the heart of this shadowed valley, Grimnir felt this sense of scrutiny heighten. Something tracked him in the darkness. Something malignant. Something that triggered the atavistic sense of preservation that lurked deep in any *kaunr*'s soul. The son of Bálegyr desperately wanted to kill something, or to run far from this accursed valley. But he kept one hand curled around the hilt of Hátr, the blade loose in its scabbard, and forged ahead. "Seek your meal elsewhere," he muttered. "Ha! All you'll get from me is hard blows and a bit of gristle."

Sounds taunted him in return. A branch creaked overhead; behind him, he heard the rustle of dead leaves, the snapping of twigs. Something tittered, like obscene laughter; in answer, he heard a distant hiss. To his credit, Grimnir did not rise to the bait. He made that eerie light the focus of his attention, his senses wound as tight as the wires binding a sword's hilt; he paid special attention to his footing. To fall among the twisted roots, he was certain, would be to invite an attack from his unseen pursuer. Thus did he move in careful predatory silence . . .

The creek widened and was joined by other freshets, becoming a broad stream that wound through the trees, its marshy banks thick with weeds and a scrub of old bulrushes. Dry stalks rattled as black water spooled through the shallows. As he slunk nearer to the light, Grimnir began to discern details. The silhouette belonged to a female, a *kaunr*, as far as he could tell. She was as tall as he was, though thin and as wiry as a starveling she-wolf. Her hair was dark and stringy, worked with silver beads, and bone and amber fetishes; she wore a thigh-length tunic of ragged green, woven—near as Grimnir could discern—from moss and ivy. Around her neck he spied the iron collar of a thrall. What's worse, Grimnir could not shake the niggling feeling he had seen her before. The way she moved. Her voice ...

"Mímir's wisdom I seek, | Raven-lords
Through dvergar gates; | where tread the Æsir
And the bright álfar, | the far-seeing Vanir
And the sly troldvolk."

She stood on the banks of the stream, near an outcropping of flat rocks where her lamp was perched. It was, indeed, forged from gold and inlaid with silver; silver runes were set in the green crystal panes, as well—a cunning bit of work. Before her, rising from the cold black water, stood the trunk of an ancient ash tree with only two branches remaining, both thick and bare of leaves. Unknown hands had cut a circle of deep runes in its rot-softened bark, and inside the circle was a stylized raven. With a frown, he realized she was trying to work out an incantation, but to what end? While he wasn't *seiðr*-wise like old Gífr, Grimnir knew enough to wonder how invoking Thought and Memory—Huginn and Muninn—might work as part of some desperate bid for freedom. Perhaps she wanted the giant ravens of Odin to spirit her away? Even to him, that smacked of folly.

Whatever its purpose, her song faltered after the third stanza; her voice trailed off and, in place of lilting sorcery, she let loose with a salty stream of curses. As she turned toward the light, Grimnir got his first unobstructed look—high cheekbones and a blunt nose, a broad forehead, and deep-set eyes that gleamed like the amber woven into her hair.

It was a youthful face. A familiar face.

Grimnir crept closer, nearly to the edge of the emerald radiance. She caught the movement; rather than shrinking away in fear, she instead snatched a knifelike shard of flint from beside the lamp and faced him down with bared teeth and a snarl.

"You peaching sneak-thief!" she snarled. "Did those bitches send you to torment me?"

Grimnir rose, stepped into view with one hand raised in a gesture of peace. His good eye scanned the deep shadows beyond the light, looking for any sign of an ambush. "*Nár!* No one sent me. What's your name?"

She spat at him. "What's my name to you, you old scrote? Which one of those accursed sisters conjured you up? Was it Gjálp? Or did that old sow, Imðr, send you? Bah! Begone! Harrow me no longer!"

"Keep your voice down," Grimnir hissed. "Are you from Úlfsstaðir?"

"Did I say that?" She sliced at the water with her stone knife. "Feh! Be off with you, vagabond! Or tarry, and give those thrice-cursed witches another blasted thrall!"

"Where are they, these witches of yours, eh?"

She shivered; with terror-widened eyes, she glanced about. "Oh, they are here. They haunt the darkness, ever watchful. They've marked your coming, you fool. And you've brought them to me."

Grimnir snorted; still, he kept one hand on Hátr's carved hilt. "Then they'll mark my going, as well, useless hags! But what will they do if I take their thrall with me, eh? That's the question."

"They'll kill you," she said, her voice low. "Kill you and feast on your liver."

Grimnir shrugged. "*Faugh!* I'm already dead, so what does it matter?"

The sheen of madness glinted in her amber eyes as she came closer, the flint knife forgotten at her side. "Oh, you *are* a fool! A precious, precious fool! Dead you might be, but that does not place you beyond torment. Imagine returning time and time again, your body bound by chains at the bottom of a well. Oh, you'll live, aye ... for the time it takes those accursed sisters to drown you, again! Or burn you. Or cut the blood-eagle in your back. Or drive iron spikes into your eyes ... Oh, my precious fool, if you die here, you will never leave. You'll be their plaything till the Gjallarhorn calls us to the slaughter!"

Grimnir's jaw clamped shut as he suppressed a shiver of fear; between clenched teeth, he snarled. "Then we'd best leg it, you rat, and not let these so-called witches of yours catch us!"

She blinked. "You'd take me with you?"

"It's your choice. Do you wish to remain here as their thrall, or do you want your freedom?"

"Freedom!" she said without pause. Her amber eyes gleamed with fierce purpose as she hooked a thumb under the edge of her collar and held it out. "Cut this iron from my neck and I'll show you the way out!"

"Your name, first," he replied. "*Nár!* I know you, by Ymir, but I cannot recall from where."

"Skaði, I am called. I died on Miðgarðr, in the Kjolen Mountains—"

"At Orkahaugr." Grimnir cut her off as the sound of her name shattered a dam of memories. He'd last seen her face among the dead. "Twelve hundred years ago, you were slain deep in the mountain, at the crossroad called Einvigi, when you and some mates tried to stop that blasted wyrm, Níðhöggr, from reaching the Hall of the Nine Fathers. You were Hrungnir's bedmate, ere he sailed with the wolf ships, bound for Ériu and the slaughter at Mag Tuiredh."

"Who are you to remember all this? To remember what even I have forgotten?" Skaði said.

"Hrungnir's brother, I am, called Grimnir."

"I remember you. You were a runt, back then," she said, then clutched at the thrall's collar around her neck. "Free me, Grimnir!"

The *skrælingr,* though, was wary. An eerie premonition crept up his spine, as though the malignant thing tracking him had laid a trap, and now it watched with unfeigned glee as he blundered into it. This Skaði, she could be the bait . . . or she could be in on it. "I'll cut that necklace off when we're clear of this loathsome valley. Bring your lamp and lead the way."

"They'll see it," she hissed.

"And so? You said they're already on to us! *Faugh!* I'd rather meet them with a bit of light at my elbow than in the howling dark, wouldn't you?"

Skaði's nostrils flared. She went and snatched up the gold-wrought dwarf-lamp. "It won't matter," she said. Then, with a jerk of her head, she bid Grimnir follow her.

★ ★ ★

THE DOOM OF ODIN

THE PATH Skaði chose carried them away from the sluggish stream and down a trail worn to hard-packed earth by centuries of use. It wound around the trunks of giant trees, ash and oak, and over small rock bridges that spanned shallow creeks; some reeked of sulfur, while others steamed as though the water boiled up from the heart of a volcano. Pale mushrooms grew thick on either hand, amid the corpse-pale flowers of stinking nightshade and the tall purple stalks of wolfsbane.

As they walked, Grimnir peppered Skaði with questions about the thralls—how many were there, and where did the witches keep them? "And how were you captured, eh?" he asked.

"Feh! My own da did it, that sorry bastard!" she growled. "Skæfloc, he's called. A while back, one of Lútr's boys took a shine to me, so Skæfloc thought he'd barter me for a better position—which meant we'd be sneaking away from Úlfsstaðir, turning our backs on our folk. I told him no, and then let it slip to Gífr what my old da had in his mind to do. Kjallandi's son takes a dim view of blood-traitors, so Skæfloc barely skinned out of there with his head on his shoulders.

"Well, our lot, we hold grudges, don't we? I'd all but forgotten about the old bastard. Went out beyond the walls of Úlfsstaðir to hunt, one day, and was busy skinning a deer when that stinking toe-rag and his new mates came up on me and knifed me in the back! Gloated about it as I lay dying. I returned down here. Skæfloc had thrown me to the wolves, right and proper. A couple of thralls found me, and in a twinkling I had the iron around my neck and was made to work for my supper. That was—" She paused as she did a sum in her head. "—twelve deaths ago.

"There are nine of us," she continued. "Seven males and one other female. Most are from Skrælingsalr, though there is one broken fool from Kaunheimr. The other female is from Jarðvegur, and she's their favorite, that hag. They keep us in a longhouse out beyond the stream where you found me."

As Skaði spoke, Grimnir kept his good eye in motion, checking their back trail, the boughs overhead, and from side to side. He saw nothing but thickly-shadowed woodland rising around them in the pale green light. But he *heard* the sounds of pursuit—the snap of twigs, the scuffling of old leaves, the sharp click of talons on rock ... and he felt the devilish sense of scrutiny, of malevolent eyes watching, waiting.

Grimnir cursed aloud. "Why don't they attack and get it over with, these blasted witches of yours!"

"And spoil the hunt?" she replied. "Ha! The Lokaean Witches like to wring every drop of fear from their prey before they move in for the kill."

"That's what they're called, eh? The Lokaean Witches?"

Skaði nodded. "Two sisters, Gjálp and Imðr. They say there's a third, Atla, but I've only seen the two. They like to brag that they were Angrboða's midwives, presiding over the birth of the Tangled God's children off in Jötunheimr, but I think the old hags are lying. I think something else happened, something that left this Atla in chains and the other two in hiding, down here among the *skrælingar* dead."

"And you think this wretch, Mímir, knows what it was."

Skaði stopped suddenly. She whirled about, glaring at Grimnir through slitted eyes. "What do you know about that, swine?"

"*Nár!* Don't play dumb!" Grimnir jabbed a forefinger at her. "You think I've never seen the workings of sorcery before? Looked to me like you were trying to conjure something, back there ... or someone. How'd the line go? *Mímir's wisdom I seek, | Raven-lords.*"

Skaði spat and turned away. She resumed her path, her spine rigid and her stride reflecting her fury.

Grimnir chuckled and followed. "Hit too close to the mark, did I? Tell me, then, who is this Mímir whose wisdom you seek?"

"You wouldn't understand," she replied.

"Try me, you rat."

Skaði stopped, again; she turned. The lamp between them made sinister masks of their faces—hers fox-thin and sallow; his sharp like a hungry wolf and hewn from flint. "Feh! I've got a hunch, is all. When she's deep in her cups, Imðr also likes to brag about how they stole a sip of water from Mímisbrunnr, the forbidden Well of Mímir. They think they can hide out here and Odin won't find them." She set off down the path, once more.

Grimnir hawked and spat, then followed. "So they're witches *and* water thieves, now? Ymir's balls! You think that bastard raven-starver cares if they steal a nip from some pissing well? *Faugh!* He's too busy keeping his little pet alive up in Miðgarðr!"

"It's not just some well, you thickheaded ape!" she said over her shoulder. "Mímisbrunnr is the source of all wisdom, and Mímir guards it like a rabid dog. Hel's teeth! That bastard drinks from it every morning! So, when old Odin came seeking a draught of wisdom, Mímir would not let a drop pass the Allfather's lips without a fitting sacrifice. They say he contemplated it for nine days, and on the tenth day Odin plucked out one of his own eyes and dropped it in the Well as payment. Mímir relented, and the pair of them became fast friends.

"But Odin is a jealous old sot, isn't he? Aye, he refuses to let any other soul drink from Mímisbrunnr. Every night, he checks the level of water in the Well. If more than Mímir's accustomed morning draught is missing, the Allfather flies into a rage that's terrible to behold. Makes it none too wise to brag about swiping a mouthful of Mímisbrunnr's bounty, eh? Yet, here they are, these inbred sisters, banging on about having stolen a sip right out from under the Allfather's nose! And if they did? Two hags from Jötunheimr?" Skaði sucked her teeth. "Feh! That'd be a gutting offense, wouldn't it?"

Grudgingly, Grimnir nodded. "And even if they didn't, it makes for a fine bit of blackmail," he said. "If you could get the word out to this Mímir."

"That's what I was trying to do. Thought I'd plant a bee in Mímir's bonnet using old One-Eye's favorite squabs."

"Huginn and Muninn," Grimnir said. "Aye, not a total cock-up, as plans go."

Skaði, though, made a rude noise. "Except it didn't work."

This time, it was Grimnir who stopped suddenly. "Wait," he hissed, tilting his head to one side. Skaði drew up, half turned toward him.

"What?"

"You hear that?"

Skaði looked around. "Don't hear nothing."

"That's right, you rat," Grimnir said. "They've been on our heels this whole time, rustling and groaning out there in the dark. Now . . . nothing. They don't seem the sort to just give up, these witches of yours."

"They're not." Skaði raised her lamp, her knuckles whitening around the haft of her flint knife. Ahead, the trail descended into a hollow, where a stone-and-log footpath crossed a narrow crevasse. Tendrils of mist wafted from the fissure. "This is the last bridge," she said. "Cross it, and we've got nothing but a snaky road between here and the far end of the valley."

"We'd best be on with it, then." Grimnir drew his long-seax; the blade's edge gave back the eerie green glow of Skaði's lamp. As they descended into the hollow, Grimnir knew the jig was up; he knew the witches had laid their snare, and he knew his neck was in the noose as eight shapes emerged from the undergrowth on the far side of the bridge. The eight thralls of the Lokaean Witches, each glassy-eyed and half naked.

As Skaði had said, one was of the old blood, a *kaunr* from before their flight to Miðgarðr—he was more dwarflike than the others, with straight limbs and a scraggly beard, a knotty club cradled in his hands. His sallow skin bore scars from his long servitude. The one female was white-haired and spindly-shanked, fey and witchlike in the deep gloom. Her eyes gleamed brightest of all, with the amber sheen of madness. She clutched a bone knife to her breast. Four were bandy-legged *skrælingar*, swarthy and red-eyed, with lolling tongues and slaver dripping from their fanged jaws. All brandished clubs of fire-hardened ash. The last two were *scrags*, thin-flanked youths a head shorter than the others, filth-crusted and feral. They seemed the most eager to cross the bridge.

Grimnir cursed. To Skaði, he said: "Get that blasted knife of yours ready and stay close. These beggarly swine want a fight? *Faugh!* I'll oblige them! I'll give them a fight they'll not soon forget!"

Grimnir coiled his strength into his legs, muscles taut and tightening like coils in an engine of destruction. Before he could unleash his rage, however, a sibilant voice came from the thick canopy of trees, above.

"*Skrælingr,*" it said, holding the last syllable long enough to become a serpentine hiss. "We need not fight. Give us what is ours and go on your way."

Grimnir turned; his red eye gleamed with barely suppressed fury. Beside him, Skaði stiffened; her knuckles cracked around the haft of her flint knife. "Show yourself, witch," Grimnir said. "I don't deal with thralls!"

Leaves rustled; from among the branches, an eerie figure dropped to the path, landing like some obscene frog with its knees splayed wide and the long clawed fingers of its left hand forming a tripod to support its weight. The thing was taller than Grimnir, even in a crouch, and far heavier, its naked limbs impossibly long and spindly; its skin was the color of bile. Framed by wild and unkempt white hair, its face was the face of nightmares—a lipless mouth filled with teeth, two slits for a nose, and eyes like a cat, yellow with long narrow pupils. A bog-*jötunn,* Grimnir reckoned, from the fens that bordered the Ironwood, the cold forest on the fringes of Jötunheimr.

"Give us the traitor," it hissed. "And we will not harm you."

Grimnir scoffed. He glanced back at the thralls, who milled on the far side of the bridge, awaiting their mistress's command. "Which hag are you, *jötunn?*"

"Gjálp, I am."

"So-ho, then, Gjálp . . . I give you this useless bit of filth," Grimnir jerked his chin at Skaði, who glared right back at him, "and you lot will let me just breeze on by without a second glance, eh?"

The witch shuffled forward, its jaw thrust out. "Give her to me and I will not harm you. You have my word."

"*Nár!* What about them?" Grimnir glanced at the thralls; the *scrags* were champing at the bit, eager for a fight. "What about your dogs, eh?"

"They will not harm you," said the witch. The fingers of its right hand opened and closed in anticipation.

Grimnir sucked his teeth. "Aye, take the useless little rat, then," he said, shoving Skaði away. "She's served her purpose."

"*Fak þú í arsegót!*" Skaði spat. She had a wild-eyed look of terror, but still she did not blench. "Someday, I'll be free of these chains, and—by Ymir!—I'll hunt you down and make you pay! You and old Skæfloc, as well!" She took a swing at him; her flint knife skittered off the links of his Turkish mail. "You treacherous son of a whore! I'll—"

The witch, Gjálp, roared a command: "*Stoðva!*" And Skaði lapsed into silence; slowly, she turned, the power in the witch's voice stealing her will. "You will never be free, little worm," Gjálp hissed. She sidled closer; naked malevolence shimmered in the bog-*jötunn*'s eyes. "You, who dared use our sorcery against us? You will wear our collar and bear our tortures until the world breaks! Come, my children!"

Grimnir grunted and turned away. The other thralls, the crestfallen *scrags* in the lead, started to cross the bridge two abreast. Grimnir stopped, suddenly. He glanced over his shoulder, his good eye smoldering like a forge-glede. "Where's your sister, eh? Where's Imðr?"

Gjálp, who was purring threats in Skaði's ear, raised her eyes and met Grimnir's. A moment's hesitation, then: "She has business elsewhere. I said none here will harm you, *skrælingr*. Go!"

Grimnir exhaled. "None *here,* you say? *Faugh!* I thought as much ..."

As Grimnir's harsh voice trailed off, the air in the valley of the Lokaean Witches grew sharp and still; the passage of time slowed. Every breath became a drawn-out moment, a still image painted in deep blues and muddy grays streaked with jags of emerald; every heartbeat became the ponderous cadence of a drum. Grimnir's eye narrowed; over his shoulder, he saw the sheen of light on the witch's jaundiced hide as it slowly rose on gangly legs, towering over Skaði; he smelled the earthy reek of the *jötunn's* body. Its long talons scraped furrows in the ground.

It knew, Grimnir reckoned. *The witch knew Death was near.*

Grimnir was already in motion. He whirled. Hard-knitted sinews creaked as he drew his axe and hurled it, muscles bunching and uncoiling like hammer-forged springs. The *skrælingr* grunted from the effort.

Gjálp's monstrous face bore a look of sudden surprise; a command was perched on its pallid tongue, but the breath that might propel it into existence would remain forever trapped behind its teeth as Grimnir's bearded axe crunched into the bog-*jötunn's* face. The blade landed edge-on, between the witch's slit-like nostrils and its right eye, and split that gruesome visage open like a ripe melon. Gjálp's eyes dimmed; like a puppet bereft of its master's hand, the creature reeled, then crumpled at Skaði's feet in a welter of limbs and knotty joints. Black blood flecked with gray curds of brain matter leaked out over the forest path.

The next instant, the world exploded in chaos. From the darkness beyond the bridge came an earsplitting howl, a cry of rage and grief. In answer, the white-haired thrall hag shrieked and brandished her knife. The effect was immediate. Goaded by the hag, and under the vengeful eye of savage Imðr, the male thralls scuffled and elbowed their way across the bridge, each one eager to be the first to come to blows with Gjálp's killer.

For his part, Grimnir did not disappoint.

Rather than stand and await their rush, the son of Bálegyr sprinted for the bridgehead; he reached it even as the *scrags* scrambled across—one slightly in front of the other. The remaining thralls were hot on their heels. With a snarled curse, Grimnir kicked the first *scrag* in the chest. The lanky brat tumbled back, snarling the legs of the two thralls behind him. That was a death sentence on the narrow bridge; screaming, the *scrag* slid over the side, taking another thrall with him. Both vanished in the misty darkness of the crevasse, while the third clung to the bridge's edge for a moment longer before its hunger-weakened fingers gave way. Grimnir ducked the second *scrag*'s wild swing, his club whistling through empty air, and then brained him with the pommel of Hátr. Before he could fall, Grimnir seized him by the iron collar around his neck.

He used the senseless rat as a shield, and as a bludgeon. Clubs struck the *scrag* three quick blows; Grimnir felt their impacts, heard bones break. And then, he thrust forward, sweeping one of the remaining two *skrælingar* off-balance. The swine dropped his club, clutched at the *scrag*'s body for support. Grimnir felt his weight shift; rather than risk it wrong-footing him, as well, he simply gave the *scrag* one final shove and let go. Their death-screams as they plummeted brought a mirthless grin to Grimnir's face. He shifted his weight, then, and met the last *skrælingr* blade to club.

Skaði, though, did not remain aloof from the fray. Shaking off the vile influence of the witch's voice, she put her foot on the dead *jötunn*'s head and ripped Grimnir's axe free in a spray of blood and brain. Turning, she ran for the bridge.

Grimnir hacked slivers from the *skrælingr*'s club; over his shoulder, he saw the shuffling *kaunr*—that straight-legged bastard with a beard like tarry weeds—moving into his blind side. Snarling, Grimnir deflected another blow from the *skrælingr*'s knotty club, then drove the hilt of his long-seax into the idiot's teeth. Once. Twice. Blood spurted from the wreckage of his nose and mouth. A third blow snapped the *skrælingr*'s head back. The club slipped from his nerveless fingers. A fourth crushing blow sent him crumpling to the ground with a broken neck.

Even as Grimnir turned to confront the *kaunr* and that knife-wielding hag, he heard Skaði shout: "'Ware!"

And that was all the warning he had as his own axe flashed past his head, burying itself in the *kaunr*'s shoulder with a meaty *thump*.

The *kaunr* grunted, staggered.

And without missing a step, Skaði barreled past Grimnir—shrieking like one of the *mná sidhe,* the banshees of old Ériu—and threw herself at the white-haired *skrælingr* hag. They fought tooth and nail, cursing with each ragged breath; their knives flashed—flint versus bone. Grimnir watched even as he cut the injured *kaunr*'s throat and retrieved his axe. He watched as the hag slashed a furrow in Skaði's brow, nearly blinding her; watched as Skaði paid her back in kind. She tackled the hag, drove her face-first into the stone kerb of the bridge. Skaði straddled her shoulders, punched her with her free hand. The hag squirmed, bucked, and came close to dislodging the younger *skrælingr;* finally, Skaði screamed, spittle flying, and planted her flint knife in the back of the hag's skull like a gruesome sapling.

"*Fak þú!*"

THEY DID not have long to relish their victory. Skaði rocked back on her haunches, wrung thick black blood from her eyes. The gash in her forehead burned. Her breath came in short, sharp gasps. Grimnir loomed over her.

"Make ready," he said, hauling her up by the scruff. "The other one comes."

Skaði could hear it, then, over the throbbing of blood in her ears—the crack and crunch of boughs bending, of limbs breaking, under the weight of an enraged *jötunn*. "Imðr," she hissed.

"Is she like this one?" Grimnir jabbed a thumb back at Gjálp's corpse.

"Gjálp was the runt."

Grimnir glared sidelong at Skaði. "*Nár!* So we're getting the pick of the litter, now, eh?"

Skaði scooped up the hag's fallen knife. "You got a plan, though, don't you? Some cunning bit of trickery up your sleeve?"

"Oh, aye," Grimnir scoffed. "And it's an easy one, you rat. Move, fight, and don't let that miserable bog-witch kill you."

"Feh! That's it?"

They could see flashes of pale flesh amid the trees; glimpses of gleaming fangs and eyes that burned with a lust for blood. Imðr came through the foliage like a giant ape, poised to crush these *skrælingar* vermin to dust under her misshapen heel.

"Go left," Grimnir muttered; Skaði barely heard him over the splintering of branches. "Ready? One . . . two . . . three!"

And as Imðr came crashing through the canopy—a hunched and twisted bog-*jötunn* twice the size of its sister, with long filth-encrusted talons and crooked limbs the color of curdled milk—Grimnir vanished into the undergrowth to the right while Skaði, slower off the mark, stumbled away to the left.

Rage guided the *jötunn,* and vengeance fed its gnarled thews; but rage and vengeance were narrow in the scope of their vision, and both easily slaked. Imðr ignored the mailed *skrælingr,* for the moment, and went after the one it could see, the easy prey—their treacherous thrall.

Skaði had enough time to bellow a curse before the bog-*jötunn* collided with her, sending her aloft in a welter of knotty joints and slashing talons. She rolled with it, tucking her shoulders in to make her lean frame as small as possible, struck the ground, and came up unharmed. As she struggled to regain her balance, Imðr struck her again.

Skaði went down hard near the crumbling and weed-choked edge of the crevasse; her breath *whuffed* from her lungs. Somehow, she kept hold of the hag's bone knife. Before she could recover, Imðr seized her leg in its viselike grip and dragged her toward it.

"I will pluck you apart like a succulent morsel!" the bog-*jötunn* said, its voice a low-pitched gurgle. "Crack your bones and suck out the marrow!"

Skaði cursed. She stabbed the witch's hand again and again, to no avail. Imðr would not release her. Instead, the *jötunn* drove the talon of its stiffened forefinger into Skaði's shoulder, as a soldier would drive a lance. Bone shattered; tendons and muscle tore, and black blood spattered the undergrowth. The *skrælingr* screamed, as much from rage as from the pain.

Suddenly, over the witch's hunched back, she spied Grimnir. Like Imðr, he had taken to the trees. Perched on a limb over their heads, he held his naked long-seax between clenched teeth; his single red eye narrowed. Then, making not a sound, he snatched his blade, held it point-down in his right hand, and dropped like a stone on Imðr's back.

The bog-*jötunn* howled. Grimnir tangled his left hand in its coarse hair.

He crouched low on its shoulders; tried to lever its head back, to strike at its throat. The witch turned Skaði loose; it grabbed for the one who rode its spine like some grotesque mare. Hard talons skittered off the *skrælingr*'s mail, but it could get no purchase. The witch whirled; it lunged against a tree. Bark exploded as it sought to crush its attacker, to scrape him off like an insect. Grimnir nearly lost his grip; the impact rattled his teeth. He recovered quickly, though; shaking off the blow, he bared yellowed fangs.

"My turn, hag!" Grimnir snarled. In answer, he punched Hátr down through the hard gristle and flesh of its shoulder; he felt it grate on bone. Then, throwing all his weight against it, Grimnir sawed the blade across the witch's upper back.

The thing's howls redoubled, then faded to a pathetic gurgle as Hátr found a chink between its misshapen vertebrae. Steel bit deep, cutting through the cord of its spine. The *jötunn*'s legs gave way; the lights of its eyes faded as it crashed headlong into the base of a tree. Grimnir rode it down, his black-nailed fingers wrapped like iron bands around the hilt of his long-seax.

Skaði clambered to her feet, her left arm and shoulder a useless wreckage of torn flesh. She staggered, fell to one knee, and retched. She stayed hunched over a moment, hand on her knee, bile drooling from her chin. "Ymir's balls," she muttered, scrubbing her mouth with her forearm. "Feh! You dead, yet?"

"Not yet," Grimnir muttered. Groaning, he rolled off the witch's back, slick now with putrid black blood. "You?"

"Almost," Skaði replied. Beneath the blood and sweat, her sallow skin looked even more pale. She spat and tried to stand, once more. This time, she made it to a tree trunk and leaned there, breathing hard.

Grimnir wrenched his blade free of the *jötunn*'s spine and stropped it clean before he sheathed it. He glanced at Skaði, then stripped off his rolled-up cloak and tossed it to her. "Use that to bind your shoulder. Can you walk?"

"I'll damn well walk out of here," she said. In short order, and with Grimnir's help, she used strips of red cloth to bandage and immobilize her shoulder. She made a makeshift sash and thrust the dead hag's bone knife through it. And with a nod, they limped side by side down the forest path, leaving a field of carnage in their wake.

4

THE WOLVES' ABODE

"Úlfsstaðir."

Grimnir spied it from the valley rim, not ten miles distant, where the forest thinned out and darkness gave way to filmy gray light; particolored shadows streaked the air, cast by the worlds burning among Yggðrasil's eternal branches.

The Wolves' Abode crowned a hill of naked rock, a single path leading up to a tall, narrow door. Even from this distance, Grimnir could see that the fortress walls were timber, jagged palisades set into a stone foundation and banded in cold wrought iron. Rising above those serrated ramparts was the upper reaches of a great *stavhǫll,* a complex structure of wood, with pitched roofs and elaborate gables, shingled like a dragon's hide in tarred pine. Curls of smoke drifted from several openings in the roof.

Grimnir grunted. "*Nár!* So that's the corpse-hall of our people, eh?"

Skaði said nothing.

He glanced back and saw her staggering up the last switchback as though drunk. Her right arm hung useless; sweat beaded her cheeks, dripped from her chin. Under the red scrap of cloth that bound the gash in her forehead, her sallow skin looked even paler than normal. Skaði swayed toward him, taking two steps before the muscles in her legs came unstrung and she dropped to her knees. Only her outstretched arm kept her from toppling face-first onto the rocky path. Her battle-torn body gave a great convulsive shudder, rattling her iron thrall's collar.

"You going to make it, you rat?" Grimnir said.

Skaði pushed herself up and sat back. "Not like this, I'm not." She grabbed the iron collar around her neck. "Cut this blasted thing off me," she said.

Grimnir examined it, passing it through his fingers, but could find neither locking hasp nor rivet-hole. He shook his head. "I'd need a chisel and an anvil to get that off."

"*Arsegót!*" She let loose a string of curses. Her nostrils flared, but she calmed herself and glanced at Grimnir. "A favor, then . . . kill me."

Grimnir raised an eyebrow. "Over that scratch and an iron necklace?"

"I show up there, wounded, looking like *this*"—Skaði plucked at her tattered tunic, torn and stinking and smeared with the fluids of death—"and with a thrall's collar weighing me down? Feh! I'll not last the night! They'll just use me, kill me, and toss me out with the night-soil! I don't have a name like you do, Bálegyr's son! I'm just some traitor's bastard, a by-blow whore fit for the sleeping furs or the kitchens! Kill me and go on your way. At least then I'll come back whole and have half a chance. Might even backtrack and snoop out the sisters' tower, down in the valley; find a decent set of war-rags so I'm not looking like some down-in-the-mouth cur."

"And the collar?"

Skaði exhaled. "After I'm dead, cut my head off and throw this blasted thing as far away from me as you can. What do you say?" She struggled to stand, grunting with the effort of simply rising off her knees. Grimnir offered her his hand . . .

She took it. And as Skaði opened her mouth to add leverage to her argument, Grimnir drew Hátr and, in one smooth motion, drove the point of the long-seax in under her left arm. It pierced muscle, plunged into the cavity of her chest, through her left lung, and buried itself in her heart.

"B-Bastard," she muttered, her weight falling on his outstretched arm. Her body jerked and twitched, but after a moment the amber light vanished from her eyes. Grimnir held her there until he knew she was dead. And then, with a snarl curling his thin lips, Grimnir did as she asked. He took her head off.

It was no simple thing to decapitate someone with a long-seax, but with a bearded axe? Like any good butcher, Grimnir knew his tools. He let her sink down; kneeling beside her, he cleaned Hátr on the scraps of the red cloak Skaði had used to bandage her shoulder, and then sheathed the blade. His brow furrowed in a look of concentration. Grimnir knotted the fingers of his off hand in her matted hair, pulled her neck taut against the weight of her body, and drew his axe.

He chuckled to himself, all of a sudden, recalling the beach, the *scrag*, Snaga, and Skollvaldr's headless corpse. Jointing beef seemed his lot in this sordid little afterlife. And, keeping that humorless smile, Grimnir set about carving Skaði's head from her shoulders. It took four blows just to hack through the dense muscle, gristle, and cartilage, wary of the iron collar. On the fifth fall of the axe, the vertebrae at the top of her spine gave way with the wet crack of bone and Skaði's head came free in his hand, still trailing torn flesh and ragged skin.

Grimnir wrenched the thrall's collar from the stump of her neck and flung it down into the shadowed valley; he heard it toll like a bell as it struck rock and bounced away. Unsure of what to do with her head, he simply laid it down on the blood-splashed path, near her shoulders, and stood. He was of a mind to do precisely as she'd asked and just shove off, make for Úlfsstaðir and leave the little rat to find her own way. He was curious about something, though. Grimnir wondered *how* this whole business of coming back to "life" worked. How long did it take? What did it look like?

He glanced around; he was in no real hurry. His kin would be there, no matter when he decided to grace their doorstep. Grimnir's gaze roamed back down into the valley. He had time, he reckoned; what he really needed was a bit of ale and some meat to gnaw on ...

IT WAS a score of hours before Grimnir returned to the rim of the valley where he'd left Skaði's corpse. He shifted the ungainly weight of a woven reed basket from shoulder to shoulder, cursing his own foolishness with every step. Grimnir had found the thralls' longhouse, all right, and he'd discovered the Lokaean Witches' lair, to boot—a stone tower on a small hill, not far from where they'd penned their slaves. He'd looted the witches' larder, finding a wheel of cheese wrapped in linen, several round loaves of bread, half a dozen good sausages, a crockery jar with some kind of meat confit, and three more wax-sealed jars that sloshed when he shook them—surely beer or mead.

He'd also found their hoard, or what passed for a hoard in this gods-forsaken patch of Nástrond: a few chests and baskets like the one he hauled up the switchbacks, with precious little coin and far too many useless baubles. In one chest, though, he discovered cast-off weapons and war-rags. He chose a leather gambeson and a hauberk of mail that would likely fit Skaði well enough, the latter of good steel, light and flexible. He found trousers of leather-reinforced cloth, and a pair of boots. To this, Grimnir had added a weapons belt with a long bone-hilted knife in a silver-chased sheath, and a broad-bladed sword of pattern-welded steel. It bore a simple cross-hilt and an acorn-shaped pommel, and rested in a scabbard of wood and leather; its locket and chape were both forged from bronze.

For himself, he added an old Roman-style dagger to his war-belt, at the small of his back, and another, a thin-bladed stiletto, tucked into his right boot. And a leather bag of coins—ancient gold and silver stamped with the likenesses of long-dead emperors and the sigils of city-states gone to dust.

Grimnir eased the basket to the ground, stretched his back, and looked around. The body appeared undisturbed. He wasn't even sure what wildlife might lurk in the forested vales of Nástrond, much less what might decide to gnaw upon a *kaunr* corpse in the wild. He was glad, though, that he hadn't missed her return to . . . life? No, they were all dead, already. Nor were they *draugar*, the undead. Grimnir sucked his teeth, at a loss what to call their existence here in the world below.

Groaning, he sat with his back against the mossy stone, the corpse in his field of vision, and attacked the crockery jar of meat confit. He tossed the flensed bones aside and slathered the remaining grease over a chunk of bread, washing it down with a long pull from a jar of mead. He ate noisily, coughing and cursing under his breath. When he finished, he wiped his fingers on the rocks around him, tilted his head, and fixed Skaði's corpse with his good eye. No change. It still looked like someone had taken an axe to a mannikin carved from a side of beef.

"Do they still sing death-songs, down here?" Grimnir asked the corpse. He laughed, then, harsh and grating. "Not damn likely, eh? I'll tell you, though: it still sticks in my craw that there is none left in the world above to sing *my* death-song!" He shifted to a more comfortable position. "I sang the last one. Sang it for old Gífr, back in the days of Karl Magnus. For three weeks, I sat on the headland where the Elbe River met the sea and sang what I knew of his deeds—for he was the eldest, then, born in the gloom of Niðavellir ere the Tangled God chose us as his servants. As the embers of the burned-out village grew cold and the corpses of the whiteskin Saxon dogs who had killed him bloated and turned to slime, I sang. I sang of the Elder Days and the Battle of the Ironwood, where the lords of Ásgarðr slew and scattered our people; of the Ash-Road and the flight to Miðgarðr. I sang of the Duel of the Four Fathers, on the slopes of Orkahaugr, and of the long wandering of Kjallandi's folk; of their war with Rome in the passes of the High Atlas Mountains, of Kjallandi's death and Gífr's return to the North, bearing the sword Sárklungr—the Wound-Thorn. I sang until my lips bled and my throat cracked.

"Miðgarðr will never again hear such a song..."

Grimnir sighed. "And what do I get, eh? A song? Ha! A pair of crossbow bolts and a shallow grave, more like! There are none left alive, topside, whose memories reach back more than a handful of generations. My memory reaches back *forty-five* generations, little rat, and my deeds would fill a few days' song, at least. But who will remember? *Nár!* It will be as if I never existed."

The realization that he faced oblivion stirred the fires of rage that were forever banked in Grimnir's forge-black heart. He shied an empty crockery jar at a rock down the path, where it shattered like glass. "*Faugh!* I was *this* close! Half a turn of the glass and it would have been over, after one hundred and thirty years of hunting. But, no!" Grimnir snorted in disgust. "That blasted Allfather, he looks out for his own, eh? Jigger some idiot's elbow at the right moment and suddenly... here I am, wandering around Nástrond with the rest of you dunghill rats, marking time till the Gjallarhorn calls us to Ragnarök."

Grimnir settled into a brooding silence.

"What happened to Sárklungr?" Skaði said suddenly, her voice as dim and phlegmatic as an old woman's. Grimnir nearly came out of his skin. He bolted to his feet, his long-seax rasping from its scabbard.

"Ymir's balls!" he roared. "How did you—" He spat and spluttered. "*Faugh!*

Not ten minutes ago you were just a hunk of worm-meat, your fool head half a foot away from your miserable body! And now . . ." He trailed off.

Skaði sat up, as hale and whole as the moment he'd found her beside the lake, down below. She stretched, cracked the tendons in her neck, and felt around her throat for a fresh scar. "Feh! And now I'm back. That's how it works, down here. No rhyme or reason to it. One minute you're a carved-up sack of useless dog meat—just some gutted fool, legless, armless, head hacked off by your mates—and the next, you're . . . *back*. Back to your old self, at any rate."

"No warning, then, eh?" Grimnir sheathed his long-seax.

Skaði glanced up at him. "Warning? Like what? A horn and a song? Some fairy-flash of golden light?"

Grimnir shrugged. "*Nár!* I don't know . . . *something!*"

"No." Skaði chuckled. "No warning. That's why you waited around, isn't it? You were hoping I'd put on a good show."

Grimnir helped her to her feet. "I've seen things aplenty," he said. "Just never some wretch come back from the dead." He jerked his chin toward the open basket. "Fetched a bit to eat and some war-rags from the witches' piss-hole of a tower. What do you remember? The last thing?"

"You knifing me without even a 'brace yourself,' thank you very much," Skaði replied. She fell on the bread and cheese like a ravenous dog; the sausage she gave a wide berth. "It's *scrag*," she said around a mouthful of bread.

Grimnir picked up the sausage and took a bite from it. "So?" he said. "It's good *scrag*. That's all you remember? What about *after*?"

They passed the last bottle of mead back and forth. Skaði scrubbed her mouth with the back of her hand. "After? What do you think I'm going to remember? Dreams and memories? Feh! We don't dream down here. We're dead, already. We don't get *more* dead . . . or more *alive*. I remember a pain in my lungs, cold steel in my heart, and then I remember you talking. Telling a tale, I think. Only really got the last part."

She finished eating, then stripped off her torn and bloody tunic. Naked, Skaði's sallow-skinned body was lean and hard, stitched together with long bands of muscle and sinew; tattooed and cut with runelike scarring. Grimnir could see the bones of her hips, her ribs, the knobs along her spine as she bent over the chest and fished out the trousers and the gambeson, first.

He felt an unfamiliar stirring in his blood as he watched her dress—something hot and possessive. His nostrils flared, lips curling in a snarl of desire. He swiped his tongue over his yellowed fangs. Then, as quick as it appeared, it was gone. Grimnir looked away.

"So, what did happen to Sárklungr?" she said, lacing up the leather gambeson. "I remember that sword, and *that*"—she nodded at his long-seax—"is not the blade of Kjallandi."

Grimnir patted Hátr's carved hilt. "*Nár!* Its bones are Sárklungr's. That pathetic wyrm, Níðhöggr, broke Kjallandi's blade at Holmgarðr, on Volkhov River, back about fifty-odd years ago."

Skaði drew on her boots, then shimmied into her mail, settled it around her shoulders. The fit was off, slightly. No matter. She twisted, flexed her shoulders, and nodded in approval at Grimnir's choice of garb. She glanced up as she buckled the weapons belt around her lean hips. "Níðhöggr, eh? Good one. Better get your story straight, then," she said. "Old Kjallandi's going to want to hear why you turned his precious dwarf-sword into a knife. Ready?"

Grimnir hitched at his belt. "Aye, lead on. You know the way to Úlfsstaðir better than I."

THE ROAD to the Wolves' Abode proved to be little more than a winding path up the rocky hillside, cut in places by shallow steps. Every inch of their ascent was under the watchful eyes of any guards posted at the tall door—surely a postern, Grimnir reckoned, for it was too small to be a proper fortress gate. Even so, Grimnir got a prickly sensation on the back of his neck, as though something was off.

Skaði gave his concern a voice. "Unless things have changed, these rats should have hailed us by now," she said.

"Not the front door, is it?"

"This?" Skaði replied. "Feh! This is the back porch."

They reached the level of the door. It was more than twice Grimnir's height, its jambs and lintel deeply carved with intertwining wolves, ravens, and long-necked dragons; he could see neither hinges nor handles. They stood for a moment, looking up. Still, no one accosted them. Grimnir frowned. He drew his axe, reversed it, and pounded on the door with the blunt end. "*Holá,* you swine!" he roared. "Open up!"

The echo of his axe blows, of his voice, faded away.

Nothing.

"Let's try the front," Skaði said. She led them around the foundations of the palisade, along a narrow path littered with loose scree and half-buried boulders—most bearing rude graffiti left behind from when the fortress walls were raised. In less than a quarter of an hour, they rounded the last tower and clambered up a short incline to stand on the main road that led to Úlfsstaðir.

The land around the fortress was bare and windswept, riven by gulches and gullies and stands of gnarled trees on either side of the road. There were other landmarks, as well: jumbled piles of scrap wood and broken iron, the detritus of countless years—and countless sieges—rising like cairns raised over the shattered dreams of conquest; he saw a forest of upright spars, each sporting tattered banners that snapped in the wind—a serpent, a stylized crown, and a raven with wings outstretched being the most numerous. How many *kaunar* had arisen from the grave to find new purpose here in the grim gloom of Nástrond? How many nursed the same desire that thundered in Grimnir's own breast—to conquer and slay and grind the bones of his enemies under heel? And how many had these desires checked by a swift blade, a spear thrust, an arrow hissing from the cloud-wreathed sky? Only the Tangled God knew these answers . . . .

Behind him, the front gate was more to Grimnir's liking: an immense set of double doors built from thick timber and banded in bronze and iron, scarred and blackened, set between two short towers. A carved stone wolf's head snarled down at them from atop the lintel. But even here, Grimnir could tell something was amiss.

The left-hand door stood ajar.

Grimnir drew his long-seax and edged closer. Behind him, he heard Skaði loosen her sword in its sheath. With his off hand, Grimnir pushed the door open, enough for him to slip through. Inside, a short, deeply-shadowed tunnel led to a courtyard.

Just inside, Grimnir found the first corpses—two *skrælingar* locked in Death's embrace, both with knives buried in their throats and their black-nailed fists knotted in each other's hair. Grimnir nudged them with one booted foot. "Maggots knifed each other," he said.

Skaði gestured at the courtyard, drawing Grimnir's eye. "There's more."

And there were. Dozens of corpses, singly and in pairs, littered the flagstones of the courtyard before the open doors of the *stavhǫll,* framed by soaring posts carved with wolf and stag symbols; rivulets of black blood oozed from severed heads, from eviscerated torsos, from lopped-off limbs, from arrow-pierced eyes and throats. The stench of death hung like a shroud in the heavy air.

Grimnir walked carefully among the bodies. He spied brothers and cousins he'd not seen since he was a whelp; sisters, too. Most of the dead wore the badge of Bálegyr—a red eye with a slitted pupil; Grimnir saw another badge among them, a stag's skull done in white paint. None of his father's folk were clad solely for battle. Some had only a gambeson, stained from drinking; others wore mail. Those who wore the stag's head, however, were kitted out in their finest war-gear.

Grimnir rolled one of the stag's-head swine over onto his back, revealing a face hacked apart by an axe. "*Nár!* Whose emblem is this, eh? Lútr's?"

"Kjallandi's," Skaði replied, coming up behind him.

Grimnir gave her a sharp look.

"No, it's true," she said. "These are Kjallandi's dogs, here. Most likely, he and old Bálegyr quarreled over something—some insult, some point of honor, who gets what . . . truth be told, the two of them can't stand each other. They stick by one another because they're each too weak on their own. Bálegyr's folk are more numerous and more cunning; Kjallandi's folk are better fighters."

"You lie," Grimnir said.

Skaði made a rude hand gesture; she pushed past him and led the way, up a short flight of steps and into the great hall. Grimnir followed, pausing on the threshold to get a good look at the heart of the kingdom ruled by his father and grandfather.

It reminded him of his old longhouse, back in the land of the Raven-Geats, but larger and far more grand. Large enough to hold an army of his kin— three or four hundred, easily. It boasted three fire pits and a hundred rough tables amid a forest of carved wooden columns, where lanterns of hammered iron hung from thick nails. There were trophies, here, too, like they'd had at

Orkahaugr; banners and shields taken from defeated foes, a niche-cut wall of severed heads—a score in all; some fresh, others nothing but scraps of flesh hanging from yellowed bone. Open doorways with intricate carvings on their jambs and lintels, the same carvings he'd seen on the back porch, led off into the bowels of the hall. At the far end, opposite the great doors of the entrance, hung the war-standards of his kin, the Eye and the Stag-Skull. Under these, Grimnir saw a dais rising three steps from the floor; atop the dais were the carved thrones of the kings.

"Welcome to Varghǫll," Skaði said, spreading her arms. "The Wolf's Hall."

And like the courtyard, Varghǫll was carpeted with the dead, its stone floors slick with spilled blood. The fires had gone cold, and a thin gray light seeped in from the door and from a long clerestory in the roof. Grimnir sheathed Hátr. Slowly, he walked the length of the hall. "*Faugh!* How often do these rats decide to scrap and scrum amongst themselves?"

Skaði sprang up on a bench, and thence onto the top of a scarred timber trestle, where the sprawled corpse of a stag-marked war-hag lay, a broken bottle thrust half down her throat. She paced Grimnir, leaping nimbly from table to table. "More than you'd reckon," she replied. She looked up. "I've lost count of the number of times I've been knifed under this roof. By Ymir, it's good to be home!"

Grimnir kicked aside the body of one of his myriad brothers, whose name he'd long forgotten, and ascended the dais under the twin banners. Both carved thrones sat vacant. Grimnir sprawled in the left-hand throne, throwing one leg over the rune-carved armrest. "I guess there's naught to do but wait," he said. "Wait for these idiots to return."

Skaði turned and raised an eyebrow at him.

"What?" Grimnir snarled.

"Your old da blood-eagled the last of his sons who dared sit on his throne."

Grimnir bared his teeth in a fierce grin. He stroked the carved armrests. "Just getting a feel for it, is all."

"Don't go getting any bright ideas." Skaði dropped back onto a bench, and then down to the corpse-strewn floor. Even as she did, she fell into a fighting crouch, her sword ringing as she drew it from its scabbard. A feral hiss escaped her lips.

Grimnir followed her hard-eyed gaze.

Two figures stood on the threshold of Varghǫll, limned in gray light. The first was a tall *kaunr*, one of those straight-legged bastards, who boasted of their so-called pure blood; more akin to a *dvergr* than a true son of Loki. He was clad in a hauberk of steel chain. A beast-faced helmet obscured his swarthy features. Around his shoulders was draped a rich red cloak, and where his sword should have been Grimnir noticed an empty scabbard. He held a white-fletched and white-painted arrow aloft, pointing down.

The second figure was the *scrag* Snaga.

"SNAGA! MY old cock-sparrow," Grimnir roared. He did not move off the throne, nor did his hand stray to the hilt of Hátr. Even so, he exuded a quiet menace. His single eye glittered like an ember in the gloom. "*Nár!* Come to pay your respects already, eh?"

Snaga looked around at the bodies of the slain. "Like what you've done with the place, long-tooth," the *scrag* said.

Grimnir's jagged smile was unsettling. "A family spat, is all. Who's your friend? Looks like one of them blue bloods from the Root-end of things, all high-and-mighty in their little city."

The *kaunr* ignored Grimnir's taunt. To Snaga, he hissed: "Is that the *skrælingr*?"

"Aye." Snaga ducked his head and nodded. "That's him, all right. He's the one that done Skollvaldr."

Grimnir pushed himself upright. He wandered down the dais to the nearest table, where a leather jack of ale sat amid the wreckage, its liquid warm and flat. Still, Grimnir snatched it up and tossed it back. He wiped his mouth with the back of his hand. "Ha! Did that little *arsegót* come back whining? Now he wants some payback, eh? So he's sent one of Daddy's henchmen, under an arrow of truce, is that it? Well, you tell that dunghill rat to meet me back on that beach! I'll hack his fool's head off, again, and feed him to the *sjóvættir*!"

Skaði chuckled—more to hide the sudden look of alarm that flitted across her lean features than from any trace of humor. "You didn't?"

"Bastard had it coming," Grimnir snarled. "Acting like he was some precious rat of consequence! *Nár!* I took the piss right out of him. Sent his head back to old Gangr with a little message scratched into his brow, and gave his corpse to those water-sprites who lurk down in Lake Gjöll. Figured those wretched *scrags* would have a right laugh, watching Skollvaldr trying to swim away from those handsy mud-maggots."

"Ymir's blood," she muttered. "Well, that explains things."

Grimnir scowled. "What are you yammering on about?"

"That's Bölthorn, yonder," she said, nodding at the *kaunr*. "He's Mánavargr's war-herald. If *he's* come, well, that means Gangr's out for blood—"

"Then tell him to fish his boy out of the water and teach him better manners!"

"It's not that simple," Skaði replied. "Feh! The lot of us, we can only die and come back again and again if our hacked-up corpses never leave the soil of Nástrond. What you did, the kings and jarls reserve for the worst of traitors, assassins, and throne-pretenders." She jabbed a thumb at the wall of severed heads, twenty in all. "Hack off their head and toss their body in the water, and they don't come back, again. Ever. So, you've gone and robbed them of any chance for glory; robbed them of their place on the great ship, *Naglfar*, that sails at Ragnarök and carries us into battle upon the plains of Vígríðr. That's why Gangr is out for blood: you robbed him of his favorite son."

Grimnir whistled. He glanced sidelong at Snaga, and saw the malevolent gleam in the *scrag*'s eyes, the triumphant half-smile on his lips, even though his head remained lowered. "And it was all *that* one's idea."

"Snaga?" Skaði grunted. "Don't surprise me. He—"

"Enough!" the *kaunr*, Bölthorn, bellowed. The beast-helm obscuring his face gave his voice an eerie ring. "You, *skrælingr*! You are Bálegyr's son, called Grimnir?"

"What if I am, wretch?" Grimnir turned to face the taller *kaunr*. "What are *you* going to do about it, eh?"

"Lord Mánavargr has declared you an outlaw," Bölthorn replied. "And an enemy of Kaunheimr. Any found giving you shelter will be held as your accomplices, and they will face Lord Mánavargr's wrath. You rats will learn, son of Bálegyr, that the True Sons of Loki are not to be trifled with! Will you come with me and face my lord's judgment, or will you condemn you and your worthless kin to face the punishment of traitors?"

Grimnir glanced at Skaði. She stared hard at Bölthorn, her amber eyes as cold and predatory as a cat's. The bones and beads woven into her hair clicked as she came around the end of the table and passed near to where Grimnir stood. She hissed a word in his ear.

A single word.

And Grimnir knew without question what tack to take.

He turned his head, his single red eye ablaze with wrath for Bölthorn and the *scrag* beside him. "Your so-called lord Mánavargr can kiss my *skrælingr* arse, you puffed-up son of a troll-born whore! He claims what he cannot hold, and if he thinks fancy titles and notions of pure blood will protect him from my axe, then he's more a fool than you! Go back to your masters, dog, and tell them this: tell them if Gangr wants the head of Grimnir, he's welcome to come try and take it! Tell him to meet me out beyond these walls whenever he chooses, for I invoke the right of *hólmganga*! Trial by combat! You know it? Good! Let him meet me blade to blade, and Ymir will decide who between us is worthy of a place in the bows of *Naglfar*!"

As if to punctuate his words, Grimnir heard a sudden intake of breath from Bölthorn; in his shadow, Snaga snapped his head up at the sound. There was real fear in the *scrag*'s eyes. Behind him, Grimnir heard the snap of a bowstring; he felt the wind off a broad-headed arrow as it hissed past his ear. Before Snaga could so much as backpedal, that arrow took him high, in the apple of his throat. It punched through gristle and bone to stand out a handspan from the back of the *scrag*'s neck.

Blood exploded from Snaga's mouth even as he crumpled back across the threshold. There, he gurgled, spluttered, and died.

Bölthorn did not dare move.

Grimnir heard a familiar voice behind him—a voice he'd heard only in his head for these past six hundred years: "Well said, little rat."

Grimnir turned. Coming through a doorway, a heavy black bow in his gnarled fists, was Gífr, Kjallandi's son. The tall *kaunr* was clad in mail and scarlet cloth, a stag's skull of silver wire woven into the breast of his hauberk. He was much as Grimnir remembered him: as thin and lean as a youth, his rawboned frame lashed together with ropes of muscle and knotted sinew. He had a long, lantern-jawed face and skin lighter than Grimnir's—his scarred hide was the yellow-gray of a fine whetstone and covered in tattooed runes and sigils; more tattoos covered his bald pate, and the fringe of hair that hung about his long ears was the color of a storm-wracked sea, woven with dozens of old bone discs and beads of silver, garnet, and malachite—some bearing the markings of sand-swept Aegyptus. Sharp eyes smoldered like coals from beneath a heavy brow.

"Ha! You miserable old git!" Grimnir said, a genuine smile curling his lips. "Wondering when I'd run into you."

"Hymn-singers finally got you, too, did they?"

"Aye. On the road to that cesspool they call Rome, no less!" Grimnir hawked and spat. "What happened here? You rats get bored and decide to knife each other?"

"Just a small disagreement, is all." Gífr chuckled, then looked past Grimnir at Bölthorn. "You have your answer, swine," he said. "Go, and take that piece of filth with you."

Hidden as it was by his beast-helm, none could see the expression on Bölthorn's face; his eyes seethed, however, and his gestures reeked of disdain as he slung the white arrow away and seized dead Snaga by the hair of his head. He dragged the *scrag* after him as he retraced his steps to the gates of Úlfsstaðir.

"Among the dead for a few hours and already you're making enemies, eh, little rat?" Gífr said, looking at the one-eyed son of his older sister. "Not that Gangr's lout didn't have it coming. If anyone deserved to go floating in the Gjöll, it's that one. But why throw your lot in with Snaga's bunch of *scrags*? Didn't trade that eye for wisdom, did you?"

"*Nár!* This one I traded for vengeance. Cleaned up Hrungnir's little mess and sent his bastard down to Helheimr, to boot. Don't go and try to hang this one on me! It was that blasted *scrag*'s idea to drop that toad in the water. Though, it was my idea to lop off the bastard's head and scrawl *argr* on his brow."

Gífr howled with laughter. "*Argr*, eh?" he said, once he got his breath back. He set his bow down on one table. "That's rich. Listen, little rat— don't let old Snaga fool you. He looks like a brat who's still two arse hairs shy of maturity, but he is the first and the eldest of us all. Your cousin, he is. In those days, he was known as Thrár the Younger, son of Thráinn, son of Thrár the Elder. His father refused our summons, refused even to treat with us under the eaves of

Mánavargr's hall. 'He is Loki,' Thráinn had said, rebuking me when I came to his door as the Tangled God's herald. 'Mischief and malice are the blood in his veins! No! We will have no part of this!'

"My words bounced off the father, aye, but they sank their hooks in the son. Thrár crept out that night to see what mischief we were up to behind his father's back. He'd seen the lights of Mánavargr's hall; he'd heard the impassioned words of the Tangled God; he'd tasted the juices of the great platters of meat Loki's servants brought out, the afterbirth of Angrboða's monstrous children. His skin grew coarse and dark; his teeth grew sharp and strong, and his eyes took on the red gleam of a predator. No poison or disease could harm him. He became one of the *kaunar*, one of Loki's chosen. One of us.

"He was just a boy. The Change scared him witless. Little bastard crawled home that night and begged his father's forgiveness. And old Thráinn, enraged by this betrayal, took his precious Thrár's head in his hands and broke his neck ... condemned him to spend the rest of his days here, on Nástrond, awaiting the echo of the Gjallarhorn and the fires of Ragnarök. He's had it out for us ever since. He picks up the *scrags* and the strays and teaches them his brand of hate. Blasted little warmonger."

"Thráinn, eh? Old Náinn's kin, by chance?" Grimnir said.

"Brothers," Gífr replied. His gaze met Skaði's for the first time, and there was a flash of recognition. "It's been a wolf's age since I last laid eyes on you, daughter of Skæfloc. Where have you been keeping yourself, eh?"

"That *arsegót* is no longer my father," she said, heat flaring behind her amber eyes. "After his bit of treachery, that feckless whoreson sold me down the river, right and proper! Knifed me in the back and tossed me under the thumbs of the Lokaean Witches. That's where this one found me." She nodded at Grimnir.

"Skæfloc dies, by Ymir! By my blade or by yours!" Gífr said. "As for those meddlesome old hags, I've been meaning to turn them out and send them packing back to Jötunheimr."

"Too late, you lazy sot," said Grimnir. He glanced sidelong at Skaði. "This one, she's handy in a fight."

"So-ho! Is she now? That's high praise coming from the likes of you! Come, little rats," Gífr said, throwing one arm over Grimnir's shoulder and motioning for Skaði to follow. "Let us drink like we did in the old days, and you two can tell me the tale of Rome, of Gangr's brat, and of the thumbs of *jötunn* witches!"

The dead returned.

They came back to life—or what passed as life on Nástrond's blighted shores—with a gasp and a curse. They came back nursing grudges, the guile in their black hearts begetting more guile; smiling as they plotted their next bloodletting. Some came back with the battle-rage still upon them, fuming and frothing in their eagerness to slay, and to die, again. These were tackled by their more levelheaded mates, who held them down till the fever passed.

But all of them returned to light, to the sounds of raucous laughter, and to a freshly-broached cask of ale.

Fires burned in the pits of the great hall of Úlfsstaðir; the lamps blazed, streaking the eternal gloom with orange, red, and yellow radiance. At the table nearest the still-empty thrones of the two kings, Bálegyr and Kjallandi, Gífr sat across from a one-eyed *skrælingr* few of them knew, his head thrown back and roaring with mirth as the newcomer spooled out a tale. Beside this stranger, snorting into her jack of ale, sat that bastard Skæfloc's long-missing daughter, Skaði—looking thin and disheveled, but otherwise hale. Already, a knot of lads had formed around them, drawn as much by the ale as by the stranger's words.

"*Nár!* So, this little bird," he was saying, "she's flailing around with her seax like she's trying to cut the wind, her arm as limp as a boned fish. No, no ... hear me out, you louts! She's dancing around, leaping from foot to foot like someone slipped hot coals into her shoes. But this little scrap, she's all of a hundred pounds, soaked to the skin! All she has to do is draw blood. She draws blood, and I'd promised I would go and drag her would-be bedmate back to Hrafnhaugr before those motherless Swedes made a fine woman out of him.

"*Faugh!* Problem is, that little bird couldn't hit the broad side of a mead hall! Not the way she's jumping and thrashing around. So, I nearly knock that seax out of her hand, and I told her what you used to tell me, you old git! I told her to move with a purpose, make your enemy see what you want him to see ... and then I all but skewered her with a feint any *scrag* worth his salt could have parried.

"Well, this little bird ... she thinks it over a moment, nods at me. Then, we go back to scrapping—but before I can close with her, she reaches down, snatches up a sock, and throws it in my face!"

Gífr nearly split his sides with laughter. "She pulled the wool over your eyes, eh?" he gasped between gales. The *skrælingar* around them hooted and guffawed.

The newcomer pounded the table with one black-nailed fist. "And, by Ymir, she nearly had me! My mail kept me from having to eat a load of crow and fetch back that prancing *arsegót* she was panting after."

"What did you do to her?" Skaði said, blowing ale-froth from her lips. "This little bird of yours?"

The newcomer glanced sidelong at her, his good eye like a smoldering ember. "Got distracted, she did. Thought she'd drawn blood. Took her eyes off me, looking for it, all smug as you please. So, I broke her skull with the flat of my seax."

The lads sniggered.

The newcomer turned, suddenly, and jabbed a finger at Gífr. "That little bird is still alive, to this day! All because your Halla called the *landvættir* up from deep in the earth to mend her, after that. Little wretch is a hundred and forty-five years old if she's a day."

"Ha! Always a good girl, that Halla. Whatever became of her?"

The newcomer spat. "Náinn's son, that maggot, Náli, lured her out into the sunlight. I got him back, though. Lured him onto the tip of Sárklungr."

Gífr *chk*'ed his teeth and nodded, then looked up. A sudden silence fell across the great hall as, from a side door, a voice tolled out like a bell, deep and clear: "Sárklungr, you say? So, you're this Grimnir who ended up with my old sword, are you? Well, drag it out, you lout! I'd like to see it again!"

As the echo faded, a giant figure emerged from the shadows—a *kaunr* to be reckoned with, surely, pale-skinned and brooding, with deep-set eyes as red as garnets; a beard the color of iron hung down to his mail-clad breast, gathered into a single plait and secured by thongs of silver-studded leather. From his broad shoulders, an embroidered cloak was draped after the fashion of the Romans, its ends clutched in his off hand; the bone and silver hilt of a gladius jutted from a baldric-hung scabbard on his left hip.

Kjallandi, the *skrælingar* whispered. Kjallandi had come.

5
HAMMER AND ANVIL

Grimnir had never met his mother's sire.

Oh, but he *had* heard countless stories. Gífr never tired of telling him about his father's duel with Bálegyr on the slopes of Orkahaugr, or of their long wanderings down from the frigid north of Miðgarðr. For the whole of their sojourn in the East, Gífr had fed him story after story—told around crackling fires, drinking wine stolen from the cellars of the Rus or meat taken from the burned-out villages of the Slavs; stories of Kjallandi's machinations against the empire of the Romans, of his battles against the renowned generals Marius and Sulla. Time and again, Grimnir had heard Gífr's account of the last battle, where Kjallandi was betrayed by his Moorish allies, who sought a separate peace with Rome. All of this had all occurred long before Grimnir was even a glimmer in old Bálegyr's eye, and stories have a way of growing with each retelling.

Seeing Kjallandi in the flesh, though, made Grimnir wonder if old Gífr hadn't held back a bit. He followed Gífr's lead and rose on unsteady legs. From the corner of his eye, he saw Skaði and the others follow suit—all the folk of the Stag-Skull stood out of deference; but only a few of the folk of the Eye paid Kjallandi this respect. And none of his brothers deigned to stand, not even those whelped by Skríkja, Kjallandi's daughter. Grimnir ground his teeth, but said nothing.

Kjallandi sat on the right-hand throne; a moment after, Gífr and the rest resumed their places. Deep red eyes stared hard at Grimnir. "I can see some of my blood in you, son of Bálegyr. This is good. Now, my sword, Sárklungr, let's see it."

Beside him, Grimnir felt Skaði's sharp elbow dig into his ribs. "Told you," she said, taking a pull on her jack of ale to hide her grin.

Grimnir stood, once more, and drew Hátr. He held the long-seax up for all to see, and then drove it point-first into the boards of the table. Kjallandi eyed the snarling beast-face carved into the blade's pommel, the wire-wrapped leather hilt, and the scarred bronze crossguard. He looked back to Grimnir and arched an eyebrow. "And what does that little cheeseparer of yours have to do with the mighty Sárklungr, the Wound-Thorn of our people?"

Fits of laughter arose. A few of the sons of Bálegyr muttered darkly to one another, as though this interrogation, this smattering of mirth, was somehow an affront to *their* honor. Grimnir, though, laughed with them.

"*Nár,* lord," he said. "This *is* Sárklungr, or what's left of her. The rest of it steeps in the muck at the bottom of the Volkhov River, to this day. At a place called Holmgarðr, on the old Varangian road, in the land of the Kievan Rus."

Gífr leaned back and stretched his legs. "Aye, I remember Holmgarðr. Place was a rat-hole. Wooden streets, wooden shacks, wooden churches under wooden steeples. Its walls were wood, and that worm-eaten bridge over the Volkhov, too. Bah! We should have burned the damned village down, back in our wandering days!"

"And salted the earth with the blood of those whoreson boyars!" Grimnir replied. "So, picture this, then: It's the dead hours of the night, in the dead of winter. There's a sickle moon, and even by that thin light the crust of snow makes it bright as daylight. All that wood, it's sheathed in ice. But that's where Níðhöggr's run off to, where—"

Kjallandi raised one long-fingered hand. "We have heard rumors. So it is true, then? Malice-Striker has returned from the dead, and Raðbolg's oath is forfeit?"

Grimnir's eyes narrowed. He glanced from Gífr to his father and then back at Skaði. He recalled her words earlier: *Níðhöggr, eh? Good one. Better get your story straight, then*. And suddenly, he understood what she meant, understood her skepticism. *They didn't know.*

"Aye, it's true," he said.

Kjallandi motioned to one of his followers. "Fetch Bálegyr, then. That cur should be here to listen to his son's accounting."

"Bálegyr is here, you swine!" a voice roared in answer. From the rear of the great hall there came a cortege of mail-clad warriors, bandy-legged and fierce, all bearing the sigil of the Eye. Around the hall, the assembled *skrælingar* showed their approval by hammering their drinking jacks against the boards. The guard parted, and Grimnir got his first look at Bálegyr in over twelve hundred years. He expected to see the fearsome boogeyman of his milk-days, the brutal overlord who had a taste for killing his own sons when they stepped out of line. He expected someone savage and regal, like Kjallandi. Someone who reeked of power, cunning, and naked ferocity, as befitting the one accounted as greatest of the Nine Fathers of the *kaunar*.

In truth, however, Bálegyr was a swag-bellied ape, dark of skin and broad in the shoulders, though not especially tall. His legs were bowed; his arms long and thick with knotty muscle. He had no neck to speak of, and a head like a ship's bollard—round and hard and covered in scars. A plaited topknot of gray-black hair hung from his scalp and down over his shoulder, its ends captured by a hollowed-out and rune-carved length of bone. His right eye was a gaping socket bisected by a terrible scar, a gift from his duel with Kjallandi; his left blazed like Grimnir's. He wore a scarlet gambeson as another might wear a robe, unlaced and open, over trousers of rust-colored cloth and leather. A black sash constrained his not-inconsiderable gut. Cradled in his arm, Bálegyr carried a mace, its head that of a snarling wolf wrought in blackened iron. This was Maugrónðr, the Corpse-Hammer.

In Bálegyr's wake came an entourage of kin and other hangers-on, from trusty lads who'd been with him since before Ériu and the great battle at Mag Tuiredh to sons who were currently in favor—Hrungnir among them. Called Grendel, the Bone-Grinder, by the Spear-Danes of Hróarr, Hrungnir was much as Grimnir recalled from their last meeting, on the shores of the Skagerrak some ten years after the destruction of Orkahaugr: slouch-backed and squint-eyed, with a face like it belonged on a cunning animal, brutal but dull. He had heavily muscled arms and legs, and hands too large for his frame—*a strangler's hands,* Gífr had called them. Here was the tree that bore the diseased fruit that was Bjarki Half-Dane, and Grimnir could see it. Hrungnir eyed him like he was some rival he meant to squash. For his part, Grimnir bared his fangs in a mocking smile and touched one finger to his brow.

Bringing up the rear of the cortege, Grimnir spied his mother, Skríkja. *She,* at least, was how he remembered her—tall, light-skinned like Gífr, but as lean and vicious as a raptor; she had eyes as feral and yellow as a cat's. Her black hair she wore in thick plaits, woven with tubes of carved gold and silver. She sized Grimnir up the same way a lioness sizes up her prey.

"So, you're one of my bastards, eh?" Bálegyr said. Grimnir bristled; his gaze shifted from his mother to the trundling sack of suet before him. He matched his father's gaze, fire with fire.

"You tell me," Grimnir replied. "Is the queen my mother, or did you get me on some two-bit whore you put it to for sport?"

"Watch your mouth, you rat!"

"Watch yours, maggot!"

The pair glowered at one another a moment longer before Bálegyr snorted and moved to sit upon the left-hand throne. "Aye, he's one of mine!" Skríkja brushed past Grimnir and went to stand between the two thrones, a hand resting upon the back of each seat. "So, you were the last one of us left topside, eh?" Bálegyr said. Without waiting for Grimnir's reply, he glanced at Kjallandi. "Proves my point, right there."

"It does no such thing," Kjallandi snapped.

"What point?" Grimnir glanced from king to king, then tilted his head to glare at Gífr. "*Nár!* What point?"

Old Gífr sighed, as though the conversation only picked at an old scab. He motioned for a thrall to fetch more ale. "Ragnarök," he said, finally. "My father believes the Twilight of the Gods should have already fallen, and since it hasn't that means something has slipped higher up the Great Ash. Some bit of treachery we're not privy to has delayed the call to Vígríðr. Bálegyr, here, believes the opposite—that things will fall out as they may, all in their own time. Aye, he believes we should focus our attention on ousting Mánavargr and breaking the so-called True Sons before we worry what goes on beyond our shores."

Bálegyr nodded. "They are the real threat, here and now! Not some half-imagined conspiracy from up Ásgarðr's way that *might* unfold!" The *skrælingar* of the Eye hooted their assent, hammering their drinking jacks and hurling curses.

"I've never said the True Sons were not a threat, you lout!" Kjallandi said. "Only that there is no greater concern to us than the breaking of the Nine Worlds!" His words brought the *skrælingar* of the Stag-Skull to their feet. Hilts pounded on trestle tables; someone shied a jack of ale at the sons of Bálegyr. Another killing seemed imminent . . .

"Silence!" Skríkja roared like a beast-mother, scolding her young. "Let them speak, you swine!"

Grimnir looked back at Gífr. "And you? What do you believe?"

"What do you think, little rat?" Gífr replied. "I side with my father, of course. I'd go a step further: Where *is* the Tangled God?" At this, Grimnir noted nodding heads among both camps. "None among us has laid eyes on Father Loki since the Elder Days. I am his herald and I have not seen him nor heard his call since the hours before our defeat in the Ironwood. Where is he? Raðbolg and a few others went out beyond Nástrond, to scout and pick up what rumors they can, but none have returned—"

"Wait." Grimnir held up one black-nailed hand. "What do you mean he *went out beyond Nástrond*? Are we not trapped here till the Gjallarhorn blows?"

Hrungnir laughed and started to say something no doubt derogatory, but the glitter of malice in Skríkja's yellow eyes stopped him cold. It was she who answered Grimnir. "Miðgarðr and the upper realms are forever closed to us, but we may come and go as we like among the lower realms. It is . . . not without its own perils, though."

"Aye." Gífr nodded. "Those who dwell beyond Nástrond, they hunt us like vermin. From trolls and *jötunn* and vengeful *landvættir*, to our blasted cousins among the *dvergar* and their allies, the cruel little *álfar*, the elves of Álfheimr. All of them want a piece of our hides. What's worse, if one of those prancing fools decides to shove a yard of steel down your gullet, out yonder . . . that's it. There's no returning from that." Gífr allowed a pained grimace to cross his features. "I fear such was Raðbolg's fate."

"Waste of good lads," Bálegyr muttered.

Kjallandi glanced sidelong at him. "I disagree."

"So the lot of you went and killed each other over it?" Grimnir shook his head.

Gífr shrugged. "We've killed each other over less."

"Do not judge us too harshly, Grimnir Bálegyr's son," Kjallandi said. His sharp eyes pierced Grimnir to the bone. "Killing is in our nature. It *is* our nature, what we were bred for—the wrack and ruin of war; it is the purpose given to us by the Tangled God. What does it matter if we kill over the least slight or the greatest insult?" He rose from his throne and stepped down to their table. He pulled Hátr from the boards, held it in his hand for a moment. "We are like the steel in this blade, son of my daughter. Age and neglect dulls its edge, weakens it. We are like this steel!" Kjallandi thrust the blade aloft. "And Nástrond is our anvil! Here, we are forged into deadlier fighters, our skills sharpened like blades ere we take our places in *Naglfar*'s blood-drenched bow. These killing fields of Nástrond, they hammer us, they fold us, they give us strength. And death? Death is but the quench. After we cool, we return to the anvil and the forging begins anew." A roar of approbation filled the great hall, rising from the throats of *skrælingar* under both banners. Even Bálegyr raised his mace in salute, though a mote of jealousy lurked in his single eye.

Kjallandi nodded. He raised his hand, motioning for silence. The tall *kaunr* flipped Hátr around, grasping it by the blade, and handed it back to Grimnir. "You have a tale to tell. Tell it, and be done. We have a *hólmganga* to plan, plots to hatch, and more killing to prepare for—you, most of all, if you mean to best Gangr." With that, Kjallandi returned to his seat.

GRIMNIR SAID nothing. He sheathed Hátr, took a long draught of ale, and wiped foam from his lips with the back of his hand. The *skrælingr* glanced about, his red eye gathering in his audience; a log shifted. Embers crackled. Grimnir let the moment drag on until he heard the impatient mutterings of his kin.

"Oaths!" he roared, suddenly. He turned in a slow circle. "*Nár!* We've all sworn them. We live and die by our word, by our oaths. But they're strange things, lads. The hymn-singers of Miðgarðr, they will swear them in one breath and break them in another—*by god* this and *by god* that. But their Nailed God, he never takes offense. You remember it, Gífr! He never strikes them down or tosses obstacles in their way. But let one of *our* folk swear even the most meaningless of oaths and suddenly every tree-humping ruffian between here and Helheimr will line up for the chance to test our mettle!" At this, Gífr—along with those *skrælingar* familiar with the world of the Nailed God—nodded sagaciously.

"We expect our oaths to matter!" Grimnir continued. "We expect the gods to honor them! *Faugh!* The oath that did me in was an old one. I heard it first on the night Níðhöggr, the Malice-Striker, came against us. Aye, the Norns wove my death-song with it: '*Hear me, Sly One, Father Loki! Bear witness, O Ymir, sire of giants and lord of the frost! By this blood, the blood of my kin, I swear! I, Raðbolg Kjallandi's son, will not rest until I've brought that wretched dragon to heel! I will not rest until Níðhöggr is under my blade!*' And Raðbolg swore it on Sárklungr, the dwarf-forged Wound-Thorn—still wet with the wyrm's filthy blood. I don't have to tell the lot of you how it played out. You've doubtless heard it from the idiot's mouth himself. And Gífr, here, has told you what went on after, I'll warrant. How that one-eyed wandering old tosspot, the so-called Allfather, took offense? Aye, the bastard cheated us! Raðbolg earned that vengeance, fair and square! But, no! *He* didn't like that one of our folk—one of us poor and lowly *kaunar*—beat him at his own game! *He* didn't like that one of us had shoved a foot of dwarf-steel right between the eyes of his precious little pet! All that meddlesome iron in the wyrm's skull meant Odin couldn't work his sorcery from afar and raise Níðhöggr from the grave, so he cheated! He sank the whole damned peninsula, sang a prophecy of return over the ruins, and bided his time."

Grimnir wet his throat with a draught of ale before continuing. "Well, you louts, here's where it gets interesting. Long after I sang Gífr's death-song on the Elbe River and took his blood-price in Saxon flesh, Odin went and lent his spirit—his *hamingja*—to a dwarf! And not just any dwarf, but a crookbacked son of Náinn called Náli, who Odin sent into the world to work his mischief!" The hall erupted with curses and imprecations.

Náinn had been a master-smith and a sorcerer, a traitor and betrayer of oaths; he had coveted Skríkja, in the eldest of days, and forged Sárklungr as a troth-gift. But when Skríkja rebuked him and refused to become his wife, the old dwarf turned bitter. It was Náinn, they believed, who warned the lords of Ásgarðr about the Tangled God's plans. On the eve of their flight from Niðavellir, the realm of the dwarves, to join Father Loki in Jötunheimr, Kjallandi slew Náinn over the banked embers of his forge and took Sárklungr off his bloody corpse. The revelation that Náinn's son was involved in Odin's chicanery only stoked the *skrælingar's* ire further.

Grimnir let the clamor die down, then nodded. "Oh, aye! He wove tales among the Nailed God's folk *and* among the bloody-handed Norse, hoping some addlepated hymn-singer or name-seeking pagan would respond to his call. He got both." Grimnir spooled out the tale of Konraðr of Skara, and of Úlfrún of the Iron Hand. He told them of the titanic battle in the ruins of Raven Hill, and of the resurrection of the dead wyrm, Níðhöggr.

"That night, by the gleam of *jötunn*-lights, I echoed old Raðbolg's oath. Sárklungr was mine, and I swore by the blood of my kin that I would hunt that wretched snake down and end it, once and for all. I would stalk the road of vengeance one last time, ere the Elder World vanished forever." Grimnir chuckled. "I thought, by year's end it would be done. But I have chased it for a hundred and thirty years! From the North, down the old Varangian road to Caffa on the Black Sea, then to Miklagarðr—what the hymn-singers call Constantinople; I chased it across Jórsalahaf, the great Jerusalem Sea, to Messina, where it unleashed a pestilence on the folk, there. I hounded it up through Langbarðaland, just outside old Rúmaborg, the ancient city of Rome." Grimnir spread his arms wide. "There, I was slain by some pox-scarred son of a whore with a crossbow, not ten steps from where the Malice-Striker was hiding."

Grimnir felt their eyes on him. He slowly turned to face Kjallandi. "*Nár!* Raðbolg didn't forfeit his oath. He saw it through, fair and square. And I would have seen mine through, as well, but Odin, that old bearded bastard, decided to change the rules again! See, at Holmgarðr on the Volkhov River, I caught the wyrm's scent early on. It had made a thrall of a rag-boned Rus merchant, a fat, chinless bastard with a wife and three sons. I followed him; watched as he delivered his youngest son to a spot at the center of the bridge. Watched him grab that little rat by the scruff and toss him over the side.

"The Malice-Striker was lurking under there, tucked up in the wooden trestles. Bastard caught the lad before he hit the ice. Gashed him open with its teeth and slurped him down whole. Three times, he came to the center of that cursed bridge. The last boy had some fight in him, but it didn't matter. His da cracked him over the head and tossed him down the wyrm's gullet. Keep in mind, last time I'd seen that snake it was hardly more than a skeleton held together by hatred and old scales, longer than the dragon-ships of the Norse and twice as broad. Well, no longer! *Nár!* Thing was still covered in plates of bone; it had the long, spiked tail it had in the Elder Days, but its body was barely larger than an ox.

"Still, the *fakr* was as slippery as an eel and as cunning as a fox . . . but I had an idea. It wanted the wife, too. Pretty little thing, with hair like gold and a heart free from guile. She thought her man was telling the truth when he told her their boys were across the river, warming themselves by the fire in their new house—*a fine house,* he called it. New wood and fresh rushes, and a huge hearth. She was happy." Grimnir spat. "She came willingly, thinking it a grand adventure on an early winter's night.

"I lit into them about a hundred yards from the bridge. Cracked her on the head and left her by the fire in a crofter's hovel. Him, I gutted like a fish—so-ho! He deserved that and more! Gaffed him up like bait and ran a sealskin rope up his craw and out his lying mouth. Then, I wrapped him in the wife's fur cloak, carried him to the bridge, and chucked him over the side.

"The old wyrm was hungry! It lunged, clamped on to the gift of warm flesh . . . and found itself with a mouthful of cold iron, instead! Ha! Hooked it like an eel! How it flopped and struggled and tried to slip away! My blood was up, then. I had Sárklungr ready . . . all I needed was to drag it up high enough to get a shot at its neck."

Grimnir made a snort of disgust. "But the Allfather looks out for his own, doesn't he? This he proved after Raðbolg put a yard of dwarf-steel into the dragon's skull. I heard my tendons crack and felt my muscles tear as I dragged that wyrm's neck over the bridge's wooden railing. I saw my opening, hammered the blade down . . . and felt the game change, again! That old snake twisted aside at the last moment, like some unseen hand had grabbed it and jerked it out of Sárklungr's path! The blade missed it, of course, and bit deep into the icy wood. And then, the wyrm's tail came screaming over the edge. It nearly spiked into my fool skull. Somehow, I kept hold of Sárklungr's hilt and was trying to wrench it free when that tail came back for a second helping. This time, it got me, but good." Grimnir gestured at his right side. "Ripped me from shoulder to hip. It splintered the wood of the bridge, shredded the sealskin rope, and broke Sárklungr off about a foot from the hilt. Snapped it like a rotten twig! Bah! I survived being torn open by that wretch's bony tail, reforged Sárklungr by the glow of a volcanic fire in the Caucasus Mountains, and had the wyrm's measure . . . only to be slain by some knock-kneed half-wit? *Faugh!*"

Grimnir's eyes shifted, the good one glaring at Bálegyr. "And you! You may think there is naught amiss so you can keep on sniping at that idiot, Mána-vargr, but I'm with them." Grimnir jabbed a thumb at Gífr and the others. "Something *has* slipped. *Nár!* Odin is hatching some bit of mischief that, like it or not, will likely bode ill for the lot of us. We should know what that old raven-starver is up to, even if there's sod-all we can do to stop it."

And with that, Grimnir turned from the thrones of the two kings and stalked away between the tables, pausing to snatch up a full crockery jug of ale. For a moment silence followed him. As he neared the doors of Varghǫll, he heard Bálegyr reel off a litany of curses; Kjallandi merely nodded, eyeing Grimnir's retreating back as he stroked his beard in thought.

When nothing more was said, Hrungnir took it upon himself to voice his father's ire. He stood. "*Hie!* You mouthy little runt! You don't turn your back on our kings, you rat, much less on your own father! Get back here and show some respect!"

Grimnir paused on the threshold. He half-turned, his gaze brushing Skaði's for the briefest of moments before continuing on to pierce Hrungnir, his single eye seething like a cauldron of hate. "And what do *you* know of respect, you arse-kissing little puppet?" Grimnir spat. "Sit down, you swine! Drink your ale and remember who it was who cleaned up your mistakes! Ymir's blood! You maggots got on without me for centuries. Surely you can last a few hours without me holding your hands? I have a *hólmganga* to plan, and a bit of killing to prepare for!"

THE DOOM OF ODIN

Grimnir slipped from Varghǫll, then, with the echo of Hrungnir's curses dogging his steps.

And Gífr—old, patient Gífr—merely smiled and went back to his cups.

SKAÐI TRACKED Grimnir down a short time later. First, she followed the rude gestures of the door wardens, who directed her out beyond the iron-banded walls of Úlfsstaðir. From there, she tracked him in truth, following the hobnailed pattern of his boots in the dust. He'd left the road and taken to a grove of ash and willow at the base of the rocky track that led around to the back porch. Overhead, a shoal of fumes from some great burning in Múspellsheimr drifted over the face of Yggðrasil, dimming its lights and bringing a hint of true night to Nástrond's shores. Still, even by the thin radiance filtering through the boiling clouds—like starlight on a clear night—Skaði was able to follow Grimnir's trail.

At the heart of the grove, she spied the glimmer of light; her keen ears caught the soft rasp of steel on stone. Around her, she was surprised to find ivy-clad ruins, low walls of pitted stone and columns broken off like rotted teeth. Though what hands had raised these works, she could not say.

There, she found Grimnir sitting beside a small fire. He had made camp next to a spring that trickled from the rocks; the son of Bálegyr had stripped out of his mail and his gambeson. Naked to the waist, he tended the edge of his axe with a whetstone. The crockery jar of ale rested beside him, and periodically he stopped to gnaw on one of the sausages he'd taken from the witches' larder. He heard Skaði approach.

"That's *scrag*, I told you," she said, nodding at the sausage.

Grimnir shrugged, took another bite. "Tastes like pig."

"You think it's safe out here, what with Gangr's folk panting after your blood?"

"As safe as it is in *there*." Grimnir jerked his head toward the Wolves' Abode, then spat a knob of gristle into the fire. "Safer, more like. I got you here to protect me."

"Feh! I'll let 'em have you, you worthless maggot."

Grimnir's lips curled in a sneer. From the corner of his eye, he saw Skaði unbuckle her weapons belt and set it aside; he watched her shimmy out of her mail hauberk. She laid it out, draped over one of the sections of ruined wall not thick with ivy, and inspected the links for rust and breakage before she sat down. Grimnir went back to sharpening the edge of his axe.

Silence. The fire crackled and popped. Stone scraped against steel. Skaði loosened the collar of her gambeson and looked up at the cloud-wracked sky.

"Do you miss it?"

"Miss what?"

"*It*. Miðgarðr. Your old home."

Grimnir looked up. He raised his eyes, following Skaði's gaze. Beyond the trees, beyond the clouds, slashes of green and gold light could be glimpsed; above it, the shimmering reds and yellows of the upper realms, alien suns burning eternal in the void between Yggðrasil's limitless boughs. "Miss it? *Nár!* The hymn-singers can have it, and good riddance! What I miss are the Elder Days. The wandering time after Mag Tuiredh, when Gífr passed the wolf-mantle to Hrungnir and let that idiot rule our folk. We took off, he and I. Ha! We were our own masters, then. Hundreds of years, we rambled—from the Baltic down to the great Stone City of Miklagarðr. Aye, we took what we wanted, went where we pleased, with no so-called *lords* to louse things up."

"Did you have many women?"

"I'm not like Hrungnir, or my old da. *Faugh!* Never understood their fascination with whiteskin *ghæsh*." Grimnir used a choice bit of slang for a woman's anatomy; beside him, Skaði stifled a grin. "Filthy creatures."

"Good," she said. Slowly, she pulled at the next lace of her gambeson. Lace after lace, until the front of it stood open. Skaði reclined, her elbows resting on the broken column behind her. She rubbed the corded muscle of her belly, toyed with the laces of her trousers. "I'd never let a whiteskin touch me, either."

Grimnir put his axe and whetstone aside. "Now, just because I don't go panting after the manling *ghæsh* doesn't mean I'll go after any smoke-colored camp whore."

Even as the words left his lips, Skaði bolted upright and backhanded him, her knuckles cracking across his cheek. "*Smoke-colored camp whore?*" she hissed, nostrils flared. "Is that what you think of me?"

THE DOOM OF ODIN

Grimnir took the blow, the sting of it only deepening the thin smile that curled the corner of his mouth. He gave a soft snort. "I think," he hissed, "you've been mounted more times than Odin's favorite mare."

"Bastard!" Skaði slapped him again. Like flint striking steel, the impact kindled something deep in Grimnir's eyes, something hot and dark and lustful. Something she knew he could see reflected in her own gaze, as well. Skaði's thin lips parted. Her tongue flicked across sharp teeth; for a third time, the slap of flesh on flesh echoed about the grove. She drew back to strike a fourth time but was forestalled when Grimnir, his manner one of almost casual contempt, seized her sallow throat in one black-nailed fist.

Skaði let out an involuntary gasp; her amber eyes widened.

"Did you come here to fight?" Grimnir said, his voice a fierce whisper; he drew her close and inhaled her scent, snuffling like an animal. "Or did you come here for something . . . *else*?"

She clawed at the corded muscle of his arm, at his shoulders, gouging furrows in his hide as she tried to drag him closer. "There's a difference?" she managed.

Growling deep in his throat, Grimnir ripped the laces from her trousers. Moist heat seeped from the juncture of her thighs. She shrugged out of her gambeson, letting the quilted cloth fall down her back. Skaði heard a hiss escape his lips; his single eye burned as his gaze roved down her lean body, hard with muscle. His grip on her neck loosened.

Skaði took advantage of this momentary distraction; she knocked his hand aside and sneered at him. She ground against him, her hips rolling like those of a dancer. She arched her back, reached up and tangled her fingers in his dark hair, pulling him closer. Nor was there anything gentle in Grimnir's touch. Hard calluses rasped across her breasts and down her flanks; unkind fingers tugged down her trousers and found her core already molten and dripping. Undulating, she writhed against him.

Snarling in ferocious lust, Grimnir found his limit. He reached down and loosed himself. Skaði replied with a primal growl; teeth bared in a vindictive smile, she spread her legs and rose to meet him. Without further preamble, Grimnir plunged into her. She harbored no illusions, Skaði did; this was no act of love. It was equally bereft of tenderness. No, this was a primeval struggle—perhaps *the* primeval struggle—a savage hammering of flesh into flesh as two animals strove and clawed their way to climax. And it was she who reached it first: screaming, hips gyrating, her body convulsing as she invoked the dark mother of their people, Angrboða. An instant later, Grimnir knotted a fist in her hair and rammed himself deep into her, bellowing as he unleashed his seed.

For a long moment, they stayed coupled together, panting, their sweat mingling as it cooled their flesh. Grimnir pulled her head back; he licked her ear. Skaði arched like a cat, still clenched around him.

She glanced up, the lustful heat from her gaze like the embers of a fire. She chuckled. "The first taste is free," she murmured. "The second one will cost you . . ."

6
HÓLMGANGA

There was no dawn in Nástrond; there was nothing like noontide, or any hint of dusk. The passage of time, here, was measured neither by the complex machinations of stars and suns, nor the mechanical sorcery of water clocks and hourglasses. No, time in Nástrond was marked by the spilling of fluids—be it ale in the great hall, blood on the battlefield, or seed in the bedchamber. By that reckoning, then, it had been one jar of ale, eight bloody furrows, and six climaxes when Grimnir heard the braying of horns.

He was in a rare moment of sleep, his head pillowed on his arm, when the brazen cacophony started. Grimnir opened his good eye, squinted at Skaði—who was already up and half-dressed. Their fire had burned to cold embers; the clouds had cleared, as much as they might in the skies over Nástrond, and behind their thin veil the lights of Yggðrasil burned brighter than usual.

"It is time," she said.

Grimnir stretched; he popped his joints one by one, cracking his shoulders and his neck as he sat up. "Any more of that sausage left?"

"That *scrag,* you mean?" Skaði wrinkled her nose at the thought of eating any sort of meat taken from the Lokaean Witches. "Feh! Get dressed. Gífr's looking for you."

Grimnir rose, drew on his trousers. "Maybe when this is done, I'll make a good sausage out of that blasted Snaga. *Nár!* This is all his doing, that maggot."

The horn brayed, again.

"Tell them to shove that horn up their arse," Grimnir snarled, thrusting his feet in his boots and lacing them up. He stood, stamped his feet, and adjusted the stiletto in his right boot. "Not like the bastards can start without me."

Skaði eyed him as he shrugged into his gambeson. "You're in fine fettle for a lout who's about to face one of the Nine Fathers."

"Should I quake and pray, instead?" Grimnir hawked and spat. He laced up the gambeson, flexed his arms and shoulders, and then picked up his mail coat. "I know a little secret about most of these so-called Nine Fathers."

When he did not elaborate, Skaði made an impatient gesture. "And? You going to share this wisdom of yours?"

Grimnir, though, merely flashed her a cryptic smile as he drew on his coat of Turkish mail, with its enameled bronze plates over the chest and belly, and buckled the leather straps, their brass fittings bright. "Tell me about this Gangr of the Three Horns."

"Feh! Keep your secrets, then, you rotter!" Skaði replied. "What did you think of Skollvaldr?"

Finally, Grimnir buckled on his weapons belt. He adjusted his axe, first, then the broad-bladed dagger in the small of his back; he half-drew and sheathed Hátr a few times to loosen it in its scabbard. "A poncey little windbag with one good fight to his name, and a losing fight, at that."

"They're cut from the same cloth, then, the son and the father. Gangr's more cunning. He won't fight fair."

"Neither will I," Grimnir replied. He pulled his long, stringy hair back; Skaði tied it off for him with a strip of leather. He turned to face her. For a moment, they eyed each other. Then, with a savage burst of passion, Skaði seized him in an embrace and kissed him on the mouth—forceful enough to draw blood. She broke their clinch, first, and slapped him hard across the cheek.

"Go kill the bastard, then," she said. "And hurry back. I still owe you for stabbing me."

★ ★ ★

THE DOOM OF ODIN

Gífr awaited them on the road. He was clad for war, as well, in a muscled cuirass of dark bronze, fitted with sleeves and a skirt of mail; he wore a leather kilt and high-strapped sandals of Roman design. A horn hung from a leather strap around his shoulder. His sword was long and straight, and he carried a shield in one hand and a heavy black bow in the other. He turned as they emerged from the grove.

"If you lot are done with your little slap and tickle," he said, "we've got business to attend to." He handed the bow to Skaði. "You still recall how to use this?" She nodded. "Good," he replied. "Head toward Gjöll's Inlet and make yourself scarce in the woods, thereabouts. You'll see what we have in store for them, there." Skaði nodded, again, glanced at Grimnir, and then took off ahead of them at a run.

Gífr passed the shield to Grimnir. It was round and a yard wide, made of wood and banded in strips of iron, with an iron boss at its center. Its face was daubed black, and in white paint someone had drawn the stag-skull of Kjallandi—with the red eye of Bálegyr in the center of its forehead. Grimnir nodded his approval. They set off, following the road away from Úlfsstaðir, toward the Root, at a leisurely walk.

"A gift from my sister," Gífr said, jerking his chin at the shield. "Your mother."

"She's not coming to watch?"

"Oh, the whole lot of them are coming, little rat," Gífr said. "Most just won't be *seen*. The rules are plain: You challenged, Gangr accepted. He chooses the spot. You both get one shield, and whatever weapons you favor. You're allowed no more than four mates as witnesses."

Grimnir nodded. "*Nár!* Which is where he plans to cheat, that craven!"

"And where we'll match him, cheat for cheat. The place they've chosen, though." Gífr sucked his teeth. "Cheating's not going to be easy."

"Where?"

"Blasted spot of land called Gjöll's Inlet. There's the ruin of an old bridge there, on the edge of our territory. You'll have your fight atop the last remaining span."

Grimnir spat. "So neither of us are on Nástrond's soil when one of us knifes the other? *Faugh!* Then we'd better make sure it's not *my* corpse that's left up there, eh?"

Gífr chuckled. "That's the plan, you lout." He glanced sidelong at Grimnir. "Skæfloc's daughter?"

The younger *kaunr* bristled. "Aye, what of it?"

Gífr shook his head. "Nothing. Nothing at all. You could do much worse, if you ask me."

"Well, no one's asking you, are they?" Grimnir snorted.

They walked in silence, after that. The old road wound through the hills, through tangled forests and over naked ridges. It descended steadily, pine and ash joined now by black willow and pin oaks as the ground grew damp, the vegetation thick and marshy. Near as Grimnir could tell, they were on the opposite side of the island from where he came ashore, near the bog-lands where Hrauðnir's folk dwelled. As they cleared the last rise, Grimnir got his first good look at Gjöll's Inlet.

The inlet was a spike of water, some hundred yards across at the throat, that lanced into the heart of Nástrond; Grimnir was certain it had been a river, once, but now its upper reaches were thick swamps and marshy shores, while here, at its mouth, it resembled a bight carved into the island's flank. Standing half the distance between both shores, Grimnir spied what was left of an ancient stone bridge—a solitary arch rising from reed-choked footings, ivy and weeds growing from chinks in the rock; its crumbling top was an uneven surface, strewn with blocks of stone and thick with tussocks of dried grass. On either shore, attempts had been made to reestablish the bridge, with rotting timber balks rising like scaffolding from the lake bed, festooned with ropes; farther out, Grimnir saw burnt pilings protruding from the water like the fingers of the damned.

Beyond it, on the far shore, the road continued up and over a low ridge, into territory claimed by the True Sons of Loki. Gífr pointed out a pavilion on that ridge, hung with rippling banners, where Gangr's four spectators would watch. "You should feel honored. Mánavargr's come to watch," he said. "Njól and that little warmonger, Snaga, with him. That last banner . . ." Gífr trailed off, his eyes gleaming with hate. He spat. "Iðuna."

Grimnir glanced sidelong at him. "Who?"

Through gritted teeth, Gífr said: "My mother."

Those two words stopped Grimnir in midstride. In all their long years together, topside, he'd never heard Gífr so much as mention his mother; he'd never even given voice to her name, at least not in earshot of Grimnir. *Iðuna*. Grimnir always assumed she'd died ere they reached Miðgarðr, or had never made the Change; the look on Gífr's face promised there was more to the tale—as did her presence in the enemy camp. Not as a prisoner, either, but displaying the banner of an equal.

"*Fak mir,*" Grimnir muttered, following the older *skrælingr*. "What in Hel's name is she doing over there, with *them*?"

Gífr did not reply.

A similar pavilion was erected on their side of the inlet; under it, Bálegyr sat alongside Kjallandi, with Skríkja between them. Gífr would be the fourth. He snarled at Skríkja. "The cupbearer brought the witch with him, I see."

"Mánavargr is a fool," Skríkja replied, with a sidelong glance at their father. Kjallandi sat perfectly still, composed. Only his eyes betrayed him—they'd gone red as blood with suppressed desire to kill. Skríkja continued: "He thinks we are as stricken by nostalgia as he is. That her presence, here, might temper our response to his trap. Do not let it trouble you." She turned and looked at Grimnir, her eyes gleaming yellow. Her words were directed at Gífr, still. "Is everything ready?" He nodded to her.

"Good. Let's get this over with," Bálegyr said. "We're too exposed, out here, and I don't trust those toe-rags not to try and slip in behind us."

"*Nár!* For the first time, we agree on something." Grimnir pushed through the pavilion.

"Kill him quick and don't toy with him," Gífr said. "Gangr's not his son."

"I'll kill him how I please, you old git. Let them know I'm coming."

Gífr raised his horn and blew three blasts; from across the water came three blasts in answer. Immediately, a broad, straight-legged figure set off from the enemy pavilion. The *kaunr* sported a long mail coat and a helmet decorated with three polished horns—one in the forehead curving down, and one in each cheek, curving inward. He cradled a large axe in his arms, and carried a teardrop-shaped shield slung across his back.

Over his shoulder, Grimnir hollered: "Gangr of the Three Horns, eh?"

"That's him," Gífr replied.

Grimnir hawked and spat. "That tin pot will make a pretty little trophy."

The son of Bálegyr walked on. Down by the water's edge, where a rickety pier jutted out into the inlet, he found a narrow, flat-bottomed skiff tied to a rotted piling. It was fifty yards to the ruined bridge, and by the look of the water—milky and gray, with the hint of *something* lurking just under the surface—it would be folly to try and swim it. Grimnir clambered aboard the skiff, slung his shield down, and untied the painter. He pushed away from the pier; it took only a handful of strokes with the oar to reach the marshy foot of the ruin. Grimnir looked up, head cocked to take in the sight of the bridge with his good eye. The ruined span soared some thirty feet over the water, and a knotted rope led up to what would be the site of their duel. Nodding, he made the skiff fast to a willow sapling.

Grimnir's shield had no shoulder strap; so, he improvised. He tied the end of the rope to the hand grip of the shield, behind the iron boss. He tucked the excess into his belt, exhaled, and started his climb. Hand over hand, knot after knot; he ascended the rope like an ape, with his shield scraping and banging in his wake as he drew it up behind him.

He reached the summit of the ruin before Gangr. Grimnir took care of business first, hauling his shield up the rest of the way, and coiling the rope just *so,* where it might do in a pinch if he needed to make a quick exit. Only then did he allow himself to stray to the edge and peer over. Below, the water frothed and boiled. *Sjóvættir,* he reckoned, frowning. Throngs of them were gathered in the shadow of the ruined bridge, just under the surface, and they had come knowing there would be a meal of blood and blade-torn flesh. *But how? How did they know?*

Grimnir straightened. He felt eyes on him—more than his kin and his enemy's mates, to be sure. He scanned the far bank, which boasted a thick canopy of undergrowth; he was certain there were rats and maggots aplenty hiding in those thickets. He spied Mánavargr sitting on an ostentatious throne under the awning; a bearded *kaunr* stood to one side, and Snaga lurked in the shadows of the pavilion. *Make that Thrár, son of Thráinn,* Grimnir corrected himself. Standing in the open, however, was a white-haired female draped in robes of smoke and silver, pale like an albino, with piercing eyes that gleamed like citrines. She leaned on a staff of carved wood. *Iðuna.* Knowing old Gífr was *seiðr*-wise and lore-cunning made Grimnir more than curious about his mother.

He did not, however, have time to speculate. Rope creaked as Gangr of the Three Horns finally heaved himself up and over the edge of the ruin.

"Taking your sweet time, are you?" Grimnir said, by way of greeting. "Starting to wonder if you needed me to haul you up, you lump of suet."

"Keep talking, you cocksure little shite," Gangr said, exhaling hard. "Your death will be here soon enough."

Grimnir, though, merely smiled and looked over the edge, once more. *How did the* sjóvættir *know?*

"Do you see your doom, *skrælingr*?" Gangr said, unlimbering his teardrop-shaped shield, daubed black with three horns painted in white, red, and green. "For yonder it is!"

Grimnir *tsk*'ed and spat. "*Nár!* I was looking for your son, swine!"

Gangr drew himself up to his full height. He towered over Grimnir; his limbs were straight and heavy with muscle; his eyes blazed like chips of red-hot iron. He was dark-skinned, Gangr was, with a thick beard braided into three plaits and a jutting chin. His fangs were long and stained black with his own blood from where he gnawed on the inside of his lips. He swung his axe in a tight arc, shield at the ready. He spat a gobbet of blood. "We'll see how cocky you are with your head split to the teeth, bastard of Bálegyr!"

Grimnir readied his shield. He drew Hátr. Gangr sneered at the long seax, at the ragged state of it.

"You're an idiot, little *skrælingr,* to bring nothing but a knife to war!"

Grimnir glanced down at the blade, raised an eyebrow at the *kaunr.* "This? So-ho! You don't approve, eh, maggot? Well, this blade has a history. The last wretch to fall to it was your sweet *argr*-loving son!"

With a low growl of rage, Gangr attacked. He came on like a tempest, his axe weaving a curtain of death around his body. Grimnir gave ground, and Gangr followed. He was as flashy a fighter as Skollvaldr, though far more dangerous; his axe wove figure-eights in the air; he swung wide and swung heavy, hacked chips from the rim of Grimnir's shield, and struck sparks from the crumbling stone when he missed.

As Grimnir dodged and danced aside, he kept talking, breath whistling between clenched teeth: "Your pretty boy screamed your name as he lay dying, did you know that?" he said, swaying away from a whistling blow of Gangr's axe. "Of course not. You weren't there! Oh, how he bellowed when my blade—this blade!—slid into his guts! All the way to the hilt! Again and again, I rammed this knife, as you call it, into him! He wept, you swine! Wept and cried your name, hoping dear old Dad would come to save him." Grimnir backpedaled, wary of his footing on the uneven ground. "I can't say if he was dead when I took his head off . . ."

"WHAT IS she playing at?" Gífr muttered, his keen eyes narrowing. He walked out beyond the pavilion, toward the water; unconsciously, his steps mimicked Iðuna's movement. Skríkja came to stand next to him. She was clad in mail and leather as befitting a war-queen of the *kaunar*. She carried a spear—as slender as an ash wand, but banded in silver and iron; of iron, too, was the broad, lugged head, and on it were carved runes that spoke of destruction. "What is she doing?"

Skríkja followed his gaze. Across the inlet, she could see the pale shadow that was Iðuna, their mother, walking nearer to the edge of the water with her staff held aloft. "What she always does," Skríkja snarled. "She's working something, some fresh bit of deviltry!"

"Something with the *sjóvættir*?"

"Aye. Look. Under the arch of the bridge . . . do you see it?"

He did. A horde of silvery-white spirits foamed the water, their fleshless faces upturned as though they expected a gift from on high. *Not a gift,* Gífr realized, *but a sacrifice.* "Damn her to Hel's deepest hollow! She's made the whole of Gjöll's Inlet into their trap!"

"Launch your attack now, husband, or withdraw!" Skríkja said, turning. "Quickly, for there is sorcery afoot!"

Bálegyr sat upright, squinting at Kjallandi. "What say you, brother-king? Throw the dice or live to fight another day?"

Kjallandi stood. "Sound the attack," he said, his voice like ice. "But forget that peacock, Mánavargr, for now. Bring me the head of that witch! Bring me the head of Iðuna!"

★ ★ ★

THE DOOM OF ODIN

FRUSTRATED, GANGR hurled his shield away and took his axe's haft in both hands. He raised it above his head, intending to strike a blow that would split Grimnir's shield, his arm, and the head they protected in twain.

The *kaunr* roared. "Bastard!"

And there was the opening Grimnir was looking for. Growling in menace, he sidestepped that titanic blow. Before Gangr could recover, the son of Bálegyr sidled in and punched him in the neck with the ragged edge of his shield. He punched him a second time, a third; iron scraped against the steel of Gangr's helmet as Grimnir rained blows on the side of his head. The *kaunr* stumbled sideways, turned, and with a serpentine hiss he swung his axe up and out in a backhand blow that would have split Grimnir hip to shoulder ... had it connected.

A blow that left Gangr wide open.

As a long, skirling note from Gífr's horn echoed across the water, Grimnir moved inside his foe's guard and rammed the point of Hátr into the hollow of Gangr's throat—between the collar of his mail and the bottom edge of his helmet. It pierced muscle and sinew, sawed through gristle and tough cartilage.

The axe fell from Gangr's nerveless fingers; his trembling hands sought the blade lodged in his windpipe, sought to stem the freshets of black blood that pulsed from the wound. He stared hard into Grimnir's single eye. Red hate matched red hate.

"Got you, maggot," Grimnir said. He spat in Gangr's face, ripped the long seax from his throat, and was on the verge of kicking him over the edge of the ruined bridge when the pieces of the puzzle finally fell into place. The *sjóvættir*. They were waiting for blood ...

He risked a glance at the enemy-held shore and spied that witch, Iðuna, standing near the water with her staff raised. She was shouting something, some word Grimnir could not quite make out.

And she, too, was waiting.

Waiting for one of them to fall, torn and bloody, into the arms of the *sjóvættir*. Waiting for one to deliver the other as a sacrifice ...

Gangr staggered backward, gagging on blood, his heels over the ruined edge. Before he could tumble back and over and into the water, Grimnir dropped his shield; that hand snaked out and caught a handful of his foe's gore-soaked beard. He dragged Gangr forward and slung him to the stones, watching as the bastard gave one last convulsion and died.

The blast from Gífr's horn echoed; in answer, Grimnir heard the sound of keels crunching against rocky soil; he heard shouted commands, and the rippling splashes of oars striking water. The son of Bálegyr turned as, from the dense cover of the tree-lined bank, a dozen four-oared longboats took to the water of the inlet. Besides rowers and a steersman, each of the high-prowed vessels also carried ten lads from Úlfsstaðir—a mix of Kjallandi's disciplined *kaunar* and Bálegyr's *skrælingar* brawlers; even a few *scrags* with bows and slings. In the prow of one boat, he caught sight of Skaði, already loosing her arrows. They would cross at speed, to reach the far shore before that witch, Iðuna, got any ideas. Mánavargr was another matter. That villain motioned; Njól roared a command, and over the far side of the ridge marched a ragged phalanx of red-cloaked *kaunar*—easily two hundred, maybe more.

Things were about to get hairy.

Grimnir put two fingers to his mouth and whistled at the nearest boat. The hand on the rudder belonged to a gnarled old salt called Elðr, one of Kjallandi's lads, who wore a pilfered Roman corselet and carried the shield of a long-dead legionary. He slewed hard on the rudder and brought the boat as near as he dared to the base of the ruined bridge.

"Hold steady," old Elðr barked to the rats manning his oars.

Grimnir, though, was already in motion. He sheathed his long-seax; then, dropping his shield, he snatched up Gangr's and slung it across his back. He caught up his coiled rope. Grimnir backpedaled; as he moved, he took out some of the rope's slack and wrapped it around his off hand. He stopped, dug in his heels. The son of Bálegyr paused, exhaled, and then sprinted for the opposite edge, away from the boat . . .

At speed, Grimnir threw himself off the bridge.

He plunged toward the water, its surface thick with swirling faces, with gleaming eyes; the *sjóvættir* reached for him, their mouths open and awaiting their expected sacrifice. They lusted after the blood, after the flesh they were promised.

At the last moment, the rope snapped taut; it held, and the iron piton securing it to the bridge held, as well . . . and Grimnir swung over the *sjóvættir's* heads. His hair streamed behind him as he described a tight arc around the end of the ruin.

"Ymir!" he roared.

And then he was over the boat; over the head of old Elðr, his hand firm at the rudder. He saw the wild eyes of his rowers, saw the *kaunar* and the *skrælingar* duck and scatter, making for the safety of the strakes. Judging it now or never, Grimnir turned loose of the rope. He tucked himself into a ball of muscle and sinew as he came in hard, crashing into the port-side gunwale toward the prow. Wood joins popped; the boat rocked.

"At it, you rats!" Elðr bellowed a heartbeat later. "Now! Unless you want *them* swimming up your useless arses!" He jabbed a thumb off to their starboard side, where the water churned and roiled as the enraged *sjóvættir* gave chase. The rowers bent their backs to the oars, and off the boat shot.

Grimnir lay there a moment, stunned. His ribs ached, and he was sure the impact had knocked his teeth loose. He shook his head to clear it. Around him, *skrælingar* rowed in unison. Breath hissed through clenched teeth; muscles cracked and tendons creaked like wind through the cordage of a sailing ship. They were almost there when something seized the boat from below and lifted it out the water like a child with a toy. Oars sliced the air; old Elðr sagged against the rudder, fell-eyed and furious.

"Brace!" he screamed.

Grimnir had a split second to contemplate *what* it was before the forces that snatched them up slung them forward—again, like an angry child, caught in the throes of a tantrum. The boat speared through the canopy of trees shielding this part of the bank. Oars snapped; lads screamed as they were plucked from their seats by heavy limbs. Wood splintered. Grimnir felt the prow come apart as they caromed off an ivy-choked pile of rock—one of the ancient pylons that held up the landward side of the bridge. And what was left of the boat plowed through leaf mold and soil, and came to rest a dozen yards from the water's edge.

THE LORD of Kaunheimr bolted up from his throne. Not a lumbering giant like the others of his ilk, Mánavargr was snake-thin and cunning, befitting his status as Father Loki's cupbearer in the time before. A serpent, he was, a son of

Jörmungandr, and the serpent was his sigil; under a cloak the color of human blood, he wore finely meshed mail and carried a barbed whip at his side. And like the serpent, he had laid this plan with speed and confidence—knowing he'd likely never again have the potential for such an opportunity: to get Bálegyr and Kjallandi, together, out in the open. In one strike of his mailed fist, he could add the lands of Úlfsstaðir to his own. Thus, when Bölthorn brought him word of this Grimnir's arrogance, Mánavargr alone had sensed burgeoning opportunity.

It was *he* who had reeled in the impetuous Gangr, who was content to scurry off alone and do battle. *He* had chosen the ground. *He* had enlisted Iðuna. *He* had even honored that ancient guttersnipe, Snaga, to borrow a disposable force of *scrags*—though Njól had insisted he and his dogs be allowed to partake in the fun. Despite all that, the whole of Mánavargr's plan hinged on Iðuna.

Oh, she had promised she could deliver the power of the *sjóvættir* to his cause; promised she could forge a bond with them that would make them Kaunheimr's allies. "It will require a sacrifice," she had told him, in confidence. "And not just any dollop of blood will do. Gangr or Bálegyr's brat. The spirits will take either . . . or both."

Mánavargr had consented, calculating the loss of Gangr to be an acceptable risk if it meant wiping out Bálegyr or Kjallandi, or both. "See it done, for the glory of Kaunheimr."

Now, though, his immaculate plan was unraveling. That worthless *skrælingr*, Grimnir, had somehow deduced Iðuna's pact; he denied the *sjóvættir* their sacrifice, and then taunted them until their rage boiled over. Those blasted spirits surged and writhed, driving the *skrælingr*'s boat faster and faster, until it was as if a hundred watery hands snatched it up and flung it into the trees.

Over the snap of timber and the hiss of water, Mánavargr heard the thin wailing of the *sjóvættir;* he could see their twisted bodies, their sharp-toothed faces in the milky gray froth. They were screaming for blood. Grimnir's blood.

And Mánavargr was in the mood to oblige.

Iðuna hurried back to the lord of Kaunheimr's side. She was panting, out of breath; she leaned on her staff like a crone. "We are betrayed!"

"Or," Mánavargr replied, his red eyes as lifeless as a snake's, "you underestimated him."

Iðuna laughed. "Bah! There's nothing there to underestimate! That one is as dull as rust! Nor are my idiot children wise enough in the arts to thwart a plan of mine! No, someone spoke of our plot, and their loose tongue betrayed us!"

Mánavargr gave her the thinnest of smiles. "Regardless, we still have the initiative. Njól! Sound the advance! Deny their boats a beachhead. *Scrag!*" He turned to where Snaga was standing. "Fetch me that *skrælingr*, or his head."

Snaga did not move. Red eyes squinted in a white skull-painted face. "Then we ain't beholden to you no more, right? Our land's ours, fair and square?"

"That was our agreement. Bring him to me alive and I'll sweeten the deal. I'll make you a prince among *scrags*."

"Aye, we'll do it, but I ain't looking to be no prince. We just want that stretch of land Lútr's done gave us, is all, and a bit more for our mates." And with that, Snaga vanished out the back of the pavilion.

Iðuna spat in Snaga's wake. "There's your traitor, I'll warrant. That worm seeks to carve out a kingdom of his own, right under our noses! And he's the one who brought this tale to us ... likely he's been in league with Grimnir this whole time."

Mánavargr ground his teeth. "I will burn that village when I get to it, witch. For now, Odin's weather looms! Blades will sing and shields will break, ere long! Make yourself useful or make yourself scarce."

At a nod from his lord, Njól raised his horn, blew a long and brazen note. Horns answered; slowly, the swine and rabble of Kaunheimr found their marks, their shields rasping together to form a ragged wall. The serried teeth of their blades reflected the savage radiance of Yggðrasil, glowering through the fume and wrack overhead.

THE ECHO of horns roused Grimnir from senselessness. He opened his eyes. The son of Bálegyr lay on his belly, in the shattered ruin of the boat, fetched up against the knotty bole of a black willow. Thin slashes of Yggðrasil's light pierced the canopy; he heard groans and snarls around him as others of the crew staggered to their feet. Grimnir clambered to his knees, shook his head to clear it. He looked about. Old Elðr was dead, his neck broken, his fingers still clutching the splintered ruin of the rudder. Three of the rowers were missing, likely swept from the boat after it had gone airborne; a fourth was bleeding out in the remains of the strakes, his belly pierced by a wooden spar.

Grimnir looked at him.

"Get it over with," the rower gurgled around a mouthful of blood. Nodding, Grimnir rose on unsteady feet, crossed to the rower's side, and drew his broad-bladed knife. He seized that rat by his hair. Wrenching him forward, Grimnir plunged the knife into the base of his skull. The dying *skrælingr* went limp.

Grimnir left him slumped over. He wiped his blade, sheathed it, and turned. "Up, you laggards! Up! The day's not done! Find a way over to that clearing and let's get in this damnable fray!" Eight others milled about, snatching up shields and weapons from the ruin of their boat.

One of the big *kaunr* grunted and spat. "Who died and made you lord and master, eh? You're not the only son of Bálegyr, here, you runt!" Grimnir recognized him by the wreckage of scar tissue, thick callus, and exposed teeth on the left side of his face—the death-gift of an arctic bear. This was Sægrár, one of his half-brothers.

"No, but I'm the only one not a wretched bastard!" Grimnir snarled in answer. "Get out there and fight, you lout! The rest of you, move! Damn your eyes!"

"This way!" one of them hollered. In a straggling line, the eight *skrælingar* and *kaunar* threaded through the trees, around the stone balks that once held up the ancient bridge, and hustled for the clearing.

Grimnir stopped short, peering through the undergrowth at the clearing where Mánavargr's pavilion stood. Where a shield wall was forming to repel the assault of Úlfsstaðir's boats. Grimnir and his handful were *between* the shield wall and the pavilion. He could see Mánavargr and his pet witch Iðuna under the gold-tasseled awning; Njól he could see leading the shield wall. Of Snaga, Grimnir saw no sign.

"Useless *scrag*," he muttered, turning. "Look lively, lads. Yonder's our target." But at his back Grimnir counted only five other heads. Four *skrælingar* and that big *kaunr*, Sægrár. The other three had gone missing. Grimnir scowled. "Where's your mates, eh?"

Sægrár spat through the scarred ruin of his cheek. "Skinned out, most likely. Bah! What of it? We get that one," he nodded at Mánavargr, "and old Bálegyr will make us lords."

"Use your head, you lout," Grimnir snarled in answer. "No one's skinning out from this fight. If three are missing, that means there's some deviltry afoot. What's likely is Mánavargr's got some of his rats in here, picking us off one by one."

Sægrár laughed. "Stay here if you're afraid, runt! The rest of us will take 'em! C'mon, lads! We've hit pay dirt! Up, and at them!"

Grimnir's logic fell on deaf ears. The other four whooped and howled; that dull-witted giant led them through the undergrowth, aiming for the pavilion of purple and gold cloth and the rich bounty within . . .

Three of Sægrár's mates died within two steps, iron broadheads slashing into their broad backs, piercing their spines, their hearts, and their lungs. Sægrár himself made it less than a dozen paces before a black-feathered arrow sprouted from the base of his skull. He stumbled and fell. The fourth *skrælingr* turned to scamper off even as an arrow pierced his temple.

Grimnir whirled about, facing the way they'd come, and sank down behind Gangr's tear-shaped shield.

"You ain't as dumb as those others," said a voice from the undergrowth. Snaga stepped into view, flanked by Köttr and Blártunga, the rest of his mates around him. A score of *scrags*, altogether—from snot-nosed brats with murder in their eyes, barely reaching to Grimnir's knee, to lean youths on the cusp of maturity. They sported piecemeal armor and makeshift weapons—knives and cleavers, short spears and stone-headed maces, bows and arrows. The lot of them stared at Grimnir like a company of butchers contemplating a side of beef.

"I thought we were mates, Thrár, Thráinn's son," Grimnir replied around the shield's edge. Snaga's face darkened.

"That name's dead, you cur!" the *scrag*-lord said. "An' you'll be dead, too, soon enough!"

Grimnir drew Hátr. He sidled back. One step. Two. Until he was clear of the undergrowth. "You think there's enough of you rats to do me in?"

"Be finding out soon enough, ain't we?"

"Fight me yourself," Grimnir said. "One-on-one."

Snaga snorted. "You ain't dumb, but I ain't dumb, neither. You just took old Gangr apart. Even so, I think you ain't going to find us that easy to kill. We—"

Grimnir did not let the *scrag* finish. Like a tiger springing upon its prey, the son of Bálegyr leapt into the midst of the *scrags*. They howled and scampered aside, but Hátr was like a living thing in Grimnir's fist. The blade flashed in the shadow-light of Yggðrasil; in one swipe, he gutted the tallest of the *scrags*, and his riposte sent Hátr plunging to its hilt in the throat of another. Grimnir smashed one of the smaller goblins to the earth with the rim of his shield, and ended him with a stomp of his heel—breaking his skull like an eggshell. Nor did he let them rest. Wheeling, he hit them again.

In the blood-soaked twinkling of a murderous eye, Grimnir killed half of Snaga's mates. They were gutted, slashed, torn, and stomped. Some died instantly; others yet writhed on the ground, their piteous cries ignored. Black slime dripped from Hátr's blade. "You were saying, *Thrár?*" Grimnir snarled.

"It's *Snaga*, you bastard!" Snarling, the *scrag* led the last of his mates into the fray. Grimnir showed them no mercy. He punched Blártunga in the throat with the rim of his shield and sent the fat *scrag* reeling; swept Köttr's legs when she tried again to creep into his blind side, then stove in her ribs with the heel of his hobnailed boot. Grimnir slaughtered the remaining *scrags*, leaving only Snaga.

They stared at one another over the corpses of his mates, over the writhing bodies and the mewling things. Grimnir hawked and spat.

"Let's make it even, *Thrár*," he said. Grimnir slung down his shield; with one hand, he unbuckled his weapons belt, then loosened the straps on his mail coat and shrugged out of it. He ripped the laces out of his gambeson, peeled it off, and threw it on the ground, as well. He stood opposite Snaga, naked to the waist. Crouching, he drew his axe from the tangle of leather and mail.

Snaga had no armor. He bent and caught up a fallen knife to go with his stone-headed axe. He risked a glance at the water's edge, where the *sjóvættir* still frothed and boiled.

"Winner takes all," the *scrag* said.

Grimnir chuckled. "When has it ever been any different?"

With a nod, Snaga attacked.

The *scrag* was quick, quicker even than Grimnir; he feinted high, stabbed low, reversed the knife and slashed out across Grimnir's corded belly. Axe haft clacked against axe haft; breath exploded in sharp *whuffs* as their blades flickered and sparked. And Grimnir grunted as the *scrag* scored the flesh of his off-hand biceps with the edge of his knife. A ribbon of blood drooled from the blade as they sprang apart.

Snaga—Thrár, Thráinn's son—was a better fighter than he had any right to be; better than any *kaunar* Grimnir had faced, and a damn sight better than most of the *skrælingar*. Grudgingly, Grimnir admitted he was nearly his own equal. *Nearly.*

The rat was fast, but he was too light. Not enough weight behind his blows. And if there wasn't enough weight for an effective strike, there wouldn't be enough for an effective block, either. Snarling, Grimnir went on the offensive.

Snaga's arm became Grimnir's anvil. He hammered the *scrag*'s axe haft, his knife's guard; he wound the blades up in a bind and used his weight to drag Snaga's guard open. Grimnir head-butted him, smashing his nose. He dropped his own axe and drove an elbow into Snaga's gut, stripped the stone axe from his grasp, and caught his descending knife hand in a viselike grip.

Grimnir bore him to the ground, straddling his thin body. Snaga's breath came in ragged gasps as he struggled and strained against the son of Bálegyr's heavier weight. Grinning, Grimnir turned the blade of the *scrag*'s knife toward its owner and slowly, inexorably, pushed it into his flesh.

"Stop!" Snaga panted as the cold steel touched his sallow skin. "No!"

And with a final convulsion of his muscular arms, Grimnir drove the knife into Snaga's thin chest, through muscle and bone, through lungs burning for want of air, and into the pulsing wall of his heart. Blood spewed from Snaga's slack lips, and the ruddy glow of the *scrag*'s eyes flickered and died with him.

Grimnir raised himself. He exhaled, the beginnings of a malicious smile on his lips. Suddenly, behind him he heard the stamp of a foot. And before he could so much as react, Blártunga—fat, forgotten Blártunga—rammed a fallen spear into Grimnir's back, to the right of his spine, and drove it through his body.

Grimnir howled like a dying wolf. The pain blinded him; he wanted to lash out, to kill—and he knew he should, but the epicenter of his sudden agony, this length of iron-tipped wood transfixing his body, hijacked his every thought, his every nerve, his every synapse. He felt it pull, this black-slimed intruder, and without question he went in the direction it indicated—up. Off Snaga's corpse. It moved toward the edge of the still-roiling water and he followed on unsteady legs, trembling legs. He heard screaming; he heard someone calling his name.

Grimnir!

"How does it feel, you son of a bitch?" Blártunga bellowed in his ear. Then, *nothing*. Grimnir shuffled slowly, the spear yet bisecting his body. *No sound reached him but the slow beating of his heart.* He staggered. *His heart . . . winding down like a clockmaker's engine. Each beat . . . slow. Slower.* The fat *scrag* was behind him, spittle flying as he hurled curses at him. *Slower, still. Two beats. One. Slower.*

"Here's your blood! Your sacrifice!" Snarling, Blártunga dragged the blood-slimed spearhead back through Grimnir's body and, with the shaft, rammed him into the boiling froth of Gjöll's Inlet.

Grimnir Bálegyr's son struck the water face-first. He heard the laughter of the *sjóvættir* as they came for him. He could see their corpse-pale flesh in the depths below; their eyes black sockets, their hair like lake grass floating around skeletal faces. Their hands reached for him . . .

And as their slimy fingers caressed his limbs, he felt the reprieve of darkness; as the silence of the grave wrapped him in its eternal embrace, Grimnir heard one final sound—a deep and powerful voice. A familiar voice. A voice that silenced the *sjóvættir;* a voice that echoed even under water.

"*NO,*" it said. "*HE IS MINE.*"

7
THE ROAD TO ROME

"HE IS MINE!"

The power in those words struck Grimnir like an open hand to the cheek. The shock of it, the sudden return to consciousness, wrenched a gasp from his throat. His eyes flew open—one cold and dead, like carved corpse-bone; the other a red and gleaming ember in the night.

"MINE . . . Mine . . . mine . . ."

The echo faded, leaving in its wake a strange sensation of familiarity. He knew the voice; knew it from a dim and half-forgotten memory, but every time the recollection drifted closer something snatched it away. "*Faugh,*" he muttered. He lay on his back in the cold shallows—*where was he?*—listening to the soft night breeze—*was this Gjöll's Inlet?*—as it ruffled the reeds around him. He felt the weight of his body. His bones ached, as though some brutal god had threaded his marrow with red-hot wires and cinched them tight. Overhead, through rips in the clouds, he could see cold bright stars wheeling in silent majesty.

Stars. He could see stars.

He groaned, snarling as he rolled onto his belly and slithered up the mud-slick bank, clawing at reeds and digging his elbows in. Two crossbow bolts hung like fetishes from the links of his Turkish mail . . .

Mail? He'd worn no mail, there at the end, when that wretched *scrag* Blártunga rammed a spear through his body. He remembered; *he'd loosened the straps on his mail coat and shrugged out of it. He ripped the laces out of his gambeson, peeled it off and threw it on the ground, as well.* He remembered the pain. The agony ...

"By Ymir, where—?" he muttered. His vision swam. He blinked, tried to clear it. *Where was the spear? What had happened?*

In answer, he heard a rasping voice, speaking Sicilian with the hard accent of Aragon: "Christ's bones! The devil yet lives?"

From nearby came grunted denials and imprecations, guttural prayers; he heard the creak of steel laths as unseen hands struggled to reload a crossbow. Had he dreamed it all? The dark shores of Nástrond, the Wolves' Abode, the duel at Gjöll's Inlet? He looked down at the bolts tangled in his mail and remembered ... *ancient ruins in the heart of a marsh, blackened and rotting. Domes of old marble cover shrines to heretic gods and forgotten nymphs. A road; hobnailed boots crush stone flakes. A wagon, gaudy and broken, canting on its shattered axle. He stops. He snuffles the air; he smells them. He smells their fever-sweat, their corruption; he smells the pus that leaks from the sores on their wasted bodies. He bares his teeth in anticipation. They're dead men, the creature's Sicilian thralls.*

Sicilians. One of them had shot him from the back of the pageant wagon ... *a sweat-slick hand gripping too tight the carved oak stock of his weapon. The crossbowman looks away. Two fingers convulse around the triggering mechanism. The flat crack of the steel laths is only barely heard. He feels it as a fist to his sternum ...*

The bolt hit him, of that he was certain, with a second hard on its heels; their combined impacts must have addled him. Had his body meeting the cold water of the marshes driven all sense from him? Had he hallucinated every scrap and scrape since these two bolts slammed into him? *Nástrond? His dead kin?*

"Get in, after him!" he heard the rasping voice command. "Fetch a brand, by God! Fetch it and bring it close! I'll not leave it to Chance."

Grimnir hawked and spat. This was Langbarðaland, then. Italy. Which meant he was still alive. Still on the Appian Way where it crossed the Pontine Marshes, a fortnight north of the plague-ravaged ruin of Messina. Still on the hunt for that skulking wyrm, the Malice-Striker. *But how was he not dead?*

THE DOOM OF ODIN

"Do not toy with it, Pandolfo." This new voice set Grimnir's teeth on edge. It was sibilant, and pitched high enough to belong to a castrato. The priest, he was certain. The priest of Messina. The fool responsible for spiriting Níðhöggr from Sicily to the mainland. "You've seen the evil it can do. Have your men spear it and be done."

Dripping and muddy, Grimnir rose from the reeds at the edge of the marsh. His hair hung in lank strands, veiling his features; his single red eye flared in the fire-streaked night. The one called Pandolfo was the same giant of a man Grimnir had rammed with his shoulder after taking his ear. There was hatred in his red-rimmed eyes, set deep in a haggard and plague-scarred face. Drooping black mustaches, slick with mucus and weighted by beads of gilded copper, framed his thin lips. Blood dripped from the ruin of his ear as he raised his longsword.

With him were four others: a crossbowman with long greasy hair and pus weeping from his eyes; two footsore *condottieri* in mud-spattered mail bearing heavy spears, their limbs plague-trembling and weak. The last one stood apart, a lad barely on the cusp of manhood; surrounded by corpses, he struggled to hold a torch aloft. Beyond them all, Grimnir glimpsed the black-cassocked form of the priest from Messina—pale as a winding sheet and sporting a close-clipped tonsure. Grimnir reached up with one black-nailed hand and plucked the spent bolts from the links of his mail.

"Aye, *Pandolfo*," he said, yellowed fangs bared. "Spear me and be done. *Nár!* If that cockless scrote, yonder, wants me dead, let him come try! You hear me, priest? It's time you put steel in your blasted hands and test your god against mine!"

"You have no gods, spawn of Hell!" Pandolfo replied. "And soon enough you'll have no head!"

Grimnir looked at each man, in turn; he sucked his teeth. "You couldn't take my head with twice the louts you have, now. Ha! My head's safe as a babe at its mother's teat."

Pandolfo took a shuffling step to his left, boots scraping like claws on slate. The *condottiere*'s eyes turned icy; a command formed on his cracked lips, but the breath that would give the word a voice was yet contained in his expanding lungs. He drew his longsword back, its blade rising into a high guard. The other two soldiers glanced at one another, knuckles whitening around the shafts of their spears. The torchbearer shifted, embers crackling, while the crossbowman raised his weapon with agonizing slowness. A light breeze whispered through the tall grass.

Suddenly, Grimnir moved; in one smooth motion, he drew the bearded axe at his hip, twisted at the waist, and slung the weapon at the crossbowman. It tumbled once, end-over-end; it missed striking the rising arbalest by a hair's breadth and instead took the man in the face. It struck at an angle between his nose and the tip of his chin, cleaving flesh and bone and breaking teeth.

The man screamed and stumbled back, a bloody froth spewing from his blade-split jaw. He flailed. His hand convulsed the triggering lever.

Steel laths *spang*ed.

And there came a sickening *crunch* as the bolt drove into the back of the nearest spearman, through his mail, and buried itself up to its wooden fletchings in his spine. The man stumbled forward. He uttered a piteous groan as he crashed face-first to the ground, his harness clattering.

The next instant was a mix of chaos and pure terror; cries of alarm erupted from the torchbearer and the remaining soldier. The crossbowman's muffled screams, the whimpering cry of the fallen spearman, and the priest's bellowed orders added to their panic. Pandolfo, alone, kept his wits about him. He cursed and leapt.

And Grimnir met him halfway.

Mail rattled and clashed; wiry muscle forged in the fires of the Elder World collided with Sicilian-born flesh and bone. Pandolfo's bloodshot eyes widened; the *skrælingr*'s thin lips peeled back in a sneer of contempt as Grimnir caught the blade of the Sicilian's longsword near the hilt and wrenched it aside. Before Pandolfo could jerk the blade free, before he could strike at his foe with his off hand, Grimnir drove the spent bolts in his fist up and into the *condottiere*'s exposed neck. Iron scraped bone as one bolt lodged in the Sicilian's jaw hinge; the other bit deep, piercing the gristle of his windpipe. Diseased blood pulsed from the deeper wound.

"Take *my* head, will you?" Grimnir snarled. "*Faugh!*" He wrenched the longsword from Pandolfo's slackened grasp and kicked the dying man away. He glared over his shoulder at the remaining spearman and the torchbearer.

THE DOOM OF ODIN

"And you ... have you come to play or will you just stand there like useless lumps of suet?"

"Kill him, you fools!" the priest screamed.

"Aye, step lively now, maggots! Raise that spear, you wretch, if you mean to use it!"

Death was near. These men felt it—the cold iron scythe of skeletal La Morte pressing against the backs of their necks. This place would be the end of them; here and now or in a few hours, the outcome would be the same, nonetheless. The Lord's Prayer dripped unbidden from the soldiers' lips: "Our Father," they muttered, almost in unison but not quite. "Our Father who art ... who art in heaven, hallowed be th-thy name ..."

The priest raged. "What are you doing, you imbeciles? The Angel of the Lord demands your service! Your sacrifice!"

"Shut that hole in your face, priest," Grimnir hissed. He turned and spread his arms wide. "Will you pray or will you fight?"

The remaining spear clattered to the ground. The young torchbearer tossed his brand at Grimnir's feet. An explosion of sparks and embers swirled up, wreathing the *skrælingr* in a halo of fire. "We will pray," the spearman said, clutching his companion's arm for support. Both men swayed and trembled, the plague ravaging their bodies nearing its end. They backed away toward the crackling fire at the heart of the ancient plaza. "And may God have mercy upon our souls."

"Mercy?" shrieked the priest from Messina. "There is no mercy for the betrayers of God! His angel—"

"I said shut your hole, hymn-singer!!" Grimnir drove Pandolfo's long-sword point-first into the soft loam at the marsh's edge. "Is that what you think you've been doing? Nursing an angel of your precious lord? Bah! Open your eyes, swine! You've been gulled by a hate old as Time!" Two long strides brought the *skrælingr* to the mewling crossbowman, still alive despite the ruin of his face. Grimnir sucked his teeth.

Without preamble, he put one hobnailed boot on the man's chest. The Sicilian clawed at Grimnir's leg as he bent at the waist and wrenched his axe free. Blood burbled and spewed, a froth that masked his agonized scream. In the same motion, Grimnir struck him once more—this time, splitting the crossbowman's skull across his brow. Death rattled in his chest as the Sicilian's body went limp.

"Níðhöggr, it is called," Grimnir said, looking askance at the priest. "The Malice-Striker! It drinks blood and breathes the fumes of Niflheimr, a black pestilence that already spreads among you piss-eyed beggars of Miðgarðr!" Grimnir sheathed his gory axe and took up the fallen arbalest. He had no need for the goat's-foot mechanism on the dead crossbowman's belt. He stuck his boot in the stirrup; then, gritting his teeth, he drew the arbalest's cord back, his hands protected by thick ridges of callus. "The East burns with plague," he said, grabbing a pair of bolts from the bag at the dead man's waist and slotting one in the groove. "Messina is lost. Neapolis, Tarracina, the rest of the villages in your wake? They're next. Call your angel forth, priest. We can end this now . . ."

"Liar!" the priest replied, striding forward. "The Blessed One was sent by the Lord God Almighty! Sent to judge us! Sent to bring us the good news: The Lord cometh! Evil shall pass away, and the Kingdom of Heaven shall arise! As for you and your kind, spawn of Hell, God will punish you! God will cast every last one of you into the Abyss! God—"

Grimnir shot him. The weapon thumped as it discharged, sending the bolt across the short interval and into the priest's belly. The man gasped, suddenly at a loss for breath. Grimy hands clutched at his midriff. The bolt had pierced cloth, muscle, viscera, and bone to exit out his back. It struck the wood of the pageant wagon with an audible crack. Grimnir spat at him. "Your god is useless, you cack-handed kneeler."

The priest staggered, unable to speak. He turned from Grimnir; turned toward the pale ribbon of stone marking the Via Appia. Wheezing and gurgling in agony, he shuffled into the night . . . following something only his dying gaze could see. Grimnir grunted; he drew back the bow and slotted his last bolt. He eyed the two soldiers who yet lived, looking for signs their courage had returned, but both men kept their gaze averted. They stared hard into the heart of their crackling fire. Sweat beaded their fevered brows.

Nodding, Grimnir crossed to the rear of the pageant wagon. To the place where he'd been skewered by the first crossbow bolt—*Bah! How am I not dead?* In a patch of sedge grass still sticky with black blood he found his long-seax, Hátr, with its hilt of bone carved to resemble a great Northern dragon. He snatched it up. Iron rasped as he slid it into its scabbard.

Grimnir stood to one side and levered the broken door to the pageant wagon open, crossbow at the ready. A voice, weak and thready, thick with mucus, greeted him: "Is ... is it done? Did I k-kill it?"

The *skrælingr* peered in. By the thin firelight, he beheld a disease-ravaged Sicilian in a filthy gambeson, his haggard face a welter of pus-filled buboes and necrotic ulcers; the man lay among the baggage, unable to walk. A spent crossbow rested across his knees. "D-Did I ... ?"

"Takes more than the likes of you to kill me, you hymn-singing maggot," Grimnir said, stepping into view. Fear shimmered in the man's watery eyes. He clawed for the butt of the crossbow. His fingers, though, lacked the strength to grab on to it, just as his arms lacked the strength to reload it. He sagged back down. Grimnir nodded toward the front of the wagon. "Where is it, this so-called angel of yours, eh? Where does it hide?"

"It's gone," the fellow replied.

"Gone? Gone where? Up the road? Into the marsh? Speak up, you dung-hill rat!"

"I ... I do not know. Just ... g-gone."

"*Faugh!* What use are you, then?" The man started to speak, but Grimnir raised his crossbow and put a bolt through the dying Sicilian's open mouth. He tossed the spent weapon aside as the dying man gurgled and kicked. Grimnir rummaged a moment through the bundles and bales of supplies, coming up with a squat, long-necked bottle of wine. He pried the cork out and took a long draught. Wiping his mouth on the back of his hand, he turned and glared at the two soldiers by the fire. They were trembling, feverish; wracked by chills and coughing, they huddled together, praying, lost in their own thoughts. The men started as Grimnir approached. He nudged one with the bottle.

"Drink up," Grimnir said. "You need it worse than I do." He crossed to the far side of the fire and squatted on his haunches.

"Will ... Will you k-kill us, now?" the spearman asked, taking a drink of wine and passing it to his companion.

Grimnir scowled. "Why would I? *Nár!* I took care of the ones who had it coming, like that mouthy priest and his lapdog, Pandolfo! And those two louts with their blasted arbalests! The rest of you ..." Grimnir *chk'*ed his teeth.

The torchbearer shivered and blinked. "There ..." he began, glancing at his companion. "There's a legend from down around Neapolis. The graybeards there talk of a beast called the *huorco,* which takes the shape of a man. Are you ... ?"

Grimnir laughed, a sound like rocks grating together. "Aye, you precious fool," he replied. "I am that, and more besides. Where were you lot headed, eh? How'd you get tangled up in all this?"

The spearman took the bottle from the other and turned it up. "Messina," he said, knuckling droplets from his lower lip. "We were bound for Messina."

"Enrico ..." the torchbearer said, a note of caution creeping into his voice.

"What of it, Ugo?" replied Enrico, gesturing with the half-empty bottle. Tears dampened his cheeks. "What does it matter? We are dead already, you and I." He wiped his eyes with the back of his hand. "Messina, like I said. We were coming back from Croton, where Pandolfo was on the duke's business. We came across Fra Benvenuto—"

"The priest?"

"Aye, we came across him in the hills of Rhegium, and he needed our aid. At first, Pandolfo refused, but the priest revealed the Angel of the Lord to us and we were humbled."

Grimnir made no attempt to hide his sneer of derision. "And the priest? Where was he headed?"

"Avignon," Enrico replied. "By way of Rome. But he could not make it alone, for—as he put it—the Devil was in pursuit. Pandolfo volunteered our services, Duke Giovanni be damned. And then you started killing us." Both men finally looked up and met his gaze. He saw anger, there, simmering amid the zealot's gleam, and a thirst for vengeance.

"Aye," Grimnir said, eyes narrowing. "I did. And so? Draw steel, if you seek a reckoning."

Young Ugo coughed blood into his clenched fist, shivered, then looked away. Enrico glanced at him; as quickly as it appeared, the fire in his gaze vanished. He sighed, wiped his eyes again, and shook his head.

Grimnir snorted in contempt. "Where's your angel, now, eh? Where has it slithered off to?"

Enrico shrugged. "It left us here at dusk, after the wheel broke on the wagon. Told us to follow it to Rome."

"What happens, now?" Ugo's voice cracked.

Grimnir rose. He *tsk*'ed a line of spittle between his teeth; it crackled among the embers of their fire. "Drink your wine, mutter your filthy prayers, and die. Slit your own miserable throats if it's a quick death you crave. No skin off my teeth. Me—" He shrugged, turning. "—I have a wyrm to kill." And with that Grimnir set off up the Appian Way, leaving the dead and dying to their own devices.

A dozen yards on he found the priest of Messina, Fra Benvenuto. The man had fallen to his knees and was crawling across a crumbling stone bridge, muttering the name of his God with each gasping breath. His life's blood drooled from slack lips.

"*As I was walking all alone,*" Grimnir crooned, crouching by the priest, "*I heard a sad little crow making a moan.* Where's your so-called angel, now, little crow? Where is your useless god, eh?" Fra Benvenuto tried to grasp Grimnir's arm, to lever himself upright. The *skrælingr*, though, slapped the priest's hand away. "*Nár!* Stay on your knees, you wretch! It's where your kind belongs."

"You . . . You cannot s-stop it," the priest said. "The Angel of . . . of th-the Lord. It . . . b-brings the cleansing fire! G-God's wrath! You . . . You c-cannot . . ."

Grimnir hissed. "I am the only one who can stop that blasted Níðhöggr, hymn-singer. And I will." The *skrælingr* rose up; as he did so, he snagged Fra Benvenuto by the back of his filthy black cassock, forcing the priest off his knees. "I'll bury that wyrm in your precious Rome. You, I'll bury right *here*." Grunting, Grimnir flung the priest of Messina off the cobbled bridge and into the Pontine Marshes. The man gabbled and flailed before he struck the reed-choked water. The splash echoed and died away. And then the priest of Messina was seen no more this side of Hell.

Grimnir hawked and spat. Dawn was not far off and Níðhöggr had a full night's head start. Wiping his nose with the back of his hand, Grimnir set off. His stride grew long, a loping pace like that of a hunting wolf . . .

★ ★ ★

GRIMNIR HATED the sun. He hated it in the North, where by this time of year it was a watery disc, masked by a thick fleece of cloud. He hated it in the fog-shrouded West, where it hung like a forge-glede over autumnal woods and rocky shingles. He hated the sun in the mountainous East, where it was as sharp and bright as the icy wind and reflected the snow crusting the high passes. Here in the South, he hated it worst of all. In these lands surrounding the Jórsalahaf, the Jerusalem Sea, the sun burned in Ymir's mist-wreathed skull like a brand, undimmed by the seasons.

Grimnir snarled up at it as he ran, sweat dripping from his lank hair.

From the edge of the marshes, the Appian Way ran across hill and hollow in an almost straight line, as though some dead god's finger had sketched it into the crust of the earth. Its deep-set cobbles and weed-edged kerbs cut across farmlands gone fallow; orchards grew on its flanks, with forests of pine, cypress, and plane trees in between. Smaller lanes branched off, rutted tracks and goat trails that led to solitary farmsteads or small villages. And everywhere, no matter in which direction he turned, Grimnir saw signs of Rome's ancient glories. Squinting in the glare, he beheld stone eidolons pitted by the elements, faceless statues atop age-worn plinths, tombs hung with ivy, and monuments bearing deeply incised runes that proclaimed the deeds of long-dead men.

And amid these ruins, Grimnir came across the spoor of Níðhöggr. Dead livestock, at first. A brace of oxen on their sides, torn open, flyblown and bloated; goats dismembered in bloodstained grass. Crouching by these grisly leftovers, Grimnir spied the marks of claws and teeth. The beast wasn't trying to hide, not like it had at Caffa on the Black Sea, then at Miklagarðr, and again at Messina. It seemed desperate to make it to Rome. "Why?" Grimnir muttered, rising. He glared toward that ancient city, still not much more than a smear of gray smoke on the horizon. "What's in Rome that has you all hot and bothered, you slithering maggot?"

He found his first dead man near noon. The bastard lay in the shadow of a gate, on a lane leading to some local grandee's estate—a barefooted corpse clad in a linen nightshirt, headless and drained of blood. From nearby, Grimnir caught the scent of smoke, of burnt flesh, and the underlying reek of corruption. He heard no screams. Even the dogs were silent.

With each passing mile, signs of the wyrm's depredations, of its voracious hunger, grew more obvious—a serf cut down in the field, bloodless and cloaked in flies; a pair of horsemen and their mounts torn asunder, gnawed to the bone; a woman's head sitting in a tussock of grass, dark of hair and milky-eyed, her devoured body doubtless stewing in Malice-Striker's belly. But where a man would see madness and horror, Grimnir merely chuckled.

That bastard, Níðhöggr, was making this hunt too easy.

The beast's advance, however, did not go unnoticed. As the day waned, Grimnir was forced to slow his pace. Squadrons of mailed horsemen, clad in bright yellow-and-blue surcoats, emerged from a squat round fortress perched atop a low hill. Some rode between farmsteads and villas, drawn by the columns of smoke staining the afternoon sky; others took up positions at crossroads and bridges, watching for signs of an invader. Their presence forced Grimnir to abandon the road. He crept through a field of tall yellow grass to a copse of trees, where columns jutted like broken teeth; toppled walls formed an ancient boundary, a temple, perhaps. Marble pavers were tilted and dislodged by the roots, a sacred grove where once sacred stones existed.

A spring trickled from beneath the mossy stones. Here, Grimnir crouched in a well of shadow, his back to a low wall, and scooped handfuls of water. He spat dust, cursing under his breath . . . and then stopped. He cocked his head, listening.

There.

From the other side of the grove, he heard the thudding of hooves. He flattened himself against the wall and drew his seax. Horses nickered and whinnied, and men hailed one another barely a dozen yards from him.

"Signore! Signore Caetani!" one rider sang out, his youthful voice thick with excitement. "Cola di Rienzo calls for aid! The Colonna and the damnable Orsini have made a truce against him . . . and they mean to be rid of him tonight!"

Grimnir heard a weary sigh. The voice of a much older man answered: "So, it is true, Jacopo? I knew those dogs were up to no good."

Grimnir heard the stamp of hooves and the jangle of curb chains as a third horseman pushed to the fore, younger even than the first. There was a tinge of fear to his words. "We have to warn someone, Father! Di Rienzo, Colonna, Orsini . . . it does not matter! They must be told what we've seen! This . . . This is something beyond any feud between nobles!"

"What does he mean, Signore?"

There was a sharp note of disapproval to the old man's reply: "What my son means is there are fires all along the Via Appia. Farmsteads burned out, corpses left to rot. Where young Gianni, here, sees the hand of the Devil, I see the work of marauders. Likely, they're making their way toward Rome."

"You saw what I saw!" Gianni snapped.

Jacopo spoke before father and son could come to verbal blows: "Then we must make haste, Signore! It might be more of Colonna's godless allies, seeking to divide our strength."

"So I thought, as well," replied old Signore Caetani. "Gather the men, Gianni!"

"God's teeth! But—"

The old signore's voice cracked like a whip: "The Pope is our patron, and the Pope—and perhaps God himself—wants Cola di Rienzo to remain in power! The Caetani will ride to his aid! Now, gather the men and keep your tongue between your teeth!"

There came a moment of strangled silence, then Grimnir heard the youthful Gianni turn his horse and canter back the way they'd come. The other two men walked their mounts to the other end of the grove, toward Rome.

"You have a boy of your own, do you not, Jacopo?" asked the old man, after a moment.

"I do, Signore, but he is young, still."

Signore Caetani sighed, again, his voice fading: "No man should live long enough to become a villain to his son . . ."

Grimnir crouched, there, in the shadows alongside the ruined wall until the men had moved off, then made his way across the country like a wraith. He turned over old Caetani's words in his mind. Strife in the streets meant fertile ground for the wyrm's pickings. While no one was watching, while the lords of Rome fought one another, Níðhöggr would seek out the poorest, the meanest, the most desperate among them and twist their minds; it would make thralls of those no others would use . . . but this could work in Grimnir's favor.

It meant he would find the wyrm among Rome's dregs.

Near sunset, Grimnir crested a low ridge and got his first look at the

THE DOOM OF ODIN

Eternal City. Oh, he'd heard stories from old Gífr, who'd visited Rome in its heyday; tales of a sprawling labyrinth of limestone and marble spread across seven hills, home to a million whiteskins, their wives and offspring, and their slaves. A city of temples and monuments, spirits and gods, where piety and perversion lived cheek-by-jowl with civility and savagery. The old sot's eyes would gleam like embers when he spoke of his time there.

That wasn't the city Grimnir bore witness to. No, under a pall of smoke lit by the dying red-gold gleam of the sun he saw a mean and dispirited town; a town cowering like a whipped dog at the foot of a single hill, Mons Vaticanus, with the turgid brown waters of the Tiber River between them. He saw a riot of domes and towers, bright marble and old terra-cotta alongside age-pitted limestone and brick; he spied villas and town houses rising like new shoots amid old stones. And churches. Scores of them, like maggots worming through the dead flesh of an empire. A cavalcade of saints and martyrs danced on the bones of ancient gods, nameless and fey; baleful eyes watched the hymn-singers' desecration from the shadows.

This was Rome: a midden fetched up against a stinking river, all of it protected by stone walls both ancient and formidable—battlements and ramparts, towers and fortified gates. Each point of entry was like a small village, with buildings of wood and scavenged stone going right up to the walls. Grimnir did not waste time speculating *how* a beast like Níðhöggr might have slipped into the city in broad daylight. He reckoned the snake must have crept west, into the Tiber, and swum upriver until he found a sewer opening or somesuch. Fine for that scaly maggot, but Grimnir would not go into the drink and try to follow. No, he had something else in mind.

Grimnir moved off to his right and followed the circuit of the wall as the chill of autumn descended, as the bloated moon rose, just past full. He stayed bent low, his good eye agleam as he prowled, hunting. His path carried him east, past solitary farms and villas where trembling hands kindled lamps against the fall of night. Dogs howled at his passage. Fearful eyes peered out, seeing nothing.

Grimnir chuckled. *Blind fools!*

It was an hour and more before he found what he sought. East of the Via Appia, the ground turned marshy, rank with thick grasses and groves of willow and cypress. A creek burbled in from the countryside. It ran right up to the walls and vanished into an iron-grated culvert. And at that spot where the creek disappeared, Grimnir beheld the outlines of a walled-up postern gate. It had been a small affair—a single arch boasting no defensive towers, simply a tunnel in the wall that had been barred by iron and wood. Now, it presented a façade of kiln-fired brick, poorly set in mortar chewed by Time and the elements.

That would be his way in.

Grimnir paused, scanned the wall for sentries; he saw none. Even the towers nearest to him were poorly manned, a pair of silhouettes hunched over a crackling brazier. Grunting, Grimnir bolted from his hiding place and across the open ground, reaching the foot of the wall unseen. He sprang, hooked his black-nailed fingers—hard as iron—into a seam between the bricks, and pulled himself up. Long arms and knotty legs propelled him higher; like a spider, he scaled the wall. Breath exploded in short, sharp gasps; harness clashed, and hobnailed boots scraped chunks of brick and mortar from the wall as Grimnir gained the keystone of the original arch.

He clung there, a moment, splay-footed on a ledge less than two fingers in width, and glared up at the crenellated summit. The next section of wall was even more pitted and cracked. This was nothing to a child of the distant North, of lost Orkahaugr, who had clawed his way up naked ice-slick rock at an age when white-skinned brats could barely walk. It was easier than scaling a ladder. Up, he went.

Barely winded, Grimnir pulled himself into an embrasure. He crouched like a monstrous raptor, glancing side to side, alert for sentries. The men on the tower—a score of yards away and twenty feet higher from where he stood—yet gathered around their brazier, polearms leaning against their shoulders as they warmed their hands and talked among themselves. Grimnir smirked. He dropped to the parapet. Like a fast-moving shadow, he crossed to the far side and discovered steps cut into the inside face of the wall. These he took two at a time. At the base of the wall, the creek rose again from its culvert and splashed its way down a stone-lined channel. With his single red eye burning in the moon-shadowed darkness, Grimnir followed the creek away from the ancient walls and into the pastoral heart of Old Rome ...

★ ★ ★

THE DOOM OF ODIN

He tasted ash. The chill air was thick with it, shoals of smoke drifting down from the autumnal heights. The night stank of charred wood and hydrangeas; the crisp pork-fat stench of burning corpses mixed with flowering jasmine. Grimnir prowled along the edges of a colossal ruin, ivy-clad and overgrown, where dappled moonlight filtered through the yellow-leafed canopy of a chestnut grove; to the north and east, partly shielded by the bulk of one of Rome's seven hills, the sky glowed with the color of molten copper. Savage fires burned in that direction; Grimnir's sharp ears heard the echo of clashing blades, the screams of men spitted on lances. He wondered, then, how fared the insurrection old Signore Caetani was worried about. Grimnir hawked phlegm into the dust. So long as it kept these Romans occupied, let them fight on.

This part of Rome reminded him of the landscape along the Appian Way—nothing but monasteries and basilicas nestled amid vineyards, of winding country lanes where once mighty streets had lain. And ruins. Always ruins, as though the dead had a constant need to remind the living that they, too, had once trod here.

As he came abreast of a great crumbling archway, Grimnir heard the *clink* of dislodged pebbles. He whirled toward the noise, his seax rasping from its sheath. Through the archway, vine-draped and eroded, he spied a wide plaza paved in tiny, colorful stones, pocked and weed-choked. Across this, from another arch, there was movement in the mist.

An old woman hove into view. She was gray-haired and thin, almost skeletal, her sparse frame draped in rags despite the cold. The crone raised one grimy hand, her index finger extended and pointing at him—a gesture fraught with doom.

"*Skrælingr*," she hissed, her voice echoing. "It wants you, *skrælingr!*"

"Then lead me to it, hag!" he answered, stalking through the arch. "Lead me to that wretched wyrm, and I'll end this little chase!"

The old woman laughed and drifted off, skipping like a child down an age-shattered colonnade. Grimnir bolted after her.

"Lead me to your master, I said!" he roared.

The old woman vanished between the columns. Grimnir saw her, dancing across another floor—this one a riot of age-shattered mosaics, where the faces of long-dead Romans stared at them, gapped and filthy. "Master?" she crooned. "I have no master, *skrælingr.*"

Grimnir leapt through the colonnade; he bore down on the twirling old hag, her hair a veil of silver in the moonlight. Her eyes . . . one was filmy and dead; the other gleamed like *jötunn*-lights on a storm-wracked sea. In her laughter was the shriek of ravens, the scrape of iron on bone, and the thunder of drums. Grimnir smelled it, then: a breath of frost-laden air that reeked of old wood, wet iron, and blood. A shiver of apprehension coursed from the *skrælingr's* crown to the soles of his feet. He skidded to a halt . . .

Even as the mosaicked floor cracked and crumbled under him. Suddenly, the world spun. Grimnir fell backward, arms flailing; his hands sought purchase, some wall or other to arrest his plummet.

There was nothing.

Nothing until the bones of his neck collided with a kerb of cold, hard limestone. And under his weight, bent as he was, not even the iron-threaded vertebrae of the *kaunar* could survive. Grimnir felt a burst of agony; he heard the wet snap of his spine, and a sudden paralysis ran through his extremities. He could not breathe; he could not move. His now-useless body slid down into a heap, his head perched at a grotesque angle. Looking up, he could see the crone's silhouette some thirty feet above, framed by wheeling stars.

No, he thought, darkness creeping at the edges of his vision. *Not a crone.* The figure who glared down at him bore the shape of a man, true, though hunched and as twisted as the staff he leaned upon; he was clad in a voluminous cloak with a slouch hat pulled low. A single malevolent eye gleamed from beneath the brim.

Grimnir gasped, racking his last breath through blood-starved lungs. "Y-You . . ."

The figure laughed, a sound like the thunder of war-drums:

> "Loki's betrayal, | born of filth and fume,
> Too long has thy doom been left to hang;
> Deep is thy years, but | shallow thy wisdom:
> Yggdrasil's wyrm is not for thee."

Grimnir snarled, defiant to the last. His single eye blazed. He felt his life leaching away. His face was black and congested; his lungs burned in his chest. All he could do was glare up at the cloaked figure, watching as it grew tattered and thin, as it dissipated like a night mist.

And there, in the gloom of that ancient underground chamber, Grimnir died . . .

8
BERSERKIR

There *was no solace in death; no peace.*

There was but a moment of darkness, a moment of silence; then, the memory of *his* laughter stung like a goad. The echo of it—as deep and powerful as the war-drums of the Norse—kindled the hot wrath of life in his breast. It drove him from the grave, from the embracing arms of oblivion. Water burned his eyes, clouding the good one in a milky haze. Through it, he could barely see the *sjóvættir* who circled him, their faces twisted in fear. *Fear of him* . . . no, that wasn't true. They did not fear him. They feared what had *claimed* him.

He is mine.

And as he floated up unmolested through the cowed and retreating throngs of *sjóvættir*, other memories—faded and pale—teased at the corners of his consciousness . . .

A gnarled oak as old as Miðgarðr's bones. Drifts of sodden leaves; eight stones, draped in thorn and bramble under a sky the color of iron. Scratched runes oozing traces of ancient sorcery; the movement of spirits, like a cold breeze tickling the back of the neck; the creak of tree limbs, the faint clash of stone on stone, the moaning dirge of the dead . . .

Booted feet found purchase in the shallows. He drove himself upward, breaking the surface of the water with a snarling gasp. Sodden black hair hung with fetishes of silver and bone clung to his face, and his one red eye flared like a beacon of hate as he staggered ashore.

But where?

He remembered Rome. He remembered ruins, where a trap had been laid for him—a place where the ground had crumbled under his feet. He remembered falling; the sharp crack of his neck bones breaking. And he remembered a cloaked figure in a slouch hat; a single baleful eye, watching under autumnal stars. Now, he swayed like a drunkard under a broil and fume, bathed in the eerie light of the Nine Worlds. Under his feet were the hateful stones and soil of Nástrond...

Nástrond.

Here was Gjöll's Inlet, not Rome.

Grimnir spat. One black-nailed hand clutched at his bare chest, at the spot where the *scrag*'s spear had pierced his body. He looked down, expecting to see a killing wound. There was nothing save for a fresh scar the width of his palm. He raised his head. Inarticulate rage twisted his vulpine features into a predatory mask.

Someone is toying with him.

His gaze lit upon Blártunga. The fat *scrag* had turned away, his head thrown back in a howl of triumph. The sudden absence of sound—for the *sjóvættir* had ceased their clamor—brought his attention back to the water's edge. His wolf-cry died in his throat; his eyes widened in disbelief. The blood-clotted spearhead trembled in his grasp as he took a step backward.

"B-By Ymir! How—?"

Grimnir answered with a savage grin, lips peeling back over yellowed fangs. Such was the antipathy burning in his single eye that Blártunga dropped his spear and recoiled. But even as the *scrag* shifted his weight and made to turn, to hare off for the safety of the shield wall raised by the True Sons of Loki, the *skrælingr* was upon him.

The youth gave a single bleat of terror as Grimnir's black-nailed fingers knotted in the hair on the unshaved half of the *scrag*'s skull. Mercilessly, he wrenched Blártunga around and bore him to the ground. "How?" Grimnir hissed, grinding the side of the *scrag*'s face against the flinty shore. "I don't know *how*, you wretch. Do you? *Do you?*"

Blártunga's eyes rolled in terror. Grimnir caught the vinegar-stench of piss.

"*Nár!* Of course you don't, you useless *scrag!*" With a grimace, he slammed the youth's head against the ground.

"M-Mercy!" Blártunga sobbed. Blood started from lacerations in his cheek. "Mercy!"

"So-ho! Mercy, is it? You mean like this?" Grimnir lifted Blártunga's head by the hair; muscles knotting, he drove the youth's skull against the edge-knapped rocks. Again, he hammered Blártunga's head and face into the ground. Again and again, until his teeth shattered. Until an eye burst like a rotted egg. Until the plates of his skull came apart. "Here's your mercy, you backstabbing tub of lard!" A gurgle arose from the *scrag*'s throat as, with a final savage blow, his head burst like a sack.

Blood and gobbets of brain spattered Grimnir's face. He raised his eyes, head cocked as he glared at the wall of shields a score of yards off. They were *kaunar*, tall and cloaked in red; their shields were round and sported the serpent sigil of Mánavargr. Plying haft and hilt against shield rims, they hammered out a tocsin of war.

Grimnir hawked and spat. The blood of one *scrag* was not enough to slake the murder-thirst writhing in his belly. He needed more. *It* needed more. Driven by fury, he snatched up Blártunga's fallen spear—still wet with the blood he had shed over it—and sprinted for Mánavargr's shield wall. Behind him, voices called his name; ahead, enemy *kaunar* jeered him. He was naked to the waist, blood spackled, and armed only with the rusted spear of a dead *scrag*.

"Come and die, little *skrælingr!*" one among them roared. Grimnir spied his first victim—indeed, he could not miss him—a monstrous *kaunr*, easily a head taller than Grimnir and heavier by seven stone, at least. Soot-blackened mail covered him from crown to sole; he wore an open-faced helmet with a wide nasal and a crest of *skrælingar* scalps, while in one brawny arm he cradled an axe with a broad blade, counterweighted by a spiked hammer-head.

This bastard broke the interlocked wall of shields and stepped to the fore. His cloak swirled as he slung his own shield aside. "He's mine!" he called out to his mates. The shield wall flowed together again as this behemoth took half a dozen long steps into the open. "Mine, you hear me? I am—"

Grimnir never let him finish.

With a serpentine hiss, the son of Bálegyr snapped his arm forward, driving the blade of his spear into the point of the *kaunr*'s bearded chin. His drawn breath, meant for the boastful recitation of his deeds, turned into a death-rattle as the spearhead plowed through bone and teeth; it cut through the muscle of his tongue and the soft flesh of his palate, splitting his face from jaw to brow. Blood spewed from the spear-cleft ruin.

Quick as a snake, Grimnir let loose of the spear shaft and stripped the *kaunr*'s axe from nerveless fingers. He pivoted, twisting at the waist; before the dying bastard could fall, he slammed the spiked hammer-head full into the center of his enemy's mailed chest. Grimnir howled with glee as the pierced and shattered giant catapulted back into the ranks of his mates. Shields were snarled; spears and swords made useless by the weight of their so-called champion.

And into this nascent breach leapt a ravening son of the Wolf.

Nor was he alone. He felt the breeze from crow-feather fletchings as arrows passed within inches of him. Arrows shot from behind, from the prows of boats, and bound for the eyes and throats of the True Sons in his path. He heard Skaði's voice, shouting her contempt for their enemy; he heard the crunch of a dozen keels against the shingle, followed by the war-cry of Úlfsstaðir.

After that, Grimnir was beyond hearing. He was insensate to the dull crunch of bone, to the screams that were by-products of the union between iron and flesh. He could not feel the spasms of impact running from the edge of his borrowed axe as he threshed Mánavargr's warriors like wheat. Here, in this moment, there was only the red mist of rage and the howl of blood and thunder; this was Odin's weather, and upon this ship of death he stood forth as a master helmsman.

He shattered spear blades and shafts with each blow of his axe; each riposte ended with splintered wood and crushed helmets, with cloven shields and heads split to the teeth. Blades whickered for Grimnir's heart, leaving only trails of blood when they failed to find purchase. The claws of the dying scored the *skrælingr*'s face, his arms, his naked chest. His single eye blazed with a baleful glow. It was a lodestar, drawing the restless dead back to their temporary slumber under the cloud-wreathed boughs of Yggðrasil.

THE DOOM OF ODIN

And so, by hammer and blade and unmitigated rage, Grimnir Bálegyr's son bent the back of Mánavargr's shield wall . . .

THERE WAS deviltry afoot, Iðuna was certain of it. That it was not deviltry of her own devising gave her pause. Still, she crept through the foliage on the left flank of the battlefield, following the trail of dead *scrags*, content to let the dogs of Kaunheimr snarl and snap at the swine of Úlfsstaðir. She was oblivious to their clangor and clamor, to the cries of the dying—sounds as commonplace as the wind for one such as her. No, as she neared the water's edge her whole attention was focused on what had just happened, on what she'd just witnessed.

That Grimnir Bálegyr's son had died was a fact beyond dispute. She'd watched through slitted yellow eyes as that fat *scrag* got the drop on him, fair and square. He'd skewered the useless bastard in the back; then, proving that even an idiot *scrag* possessed some shred of wit, he guided the son of her daughter to the water and fed him to the *sjóvættir,* pretty as you please. And that should have been the end of things. Their compact sealed—the blood of one or the other, as agreed upon—the water-spirits should have entered the fray, dragging her feckless husband's boats to the bottom. That's not what happened, though.

He had hit the water face-first . . . and the *sjóvættir* had fled. Then, not a heartbeat later, this Grimnir emerged from the water unscathed. *Unscathed!* And *that* was the sort of deviltry she could not fathom. How had this witless maggot managed to die and be reborn in the blink of an eye? The idea of it went against the spirit of Nástrond, where the Nine Fathers of the *kaunar* and their children made ready for the day when the Gjallarhorn would echo, its call sending them to the bloody fields of Vígríðr and the Twilight of the Gods. That time was not yet here, nor did she feel it would ever be. For now, their eternity was an endless cycle—feast, fuck, fight, and fall—and that was the sum total of their existence under the roots of the Old Ash. So, how had Bálegyr's idiot son cheated? That was what Iðuna wanted to know.

There was one way to find out . . .

The surface of Gjöll's Inlet was placid, now. Yggðrasil's shrouded lights reflected from faint ripples of current, jags of orange and red, green and gold shimmering in the mud-churned shallows. Iðuna's eyes narrowed. She knelt and touched the surface of the water with her fingertips.

It was as cold as a glacier's flow. She jerked her hand back, scowling. *Cursed deviltry!*

Undeterred, Iðuna stretched out over the still water, her palms flat against the rocks, her arms supporting her upper body. Her visage stared back at her, a mask of hate hacked from ivory and framed by snaky locks the color of milk; topaz eyes gleamed in the half-light. She leaned down and breathed on the water's surface.

"*Sjóvættir,*" she hissed.

> "*Sjóvættir, hark!* | *Heed you my voice;*
> *shake off thy fear* | *and attend me!*
> *Sjóvættir, hark!* | *Answer my call;*
> *Rise from the dark* | *beneath Nástrond.*"

Lower, she went, with each stanza until her face broke the surface of the water. The cold—*the cold!*—was so sharp it felt as though unseen hands flensed the flesh from her cheeks with knives of ice. Iðuna resisted gasping; resisted drawing water into her lungs. Instead, she pried open her eyes . . .

. . . *To stare up at a gnarled oak, its roots sunk deep into Miðgarðr's bones. A cold north wind stirs drifts of desiccated leaves. Around her, eight stones stand thorn-draped under a sky the color of blood-smeared iron. Scratched runes ooze traces of ancient sorcery.*

"*What is this place?*" *she says, turning slowly, her voice hollow and profane in the primordial silence.* "*Why have you brought me here?*"

Her skin prickles. Something moves under her feet, twisting, writhing through the crust of the earth. Something impossibly ancient. She feels . . . anger. Wrath. A thirst for vengeance. The gnarled oak looms over her, its spreading limbs taking the shape of a long-fingered hand. A voice issues from every branch, bole, stone, leaf, and blade of grass, and its power is such that it drives her to her knees.

> "*Skrælingr witch!*
> *Traitor to thy blood!*
> *Naught have ye learned*

Since Jarnfjall's end!
And naught will ye find here
But death and damnation;
So cease thy meddling,
And mark ye well:
The Hooded One is mine."

She quails, eyes screwed shut. An eerie sound reaches through her terror—a sound like the tearing of fabric, the ripping of turf. Too late, she realizes its source. Before she can rise and run, the tree's roots—pale and damp and wriggling—coil up from the ground to seize her. Her struggles mean nothing, so quickly do the roots bind her up; serpentine, the sap-wet roots lace around her legs, up her torso. They slip up her shoulders and shackle her arms to her sides. She thrashes as the old oak's roots wind around her head, choking off a scream.

And the last thing she hears, ere she is dragged into the primordial darkness from whence she came, is the oak-spirit's voice, thick with menace:

"Mine!"

Iðuna recoiled, scrambling away from the water's edge. She coughed and spluttered, her hair a wet fringe of white around a corpse-pale face. Fear clouded her yellow eyes—a bone-deep terror, savage and atavistic. With a trembling hand, she wiped her mouth with the damp edge of her sleeve.

Off to her right, through dry leaves and nettles, she heard the shield wall of her chief, Mánavargr, as it buckled under the weight of Úlfsstaðir's onslaught. The sounds of slaughter took on new meaning as this . . . this *thing* that wore the guise of Grimnir Bálegyr's son savaged the True Sons of Loki. What was he? An Outsider? Some spirit called up from the Howling Dark and given a *skrælingr's* form? Some *vættir* of old who dwelled under the roots of Yggðrasil, summoned to Nástrond by the promise of slaughter? And *who* summoned it? The only one among that lot with any blasted sense was her whore of a daughter, Skríkja. Was this her doing?

A chilling thought gripped Iðuna, then. What if this Grimnir, this Outsider who was protected by spirits even greater than himself, was that *scrag* Snaga's idea of vengeance? He was eldest of them all; he had had millennia to plumb the mysteries of Nástrond . . . what if *he* was the one behind this?

Resolve flooded Iðuna's withered limbs. She clawed for her staff, using it as a crutch to lever herself to her feet. She had to warn Mánavargr. Njól's lads were lost, but there was still time to spirit the lord of Kaunheimr from the field …

SKAÐI SKULKED in Grimnir's wake like a scavenger after a shark, eager for an easy meal. She had a dagger clenched between her teeth, and her last arrow on the nock. Stumbling over the carpet of dead and dying *kaunr*, she somehow kept her footing; at the last moment, as some evil-eyed bastard from Kaunheimr came at Grimnir's blind side, she hauled back on the string and loosed in the same motion. That iron broadhead, fletched in night-black crow feathers, pierced the howling foe through the neck; she watched as it punched through that blood-spewing fool and continued on, splitting the willow shield-boards, mail, and bone of the *kaunr* next to him. And that lout's enraged bellow turned to a scream as, three paces ahead of her, Grimnir's axe sang his death-song.

Nor was she alone. All around, Skaði saw the white stag-skull emblem of Kjallandi's folk. Old Roman corselets and shields clashed and clattered as bandy-legged *skrælingar*—like gnarled spirits of rapine and slaughter—came to blows with their straight-limbed cousins, the True Sons of Loki. Bodies crashed and writhed; spears sought chinks in armor, axes flashed in the perpetual gloom, and swords rasped and sparked, splitting helmets and the skulls beneath. Black blood rained down; rivulets of it trickled into the milky waters of Gjöll's Inlet, creating a slick of reeking gore across the shingle.

The *skrælingar* followed Grimnir's lead; the blood-drenched son of Bálegyr, lost in a berserk rage, created the head of an ironshod wedge. And that wedge spiked into Mánavargr's shield wall, splitting it like a rotten plank.

Skaði plucked the dagger from between her teeth. Snarling like a she-wolf, she stomped on the throat of the mortally-wounded *kaunr* she'd shot in the neck, then knifed another who'd been hammered to the earth by a *skrælingr* shield and now struggled to rise. Other allies streamed past her, their war-gear bearing the Red Eye—an undisciplined mob that spilled along the flanks of the wedge. This respite gave Skaði time to catch her breath, to gather arrows from the slain, and to think.

She had seen some odd things, down among the Lokaean Witches; sorcery and necromancy, things that defied explanation. But such was the nature of Nástrond, where the eerie and the profane met in the business of strife, each waiting for the strident call of the Gjallarhorn. She'd never seen one of their kind shrug off a death-wound.

Feh! That blasted *scrag* got Grimnir in the back, plain as the nose on her face. Through the heart, she reckoned. And before she could intervene, before she could even set an arrow to the string, that fat little worm gave him to the *sjóvættir*.

Skaði shook her head, trying to clear it of the fog shrouding her memory of what happened next. Grimnir had gone under that spirit-whipped froth, leaking blood like a sieve; not half a heartbeat later, the water of Gjöll's Inlet became as motionless as a sheet of ice—like someone, somewhere had sent a cold wind to extinguish the *sjóvættir's* anger. He'd gone into the water dead; when he emerged, again, quick as you please, he'd come up roaring like some beast of legend ... with not a scratch on him.

"Watch yourself!" a voice warned. Caught flat-footed, Skaði whirled even as a bloody *kaunr* lurched to his feet behind her, shrugging off the corpses of the dead that had hidden him. He leveled a broken spear at her. Before he could lunge, however, Skaði moved. She danced back, lashing out with the bone-tipped end of her bow. It caught the *kaunr* across the eyes. He reeled to one side, screaming as his right eye burst like an overripe plum. Before he could recover, Skaði planted a hobnailed boot in his balls. He doubled over, gagging; with almost careless aplomb, Skaði slid her dagger between the knobs of gristle marking his vertebrae and severed his spinal cord.

The *kaunr* dropped like a sack.

She eyed her benefactor. At the head of a dozen reserves, Gífr strode up the stinking carpet of hewed flesh and riven viscera. "That one almost had you, little rat," he said, by way of greeting.

"Almost." She glanced over her shoulder at Grimnir, who roared challenges at the cream of Mánavargr's dwindling crop. "Did you see?"

"See what?" Gífr studied the fallen. Most had died by Grimnir's hand, their heads split and chests crushed. A handful had other wounds—arrows, knives, swords. "That one go berserk?"

"Don't be coy," she snapped. "You had to have seen that same thing I saw!"

He turned his gaze on her, his ruddy eyes veiled and calculating. "I don't know what I saw, little rat, and neither do you. I know, whatever it was, it has worked to our benefit, so I'll hold my judgment close to the vest until I hear what happened from *his* lips." He nodded at Grimnir, who was thirty yards distant, now, and showed no sign of his rage abating. "Agreed?"

"It's not natural, whatever it was," she grumbled.

Gífr laughed. "We are all already dead, you precious little fool. There is nothing natural about any of this." He handed her a fresh bag of arrows. "Take a couple of these lads and head around the right flank. See if you can spy Mánavargr and Iðuna, and bring them both down if you have a shot. Let's get them before they can skin out, eh? What say you?"

Skaði looked Grimnir's way, once more. She chewed her lower lip.

"I'll look after him," Gífr said, nudging her with the bag of arrows. She snatched it from his hand.

"Better hurry, then, you old sot," she replied. "He's getting away from you."

And with that, Skaði and a quartet of *skrælingar*—all bearing the emblem of Kjallandi—set off along the right flank of the fray, loping like a pack of hunting dogs.

GRIMNIR'S BREAST rose and fell; his breath hissed through clenched teeth. Though his slate-dark hide was scored by talon and blade, most of the black blood dripping down his knotty arms, down his belly, and soaking into the coarse fabric of his trousers was not his. He was bathed in the slaughter-broth of his victims, who were laid out behind him like driftwood after a storm.

He sensed others around him, allies and kin who had joined the shield-breaking. He paid them no mind. They were dogs, yapping at the hocks of the wolf. And though his fingers cramped around the haft of his blunted axe, though his shoulders ached and his legs felt leaden, the murderous daimon writhing in his belly thirsted still.

It wanted more.

More blood.

Someone is toying with you, this daimon screamed. *The voice from the deep, the gnarled man in a slouch hat, his mocking laughter . . . he is toying with you!*

The raven-starver, Lord of Ásgarðr!

THE DOOM OF ODIN

Grimnir snarled. From the last milling rank of the enemy formation, a *kaunr* shield-maiden lunged for him, her eyes like slitted yellow lamps in the eternal gloom. He batted her sword aside with the palm of his hand; her riposte thrust through empty air. As she recovered her balance, drawing her sword back and resetting herself for another flurry of blows, Grimnir stepped inside her guard and rammed his head into hers. Driven by wiry cables of muscle lacing his neck, the iron-hard bones of Grimnir's forehead smashed the nasal of her helmet and the nose beneath. She stumbled back; curses poured like blood from her lacerated lips. Her screams of rage became agonized gurgles as Grimnir's notched and gore-caked axe half-sheared through her sword-arm at the shoulder. The maiden staggered and fell to her knees; the *skrælingr's* backswing crushed helmet and skull, extinguishing the hateful gleam in her eyes. Those who had stood at her shoulder looked poised to break.

"Run, dogs!" Grimnir roared. "Run and hide! Where's your chief, eh? *Faugh!* Send the bastard to me!"

"Here!" a voice replied. "Face me, you piss-blooded *skrælingr!*"

Grimnir whirled toward the challenger. It was Njól who stepped to the fore. Grimnir had seen him only from a distance; up close, Mánavargr's warlord—also one of the Nine Fathers—was as nondescript as the others. Another straight-limbed *kaunr;* another red-eyed and yellow-fanged bastard with a black thatchy beard, a holdover from his days as one of the *dvergar.* Another idiot who would crow over the purity of his blood. Grimnir smiled.

There was no preamble to their duel; no sizing each other up or exchanging taunts. Grimnir simply pivoted and launched himself across the short interval. Using a mound of bodies as his springboard, he leapt into the air; his gore-clotted axe whistled as it descended. Njól took the blow on the round shield, its face emblazoned with the serpent of Kaunheimr. The second blow staggered him; the third blow split his shield's face. Grimnir drew back for a fourth ...

Thinking he had his enemy's measure, Njól went on the offensive. He drove forward, a red-cloaked tempest of steel and silvered mail; his sword darted snakelike for Grimnir's throat. The *skrælingr* swayed and backpedaled, batting Njól's thrusts aside with his axe. Enraged, the *kaunr* brought his shield to bear as a weapon, intent on hammering Grimnir to the ground with its iron boss.

Made of sterner stuff, was the son of Bálegyr. He took that mammoth blow on his left shoulder and his side, oblivious to the flesh-tearing of the ragged iron or the bone-deep bruising. He took that impact with naught but an aggravated grunt. Before Njól could hit him again, however, Grimnir let fall his axe; like iron chains, his arms seized the shield rim and spun it to the right—cranking the *kaunr*'s arm with it, wrenching it at an impossible angle. Nor did Grimnir stop until he was rewarded by the snapping of joints and the splintering of bones in their sockets.

Njól bellowed in agony. "Filthy little rat!" he screamed, spittle flying. His shield arm was useless; nevertheless, he spun his body around in a tight circle—a backhand blow meant to divest Grimnir of his head.

The *skrælingr* watched Njól's sword, the razor-edged iron hot for his blood. Smiling, he caught his foe's wrist as the blade came round. And though he struggled and thrashed, Grimnir held Njól's arm extended, kicked one leg out from under him . . . and brought the bastard's elbow down across his knee.

Bone snapped.

The sword fell from nerveless fingers.

And Njól, who was the warlord of Kaunheimr, Mánavargr's right hand, who died in the Battle of the Ironwood against the Æsir, screamed and spat as Grimnir's long, black-nailed fingers dug at his throat. Then, with a sneer of triumph, Grimnir tore out the gristle that was Njól's windpipe, taking the arteries on either side with it. The *kaunr* gurgled and died.

The remaining True Sons of Loki fled.

Grimnir slung Njól's corpse aside. Through the mob of routing *kaunar*, he spied the master of Kaunheimr himself—slender Mánavargr. Beside him stood that witch, Iðuna. Grimnir's smile widened; he licked the blood from his hand, caught up Njól's fallen sword, and went after them.

"Dogs and sons of dogs!" Mánavargr drew himself up to his full height. His whip split the air with a thunderous crack. "You would flee from these swine?" Scorn dripped from each syllable. "These *skrælingar*? Where are your spines, you louts? Where are the fearless lads who stood by my side against the tyrants of Ásgarðr? Where are my True Sons of Loki?"

His fiery-eyed presence, his contempt, stopped his fight-ravaged *kaunar* in their tracks. Without Njól to lead them, they simply milled about, breathing heavily. Some turned and locked their shields once more, drawing shreds of courage from their mates on either side. Slowly, their battered shield wall re-formed.

"Let them screen your withdrawal," Iðuna said as she came abreast of Mánavargr, her voice a low hiss. "The day is lost."

"Is it?" he snarled, turning. "I should choke the life from you, witch! This defeat is your—"

"We were betrayed!" she replied, striking the ground with the butt of her staff. "Did you not see? The offering was made! The pact was complete!"

"Then why are we giving *them* ground?"

"Because the *sjóvættir* fled," she hissed. "They fled from *him!*" She jerked her head in Grimnir's direction. The bare-chested and blood-smeared *skrælingr* had his fingers around Njól's throat.

"Impossible!" Mánavargr said.

Iðuna's yellow eyes slid back to the chief of the True Sons. "Not for something called up from the depths of Ginnungagap, from the Howling Dark."

"You think this Grimnir is that potent a sorcerer?"

"No," she said. "I don't think he is one of us, at all. I think he was summoned, an Outsider, and clothed in the flesh of a *skrælingr*. I think someone seeks to drive the True Sons to extinction, my lord."

This revelation rocked Mánavargr back on his heels. "Who? Bálegyr? Kjallandi?"

"Perhaps." Iðuna's lip curled in a grimace of distaste. "But I think the true culprit was the one who calls himself Snaga."

"That *scrag*?" Mánavargr started pacing, a lion caged by his foes. "How?"

"I will find out, my lord," Iðuna said. She glanced across the field. Grimnir met her gaze; his single eye flared in the gloom as he licked Njól's blood from his fingers. He stooped and snatched up a fallen sword. Others streamed toward them, including—she noted with grim amusement—that idiot son of hers, Gífr. "But not now. We must be away, while there's still time."

Mánavargr followed her gaze. His lips thinned. "Lads!" he said. "Take your positions! Form a line! Lock shields! Do not sell your lives cheap! Die here, die now, for the glory of Kaunheimr!" The remaining True Sons echoed his cry, turned, and stared hard-eyed into the face of their doom. To Iðuna, Mánavargr said: "Work your sorcery, witch!"

Iðuna scowled. While she could not match the deviltry of the Howling Dark, the Witch of Kaunheimr was not powerless. Words spilled from her lips, linked stanzas and couplets of power. With her staff—and using Mánavargr as an anchor—she sketched a wide circle around them, chanting as the wood scraped the ground. Where her staff touched, the tall grass grew in a twisting riot, coiling and lashing around itself to form a cage, of sorts. Mánavargr looked askance at the witch, who drew from her robes a small silken pouch. Into the palm of her hand, she poured a measure of silvery dust. Kneeling, she hollowed her cheeks and blew dust around the circle. The woven grass at their feet took on a metallic hue. Iðuna stood, raised her arms to reveal pale white flesh tattooed with whorling patterns of vines and runes, and shouted:

"*Veðrfölnir!*"

The world around them went silent. From the roots of Yggðrasil, a hot breeze kicked up, driving dust and particles before it. The sky over Nástrond boiled and seethed as something stirred far above the endless storm-wrack. *Kaunar* stood in their single rank, their shields locked together; through gritted teeth, they muttered curses and imprecations.

Behind them, Iðuna shrieked: "*Veðrfölnir!*"

Grimnir stalked nearer. He stopped just out of range of their spears and swords. Gore-splashed, breathing heavily, his red eye gleaming with unchecked rage. "Stand aside," he said, his voice like iron on stone. He gestured past them; gestured at their chief with the tip of his purloined sword. "It's that one I want!"

Mánavargr snarled at him through the woven grass bars, still tightening and creaking. "Open this cage! I will take that bastard's head back to Kaunheimr!"

Iðuna, though, could not hear him. She stood rigid, her eyes rolled back in her head, her arms upthrust. "*Veðrfölnir!*" she screamed.

From the cloud-wracked heavens came an ear-splitting screech. Mánavargr's folk cowered behind their shields; the *skrælingar* of Kjallandi and Bálegyr ceased their advance, their necks craned, their eyes canted to the roiling sky. Long grass rippled as the hot breeze turned to a howling gale, a squall of dust driven by something immense, something unseen. For a moment, the veil of

THE DOOM OF ODIN

clouds cloaking Yggðrasil parted and the radiance of the Nine Worlds bathed Nástrond in its particolored glow, the greens, yellows, reds, and oranges all sharp as stained glass. *Kaunar* and *skrælingar* quailed; even Grimnir averted his eyes, shielding the good one with a blood-streaked forearm.

It wasn't the sudden gleam of distant worlds that caused Mánavargr's folk to break and run, or that sent the folk of Úlfsstaðir scurrying for cover. No, it was the winged shadow that swept across Nástrond . . . a shadow that belonged to something large beyond all reckoning.

A feathered titan. A raptor. Veðrfölnir, it was called, and the highest point of Yggðrasil was its home. From there, it soared through the light-streaked void, hunting the branches of the Great Ash for that chisel-toothed gossipmonger, the squirrel Ratatoskr.

The monstrous hawk stooped on Gjöll's Inlet as though it had found its prey.

Grimnir stood alone in the beast's shadow, his eye a gimlet of raw fury. The earth trembled as Veðrfölnir touched down, briefly. The talons of one foot gouged four deep furrows in the hardpan of Nástrond as it settled its weight; the other, with a gentleness that belied its size, caught up the woven grass cage. Screeching, it drove itself aloft with a sweep of its powerful wings. Hunched against that withering tempest, Grimnir looked on as that titanic hawk took to the somber skies, darkened by shoals of forge-smoke billowing out of Múspellsheimr. It banked, circling on an updraft, then turned its beak toward the great root of Yggðrasil, toward Kaunheimr, its shadow dwindling.

For a long moment, Grimnir stood as still as a statue hewn from bloody gristle. The knuckles of his blade hand whitened and cracked around the hilt of Njól's sword; his off hand clenched and unclenched, muscle rippling along his gore-slaked forearm. Nostrils flared; thin lips writhed over yellowed fangs, drawing back into a sneer of malice as murder danced in the ruddy depths of his good eye.

"Ho, there, little rat."

Grimnir's head half-turned at the sound of Gífr's voice.

"Stitched those louts up good, you did."

The son of Bálegyr whirled. "I was no one's pawn in life, by Ymir!" he snarled. "And I will be no one's pawn in death! Do you hear me, you old sot?

I am no one's pawn!" He spied movement in his periphery; glancing sidelong, he saw Skaði approaching. "Do you hear me?"

Her brow furrowed. She started to reply, but a gesture from Gífr brought her up short.

"You are no one's pawn," the old *kaunr* repeated. "Not in life, and not in death."

Grimnir looked hard at his kinsman. Finally, he nodded. Tension drained from his knotty shoulders. He glanced down at the sword in his fist as though he could not recall from whence it came. "*Faugh!*" he muttered, slinging the blade away as he turned. Behind him, from the crest of the ridge to the edge of Gjöll's Inlet, bodies lay in lines and piles; corpses and parts of corpses, hacked and bloody. Black-taloned hands frozen in death reached up from trampled grass. Spears canted, their pennons limp in the heat. Black blood pooled and stank. Splintered shields and broken swords, arrows like crow-fletched weeds, axes dropped by the wayside ... and nearly all of it Grimnir's doing. He licked blood from his parched lips, looked askance at Gífr.

"Any of you maggots think to bring a drop of ale?"

9

PAWNS AND FOOLS

The sky above Úlfsstaðir was the color of old steel, whetted and bloody.

Victory fires lit the underbelly of low scudding clouds; storm-wrack thundered out of Múspellsheimr, mingling with the forge-fumes from Jötunheimr and an icy mist rising from Helheimr. Where these shoals met, great trunks and branches of lightning illuminated the billowing murk. So thick was it that a darkness akin to true night descended across Nástrond.

From behind Úlfsstaðir's walls came a cacophony of noise—wolf-howls and raucous laughter, the clash of steel and cackles of black mirth, shrieks of rage and snatches of obscene songs. All of it drifted on a hot wind spiced by the stenches of spilled ale and roasted pig. The banners of their defeated foes fluttered from the battlements. Their shields, too, some defaced by the symbol of the Eye scrawled in red paint. Grimnir Bálegyr's son had handed them this victory, but it was not his name the folk of Úlfsstaðir roared over their fire pits and their mead. His sire had claimed credit.

But if Grimnir heard the voices chanting Bálegyr's name from the ramparts, he did not acknowledge them. No, he sat by a crackling fire out beyond Úlfsstaðir's walls, surrounded by a grove of oak and willow—the grove he'd taken for his own. He'd sluiced the blood and broth of slaughter from his gnarled frame, mended the cuts and scrapes as best he could; clad, now, in a pair of silk-slashed leather breeches taken off some dead *kaunr* and his own stained gambeson, open down the front, he nursed the edges of Hátr's blade with a whetstone. A half a dozen paces away, at his back, a creaking rope supported the *scrag* Blártunga, who hung by his ankles from the limb of an oak.

The angry susurration of stone against steel was punctuated by growled curses. Grimnir's good eye gleamed like a banked fire, his rage abated for the moment but ready to burst forth anew at the least provocation. This is how Gífr found him, hunched over, elbows on knees, glaring at the edge of his blade. He glanced up as the old *kaunr* appeared across the fire, Skaði in tow. Both carried corked bottles of mead.

"Wondering when you louts would show up," Grimnir muttered, stropping the stone down Hátr's length. "Got tired of celebrating Bálegyr's great victory?"

Gífr replied with a chuckle. He handed a bottle of mead to Grimnir, then eased himself to the ground near the fire, his back against a moss-draped boulder.

"*Feh!* It's not right," Skaði said as Grimnir pried loose the bottle's cork, spat it aside, and drank a long draught. She took a seat on the low ruined wall. "Your idiot brothers are taking credit for what *you* did, out there. Sægrár and that lot! Bálegyr lauds them when that fat fool should be thanking you!"

Grimnir wiped dribbles of mead from his chin with the back of one hand. "Sægrár, eh? That maggot died before the battle even started! Killed by a *scrag*. One of that one's mates." Grimnir jerked a thumb at Blártunga.

"That's why you should be in there, to set those swine straight!"

Grimnir's lip curled in a sneer as he studied the edge and blade of Hátr once more. "Let the dogs boast," he muttered. "What do I care about their lies, eh? I've got bigger problems than that."

Gífr glanced sidelong, watching Grimnir through slitted eyes as he attacked a nick in Hátr's blade near the hilt, spitting on the stone and rasping it back and forth. "Bigger than setting straight those filthy braggarts out there pinching your deeds, little rat? Doesn't sound like the Grimnir I know."

"Doesn't it?" Grimnir snarled. His nostrils flared; stone ground on steel, and his good eye flared into a rage-filled ember of hate. "Let those useless *scrag*-fucking bags of rot who call themselves my kin say whatever they want! *Faugh!* It's no skin off my nose, is it? Let them be oblivious to what's going on around them!"

"And what do you think is going on?" asked Gífr quietly.

"What do *I* think? I think if I knew the answer to that it wouldn't be a problem, now, would it? Ymir's balls!" Hátr's edge carved a furrow on the whetstone as Grimnir bore down on it. He stared hard at the stone in his hand, and at the blade—its bones culled from the shards of ancient Sárklungr. Suddenly, growling under his breath, he straightened and shied the whetstone off into the darkness. It clattered against the trunks of gnarled oaks. He gestured at Gífr with the long-seax's point. "Answer me this, you old sot: How many times have you died here?"

Gífr gazed into the fire's heart, a moment, before shrugging his shoulders. "Too many times to count."

"And what happens after some lout sticks a dagger in your craw? What do you remember?"

"You don't remember anything." Gífr shrugged. "You remember the death, of course, but after? There's nothing to remember. After a day and a bit you wake up. Thirsty, hungry, and ready to crack the skull of the bastard that put you down."

Grimnir glanced at Skaði. "Same for you?"

She nodded. Her amber eyes narrowed. "But not for you, was it? I saw it. You came right back."

"Like I hadn't even been put out of the fray," Grimnir replied.

"How is that even possible?"

Gífr took a long draught of mead. Finally, he replied: "It's not."

"Then, how—?"

"Oh, that's not even the half of it. Tell me . . ." Grimnir paused; his eye shifted from Skaði to Gífr. "How many times did you die up top, eh?"

Gífr scoffed. "Don't be daft."

Grimnir, though, wasn't laughing. "The blasted Saxons did you in near the mouth of the Elbe River. I know this because I burned your stinking corpse on a pyre made from the bones of dead hymn-singers and sang your death-song."

His eye fixed on Skaði. "And you? You said that snake, Níðhöggr, got you in the tunnels of Orkahaugr?"

"At the crossroad, Einvigi," she replied, nodding. "Feh! We tried to stop it before it could reach the Hall of the Nine Fathers, but that scaly bastard got the drop on us. Its tail got me, I think. I don't remember . . ."

"Me, I died in Langbarðaland," Grimnir said. "In the Pontine Marshes, on the road the old Romans called the Appian Way. Took a pair of crossbow bolts." He tapped his sternum. "Right through the heart. *Faugh!* What a shabby death that was, too! The Norns shortchanged me, by Ymir, but those were my lumps and I took them." Grimnir stretched his legs. "Well, imagine my surprise when—after *that* one," he jerked his chin toward Blártunga, "rammed a spear through my gizzard—I woke up right back where I started: in a canal in the Pontine Marshes. *Nár!* Not even a ten-count after two of those Sicilian laggards had skewered me! I rose up like their Nailed God! Fresh off the cross and ready to draw steel."

The bottle in Skaði's lap shattered on the rocks as she bolted to her feet. "Liar!" she snarled. "You can't die *here* and wake up *there,* in Miðgarðr!"

Grimnir's eyes narrowed. "I'll give you that one for free, because none of this makes sense. But it happened exactly as I said it did."

"How?"

"That's not the question, though, is it? *How?* Who cares *how. Why* is what nags at me."

Gífr, who had remained silent and pensive, stirred. "If you're here, that means you died *again,* did you not? Up in Miðgarðr?"

Grimnir hawked and spat into the fire; his saliva sizzled. "Again, aye. And this one was just as shabby as the first."

"What happened?" said Gífr.

"Well, I wasn't about to let those Sicilian dogs off easy, so I took care of my business with them—killed the ones who needed killing—and then legged it up the road to Rome, hot on Malice-Striker's trail." Grimnir again leveled the tip of Hátr at the old *kaunr*. "Not a damn thing you used to tell me about that place was true, you old sot! Might have been grand in your day, but it's a maggot-infested lump of shit, now, steeping in the ruins of its old empire. Took me no time at all to figure out how that snake, Níðhöggr, got in."

"Slipped in by the Tiber, didn't it?"

"Aye," Grimnir replied. "But I'm not about to get soaked to the skin following that swine's footsteps, so I found a way in through those blasted walls. Pretty as you please, eh? And, I'd sussed out how to find one maggot in all that rot—scaly bastard's nothing if not predictable—when I fell into a trap."

"One of Níðhöggr's?"

Grimnir shook his head. "One of its allies. Used a glamour to trick me onto a patch of ground that gave way beneath my feet. Went tumbling into an old cistern and broke my neck at the bottom. Oh, but that's not the best part. No, the best part is *who* lured me onto that patch of ground..."

"Who?"

"That old raven-starver, the Lord of Ásgarðr!"

Skaði cursed. Gífr glanced Grimnir's way, red eyes sharpening to points. "Odin? You're certain, little rat?"

"I saw him as clearly as I see you, now," Grimnir replied. "Perched at the edge of that blasted hole, gloating like some milk-lipped war-virgin ere he vanished. *Nár!* I reckon he was there to protect his investment." Grimnir indicated Úlfsstaðir with a sharp jerk of his chin. "But these idiots want to prance about and play their little games as if Nástrond matters, when something really *has* slipped up top. At the very top!"

"Feh!" Skaði said. She moved closer to the fire, rubbing her hands together as though a chill had gone through her. She glanced at the cloud-girt heavens, where the dim glow of Yggðrasil could still be seen. "If old One-Eye is prancing about Miðgarðr, who's pulling the strings, eh?"

"She's got a point." Gífr, too, turned his gaze to the skies. "Kjallandi told me, once, that there was a compact between the gods. An agreement. Miðgarðr was to be the board upon which they played their games of domination, but all were forbidden from setting foot upon its soil. They could influence, but not intercede. Not directly. If Odin has broken this compact..."

"You think someone might be playing me against the so-called Allfather? There's an idiot's gambit for you." Grimnir chuckled, then bared his teeth. "It makes sense, though. When the time came for Níðhöggr to rise, it wasn't that old rhyme-spitting tosspot I dealt with, but his stand-in, Náli Náinn's son. So he was abiding by this compact of yours at least a hundred and thirty-odd years ago."

"Could be the answer to *why*," Gífr replied. "You skewer that wyrm on what's left of Sárklungr and Odin loses that vital part of himself in the bargain."

Grimnir nodded. "His *hamingja*."

"Could all of this be the Tangled God's doing?" Skaði asked.

Gífr sucked his teeth a moment, then shook his head. "Unless Raðbolg's somehow got through to him, I don't see how. There's been no sign of Laufey's son since the Elder Days, since he called the Nine Fathers to him on the eve of the Great Battle. You little rats should have been there! We passed the oath-cup, our blood mingled with his, and he gave us our orders. He knew the Æsir would hit us at dawn, and it was on our shoulders to delay them long enough for Angrboða to spirit the Tangled God's children away. We did that, at first. We rocked the swine of Ásgarðr back on their heels, but then their lords waded into the fray and that was the end of that. Those among us not slain took flight. It was Iðuna who opened the Ash-Road, and Kjallandi who led the few of us who remained to Miðgarðr—" Gífr cocked an eyebrow, as if something about that old tale finally made sense to him. "Because Kjallandi *knew* about the compact. He knew Odin or his sons could not follow. No, this is not the Tangled God's doing."

"Then whose?" Grimnir stropped Hátr's blade against his thigh, then sheathed it. "And who would know? Who among the swine up or down the Tree would listen to the likes of us long enough to hear what we have to say, and tell us the truth in answer, eh?"

To this, Gífr made no reply. There was silence for a long moment; silence broken only by the crackle of their fire, by the moaning of the wind through the trees of the grove, and by the creak of the rope that kept the captive *scrag*, Blártunga, aloft.

"Mímir," Skaði said suddenly. "Mímir would know."

"Would he?" Grimnir's singular gaze shifted from Skaði to Gífr. The old *kaunr* stroked his chin. Grudgingly, he nodded.

"If anyone has an inkling, it would be that one."

"How do we find him?"

"That's the tricky part." Gífr took up a stick and shoved its tip into the fire. Embers coiled into the eerie darkness. "There's two ways off this rock. First is the Ash-Road. Makes sense, eh? What with a root of Yggðrasil jutting out there at the far end of the island. The gateway to it sits right under Mánavargr's nose. That's how Raðbolg and his mates slipped off of Nástrond—paid homage to the old snake of Kaunheimr, a bit of flattery and a bit of arse-kissing. But after the drubbing you gave Mánavargr no amount of honey will sweeten that vinegar."

"And the other way?" Grimnir stood and laced up his gambeson.

Gífr raised the stick from the fire and blew out the tongue of flame that clung to it. "Hárbarðr."

Grimnir heard Skaði gasp, a sharp inhalation; he glanced her way, saw her eyes shining like yellow lamps in the gloom. "Who is this Hárbarðr?"

"Feh! A myth, I'd always heard. That bastard who whelped me always held Hárbarðr over my head as a threat. *Toe the line,* he'd say, *or I'll take your head to old Hárbarðr!*"

"He's as real as you or I, Skæfloc be damned," Gífr replied; he went back to prodding the heart of the fire. "Hárbarðr is a miserly git of a *jötunn*, but he has a boat. His ferry, he calls it. For a price, he'll take us wherever we want to go."

Grimnir's eyes narrowed as he reached for his hauberk. "What's the catch?" He jerked his chin at Skaði. "That one's put off by his very name, thinks he's a boogeyman from the Elder Days, but you're telling me he's just some lout with a skip? *Nár!* Pull my other leg, you old sot!"

Gífr grinned, teeth like yellow knives in the dim firelight. "No wood will float on Gjöll's breast, not long enough to reach the far shore, at least. But bone will. Hárbarðr's ferry is made from the bones of the sacrifices he demands. He hangs the poor unfortunate from the keel and laughs as the *sjóvættir* strips him clean of flesh."

Grimnir shrugged into the Turkish mail and fastened it across his chest, his brow furrowed in thought. "So, this Hárbarðr trades in blood. Well, that's an easy enough price to meet, eh?"

"Not just any old *scrag* will do, either," Gífr said, eyeing the slowly spinning form of Blártunga. "Hárbarðr is picky about what form his payment takes. He prefers quality . . ."

"Then we make sure we have a choice bit of flesh ready to trade." Grimnir settled his weapons belt about his waist. "And once we're off this thrice-damned rock, where then?"

"Mímisbrunnr," Skaði said. "The Well of Mímir."

"You know the way?"

She spat and shook her head. "I know it's under the roots of Yggðrasil, somewhere, deep inside the borders of Jötunheimr."

"How about you?" Grimnir put the question to Gífr. "You know what road to take?"

Leaving the stick to burn, Gífr clambered to his feet. He dusted his palms together, ancient skin scraping like leather. "If Hárbarðr can be paid off, we get him to take us across the lake and into the mouth of the River Gjöll, under the accursed slag-bridge that stands there—the Gjallarbrú, where the dead cross to Hel's gates—and up as far as the Hræholt Road. There, we'll make our way through the Ironwood, and then across the moors and fens bordering the Myrkviðr, where the veil between the Nine Worlds and the Ginnungagap is thinnest. Mímisbrunnr is beyond those foul moors."

"Sounds like you just signed on as a guide, you old sot," Grimnir said. He looked at Skaði. "You coming, too?"

She chuckled. "Wouldn't miss it."

Gífr stood there a moment, his face lit from below by the fire's greasy orange glow. His eyes burned like embers; they narrowed as he took in his two companions. His inscrutable gaze searched for something in their faces, in their demeanors—he looked for steel, Grimnir reckoned. Steel and whalebone. Finally, the old *kaunr* nodded. "All right, little rat, but until we're off this blasted rock, we're going to do things my way, just like in the old days." He did not wait for Grimnir or Skaði to acquiesce. "We're going to need allies. Kjallandi will be loath to lose another son to the lands beyond Nástrond, but leave him to me. And Bálegyr's not about to let you out of his sight. Not without good reason—and not at all if he gets wind of what you've told us."

"That'll be the froth on his ale," Skaði muttered.

Grimnir's jaw jutted, his lips thinning into a sneer of contempt. "I am no one's pawn, and I ask no one's permission," he said through clenched teeth. "I decide where I go and what I do, not that old wine-bag who plays at being king! *Faugh!* King of what? King of the shit-house rats?"

Gífr took his outburst in stride. "Call it what you will, we're still going to need allies, you little fool."

THE DOOM OF ODIN

"Who can we trust?"

Gífr scratched his jaw. "Kjallandi, once I've had a moment with him," he said, ticking names off on his fingers. "Old Narfi, his sons and brothers. Likely all the folk of the Stag, once they realize what's at stake—"

"My mother?"

Gífr's nostrils flared. He waggled his hand from side to side. "With Skríkja, it all depends."

"Depends on what?" Grimnir replied.

"On if she believes you. She has a foot in both war-camps, but she will only act contrary to Bálegyr's wishes if she thinks the end result will mean a triumph for the folk of the Eye. Be wary around her. She will cut your heart out, son or no, if she thinks you're a threat to her standing. She likes being queen, that one."

"Get me a moment alone with her and I will make her believe."

"Be careful what you wish for, little rat," said Gífr. "Let's go, both of you. Time to put in an appearance. And mind your tongues! Bálegyr's got spies everywhere. We might not stay dead, around here, but that old bastard can make coming back to life a torture in its own right."

Grimnir, though, did not move. His attention was fixed on the captive *scrag*. "You louts go on ahead."

"What about you?"

"I'll be along," Grimnir replied, his single red eye a deep well of malice as he turned his gaze back to Blártunga's slowly twisting body. "I have some unfinished business, yet."

And with a knowing chuckle, Gífr caught Skaði by the scruff and walked with her from the grove ...

GRIMNIR PROWLED around the fire, his thumbs thrust into his weapons belt; he regarded the *scrag*'s fleshy body the way a butcher regards a side of beef. He stopped, head cocked to one side. His nostrils flared. Without warning, he lashed out, bony knuckles catching Blártunga in his kidney.

The *scrag* gasped.

"*Faugh!* You can quit pretending to be dead, now, you little weasel," Grimnir said. "They've gone." He spun Blártunga around until they were facing one another. "You heard everything, didn't you? Ha! Of course you did, you nosy little sneak! Now, how do we keep that treacherous tongue of yours from spilling all our secrets, eh?"

Face suffused with black blood, snot and spittle glistening from his forehead, Blártunga stammered: "I . . . I c-can help you! I c-can! Let me . . ."

"Help me? How?" Grimnir spun the *scrag*'s body, rope creaking under the strain. "How can a piece of filth like you help me?"

"There's another way," he mewled. "Your long-toothed mates don't know about it, b-but there's another way!"

"Another way?" Grimnir arrested his spinning; he crouched, bringing his feral red eye on the same level as Blártunga's. "Another way off Nástrond?"

The *scrag* bobbed his head. "A cave . . ."

"Tell me."

"I'll sh-show you if . . . if you cut me loose."

"*Nár!* I cut you loose and I already know what will happen. You'll scamper back to that idiot, Thrár, at first chance and tell him all manner of tales. When you're done, that little bastard will take those tales to Mánavargr. And *that* fool can cause all manner of mischief for me ere the Gjallarhorn blows. No, you'll tell me, and if I believe you *then* we can haggle over the price of your freedom."

"N-No! I'm done with Sna—with Thrár! I'm your man, now! I'll give you my word!"

"Your *word*?" Grimnir laughed. "Your *word* is worth about as much to me as the wind from Odin's arse, little fool! Start talking! I'm starting to grow weary of your blasted games. Tell me of this cave you claim to know about."

"It . . . It's tucked away at the bottom of a hollow, on the edge of Lútr's lands," Blártunga began. His voice was halting. "We f-found it by accident, Snaga and me and the Cat. The *scrags* of Jarðvegur, they tried to waylay us, to get back the spoils we'd earned fair and square from raiding *them*. Well, Snaga thought we'd give them the slip by heading toward the Root from Skrælingsalr. That's when we fairly tripped across it—a fold in the earth filled with trees. There's water at the bottom, and a cave." Though he was bound and hanging by his ankles, the memory of that place wrenched a shiver from Blártunga.

"There ain't gold enough in all the Nine Worlds to get me to go back in there! *Garn!* It ain't natural! *Things* whisper from the darkness..." The *scrag* fell silent.

"Go on," Grimnir snarled.

"Well, if you can stomach it and follow it to the end, it comes out under some ruins near the same place your old long-tooth was talking about, the Corpse-Wood Road. Hræholt, he called it. How about you cut me loose, eh? I'm telling you what's true."

Grimnir *chk*'ed his teeth. "Aye, I believe you."

"'Cause I'm a truthful little rat, ain't I? Aye, so you'll take me into your service, then? My word, I'll serve you till the Horn blows!"

"Will you?" Grimnir's voice grew flat and hard; like steel scraped across flint, there came the ominous rasp of Hátr leaving its sheath. "There is another matter..."

"N-No," Blártunga sobbed. "You ain't got to do this."

"Do I not?" Grimnir crouched once more, their faces mere inches apart. His hot breath burned the *scrag*'s cheeks. "So, I'm supposed to forgive a two-bit nobody like you for spitting me on the end of a blade? Gífr—*old long-tooth*, you call him—taught me a lesson, back when I was yet a fresh-off-the-teat *scrag* like yourself. He said, 'You let a wolf get a taste of your blood and they'll be at your throat for the rest of their days.' Wise words, eh? Well, you've tasted my blood, little wolfling. And a taste is all you get."

Blártunga writhed against his bonds. "P-Please...cut me d-down, at least...Ple—"

With Hátr's freshly-honed edge, Grimnir opened the *scrag*'s throat. Stinking black blood bubbled from the ragged cut, thick rivulets running over Blártunga's chin. Grimnir stepped away; he flicked droplets from his blade as the quivering corpse bled out.

"You lot will learn the same lesson those pathetic Sicilians learned," Grimnir muttered. "*Nár!* You kill me and I'll make sure you regret it!"

The *scrag*'s blood slowed to a trickle, and then to mere drips and splatters. Nodding, Grimnir sidled up to the corpse. Seizing a handful of gory hair, he put Hátr's blade to work removing Blártunga's head...

And Grimnir Bálegyr's son carried that grisly token with him when he left the grove, leaving the *scrag*'s body hanging above the soil of Nástrond as he retraced his steps to the raucous heart of Úlfsstaðir.

The Wolf's Hall was ablaze with light and shadow. Lanterns dripping tallow added a thin yellow sheen to the guttering of iron cressets, their flames reeking of rosin and pitch; from the three fire pits came a haze of smoke and crackling embers as axe-split logs burned with a greasy orange glow. Shadows danced as hundreds of *skrælingar* cavorted from one end of Varghǫll to the other, the folk of the Eye mingling with those who bore the sigil of the Stag.

Grimnir paused on the threshold, a derisive grin twisting at the corners of his mouth as he took in the spectacle of savage debauchery enacted by his kin. Ragged thralls fetched food and drink—wine and mead from the cellars, ale from broached casks resting on wooden trestles; platters of flesh carved from whole pigs, roasting over hearths along the right-hand wall. The stench of pork fat warred with that of smoke, blood, and sweat. Shrill screams erupted from tables where dice clacked and gold tinkled, where thralls fought off the clutching talons of their amorous masters. Blades flickered in the light, teeth clenched and eyes flared; in a twinkling, another dead *skrælingr*—or another dead thrall—dropped to the filth-slimed rushes, throat-cut and stabbed, kicked aside and forgotten until they returned.

Grimnir heard laughter and croaking snatches of song as he slung Blártunga's severed head into the heart of the nearest fire pit. Hair crackled and flamed; logs shifted, and the *scrag*'s death-frozen visage was lost for all time. That done, Grimnir wiped his hands on a thrall's smock, then sauntered into this nest of madness.

He spied Skaði sitting with a knot of Stag-Skulls, the lot of them war-maidens and battle-crones. Gífr he did not see, nor old Kjallandi—the right-hand throne stood empty. Bálegyr was in attendance, sprawled across his carved seat with the mace Maugrónðr standing before him, his broad black-nailed hand draped over its pommel. He had one foot propped on Gangr's triple-horned helmet.

His brothers he saw, as well. All twenty-two of them, led by Hrungnir and the giant Sægrár, clustered around the table closest to the throne. Those idiots preened and boasted, eager for their father's recognition and jealous of Sægrár, who basked in stolen glory.

Grimnir hawked and spat.

He'd cleared half the distance to the thrones before any of these dunghill rats paid him any mind. Curiously, it was Elðr who spotted him, first—old Elðr, whose boat had plucked him off the bridge at Gjöll's Inlet; that grizzled *kaunr* rose on unsteady legs, and staggered into Grimnir's path. Through squinted eyes, he peered at Bálegyr's son; then, with a nod, he hoisted his mead horn on high and roared Grimnir's name.

That bellow of approbation spread from table to table.

"GRIMNIR!"

Fists pounded the boards in unison as his name became a chant. Soon, the rafters shook with acclaim for Gangr's killer. For his part, Grimnir played to the crowd. He bared his teeth in a savage grin, describing a slow circle so all could lay eyes on him.

"GRIM-NIR!"

"GRIM-NIR!"

As the noise reached a crescendo, a black-nailed hand thrust a frothing mead horn at Grimnir. He took it. Old Elðr staggered into view.

"To Gangr's slayer!" he bellowed, raising his own horn.

Grimnir heard Skaði's voice above the cacophony: "To the rat who humbled that glad-handing rogue, Mánavargr!" Laughter rippled among the *skrælingar*.

"By Ymir!" Grimnir roared in answer. "I'll drink to that!"

And he did. He drained his horn in one long draught and tossed it aside. Mead dribbled from his pointed chin. Grimnir growled, teeth displayed in a snarl of challenge as he stalked closer to the thrones. Across the heads of their kin, Grimnir and his father's singular eyes locked; the air between them crackled with menace.

Bálegyr stirred. He twirled Maugrónðr's haft between his fingers. "Finally decided to join the revels, eh?"

"*Nár!*" Grimnir replied, hitching at his weapons belt, his hand near Hátr's dragon-headed pommel. With a jerk of his head, he indicated the helmet under Bálegyr's heel. "Came to collect my spoils. That's mine!"

"This?" Bálegyr glanced down. His thick lips curled and peeled back, unsheathing a serrated grin. He rocked the helmet back and forth. "You think you've earned this, eh? Take it, then." He gave the three-horned casque a contemptuous kick. It clattered down the dais and came to rest half a yard from Grimnir's feet. "Smells like *scrag*, to me."

The hall had fallen silent, but that gibe sent a smattering of coarse laughter through the closed ranks of his brothers. Loudest of all was Sægrár.

"Why do you laugh, you scar-faced imbecile?" Grimnir said, singling him out. He propped himself against a table in front of Kjallandi's empty throne. "It was a *scrag* that did you in! Did he not tell you? Aye, your favorite bastard, there, was outsmarted and killed by old Snaga himself, long before the battle was ever joined."

"Liar!" Sægrár lurched to his feet, his hand going to the heavy-bladed sword at his waist.

Grimnir raised his chin, his voice silken, his single eye gleaming with menace. "Air the edge of that onion-chopper and I'll make you wish someone had thrown *your* carcass to those *argr*-loving water-sprites."

The threat hung heavy in the air. No one moved; all eyes watched the pair of them—Grimnir leaning back with studied insouciance; Sægrár vibrating with a barely-suppressed desire to kill. Grimnir's black-nailed finger tapped a staccato rhythm against the pommel of his long-seax. Sægrár's knuckles darkened around the hilt of his sword.

A humorless chuckle broke their stalemate. Bálegyr cocked his head to one side, flicking his long, plaited topknot over his shoulder. He fixed his one grim-hued eye on his youngest son. "You yap and growl like a little dog, runt! You think there's one of us gathered here who gives a fig about what you claim to have done? Bah! You've not earned the right to challenge even the meanest thrall under these eaves! Whatever you think you were up top, you are less than nothing, here! But I am a generous lord. Fetch this runt some ale! It's the least we can do to repay him for his small part in my victory!"

A smattering of cheers came from around the hall. "Hail Bálegyr!" someone bellowed.

Grimnir's manner remained unchanged. He mimicked his sire, tilting his head to fix him in his one-eyed gaze. "Your victory, was it? Funny, but I don't recall you leading the boats across the water. What about this one?" He stooped, caught up Gangr's helmet by one horn and held it aloft. "Did you scale that ruined bridge to fight a *hólmganga,* too? By Ymir, that must have been something to see!"

"Prattle on, runt," Bálegyr snarled. "Prattle on. My goodwill is all that stands between you and a thrall's collar."

Grimnir glanced about the hall, raking the assembled *skrælingar* with a withering stare. Some looked at him with expectations, seeing in him the shadow of a great war-leader; others simply glared back, impatient for the bloodletting to begin. In an alcove, he spied Gífr standing with Skríkja. He was animated, arguing. She merely watched, aloof and cold. Grimnir's nostrils flared. "Then I crave your pardon, great Bálegyr. Give me a chance to get back in your good graces, eh? Let me make up for that poor showing I made at Gjöll's Inlet and all."

"Keeping your tongue between your teeth and doing as you're told by your betters will make a good start."

"My ... *betters*?" Grimnir looked from his father to his brothers. "You mean *this* ragtag collection of idiots, grinning fools, and glad-handing sons of whores? These are what you call my *betters*?" Grimnir snorted. "You're saying I should just keep my head down and earn the right to be heard, eh?"

"Now," Bálegyr replied, "you begin to understand."

"You're an outsider!" Sægrár spat.

"Aye," said Hrungnir, rising to his feet. "You've not bled with us, you maggot!"

"Not bled with you? Is that the price, then? Lick your boots and bleed a little?" Grimnir set the helmet down on the table beside him. He leaned forward, rubbing his hands together like a miser eager to haggle over a pittance. "*Nár!* What price to skip all that?"

The question took his brothers by surprise. They exchanged glances, unsure how to answer.

"What price, I said!" Grimnir spread his arms in a gesture that encompassed all twenty-two of his siblings and their father, as well. "What price must I pay to skip to the head of the line, eh? Where my voice is worth more to you than anything this collection of stammering half-wits might say?"

Bálegyr's hand tightened around the haft of Maugrónðr. "Do you test me, runt?"

"This is no test, *my lord,*" Grimnir replied. "Pick one of these louts. Pick the one you cherish the most, whose counsel you place above all others. Name him! And I'll put his blasted head in your lap!"

A clamor arose among the brothers. They all wanted to be chosen; all wanted to be the one to humble their upstart little brother. Hrungnir and Sægrár elbowed each other in their fervor. Rawboned Næfr, who was the eldest of all, rose to his feet and looked for his axe. Salfangi, the Eunuch, who sacrificed his jewels for wisdom, snarled and spat; even tongueless Frægr, who was boss of Úlfsstaðir's *scrags,* grunted and shook his spear.

Bálegyr looked over his collection of sons before returning his gaze to Grimnir. He leaned forward, his weight resting on the pommel of Maugrónðr. "Why, you pitiful little fool," he said, his serrated grin dripping malevolence. "I cherish them *all.*"

10

A WOLF AMONG DOGS

Bálegyr of the Eye sank back on his throne.

He glanced sidelong at the collective of his sons and bastards, his gaze flaming with wrath. "One of you louts," he said, nodding at Grimnir, "fetch me this runt's head!"

And with a bellow that rang to the roof-timbers, Sægrár charged forward to do his father's bidding. He was like a mastiff unleashed. The wreckage of his face—all thick scar and exposed teeth—was drawn back in a rictus of hate as he flung his brothers aside, eager to be the one to lay the upstart out. His sword scraped from its scabbard.

For his part, Grimnir did not recoil from this lumbering giant. Snarling, he snatched up the three-horned helmet and leapt to meet Sægrár. Grimnir swung that casque like a bludgeon. The arm that drove it was a bar of twisted iron; its muscles woven from steel wire and fueled by pure spite. There was an instant of bone-crunching contact. A moment of uncertainty punctuated by a sickening sound, like a melon dropped from a window ledge. Then, Grimnir sprang away, untouched, while Sægrár staggered and fell, his skull shattered by the sledgehammer impact of steel with bone.

"*Faugh!*" Grimnir said, looking at the dented and blood-slimed helmet before tossing it aside. "Is that the best you've got?"

Bálegyr chuckled, though there was no trace of humor in his seething red eye. "That was but the bread. Now comes the meat. Lads? Take him!"

A tide of harsh voices arose from around the hall; from hundreds of throats came a mix of cheers and curses, imprecations mingled with gales of black mirth. Wagers flew thick and fast, with the *skrælingar* of the Eye laying their lot with Bálegyr's brood, while those of the Stag-Skull put their coin on bloody-handed Grimnir.

Even as the echo of that sanguinary cry faded, Grimnir's twenty-one remaining brothers—full-blooded, half-blooded, and bastards, alike—bolted over their table, kicked the benches aside. They scrambled in ill-fated Sægrár's wake, whooping and baying like an impatient rabble of dogs. This time, Grimnir gave ground. His eyes narrowed, one dead bone and the other an ember of hate; he raked their ragged front. The lot of them were clad in piecemeal armor, with a gambeson here or a hauberk there. None bore shields, and their weapons were whatever they had at hand—blades, axes, and a solitary spear in the hands of Bálegyr's pet *scrag*, Frægr, who'd had his tongue ripped out by the roots long ago. Aye, a rabble in truth. Twenty-one would-be champions, and that was the tactic they took with him—every rat for himself as they closed the interval. Grimnir reckoned facing a horde of trip-footed idiots rather than a wedge of fighters would tip the scales in his favor.

He backed up farther, still, placing himself between the trestle-table with its heavy benches and Kjallandi's empty throne. Here, Grimnir dropped to a fighting crouch, poised on the balls of his feet, his blade-hand resting on Hátr's carved pommel even as the first clump of brothers reached him. In the lead was old Næfr—gaunt and spindle-shanked, his lank hair braided with bits of rune-etched bone and ancient amber from the limbs of mighty Yggðrasil; old Næfr, who had died under Bálegyr's knife, sacrificed to Ymir on the cloud-wreathed crest of Orkahaugr. Even in death, he bore a livid scar across his throat to remind him of his worth. His voice was like gravel scraped against iron.

"Tired of running, little fool?" Næfr rasped, drawing back his bearded axe. "Good! Now stand there and let me take your head!"

Grimnir, though, did not oblige him. Moving fast, he closed with Næfr and caught the haft of that descending axe with his off hand. They collided chest to chest, faces inches apart, yellowed teeth bared in snarls of malice. In that brief struggle, Grimnir aired Hátr's edge in a cross-body draw and plunged it into the left side of Næfr's belly. He gave a croaking bellow, spat in his little brother's eye. Grimnir's answer was to saw the blade to the right, opening Næfr's gut as pretty as you please. Wreathed in the reek of blood and offal, slippery ropes of intestine spilled from that ragged slit to coil at their feet. With a shove, Grimnir stripped the long-handled axe from his grasp and struck him in the side of the head with the flat, catapulting him up against the dais.

By then, the others were upon him.

Their faces were familiar, but Grimnir could not recall their names. Nor did he want to. To him, they were merely the dogs of Úlfsstaðir, scrawny hounds who fought over the scraps of their master... and he was the wolf in their midst. Nor did he sit back and wait to be overwhelmed by their numbers. No, with a snarl and a howl Grimnir took the fight to them.

Næfr's axe was too long for this kind of work, so he buried it in the skull of the first yapping cur who charged from the pack and left it there. The point of a knife tested the links of Grimnir's Turkish mail, a punch to the gut that rebounded; another blade skittered off his armored shoulder. In answer, Hátr sang a gory paean, a funereal dirge of slaughter accompanied by a choir of gurgling screams and panted curses. Flesh and muscle parted under its edge; bone cracked and gristle popped as the remnant of mighty Sárklungr carved a path through this seething knot of his kin.

Seven more of his brothers lay in his wake—their bodies pierced, slashed, or stomped; the last vestiges of their strange unlife seeping from opened arteries. Twelve remained. These formed a loose half-circle around him; Hrungnir goaded them on. That brother stood with his sword drawn, his free hand clamped on the shoulder of the spear-*scrag*, Frægr, who served him as a living shield. Together, they made menacing advances toward Grimnir.

Warned not so much by a sixth sense as by long experience, Grimnir suddenly whirled in the direction of his blind side. There, he found Salfangi—that bald and fey-eyed eunuch, sleek-skinned and fat, whose robes of Byzantine silk rustled like the murmur of an Eastern wind—creeping up with a curved knife poised to strike. Grimnir *tsk*'ed; before Salfangi could recoil, Grimnir's bony fist, stiffened by Hátr's hilt, flashed out. The eunuch reeled from that precipitous impact. Blood spattered the breast of Salfangi's robes as Grimnir hit him twice more, crushing the bones of his face.

As he fell back, Grimnir caught a handful of rich silk, twisted, and slung his stunned brother at Hrungnir. Tangle-footed, Salfangi stumbled, then gave a gurgling shriek as Frægr's iron-headed spear pierced his liver. The weight of his falling body took tongueless Frægr out of action for a moment, leaving Hrungnir bereft of his shield. Yet, even as Grimnir moved to exploit that sudden hole in his brother's defenses, the other nine crowded in upon him. Blades whickered and thudded, scraping along his mail; some drew rivulets of black blood from his arms, his thighs, his neck. The edge of an axe flashed perilously close to his single blazing eye, shearing away locks of hair as it passed.

Grimnir, though, dished out more than he received. He wove and danced among this knot of his kin, never still. Hátr's blade was a blur as he struck left and right. The axe-brother lost half his face—from his forehead to his teeth—to Grimnir's riposte; another savage thrust he parried, driving the offending blade into the groin of his closest brother. Grimnir whirled and leapt, splitting open the one's belly and piercing the other's temple, releasing a tide of black blood, brain matter, and viscera into the fray.

The same alacrity that drove the brothers forward now sent them scurrying, suddenly fearful of Grimnir's fury. Five of them bled out on Varghǫll's rush-strewn floor. But Grimnir himself did not pass through that crucible unscathed: the axe blade had opened his scalp above his ruined eye; hot blood trickled down his forehead, through the bone-colored orb that filled the empty socket, and off his pointed chin. More blood leaked from wounds in his torso, where dagger points had twisted mail links aside and found their mark—the deepest of these bubbled with each wracking breath. Grimnir's nostrils flared; his good eye was fixed on Hrungnir.

Hrungnir—called Grendel, the Bone-Grinder—bared his teeth in a savage grin.

Nor did that grin falter as Hrungnir palmed Frægr's head, lifting that mute *scrag* off his feet and slinging him at Grimnir. It was like throwing a hundred-pound sack of scrap iron; the pair *should* have collided with bone-crunching force—hard enough to yank Grimnir off his feet and put him on his back. And if it were one of his idiot brothers, likely the fight would have ended right then, dusted and done.

Grimnir, though, merely sidestepped.

Frægr flailed past him to strike a table's edge. His spine snapped like dry-rotted kindling; the tongueless *scrag* loosed a bellow of rage and agony as he slid to the floor in a tangle of useless limbs.

Now, Hrungnir's grin died on his lips.

"In, you rats!" he screamed. "Get in there and finish him!"

"Just like you," Grimnir replied, "getting others to do your dirty work! Not this time, *dear* brother!" Lips peeled back in a snarl of wrath, Grimnir launched himself at Hrungnir. For his part, Hrungnir did not shirk. He sprang to meet him. Sword met long-seax with the crash and slither of iron. Grimnir parried and ducked, never still; as Hrungnir opened his fanged maw to bellow a frustrated oath, however, he suddenly found his mouth full of gore-streaked iron. Red-tinged eyes widened when he bit down on Hátr; a heartbeat later, those eyes lost that bright gleam of life as Grimnir dragged the blade out through the hinges of Hrungnir's jaw, across the opening of his gullet, and through the stem of his brain.

Nearly beheaded from the nose up, Hrungnir swayed and crashed to the floor, sword clattering against the dais. Grimnir stood, a moment. His chest rose and fell; blood dripped from his fingers, from his chin. He spat, nostrils flaring as he raked the assembled *skrælingar* and *kaunar, scrags* and thralls, with his single gleaming eye. Bálegyr watched him, pale with rage; he spotted Kjallandi standing with Gífr; Skaði stood alongside his mother, Skríkja—both wide-eyed at the breadth of slaughter Grimnir had wrought.

Four brothers remained. These were not the boldest of his kin, nor the best fighters; they were the laggards, the bench riders who'd rather boast of their prowess than prove it. Near him, Frægr struggled to rise—hissing and mewling as his broken vertebrae ground together. Grimnir's lips curled into a smile of pure malice as he wandered over to him. Frægr glared up at him, clawing at the bench that supported his weight. The *scrag*'s head lolled to one side. And Grimnir, his smile never shifting, raised one hobnailed boot and *stomped* Frægr's skull, shattering it and the bench beneath. He glanced over his shoulder at his four brothers.

Still nothing. No flare of courage. Casually, Grimnir raised a stoneware tankard of ale from the table; he sniffed at it before upending it. Some went down his throat, the rest sluiced blood from the breast of his mail. Smacking his lips, he wiped his chin on his sleeve, turned, and gestured at the four, arms wide.

"Kill him, damn your eyes!" Bálegyr roared. His voice cracked like a whip over the four brothers' heads; only then were they stung to action.

Screaming obscenities at one another, they hoisted their weapons and charged, falling into staggered pairs. The brother in the lead had snatched up a bearded axe. Its rust-spotted blade came whistling for Grimnir's life. The *skrælingr* sidestepped that blow; without breaking stride, Grimnir backhanded the axe-brother with the heavy stoneware flagon in his off hand, shattering it against the side of his head. That brother staggered and stumbled, blood mixing with the crockery fragments raining to the floor . . .

Grimnir shifted his weight. The second brother in line, arms cranked back to deliver a sword blow that would have felled a small tree, died with the handle-fragment of the flagon jammed into his neck. Grimnir sawed it across muscles and arteries, then left it lodged near the apple of his throat. That brother gobbled blood as he crumpled . . .

Grimnir whirled to his right. He ducked under a wild sword cut; Hátr lashed out, ripping through leather, skin, muscle, and viscera to gut the third brother like a trussed hog. Grimnir stiff-armed him from his path . . .

The last brother tried to stop. His booted feet lost their purchase on the blood-slimed floorboards. He skidded; fell backward. Even as he struck the floor, Grimnir was there. That brother died with Hátr piercing his sternum, his lungs, and, finally, his heart.

Grimnir rose smoothly to his feet. He left Hátr sheathed in his brother's corpse while he finished one last piece of business. The brother who had the flagon broken over his head struggled to rise. He clawed for his axe even as Grimnir seized him around the neck and grabbed his shoulder with one hand, and then grasped his chin with the other. With an explosive grunt and a violent twist, Grimnir broke his neck.

Silence reigned under the eaves of Varghǫll. The only sound was the explosive *shuff* of Grimnir's breath, whistling as it did between clenched teeth. He glared at his assembled kin, his cousins of every degree, maternal and paternal. A sardonic grin flirted at the corners of his mouth.

"Cherish them *all,* did you?" he said, turning toward the throne of his father. "*Faugh!* Why—"

Bálegyr chose that moment to strike. The wolf-headed mace, Maugrónðr, came from Grimnir's blind side. It caught him between his ear and his missing eye; blackened iron tore skin and shattered bone. Grimnir's head snapped to the right as his skull gave way beneath that unexpected blow, sending fragments knifing into his brain.

And Grimnir Bálegyr's son was dead before his body could come to rest, draped over the corpses of his brothers.

BEYOND ÚLFSSTAÐIR'S walls, under the storm-wracked firmament, chains of eerie lightning crackled between cloud-shoals and pillars of forge-fume; each searing blast set clotted shadows dancing by its unnatural light.

Moving among those warped and twisted shades were a company of *scrags.* They came from the battlefield at Gjöll's Inlet—still clad in the bloody rags they'd died in—and they followed a trail only one of them could sense. That slight murder-wisp, Köttr, moved a dozen paces ahead of her feral pack. The Cat was bent low, almost double, and her thin nostrils flared as she caught the ghost of a scent. Snaga came next, his blood-flecked face grave. The rest piled in behind him.

"Did they come this way?" he whispered. They were at the foot of the hill that Úlfsstaðir sat upon, below a rocky escarpment that led around to the so-called Back Door. There was precious little cover here, amid the scree and loose rock—though even Snaga could discern trails and paths among the rubble. "Or are we barking up the wrong tree?"

Köttr waved him off. She swayed this way and that, uncertain. At one point, she looked like she might go left, back toward the road from Úlfsstaðir to Gjöll's Inlet, rutted and hard-packed from countless shuffling feet; a moment later, the slight eddying breeze brought a familiar smell to her. She stared hard to her right, eyes like yellow lamps burning behind the veil of her hair.

"Well?"

She said nothing. Then, the Cat leveled one of her knives at a grove of ash and willow rising from the uneven ground, a few dozen yards away. There was water there. And something else. Snaga could smell it, now: the iron-rich stench of blood.

"There," Köttr rasped.

Snaga drew himself up to his full height. The lord of the *scrags* carried a different axe, this time—a bearded axe of blackened steel and iron-banded oak taken from the battlefield. He hefted it, used it to gesture at the others. "You lot, fan out. Köttr and me, we're going in there to fetch our mate back. The long-tooth that's got him, he ain't no pushover like most of the others, so make sure you got enough sand in your bellies. Ain't no running from this fight. You get me?"

"We get you, chief," the *scrags* murmured. They, too, hefted their weapons and tightened their belts.

Snaga nodded. Then, with Köttr leading the way, the pair of them crept off into the grove. A fire had burned here, within the hour; he could smell the smoke of its embers, mixed with the reek of burning meat. Köttr drew her second knife. They drew near a small clearing at the heart of the grove. Lightning from the heavens crackled and blazed, casting traceries of light and shadow across strewn rocks and hewn wood, on an old basket of woven reeds and empty bottles of mead, on the still-glowing bed of a fire. A dull susurration filled the air; a hiss, like water on too-hot stones.

And from the limb of a gnarled ash tree, rope creaked as a headless carcass twisted slowly; it hung by its feet, stripped and ready for butchering. Blood still dripped from the stump of its neck. Rivulets of this black slaughter-broth reached the fire's roots and cooked in its embers. Outstretched arms reached for Nástrond's rocky soil, but to no avail.

A muffled snarl caught in Köttr's scarred throat. Snaga lowered his axe, his eyes alight with naked fury. "Blártunga," he said.

The Cat started toward him. "Grab him! I'll cut the rope. There's still—"

"No."

"There's still time!"

Snaga squatted on his haunches beside the embers of the fire. "No, Köttr. He ain't coming back. Not this time. That ol' long-tooth made sure of that."

From deep within Köttr's breast came an eerie rasping scream—a piercing sound, like the hinges of her murderous soul squealing for want of slick, hot blood. She fell to her knees, yellow eyes screwed tight and her slight weight propped on the hilts of her knives. "I want him, Snaga!" she panted, glancing up at her chief. "I want his heart on a platter! I want him roasted alive and fed to the dogs!"

Snaga's eyes narrowed. "Grimnir Bálegyr's son will get what's coming to him, mark my words. But we ain't going to get nowhere unless we keep our wits about us. You savvy to what I'm saying, Cat?"

Köttr spat each word of her answer: "I . . . want . . . him . . . under . . . my . . . knives!"

"Then heed what I'm tellin' you and do as I say."

Her thin nostrils flared. "You got something in mind?"

"Ain't nothing solid, yet." Snaga pushed himself to his feet. "But this I know: it's high time we shook things up. Mánavargr took a beating, by the looks of things back at Gjöll's Inlet. Poncey bastard like that, he'll hole up and lick his pride. So, maybe we go to Hrauðnir and his lot down in the swamps, instead. There ain't no love lost between him and Bálegyr . . . or between him and Kjallandi, I reckon. And this victory ain't gonna do nothing but make those bastards bolder than ever." He walked over to where Köttr sat on her knees and thrust out his hand. "Couple of well-placed lies might be all it takes . . ."

The Cat took his proffered hand and let him haul her to her feet. "And what do we do with . . . what do we do with Blártunga?" Her eyes were dry, but the pain etched into her young-old visage looked like the work of hammer and chisel.

Snaga sighed. "Leave him. Ain't nothing but crow-meat, now. No use trying to bury him."

From beyond the heart of the grove, back the way they'd come, Köttr and Snaga both heard a harsh whisper: "Chief!"

"Here, Rat-bone," he replied, recognizing the voice as one of his *scrag* lieutenants. Rat-bone hove into view. Red-eyed and sporting a shock of mud-stiffened hair, Rat-bone was as tall as Snaga but thinner, like a fleshless mannikin covered in poorly-stitched skins. The tattered remains of a mail shirt hung from his sparse frame, and he leaned on a short spear. "What goes?"

"Somethin' odd's a-going on, up yonder." Rat-bone jerked his sharp chin at the walls of Úlfsstaðir, barely visible through the canopy of leaves. "Ain't none of us know what to make of it."

Snaga took one last look at the slowly twisting corpse that had been Blártunga—fat, loyal Blártunga, who was always eager to serve. Now ... nothing. Meat on a rope. A stark reminder that the inequities of the upper worlds repeated themselves in the lower. At least, for now. Though he did not invoke any god—for what god cared about the likes of him and his *scrags?*—Snaga nevertheless swore vengeance. He swore it on his blood, on his eternal life. Grimnir Bálegyr's son would pay.

And he did not care how.

"Show me," he said, turning to Rat-bone.

MAUGRÓNDR ROSE and fell, again. The spikes around the collar of the wolf-headed mace pierced mail and bone to lodge in the wall of Grimnir's chest. There, Bálegyr left it, like a woodsman's axe in a stump at the end of a hard day's work. "Useless little bastards!" he said, turning. "If you want something done right, you'd best do it yourself, eh?"

Varghǫll erupted in screams of mirth and howls of fury. Bettors punched and kicked to retrieve their stakes; fights broke out, for none among them had foreseen *this* outcome. The Lord of the Red Eye raked the crowd. He spread his arms wide and drank in in equal measure their approbation and consternation.

Gífr had nothing but contempt for that fat fool. *Look at him,* he wanted to say. *Look at him strutting and preening as though he had won a great victory! Bah!* In Gífr's estimation, Bálegyr was the worst sort of scavenger, the too-lazy hyena content to do naught but poach the lion's kills. He was careful not to give voice to his scorn. Even the hyena had teeth that could rend and jaws that could crush. So, Gífr smiled; he laughed along with the rest of them, though his eyes glittered with the banked heat of his disgust.

Beside him, Kjallandi muttered under his breath: "Where is this miracle you spoke of?"

"Wait," Gífr replied, turning slightly. "Watch." And with bated breath, father and son did just that: they waited, and they watched.

Grimnir had not lied. It came quick, and without warning. At first, it was barely noticeable—a tremor that ran up the iron-wrapped haft of Maugrónðr; then, it became more pronounced. The butt of that great mace trembled; it tilted as though some unseen hand was trying to work it loose from Grimnir's gore-splattered corpse. Finally, it toppled over, falling to the floor with a muffled clatter.

The corpse stiffened.

"There," Gífr hissed. "Do you see?" In answer, Kjallandi clutched his son's arm. Across the hall, Skaði and Skríkja also took note. The daughter of Skæfloc's eyes grew wide, while the queen's face lost all color, turning as pale as clotted cream. Nor were they alone. Singly and in pairs, others noticed *something* happening; a dismayed silence crept across Varghǫll.

Bálegyr, however, was oblivious. Instead, he pointed one dirty black-nailed finger at Kjallandi. "Twenty-two sons I have, twenty-three if you count *this* upstart." Without looking, he jerked his thumb back at Grimnir's corpse—its muscles knotted and trembling, now. "And still, not one among them is worth even a dram of your lad's spittle! None of them! What gives, Kjallandi? What secret do you possess, eh? Must I capture that frigid bitch of a wife of yours and get a few bastards on her?" He glanced from Kjallandi to Skríkja, expecting a response. He got nothing. Gífr saw a scowl crease Bálegyr's forehead when those *skrælingar* nearest him stumbled back, their eyes gleaming with atavistic terror.

The air itself grew still; the smoke ceased its curling, and the wood in the fire pits refused to crackle for fear of drawing attention. In that unexpected wellspring of silence, Gífr heard a sound that chilled even his ancient black blood: the sudden inrush of breath; upon exhale, the low growl of a predator.

Bálegyr heard it, too. He whirled, his face slack with disbelief.

There, rising to his feet, was Grimnir—red-eyed and fell-handed; blood-splattered like a *draugr* of old, a creature of cairn and barrow whose cruelty, greed, and bloodlust in life lent it power after death. Through a disheveled veil of hair, Gífr saw Grimnir's lips skin back in a snarl of hate; clawlike fingers tightened around the haft of Maugrónðr.

"Ymir's balls!" Bálegyr exploded, his hand going for the knife at his belt. "You can't—"

Grimnir, though, moved faster.

The wolf-headed mace swung up and out. With the dull crunch of bone, it connected with Bálegyr's left hip. The Lord of the Red Eye howled as the blow lifted him off his feet, all but twisting him around the mace's head. Grimnir wrenched Maugrónðr free; Bálegyr collapsed, his left side unable to bear his not inconsiderable weight. He clawed at Grimnir's boot, bellowing curses. Maugrónðr's iron spikes sloughed a welter of blood as he drew it back once more.

He held it aloft for a heartbeat. There was no mercy in Grimnir's singular eye, and precious little to be had in the eyes of those who looked on. Some still registered disbelief, as though Grimnir's rapid return to the unlife they all shared had been some sly ruse; others watched with a mixture of terror and awe. There was eagerness on display, as well as a thirst for spilled blood. The weak saw this as a change in the status quo. The powerful saw it as a threat to their existence. Still, not a soul among them moved to intercede.

All of this Grimnir beheld in the split second Maugrónðr remained on high. Then, with an air of finality, he let the mace fall. Bálegyr's curses ended with the dull *thock* of iron meeting flesh. The sutures between the plates of his skull came apart under the impact, and his head popped like a piece of ripe fruit, sending a slurry of brain, blood, and teeth across the floor in a roostertail of gore. Again, Grimnir hit him. And again. Each blow pulped flesh, splintered bone, and spattered blood across the thrones of the kings of Úlfsstaðir. After half a dozen such impacts, Grimnir slung Maugrónðr aside.

His body rigid, his muscles standing out like cables of woven steel lashed to a frame of bone, Grimnir threw back his head and roared to the smoky rafters, to the heavens beyond—an inarticulate cry of rage and frustration. He stood there as the echo died away; his chest rose and fell, and with each panted breath the killing lust abated. In the scarlet gleam of his single eye, Gífr beheld once more the curious intensity he'd seen as they left the grove—and left Grimnir alone with that fat *scrag*.

"One of you louts grab this pus-bag's feet!" he snarled. With a sudden gesture, he encompassed the wreckage of flesh that had been his brothers. "*Nár!* The lot of you, heave to and bring them all! We'll fetch them down to the water's edge and feed them to the fishes, eh? Give those blasted *sjóvættir* a chance to eat well tonight."

A handful of *skrælingar* started forward, eager to do his bidding, but a sharp voice brought them up short.

"Stop!" Kjallandi stepped to the fore, crossing the bloody interval to face Grimnir. His pale visage was hard and unflinching; his eyes gleamed with millennia of wisdom tempered by the knowledge of dark deeds done by the light of the Nine Worlds. "True death is reserved for traitors, you lout, not for any rat who vexes you. Let them be."

Grimnir glanced up. "Well, begging your pardon and all, but I don't think I will. There's too much at stake to just let these idiots amble about, plotting their little acts of vengeance against me. This one, especially." He dealt Bálegyr's corpse a savage kick. "I'm proof that something's slipped, up top. That we're hip-deep in it, and that not a thrice-damned one of us knows what in Ymir's name is going on! So, no, I don't think I'll stop. I think I'll haul these cack-handed beggars down to the water and let the *sjóvættir* have their way with them. And the rest of you rats, take heed! If you're not on board with the solution, you're part of the problem!"

"Listen to you, all high-and-mighty," Gífr said, coming to stand at his father's side. He thrust his thumbs into his weapons belt. "You'll do this and you'll not do that, eh? We'd better toe your line or else?" Gífr sneered. "You sound like one of those blasted hymn-singers!"

"And you sound like you've gone soft, you old sot! Was it not you who taught me to never leave an enemy alive? Was it not you who said an act of mercy today meant a knife in the gullet tomorrow?" Grimnir spread his arms, as if proving his point.

"These?" Gífr replied, jabbing a finger at the sprawled corpses. "These aren't your enemies. None of us, here, are your enemies."

"That's a steaming load of dung, and you know it! *Nár!* The moment they spring back to life, these slags and whoresons won't rest till they get a little payback, that other matter be damned! You said it yourself." Grimnir nodded to Kjallandi. "Killing is in our nature, what we were bred for, the purpose given to us by the Tangled God. We kill over the least slight or the greatest insult, remember?"

Before Kjallandi could answer, however, a low and humorless chuckle brought them around. They turned to face Skríkja, and the disdain in her voice as she spoke pierced each one as deep as the darts of an enemy. "Behold, the sons of the Wolf! See them, Skaði? See them barking and baring their teeth? That's because they have forgotten." The queen gestured and the cordon of curious *skrælingar* parted, allowing her to pass. Skaði followed on her heels.

Grimnir straightened, a pugnacious jut to his sharp chin. "Forgotten? What have we forgotten?"

"You've forgotten that everything here—every board and cup, branch and bole, hill and hollow; every bottom-feeding maggot and grasping worm; every *kaunr*, *skrælingr*, and *scrag* who calls Nástrond home, pure blood or bastard, prince or pauper . . . all of this and all of us belongs to the Tangled God. And not even you dare put yourself above Father Loki." She pushed past Grimnir and ascended the dais. Turning, she raked the crowd with a gaze as cold and hard and bright as frozen sunlight. "Step up, if you dispute my right to rule in my lamentable husband's stead! Step up now if you think yourself better suited to sit on the Throne of the Red Eye!" None among them moved; not even the staunchest of Bálegyr's followers dared risk the wrath of Úlfsstaðir's pale queen. "No? So be it, then! I'll tell you three great and mighty sons of the Wolf what else you've forgotten . . . you've forgotten that we are also brothers and sisters of the Serpent. Now, pick up this carrion and follow me! I'll show you how to keep these swine out of your hair . . ."

RAT-BONE LED Snaga, Köttr, and the others back the way they'd come, through a landscape riven by eternal fighting. They crept down long, jagged ravines where pallid dust caked the corroded remnants of a thousand different sieges. The *scrags* ducked under dry-rotted beams from broken engines of war; around them, roofed galleries with ironshod rams and rolling mantlets that could shield a dozen archers lay forgotten in Úlfsstaðir's long shadow, swept from the road overhead by sorties and raids and furious charges. Desiccated arrow shafts crackled like leaves underfoot. Nowhere were there to be seen any bones larger than that of an animal, for their kind did not leave corpses behind; they did not carve eidolons in the rock to honor their fallen chiefs, then decorate them with the skulls of the defeated. No, the long-tooths had no need to raise cairns and barrows.

Rat-bone stopped near the base of the hill, where the road rose to meet the open gates of the Wolves' Abode. Here, cloaked in shadow, they had a good view of what was going on.

Under the watchful eyes of Bálegyr's frightful queen, pairs of *skrælingar* shuffled through the gate dragging burdens behind them. Corpses, by the look of things. They brought them as far as the edge of the road before hoisting them by wrists and ankles and, with a swinging two-count, heaving them off down the slope. Jeers and howls of laughter met each wet impact.

"Strip them, Skaði," the queen commanded. Another female—thin and sallow, with eyes like glittering topaz—cut away belts and fastenings as each corpse passed by her. "Take their weapons. Leave them not even a button they can sharpen!"

"She's cleaning house," Snaga muttered, scowling. "Look there."

He spied Grimnir and that old long-tooth, Gífr, struggling with a fat corpse that could only be the illustrious Bálegyr himself. The other king, that bearded giant, Kjallandi, walked alongside them.

"You're certain of this, daughter?" Kjallandi asked, his deep voice echoing.

Skríkja gestured for Grimnir and Gífr to rid themselves of their burden. A snarl twisted her thin lips. "Throw him out with the rest of this trash!" The two of them exchanged glances, then did as they were told. Bálegyr's corpse arched and twisted; it struck the road and slid to the edge, teetering there a moment before slipping over the side and into the ravine. Splintering wood marked the moment of impact with the ground.

"A little hardship will do the bastard some good," said the queen, turning. "While he is fuming and scheming to get his throne back, you lot can go about your business. And there is no offense given to the Tangled God."

"Shrewd," Kjallandi said, nodding.

Grimnir stopped the last pair of *skrælingar*, who were shuffling and cursing under the weight of the last corpse. Snaga recognized the body as that of the scar-faced giant, Sægrár. He looked as though someone had staved in his skull with an anvil. "Not him."

Snaga heard the one called Skaði say: "*Feh!* What are you thinking?"

Grimnir glanced over at Gífr. "This ferryman of yours has a price, you said, and that he's picky. Consider it Sægrár's chance to do some good with his miserable life. Take him inside and keep him quiet. Bastard's coming with us."

Snaga sank down, Rat-bone and Köttr beside him. They heard the gates of Úlfsstaðir as they trundled shut, followed by the crash of the bar falling into its moorings. The wind kicked up, its warm breath spiced with blood and offal. Overhead, the fume and wrack thinned, the shrouded light of Yggðrasil stealing their shadow.

"The ferryman, says he?" Snaga glanced at his mates. "The Bone Ferry, I'll warrant. They mean to slip off this rock. Time we go play nice again with that long-toothed old pris, Mánavargr, ain't it? He's going to want to know there's been a shake-up, down here. And, send a couple of lads around to fetch Bálegyr. Ain't nothing like the head of a sworn enemy as a peace offering, is there ...?"

As THE heavy iron-banded bar securing the gates of Úlfsstaðir fell into place, the pairs of *skrælingar,* those of the Stag-Skull and of the Eye, followed Skríkja and Kjallandi back into the firelit heart of Varghǫll. Soon, only Grimnir lingered in the short tunnel between the gates and the inner courtyard. Like a beast in its cage, he paced back and forth, his agitation growing with every step. He muttered under his breath; black-nailed fists clenched and unclenched.

Gífr, who was crouched by Sægrár's discarded corpse, finished securing the bastard's thick wrists with manacles of hammered iron and rose to his feet. He cast a sidelong glance at Grimnir. "What is it, little rat?"

"We're wasting time," Grimnir answered, nostrils flaring. Beads ticked as, with a jerk of his chin, he gestured into the heavens. Thinning fumes revealed the light of the Nine Worlds. "That one-eyed rider of benches, up yonder, he's starting to realize something's amiss. How many *skrælingar* do you think are left to be killed, up there? And he's done away with *two* in one night? *Nár!* He's no fool, that one. He suspects something."

"He doesn't *suspect* anything. He *knows* you're trying to stop him, doesn't he? You've been after that wyrm for, what? A hundred and thirty years? This is how the mill's run. He knows it just as well as you do."

Fuming, Grimnir stalked half the distance toward Varghǫll's wide open doors, then returned to Gífr's side. When he spoke, his voice came as a flinty hiss. "Doesn't matter. We need to be on the road. We know nothing ... *nothing* about the why or how of it all, nothing about how long we might have. We need to get to Mímir before it's too late."

"Why?" Gífr scowled. "You said it yourself, barely a moment passes between deaths. That means time is on our side, little rat."

"*Faugh!*" Grimnir snarled and turned away. "You don't understand!"

"Then explain it to me, by Ymir!" Gífr did not shy away from Grimnir's rage. He caught the younger *skrælingr* by the arm and spun him back around. "Hel's tit! What's got you so spooked?"

Grimnir tore himself loose from his elder's grasp. He stalked to the open doors of the Wolf's Hall and peered inside. He saw Skríkja as she ascended the dais, turned, and settled into the Throne of the Red Eye. Kjallandi himself handed her Bálegyr's crown—a circlet of hammered iron with a bloodred jewel set into its face. Without preamble, she snatched the circlet from his hands and placed it upon her own brow. Skríkja's lips peeled back in a self-satisfied grin as the folk of Úlfsstaðir roared their approval. Outside, Grimnir glanced back at Gífr, who trailed a pace behind him. He chewed over his words.

"Just spill it, little rat. After that fat fool cracked your head open, what happened?"

Grimnir spat. "Things happened the same as before . . . died *here,* woke up *there.* This time, though . . ."

11
LUPA ROMAE

"This time, I woke up cold. *Nár! Not shivering like some milk-blooded whiteskin, you idiot. But with the fires of rage tamped down. I woke up and knew what had happened. I knew that that reeking bag of suet who claimed to have whelped me had gotten in a cheap shot. And I knew it would do him fat little good, in the end. I knew who I was, this time. Not like my first death, or my second. I knew where I'd been and what I'd seen. And I knew where I was bound—Rome or Nástrond, it's all the same. I felt* aware..."

When Grimnir roused himself from the sleep of death for the third time, he did not thrash or writhe in confusion. No, he woke with a snarl on his lips, teeth clenched against the return of feeling into his knotty limbs, and with it the dull ache of the Nailed God's presence. He opened his eyes to thin slits—an ember of hate kindled in the good one as his gaze swept the darkness of the ancient chamber. He lay where he'd fallen, still in a heap on the cold stone floor. The *skrælingr* stifled a curse; exhaling through flared nostrils, his eyes shifted to the star-flecked firmament some thirty feet above his head. Tendrils of mist faded where seconds before a cloaked figure had stood, one-eyed and malevolent. And as he had before, he recalled the dim echo of a memory—

"This memory, tell me about it."

Grimnir glares at Gífr for this interruption. "Faugh! *It's nothing. Some dim recollection, is all. Must be something I laid eyes on over the years, up top. Or else it's something I heard about.*"

"Tell me."

Grimnir exhales. His brow furrows. "*There's an oak as old and gnarled as Miðgarðr's bones. Around it, under drifts of wet leaves, are eight stones, draped in thorn and bramble beneath a sky the color of iron. Some hand has scratched runes into these stones, and they're oozing traces of ancient sorcery; I feel the movement of spirits, like a cold breeze tickling the back of my neck; I hear the creak of tree limbs, the faint clash of stone on stone, the moaning of the dead . . .*"

"And that's it?"

Grimnir ducks his head. "That's all I remember," *he mumbles.* "*If I've seen it, I can't place it. If I heard about it, then it had to come from you, you old sot. Does it ring any bells?*"

"None."

"*Then, no matter. I felt its echo, is all. I lay there for a bit, listening to see if that old raven-starver had truly gone. Once I judged it safe, I started to move . . .*"

Mail rustled as Grimnir clambered to his feet. He rolled his shoulders, cracking the muscles and tendons in his neck as he shook off the torpor of death. Brick dust and dry leaves trickled from the edges of the hole above his head; bits of the broken mosaic clattered to the floor, their echo revealing the limits of the chamber in which he stood, surely the cellars under some long-dead patrician's villa, or the palace of a forgotten Caesar. The clash of a pebble striking steel drew Grimnir's attention.

He dropped to a crouch; his good eye swept the floor. Not far away, he caught sight of the bone-hilt of his seax, half buried under debris from the roof's collapse. With a muttered curse, he scrambled over to it, clawed through the detritus, and snatched up the fallen blade. Grimnir straightened. Hátr slid back into its scabbard with an angry hiss. Around him, the darkness was oppressive, the air stifling. The faint glow of distant stars filtering down through the hole overhead was the only light. Even the most cat-eyed whiteskin would have been blind, stumbling about in growing desperation. Not so, Grimnir. Even one-eyed, the feeble sheen of the firmament offered him enough light to see his predicament.

He was in a vaulted chamber, under groins of stone and buttresses of reddish brick. The rent he'd fallen through was thirty feet over his head, its edges unsteady; the bricks around it were crumbling, with gaps where pieces had fallen away. The stones were slick with patches of mildew left over from the autumnal rains. He reckoned the stomp of a foot would bring the whole blasted thing down on him. Grimnir hawked and spat; no escape lay in that direction, so he shifted his efforts to finding another way out.

"That wretched cellar." Grimnir tsk's a line of spittle between his teeth. "Away from the hole, things got as black as Hel's arse, and quick! A maze of nooks and crannies, all of them going nowhere. Ha! Nothing but rats and old pottery. Couldn't see my hand if I flapped it in front of my face. I was right buggered. Ymir take that one-eyed bastard and his tricks!"

"How'd you manage your way out, unless you died in there, again?"

Grimnir flashes a serrated grin. "Got my head on right, that's how! Let my nose guide me. Got a whiff of running water, a hint of fresher air, and finally tracked it down to an old grate in the floor . . ."

Grimnir knelt. His fingers brushed against bars of rust-pitted iron. From beneath these, he felt cooler and fresher air, and heard the chuckle of running water. Down here, in the bowels of this place, not even his owllike vision could stave off the utter darkness. Though he could not see, he had the snuffling nose of a hunting wolf. He moved without hesitation, without fear. Indeed, what was there for him to fear in the darkness? An enemy? Ha! Not here; not anymore. *He* was the monster haunting the shadows.

The *skrælingr* wrapped his black-nailed fingers around the coarse bars and, with contemptuous ease, ripped the grate's iron frame from the old mortar that had secured it for centuries. He tossed it aside, heedless of the noise, and explored the edges of the opening it had shielded. It was large enough for a rat his size to pass through, though barely; he squinted, seeing nothing, but hearing the sound of water running along a man-made channel. His nostrils flared; he caught a hint of crisp night air, and with it the earthy reek of moss on wet stone.

"Not a sewer," he muttered, his voice profaning the silence. Not anymore, at least. The water he smelled was fresh—or fresh enough, at any rate. He remembered the creek that had passed under the wall, near where he'd slipped into Rome. This must be part of that watercourse. Carefully, he lowered himself through the hole until his booted feet found purchase.

The water was not deep—barely to his ankles—but it was fast-moving and cold, and the stones treacherously slick. He crouched. The water flowed down a gentle incline, Grimnir reckoned, likely from the hilly region around the Appian Gate, past this ruin, and into the heart of the ancient city. The way forward was tight. He could not stand upright; the tunnel's narrow confines and low ceiling would force him into a deep crouch, and he'd have to scuttle like a crab if he hoped to move through it. And, he thought with a slow curl of his lip, he'd have to shed his mail to do it.

Grimnir stood. He braced himself against the walls of the tunnel and stripped off his weapons belt, setting it aside. Next, he tugged the leather straps of his hauberk from their brass buckles and shrugged out of it. By touch, alone, he folded the silver-threaded mail and rolled it into a bundle, securing it with his weapons belt. He slipped his axe into the heart of the bundle, so as not to lose it; he double-checked that Hátr was tight in its scabbard by his hand, and that the bundle of mail was secure, before crouching once more. Grimnir exhaled; he glanced from side to side at the stones around him. "Rest your bones, great Ymir," he muttered, edging crabwise into the tunnel . . .

Grimnir jabs a gnarled finger at Gífr. "Those old Romans might have been a boil on the arse of our people, once, but I'll say this about them: the olive-eating bastards knew how to dig. Tighter than a cheeseparer's fist, down there, and twice as slick, but that tunnel was as solid a piece of work as anything I've ever seen. Even after all these years."

Grimnir turns from Varghǫll's doors and finds himself a place to sit near the left-hand column supporting the carved portico. The wood is ancient, blackened by age and fire. Stylized wolves chase one another up the column, curling and coiling around the bole of a great tree—Yggðrasil, surely.

Gífr crouches. With his left hand, he scoops up a palmful of hammerscale mixed with gravel. He stirs it with one long finger, then starts flicking the gravel off into the shadows one by one. Tick. Tick. Tick. He says nothing, but watches Grimnir from under beetling brows.

Grimnir knuckles the socket of his missing eye, as though its loss pains him, still. "Is that their legacy, you think? The Romans? Will these milk-lipped Italians in days yet to come look back and say 'well, they could dig a sewer' or 'they could lay a road'?

THE DOOM OF ODIN

The Greeks before them could spin a yarn; the Egyptians before them could raise a monument. What will they say of us, eh? We kaunar? That's if those bastards remember us at all? 'By god, they slunk through the night like stoats' or 'they knew how to burn a village'?"

"*Does it matter?*"

Grimnir sucked his teeth. "To you? Nár! I doubt it. But you had a death-song sung over your bones, back in Miðgarðr. I made sure of it! A song that will echo through eternity. And you have a stone marking your death, at that fly-speck village near the mouth of the Elbe—"

"*Hathu's End," Gífr says. He flicks another bit of gravel into the gloom.*

"*I'd forgotten its name," replies Grimnir. "But not the words I had that Saxon chief carve into the rock, ere I added his corpse to your funeral pyre:* Here by Elbe's accursed shore, Kjallandi's son took the road to Nástrond . . ."

"*Now you wonder how the whiteskins will remember you, is that it?*"

"*No. I wonder if the dunghill rats will bother to remember me at all.*"

"*Perhaps," Gífr begins. He lets the hammerscale trickle from his palm, wipes the dust on the thigh of his trousers. A feral gleam plays about his gaze, a hint of mockery. "Perhaps if you quit prancing about and ram that feeble shard of Sárklungr down Malice-Striker's gullet, those precious hymn-singers up top will think more kindly of you.*"

Grimnir chuckles. "That's it, eh? That's the wisdom gleaned from experience? Thank Ymir I have you around, to remind me what I'm supposed to be doing with this gift of endless death some bastard god has bestowed upon me. Simple as that, eh?" He snaps his fingers. "Just kill that filthy wyrm and all will be well?"

Gífr's laugh is low, like the grumble of stones. "Aye. So, get on with it, little rat."

Grimnir hops from his perch. He stretches, cracking the tendons in his neck. "There's just one problem with this plan of yours, you buggering old fool. And that problem's name is Odin Bench-trembler, Starver of Ravens. His presence in the city had already upended the natural order of things. Woken things that should not have been roused from the earth."

"*Like what?*"

Grimnir's lips curled into a snarl. "Like the Mother of Rome itself. That tunnel brought me near to the heart of the ancient city, the old Forum . . ."

He emerged from earth like a revenant, a gimlet-eyed creature of waste and desolation. Clad once more in his hauberk of Turkish mail, Grimnir crouched at the edge of ancient Rome's beating heart and snuffled the night air—thick, now, with a soupy mist that reeked of the Tiber River. Stringy black hair threaded with fetishes of gold, silver, amber, and bone hung like a veil before his face. He swiped it back with one black-nailed hand and stared hard through slitted eyes.

His hackles rose. The *skrælingr* felt an alien sense of scrutiny. *Something* was watching him. Something not human. And for the briefest of moments, he wondered if he'd stumbled across Níðhöggr's bolt-hole.

"The air was different, though," Grimnir says. *"That blasted wyrm has a stench to it. It's unmistakable. Smell it once and you'll never forget it—like fish guts boiled in brine, blood, and iron. Nár! This was something else . . ."*

Grimnir scrithed into the open, bold-eyed and arrogant, one hand resting on the hilt of his long-seax. Ruins loomed in the riverine fog. Moisture glistened on pitted stone, or else dripped from the autumnal foliage draping the broken façade of an ancient temple. Between toppled slabs of marble, crude shacks sprouted like a fungus, their walls of scavenged stone and wood leaning like drunkards under awnings of faded cloth. He could sense huddled bodies hiding within; he could hear the catches in their breath as they started at every sound; their murmured prayers to their Nailed God. There was Fear, here, stalking the space between the stars. With it came its bloody-minded brothers: Madness, Violence, and Death.

Grimnir's nostrils flared. His lips skinned back over yellowed teeth in a grimace of hate. *This* was his element.

Olive trees grew on either side of the rutted dirt road that ran through the weed-choked Forum. Where cows now wandered, cropping grass, once the Romans had displayed the prows of defeated ships; where hovels now crouched among crumbling stones, once a madman named Sulla had nailed lists bearing the names of his enemies, both real and imagined; where vegetables now grew, once a scrawny popinjay named Cicero had exhorted his fellow Romans to reject the tyranny of Lucius Catilina. Here, in the shadow of Rome's glories, haunted by its restless ghosts, Grimnir stopped. He made a slow circle, arms held wide.

"Show yourself, dog," he said. "If my being here offends you, then come and take me to task, if you dare!"

THE DOOM OF ODIN

Nothing.

No sound reached his keen ears.

No shape emerged from the darkness.

"I thought as much." Grimnir sneered. "Then be off with you, whatever you are!" He hawked and spat into the night. And before him, in the mist—at the limit of his spittle's reach—a pair of yellow eyes opened.

Eyes the size of his fists.

Grimnir recoiled; Hátr scraped from its scabbard. Though himself a creature of the Elder World, the *skrælingr* nevertheless felt an unaccustomed thrill of atavistic terror dance down his spine as those eyes rose up, stretching even beyond his height; at twice the height of a tall man, a shape took form, its outline cloaked in swirling mist: the muzzle and slavering jaws of a titanic wolf.

"Bastard child of the North," it said, its voice hard and guttural. It snuffled the air, then exhaled. "*Orcadii* . . . yes, I remember your kind. The noble Marius dragged your chief back from Numidia in chains. And now you dare return? You dare disturb my rest?"

Grimnir scoffed. "None of your pig-fucking Romans put chains on any chief of my blood, you lying wretch! And as for what I dare . . . I dare go my own way without begging an ounce of your pardon! *Faugh!* Go back to sleep, *landvættr*. My business is none of your concern."

The thing snarled and gave a low growl; it circled Grimnir. "*Landvættr?* I am the Lupa Romae, the She-Wolf of Rome, and within the *pomerium* of the Eternal City all is my concern! Now answer me, child of the Orcadii, lest I snatch you up and chew the gristle from your bones!"

Grimnir, though, did not back down. "I piss on your *pomerium*," he said, with a derisive chuckle. "*Eternal City?* Ha! I piss on that, too! Your day is done, little wolfling! Look at you . . . thin and wasted, like a dog chained to its kennel and forgotten by its masters! This is the Nailed God's domain, now. Slink back to whatever hole you crawled out of and leave me in peace. My errand—"

The She-Wolf of Rome did not let him finish. With a snarl fit to freeze the blood, the guardian-spirit of the ancient city lunged for Grimnir. He swayed aside, but barely; its champing jaws missed him by a hair's breadth. Then, matching snarl for snarl, Grimnir lashed out with his off hand. Iron-hard knuckles slammed into the side of the She-Wolf's muzzle. Backed by every stone of his weight, that bone-crunching blow staggered the beast. Yellow eyes blazed anew at this affront; in answer, the forge-red rage of the *kaunar* roared to life.

And battle was joined.

There was no time for gibes or taunts. Neither could waste their breath on it. The She-Wolf, the Mother of Rome, came on like a tempest. Claws like curved sabers skittered off good Turkish mail as Grimnir ducked, whirled, and then sprang, knotting his fingers in the matted fur at the Wolf's shoulder. He meant to get close. Close enough to render moot its advantages of size and weight; close enough to straddle its neck and ram a foot of cold steel into the beast's brain. The She-Wolf was a canny fighter. Wary of both the rune-marked blade in Grimnir's fist and of letting him get astride its back, the Mother of Rome did the unexpected—it folded its foreleg up and slammed that shoulder into the ground.

A slower fighter might have been caught flat-footed by that ruse; taken unawares, unable to recover, only to be crushed into the dust of the Forum. Grimnir, however, was hacked from sterner stuff. He turned loose of the beast and flung himself back. He hit the ground, rolled, and came up on the balls of his feet.

And as he sought his balance, the She-Wolf caught him broadside with a flick of its ram-like snout. It was like getting hit by a *jötunn*'s sledgehammer. The breath *whuffed* from Grimnir's lungs; he cartwheeled, smashing through the wall of a hovel in an explosion of wood and unmortared stone. Suddenly unmoored, the moth-eaten awning that had covered the structure fluttered like a death-shroud around him.

Even though he could not draw breath, even though broken ribs grated together with every movement of his torso, Grimnir nevertheless came up fighting. His blade, Hátr, ripped through the awning; it was poised to seek the soft flesh of the She-Wolf's fanged maw, its eyes, anything he could reach before those rushing jaws sped him back to Nástrond . . .

"*But there was nothing there,*" *Grimnir says.* "*I scrambled to my feet, wheezing like an old bellows and tasting blood, and saw . . . nothing. Swirling mist, the smell of damp fur. Well, I reckoned that old bitch-hound meant to play with me a bit before coming in for the kill. And me? Nár! I was game. 'Ymir's blood!' I screamed. 'Ymir's blood!*

THE DOOM OF ODIN

Show yourself, swine!' I backed out of that wrecked hovel, turned ... and that's when the fat hit the fire ..."

An arm shot from the darkness and the mist and seized Grimnir by the throat. It was long, this arm, and knotted with ropelike muscle. The flesh was as pale as Northern ice, and inked in a tracery of runes that writhed like blue veins just under the skin. That grip was deathly cold. Grimnir felt his feet leave the ground; he dangled there, long fingers wrapped around his neck like a multitude of hangman's nooses, as this newcomer drew him close. Grimnir saw gray cloth, a loose and voluminous robe; he saw a slouch hat pulled low. Under its brim, a single malevolent eye, grim and rheumy, pierced him through and through.

Odin had come.

The Lord of Ásgarðr exhaled. His reeking breath carried the stench of ancient hoarfrost, of burning wood and salt-spume, of rich coppery blood and forge-hot iron. When he spoke, his voice rumbled like distant thunder:

> "Mögþrasir's daughters, | who dwell beneath the Tree,
> Dabble not in coincidence;
> While more of thy breed might | lurk on Miðgarðr's shores,
> Two in Rúmaborg cannot be.
>
> "Speak now, skrælingr, | though false be thy tongue
> And it sings thee an evil song;
> By what sorcery | art thou unbroken,
> When I have seen thee slain this night?"

Grimnir, however, did not answer. His single red eye blazed; his lips writhed over clenched and serrated teeth. And in that moment, in that instant where he hung between life and death, a hundred mortal lifetimes of fear and apprehension simply sloughed away, revealing the molten core of hate that burned at the heart of every *kaunr*. Yet, there was something more to it—something deeper, something feeding into this hate like a smith feeding coke into a forge. Something that wanted him to burn, to feel the hammer, and to emerge anew.

Something not of him. Though the awareness was sudden, Grimnir did not care. He seized upon that alien hatred and made it his own.

And though he hung by the neck in the fist of a god, Grimnir Bálegyr's son did the one thing none of his kind could boast of . . .

"I stabbed the son of a bitch," Grimnir snarls. "Drove Hátr point-first into that bench-trembler's forearm and ripped it back toward his wrist. Faugh! *Why not? What was he going to do, kill me? Don't look so shocked, you old git. I was dead, anyway. Might as well go down swinging, eh? Well, that's when he said it . . ."*

Odin recoiled from Hátr's cold iron bite. He turned loose of Grimnir, who landed on his knees and doubled over as he sought to draw a racking breath. He glared up at the Lord of Ásgarðr. The blood that dripped from Odin's arm was as red as any mortal's. But the rage that poured forth from the god's eye was like a buffeting wind; his voice, the howl of a gale:

"Spawn of perfidy! | Filth-born skrælingr,
*Thou would dare strike at thy betters?
(Hold the cur blameless | for being a cur?)
Tell it in Nástrond | when the death-blow falls,
That thy doom waits not for Vígríðr!"*

Odin raised his hand to the heavens, where thick swirling clouds backlit by jagged lightning blotted out the stars. A word formed on his bearded lips. A name. Grimnir knew it; he knew what would come from it. He braced himself, teeth clenched, and refused to look away. Before Odin could speak, a shadow struck him from his blind side. Slavering fangs clamped down on his bloodstained arm.

And Grimnir laughed.

For the She-Wolf of Rome had taken the Lord of Ásgarðr unawares.

The force of their collision caused the earth under Grimnir's feet to tremble. He saw the dwellers of the Forum fleeing, heard screams in the night as jagged columns were trampled and hovels flattened; a litany of prayers lofted heavenward like arrows, seeking the Nailed God's ear. But not even he would dare intervene. Not here, on ground hallowed by pagan priests, amid the ruin of Antiquity; here, two titans of the Elder World fought for primacy.

THE DOOM OF ODIN

Odin's voice was the voice of the storm, savage and bellicose. He flung the She-Wolf aside. The beast landed nimbly, whirled, and sprang again for the Allfather's throat. Its claws tore divine flesh like knives. Its snarls were like a legion of drawn swords; it drew upon the power of this place, upon the spirits of Eternal Rome. Those spirits lent it potency, and before his eyes, Grimnir saw the She-Wolf swell; its yellow eyes burned with controlled hate—the same hate Romulus bore for Remus.

The runes etched into Odin's flesh flared like beacons, glowing with the weight and majesty of Yggðrasil. He, too, grew in size as he drew upon the vigor of Miðgarðr itself. He caught the lunging She-Wolf with one iron-fingered hand and held it at bay even as it shredded his robes and pierced his flesh. His other hand clawed for the heavens, where the vortex of swirling clouds ripped a hole between worlds.

Grimnir felt the chill of Northern ice, the breath of glaciers, as a rime of frost crackled across the ground. The sounds emanating from that jagged tear were distant and phantasmal, but familiar: the clash of steel, the roar of voices, music, harsh laughter, the cries of the dying, howling, monstrous grunting. Grimnir knew it for what it was: the din of the Nine Worlds. And he had an inkling of what came next.

The *skrælingr* backpedaled. He cursed under his breath, turned, and made to run as Odin roared a single word:

"*Gungnir!*"

And suddenly, before even the echo of the Allfather's thunderous voice could fade, the world around him vanished in a harsh and actinic explosion of light. Something struck Grimnir low, in the back, catapulting him into a ruined wall. He heard a crackle, felt the hairs on his neck stir, and then he knew no more . . .

Gífr whistles.

"Aye," Grimnir says. "*I never saw what it was that did me in. A spear, a bolt of lightning from Ásgarðr, who can say, eh? But if it got me, I reckon it took care of that landvættr, too—and most likely every kneeler and cross-kissing hymn-singer left in the Forum. And you think that one-eyed tyrant gives a fig about any of them? Or any of us? Nár! He's protecting his investment in that wyrm, Níðhöggr, though to what end I cannot say.*"

"Tell it in Nástrond when the death-blow falls," Gífr mutters, half to himself, "that thy doom waits not for Vígríðr." He rubs his chin as he turns the words over and over. "No matter how you parse that, it has an ominous ring to it."

"So I thought. Like he means to strike at us before the Gjallarhorn blows. Why, though? We die and come back, just like his precious Einherjar."

"I don't know." Gífr stands, looks up at the cloud-girt sky with the lights of Yggðrasil shimmering beyond the veil. "I don't know, little rat. You're right to be spooked. And you're right about another thing: we need to get to Mímir and find out what that old raven-starver is up to, and who's behind your gift of eternal life. There's too many unanswered questions floating about."

"Twice I'm right?" Grimnir says, grinning. He hitches at his weapons belt, settles it better around his hips. "Small wonders, you old sot."

"I'll go fetch Skaði and a few supplies, make my obeisance to the queen, yonder." Gífr nods at the doors of Varghǫll. "You get your beloved brother, over there, ready to travel." Grimnir follows Gífr's gesture, his good eye alighting on the corpse of the bastard Sægrár.

"I'll get him ready," Grimnir says with a widening grin.

Gífr nods, mounts the steps, and vanishes inside. Grimnir hears Gífr's name shouted in triumph, then turns away. His smile fades. He walks not toward rope-bound Sægrár, but toward the center of the courtyard; he stops, stares up at the roiling sky. Flashes of green and yellow and blue pierce the thunderheads of smoke and forge-vapor. And under that eerie witch-light, he recalls the instant of this last death, the part he kept from Gífr's hearing; the instant Gungnir's energy stripped the life from him—as easily as a gale strips the leaves from a sapling . . .

And suddenly, before even the echo of the Allfather's thunderous voice could fade, the world around him vanished in a harsh and actinic explosion of light. Something struck Grimnir low, in the back, catapulting him into a ruined wall. As the life fled from him, he sensed something impossibly ancient looming over him—something that emerged from the earth itself, a part of it but yet separate from it. A slow, sonorous voice throbbed:

"Heed me, skrælingr!
For thy oaths we heard,
And thy witnesses borne

THE DOOM OF ODIN

Now comes a reckoning;
No rest will there be,
For thee and thine,
Until the Tree is put right.
By blood and by oath,
You are mine!"

Those words haunted him down into the darkness of oblivion ...

GRIMNIR STARES *down at his left hand, clenched into a fist. He opens it, long fingers uncurling. His gaze picks out hieroglyphs of pale scar tissue. Each one tells a tale in itself. A battle fought; a foe ended. A life snatched away by iron's edge. Even that one, the jagged scar in the heel of his left hand. Though it is long healed, Grimnir knows its origins: it was carved by his own blade, to get blood. Grimnir's brows furrow. Blood that he then smeared on the surface of the eight stones he'd found in the valley of the Avon River, more than three hundred years before.*

"It cannot be ..." he mutters. And in the cloud-draped heavens, behind the fume and broil rising from Múspellsheimr and Jötunheimr, Yggðrasil trembles in answer.

12
KAUNHEIMR

A fire crackled in an iron brazier, and by its wan light Snaga sat on his haunches, watching Bálegyr's corpse as it inched closer to the moment of rebirth, when the weird unlife of Nástrond reanimated its limbs and brought him roaring back to consciousness. Already, the edges of the half a dozen ferocious wounds in Bálegyr's head and body were knitting together. Shattered bone writhed under the skin; a new eye grew from the jellied ruin of the old, while the old empty socket rebuilt itself and stayed empty.

Near him, Köttr hissed a question, her voice the slow scrape of flint on steel: "Do you believe him?"

Snaga toyed with the necklace of finger bones that brushed his thin chest. Rat-bone was also close at hand, along with another older *scrag* called Reðr, who was chief of the *scrags* of Kaunheimr. "Reðr's a mate. He heard what he heard. He's got no cause to lie," said Snaga.

Köttr grunted. "So, if we kill the bastard, he'll just come right back? That ain't fair."

"This place . . . it ain't meant to be fair. Wish I could have seen it, though. Ol' Blártunga wading into the fray like a long-toothed hero and all? That would have been choice. Probably thought he'd finally earned his keep, avenging us and all." Snaga snuffled and wiped his nose with the back of his hand.

"Why'd Grimnir go and string him up, then? Why kill him true?"

Snaga said nothing for a long moment. He turned those questions over in his mind, wishing there'd be an answer to them worthy of the deed. He came up empty. When he spoke, his voice was hard as iron. "Same reason Reðr says the witch is trying to put the blame on me, telling Mánavargr I'm some all-powerful conjure-man disguised as a *scrag*. That lot has a problem with being all high-and-mighty. Can't fathom someone less than them, someone like us, might get the drop on them, so they soothe themselves with lies and overreactions. Ain't nothing more, nor nothing less." Snaga *chk*'ed his teeth and gestured at the corpse.

He had watched this process a thousand times, a hundred thousand, maybe more. Still, it fascinated him. Severed limbs crawled back to their masters, or else formed anew; heads that had ridden aloft on fountains of jetting blood now returned like meek wives, aware of their transgressions and prepared to atone for them. Guts writhed back into the jagged tears that had loosed them; every ill and hurt was stitched up by unseen hands and the whole refilled with frothing black blood.

And then, it was time. Blink and you'd miss it.

Snaga leaned closer as Bálegyr's lungs expanded; he bared his teeth in a serrated grin as the fat fool's body quivered, as powerful witchery punched his heart until it started beating on its own. He watched that solitary red eye fly open ...

And in that moment, when life flooded Bálegyr's limbs and rage boiled from the memory of his last death, Snaga was glad he'd had the forethought to lash the long-tooth's wrists and ankles with heavy rope.

"Where is he?" Bálegyr roared, spittle flying as he bolted upright. "Where is that ungrateful swine, Grimnir? Where—" Words caught in his throat as he toppled onto his side; he struggled with the ropes binding his hands and feet, confusion writ across his scarred brow. "Where—?"

"Now, don't go and get your innards in a twist, one eye," Snaga said. "But you ain't behind your poncey walls, no more."

"Where am I?" said Bálegyr. "Untie me, *scrag*!"

"Not yet. Not until you and me come to an understanding. Things have changed, you see, and ain't none of it was our doin'." Snaga rocked back on his heels. "Seems your queen went and got rid of you."

"Liar!" Bálegyr fought to free himself; Snaga knew he wanted nothing more than to wrap those fingers around his throat and squeeze until the *scrag*'s eyes popped out.

"Well, someone killed you, didn't they?"

"That thankless bastard, Grimnir! Showing out and acting all self-important! Took a cheap shot at me and got lucky."

"I'm sure he did. Help him up." Snaga nodded, and from the shadows on either side of the brazier came Rat-bone and Reðr. Together, they wrestled Bálegyr into a sitting position. "There," Snaga said. "We ain't no barbarians, us *scrags*. No matter what you long-tooths might think. And any rat who's cross at Grimnir is a friend of mine."

"What happened? Last thing I remember is . . . is—"

"Grimnir and his mates must have killed the lot of you. Adding insult to that injury, your queen went and tossed you and your boys out like bad meat. What did she say, Köttr?"

The Cat, her voice like the whisper of steel, said: "*Throw him out with the rest of this trash.*"

Snaga nodded. "Aye, that's it. Like trash, she said. And her old da . . . well, he agreed. Said a little hardship would do you some good."

"How do you know all this?"

"I got ears, don't I? I heard that bit straight from your blasted queen's lips. Whatever she's up to, the main thing is she's covering for Grimnir. Letting him do as he pleases."

"Mother of bitches!" Bálegyr's single eye flared in the gloom.

"Now, I ain't one to let an opportunity pass me by, so I had my lads snatch you from the trash-heap and we brought you here."

"What is this place?" Bálegyr's lip curled in disdain at his surroundings. Snaga knew what he saw: the floor of flat stones covered in threadbare rugs and rushes, the rusted iron brazier spitting forth heat, light, and smoke; walls of scavenged timber daubed with clay under a roof of charred beams. "Where have you brought me?"

"Under the Root. This here's *scrag*-town, and Reðr, there, is its chief. He's sent word up to Mánavargr, and we got a meeting with him as soon as you're able."

"Do we, now?" Bálegyr spat. "What am I? Your prize? And you're going to use me, how? To barter some better terms for you and your precious mates, is that it?"

Snaga chuckled, his sullen red eyes lacking humor. "Ain't gonna lie. That was my first thought. Beforetimes, if me and my mates brought in a catch like you we'd eat like kings. But now? Now, things have changed."

"What's changed, *scrag*?"

"Grimnir. I ain't making no claim on you because I want you and Mánavargr to appreciate this situation we find ourselves in. Your boy's out of hand. He's already true-killed one of the Nine Fathers, put Mánavargr's army on its heels, and convinced your precious queen to put you out with the night-soil. Why? What's his play? Who does he serve?"

Bálegyr scowled. "Where is Grimnir now? Do you know?"

"He and his mates have left Nástrond, or they're near to it."

"Left? You're certain?"

"I said it, didn't I?" Snaga's nostrils flared. "They chucked you and twenty-one of your boys out the gates of your fancy hall. All of you, dead and gone. The last one, that scar-faced heel-biter, Sægrár, they kept back as payment to some ferryman. I ain't as smart as you lot, or so you keep tellin' me, but that sounds like they mean to offer Sægrár as payment for passage on the Bone Ferry. And that ain't nothing but a way off this island, is it?"

Bálegyr nodded. After a moment's thought, he squinted at the wiry chief of the *scrags*. "What's in this for you, eh? And don't blow wind up my arse with some half-baked story that you've suddenly become civic-minded."

"I want Grimnir's head."

Bálegyr laughed. "You can have whatever scraps of it are left after I'm done with it."

Snaga uncoiled like a tightly-wound spring. Iron hissed on leather as he drew a knife from the sash about his waist and loomed over Bálegyr. "Wrong answer, you fat one-eyed bastard," he snarled. "I will bleed you like a suckling pig and deliver you up to Mánavargr on a platter before I let anyone kill that son of a bitch but me! I don't care what kind of claim you think you have! And I ain't backing down on this, neither. You want to be a partner or a pawn, one-eye? Choice is yours! Make it quick, 'cause I already know where I stand!"

Bálegyr relented. "Quench your iron, boy," he said. Snaga glared down at him, then after a moment he backed away. "So, what's your plan?"

"Mánavargr's shortsighted," Snaga said, dropping back into a crouch. He toyed with his knife, digging its point into the dirt between the stones of the floor. "The only thing he cares about is being lord of this blasted rock. He's also meddlesome. Now, your queen is meddlesome, too. She meant this little insult as a *diversion*, see? She meant for you to be fuming and scheming with your boys, all of you out from underfoot long enough for Grimnir, that long-tooth he pals around with, and his yellow-eyed harridan to take care of whatever business they're all involved in. You follow me?"

Bálegyr looked askance at him, nodding.

"So, don't fume and scheme," Snaga continued. "Don't waste time. Cozy up to Mánavargr. Act all contrite and humble, let him believe you'll be his puppet, but get him to commit his lads to putting you back on your throne, and fast. Kick that leg of the chair out from under Grimnir. Meantime—"

"Meantime, you'll slip off and go hunting," Bálegyr finished for him.

Snaga nodded. "Lend me a couple of your boys—hardy lads, not easily spooked . . . and not particular about taking orders from a *scrag* like me. We'll catch those three away from Nástrond and then we'll see how much luck Grimnir has."

"It's not luck," replied Bálegyr, his eyes narrowed and trembling as he remembered the speed of Grimnir's return. "That one's got a geas on him, like nothing I've ever seen. Kill him and he comes right back. Whatever that bit of sorcery is, it gives him an edge."

"That's the thing, ain't it?" Snaga stood. "Away from Nástrond, ain't none of us got an edge. Put a hole in his gizzard in Jötunheimr and he'll be just as dead as the rest of us, geas or no. Ain't no coming back from that. Mark my words, one-eye: I'll bring you his head and leave the rest of him for the maggots. We of the same mind, you and me?"

Bálegyr met the *scrag*'s gaze. "We are."

With a nod, Snaga bent and slashed the ropes securing Bálegyr's ankles.

"You can get word to my sons?"

Snaga placed the edge of his knife against the ropes binding Bálegyr's hands. "I can."

"Then send for two of them, Hrungnir and Næfr, and bid them in my name to gather up Skæfloc and that rabble of brigands he calls a clan. The harridan is *his* daughter, and if he wants back in my good graces, he'll go fetch her from the doors of Odin's Hall, if need be!"

Snaga's knife sawed through the tough fibers. With a final swipe, the last of Bálegyr's bonds fell away . . .

And like a striking tiger, the Lord of the Red Eye surged to his feet, one hand wrapping around Snaga's throat. Bálegyr bore the *scrag* back, until his thin shoulders collided with the wood-and-clay walls of the hut. The whole structure trembled under the impact. Bálegyr held his face inches from Snaga's own, teeth bared in a rictus of hate. "You dare bind me up like a slave, you piece of filth?"

Snaga did not react. When that singular red eye tried boring into his own, he did not flinch. He did not wince at Bálegyr's vile-smelling breath, nor try to twist free from his black-nailed grasp. No, Snaga's white-daubed skull-face remained an impassive mask, though the flesh beneath darkened from lack of breath. The *scrag*'s lips moved.

"What was that you said, runt?"

Snaga's voice rasped, barely above a whisper. "Partner . . . or pawn?" His eyes shifted, looking down. Bálegyr followed his gaze.

Snaga's knife was wedged between them, its point aimed at Bálegyr's heart. One shove, one convulsion, and he would once more be at these *scrags'* mercy. Slowly, Bálegyr nodded.

"You got sand, I'll give you that," he said, releasing his grip on Snaga one finger at a time before backing away. The others—Köttr, Rat-bone, and silent Reðr—stood ready, their blades drawn. "If the lot of you had balls the size of *his,* the rest of us might think twice in our dealings with you. It's your play, *scrag*. Let's go up and cozen Mánavargr, see if there's still enough honey in all this vinegar to win back my throne . . ."

Erupting from the rock and soil at that end of Nástrond, the Root was but a gnarled bit of Yggðrasil, the least of its roots; a tendril seamed and scarred and furred with gray-green moss. Even so, it towered over the island like a mountain made of ash wood. And Kaunheimr, the city of the True Sons of Loki, was hewn from its flanks.

From the festering streets of *scrag*-town, huddled in the Root's shadow, Snaga led Bálegyr over a bridge; below them, Lake Gjöll seethed in and out of a cavern created by the underside of the Root. The song of the *sjóvættir* echoed up from the depths where they lurked, hoping for the scraps from Mánavargr's table—the traitors and oathbreakers who were tossed, throat-cut, from the heights of Kaunheimr.

The bridge led to the foot of the Thousand Stairs. This was the town's only street: a flight of steps, landings, and switchbacks that wound up the island-facing side of the Root. Lanterns gave forth pools of light, illuminating curtain-hung doors leading to chambers bored into the wood itself; narrow winding alleys ran off like maggot-holes into the heart of the ash. These lower levels were given over to the *skrælingar* who pledged their support to Mánavargr's flag, the foot-soldiers and the menials, their blood too impure to claim the red cloak of the True Sons of Loki. Hard, wolflike faces looked up from their ale jacks, from their dice games, from their whetstones as Bálegyr and Snaga passed by. Their red eyes were sullen, hate-filled; the eyes of their slatterns burned with the yellow fire of ambition and greed. Among both, Bálegyr saw faces he'd not seen since Mag Tuiredh.

They heard the ring of hammers on anvils as they ascended; the murmur of voices, laughter, the harsh rasp of steel. They smelled meat cooking over a fire. On his right hand, Bálegyr had a view of the Root-end of Nástrond, the shadowed valleys and ridges cloaked in pine and cedar, the fallow fields and orchards, the trade road leading off to Skrælingsalr, where Lútr clung to power by the skin of his teeth. On a clear day—if such a thing ever existed, here—he fancied he could just see the jutting roof peaks of Varghǫll in the distance.

"The cupbearer, up yonder, wants to make this place into a neat, well-ordered kingdom," Bálegyr said. Snaga glanced at him. "A land of fields and granaries, where all the rats know their worth and their place. Bah!" He hawked and spat over the low mossy wall. "Ymir take that fool! This is meant to be a killing field, a place of endless war! The anvil upon which we're forged and reforged, tempered for the dawn of Ragnarök!"

Snaga sucked his teeth. "This Ragnarök's just an old wives' tale, ain't it? The battle to end all battles? The Twilight of the Gods and the Breaking of the Nine Worlds and all that?"

Bálegyr glanced sidelong at the *scrag*. "Kjallandi doesn't think so. Nor that idiot, Grimnir. They think something's gone off, up top."

"What do you think?"

"Me?" Bálegyr caught Snaga by the scruff of the neck and pulled him close; his voice came as a harsh whisper. "I think I'd rather fight all day, then feast and fuck all night before I'd want to sit at a table with these prancing bastards, counting my wheat and my cattle like some bloated Danish king!" At this, Snaga grinned in spite of himself. Bálegyr gave him a playful shake, then turned him loose.

At the next switchback, they met their first red-cloaked True Son of Loki. He was tall, like most of the so-called pure-blooded *kaunar*, and sallow, with straight limbs and a beard like braided wire. His mail was fine mesh; the sword riding his hip bore traceries of gold on its acorn-shaped pommel and silver wire wrapping the grip. His red eyes seethed.

"What have we here?" he said, his speech the unadulterated tongue of the *dvergar* rather than the guttural argot of a Miðgarðr-born *skrælingr*. "Find yourself a little pet, *scrag*? Or is *that* a gift for our lord?"

Snaga gave the *kaunr* a tight, humorless smile.

Bálegyr, though, was not quite as circumspect. He stopped a moment, turned toward the red-cloaked True Son, and looked him up and down. Disdain curled his fleshy lips; his singular eye narrowed as he gave a low, rough chuckle. "For a moment," he said, answering the *kaunr* in the same language, "I thought you might be one of the lords of Kaunheimr, with your fancy mail and your unsullied blade, come to bid me welcome." Bálegyr flashed a jagged grin. "But no . . . too lowborn." He showed him his broad back as he resumed his ascent.

Rage suffused the *kaunr*'s features. The layers of insult were too much for him to bear. With a strangled cry, he bounded after the two of them. "You dare—?"

"Dare what?" Bálegyr roared, rounding on the *kaunr*. "Dare match your feeble play at arrogance? Ha! You call yourself a True Son of Loki, but I do not recall your face at the high table that night. *I* was there, you dolt! I took a cut of meat from the Tangled God's own hand! What did you get, eh? Scraps from a servant?" Bálegyr spat at the *kaunr*'s feet. "Go back to your mother's skirts, boy, before I take that cheeseparer away from you and beat you with it."

Their exchange drew attention. Up and down the Stairs, *kaunar* and *skrælingar* appeared from alleys and doorways—females among them, their yellow eyes brazen with curiosity; a grumble of whispers answered their muttered questions. Red cloaks flared in the gloom as taloned fingers sought haft and hilt.

"Do it," the *kaunr* said, his courage bolstered by the sudden throng. "Do it, and see how far you get."

"You mean to test me, is that it?" Bálegyr drew himself up to his full height. "You think you can skin that daisy-cutter before I get my hands on it, eh? And then what? You'll stab me in the gizzard? Fine! I'll play your game!"

"We ain't got time for this," hissed Snaga.

"Bah! Mánavargr can wait, you runt," Bálegyr snarled, half-turning toward the *scrag*—and presenting his blind side to the sneering *kaunr* in the process. Unable to resist, the True Son of Loki took that bait like a starveling trout.

And like all fish, he was oblivious to the hook. At the first rasp of the *kaunr*'s iron blade against the silver throat of its scabbard, Bálegyr moved. Quick as a snake, he ripped the knife from the threadbare sash wound around Snaga's waist. Twisting, he struck.

At first, the *kaunr* just stood there, sword half-drawn, watching the ends of his beard flutter to the ground. He raised his eyes to meet Bálegyr's wrathful gaze, confusion writ plain across his sallow visage.

A thin ribbon of black blood drooled off the edge of the knife.

"What say you, now?"

The *kaunr* opened his mouth to speak . . . and choked on a torrent of blood foaming up from the severed arteries in his throat. A last gasp of air blew black froth from the deep incision across his windpipe. And as his lungs filled with blood, the *kaunr* finally moved. He staggered toward his mates. Ropes of gore dripped from his chin as he dropped to one knee. Too late, he tried to stem the tide of his life's blood.

Mail clashed as he toppled onto his side and slid down three steps to the landing.

Bálegyr stropped the blade clean on the thigh of his cloth-and-leather trousers before handing it back to Snaga.

The throng's reactions were mixed. Some glowered at the pair of interlopers, muttering threats and fingering hilts. Others grinned at the jest, or else laughed aloud, proving that—in spite of their vaunted blood, so pure and so unmingled—the high-minded True Sons of Loki shared a cruel sense of humor with their Miðgarðr-born cousins.

"Let's go, rat," Bálegyr said, turning from the dying *kaunr.* "Mánavargr's expecting us."

Slowly, and with swagger aplenty, Bálegyr let Snaga lead him through the onlookers and up the remaining Stairs.

Crowning Kaunheimr, at the highest point of the Root, stood Mánavargr's hall, Vingameiðr. *Wind-swept,* it was called, for it creaked like a gallows when the scorching forge-reek blew in from Múspellsheimr, and moaned when the frigid gales brought ice and the stench of death from Helheimr, beyond rocky Niðafjoll. But its foundations were strong, for they were hewn from the bones of Yggðrasil itself.

It was a *stavhǫll,* like his own Varghǫll, with peaked roofs and carved lintels. Its age-blackened walls were green with moss. Bitumen burned in giant iron braziers out front, their flames dancing in the wind and their black smoke adding to the fume. By that harsh orange light, Bálegyr and Snaga saw a figure awaiting them. He was clad in a hauberk of steel chain, a beast-faced helm obscuring his features, and around his shoulders was draped the rich red cloak of the True Sons of Loki.

"Bölthorn," Snaga said.

"The cupbearer's cupbearer," Bálegyr muttered. Still, he sketched what passed for a sincere bow, his head inclined toward the doors of Vingameiðr. "I seek your master's counsel, Bölthorn, and his hospitality. Will he see me?"

"Lord Mánavargr has heard of your misfortune, Bálegyr of the Eye. He awaits you, within." Bölthorn's helmet lent his voice a doom-laden echo. He twitched his cloak aside and gestured that the two of them should follow. Behind them, the throng of *kaunar* and *skrælingar* milled about, their curiosity outstripping their anger.

THE DOOM OF ODIN

The pair ascended the steps to the portico of Vingameiðr, following the red-cloaked herald through the giant brazen doors and into the antechamber of the hall. Here, gold and silver lamps painted living columns hewn from Yggðrasil's ash-wood heart in a warm yellow glow; copper censers spewed incense into the chill air, and thick carpets muffled their footfalls. At a nod from Bölthorn, two *kaunar* guards hauled open the inner doors.

Mánavargr's throne room—and that's precisely what Bálegyr reckoned it to be—was the antithesis of the great hall of Úlfsstaðir. It was quiet and dark, lit by fires only at one end. Drapes made from enemy war-banners and woven tapestries depicting the Battle of the Ironwood hung between columns of living ash. And within that far circle of firelight, on a platform raised up on the helmets of those slain fighting against the True Sons, Mánavargr reclined on a throne of carved wood.

Four other seats were arrayed below his. One was empty; in the other three sat the last of the Nine Fathers of the *kaunar*: mailed Njól, Mánavargr's warlord, who stroked his thatchy beard; nine-fingered Dreki, whose folk were archers, masters of the black yew war-bow that reaped such a red harvest among the lesser Æsir in the Ironwood; and sinister Naglfari, chief of Mánavargr's spies, who in the before-times was a bastard princeling of mixed *dvergar* and *álfar* blood. His eyes, alone, shone like emeralds in the dim light.

"So much for your great victory, eh?" said Mánavargr by way of greeting. "Yesterday, you were the conqueror. Today, you stand before me, hat in hand, begging for scraps."

Bálegyr snarled. "I beg for *nothing*!"

"Then, why have you come?"

Bálegyr glanced sidelong at Snaga. "I've been betrayed! Kjallandi and his blasted daughter have turned on me! They've killed my sons, killed me, and tossed us all out in the cold! I fear they mean to make that bastard of mine, Grimnir, the new lord of the Red Eye!"

Mánavargr's eyes narrowed. "My witch tells me this Grimnir is not of our world. That he is a creature called forth from the depths of Ginnungagap and given a *skrælingr*'s form. Called up by *that* one." The lord of Kaunheimr unfolded one long finger, pointing it at Snaga.

The *scrag* glanced about himself, then scoffed. "Your witch ain't got her head screwed on right," Snaga replied. "I had that kind of power, I'd have done scraped you lot off this rock and set myself up as king."

"Grimnir's my brat, to be sure," said Bálegyr. "There's a geas upon him. Some ancient bit of sorcery. Once he returns—"

"*Returns?*" This from Naglfari, whose voice was like the hiss of a viper.

Bálegyr glanced from him to Mánavargr and back again. "You've not heard? That lout and his mates left Nástrond. Taken the Bone Ferry to parts unknown. No doubt they'll be back, but for now, he is out of our hair. It's time we got ahead of whatever deviltry he has planned."

Njól started to speak, but Mánavargr held up one hand, demanding silence. And he was silent for quite a while, his mind poring over Bálegyr's words and chasing every possible motive for this change of heart. His hooded gaze sized his onetime enemy up like a feral beast, judging when it might break loose of its chains and wreak havoc. And, trying to discern a means to control it. Finally, he bestirred himself. "My hospitality is given, Bálegyr of the Eye." He motioned him closer and indicated the empty seat—Gangr's seat, surely. "Join us, and we will see what Kaunheimr can do to redress this wrong done to you. And you, *scrag*: Will you claim a boon of me, for this unasked-for service?"

"I ain't asking for nothing," Snaga replied.

Mánavargr raised an eyebrow. "A *scrag* without want? There's a twist I did not expect." The others laughed. "Very well. Go, then, but not far. I might have need of you."

With a nod, Snaga turned and slunk from the throne room. At the threshold, he glanced back and saw Bálegyr take the proffered seat, accepting a goblet of wine from a *scrag*-servant. At that moment, he knew that fat one-eyed bastard would play the lot of them like a cheap rebec.

Then, lips thinning into a tight smile, Snaga crossed into the antechamber; the guards levered the doors closed in his wake. He was halfway to the exterior doors, his mind elsewhere, when Iðuna, the Witch of Kaunheimr, drifted from behind a column and into his path. He stopped, instinctively dropping to a half-crouch. Fey-haired and pale, the witch was, her robes silk and silver; piercing eyes gleamed like citrines as she leaned on her ash-wood staff and stared hard at him. Snaga returned her gaze with simmering anger.

THE DOOM OF ODIN

"What manner of mischief are you up to, Thrár, son of Thráinn?"

"My name is Snaga, witch." He made to go around her, but her staff darted out, blocking his way.

"Whatever you call yourself," she purred, "you're out of your depth."

"Ain't what I heard," Snaga replied. "Old Mánavargr tells me you think I'm some wayward conjure-man, dragging devils from the Howling Dark and stuffing them into *skrælingar* skins. That being the case, you think it's wise to get on my bad side?"

For a moment, Iðuna did not move. Her yellow eyes narrowed; then, with a sardonic bow, she stepped from his path. Snaga brushed past her, lips curling in disdain . . . only to be caught by the barrier of her staff, once more.

"I can read you like a runestone, little Snaga," Iðuna said quietly. "*He* has done you ill, and you mean to go after him. This thirst for revenge is written across your brow."

"Bastard won't get away with murdering my friend!" the *scrag* snarled.

Iðuna sighed. "He will. Something protects him, this Grimnir. Something beyond all of us—"

"Beyond you, maybe. But I'd wager the last drop of blood in this scrawny body that once that maggot steps off this blasted rock, ain't nothing going to be there to protect him. Same as the rest of us!" Snaga pushed past Iðuna, knocking her staff aside. As he gained the outer doors, he heard the Witch of Kaunheimr, behind him.

"Only a fool goes forth from Nástrond to seek a reckoning."

Snaga, his mind elsewhere, did not answer.

No ROAD ran from Úlfsstaðir to the rocky shore of Nástrond facing Yggðrasil, but Gífr knew the way. Under skies the color of smoke, shot through with jags of gold, red, orange, and green light, he led them across knifelike ridges by way of overgrown goat trails; he blazed paths through heavily-forested valleys, down washes of loose shale and gullies thick with hellebore and deadly nightshade, skirting ruins like those Grimnir had seen at Gjöll's Inlet.

"Oy, you old sot!"

Gífr glanced back at him. Grimnir and Skaði walked side by side; between them, cunningly yoked, chained, and bent nearly double, shuffled Sægrár. That bastard son of Bálegyr had returned to life an hour ago, filled with enough piss and vinegar to drown a village. But for all his bull-like strength, Sægrár was no match for Gífr's inventiveness. He'd learned how to yoke a stubborn slave from the Romans, who were peerless. Grimnir's contribution had been the gag he'd shoved in Sægrár's mouth and tied there with strips torn from his loincloth. That cut down on the worst of the cursing and hollering. But it had been Skaði's idea to cover his scarred head with a hood of black cloth. *"Let him think we're taking him somewhere else,"* she'd said. *"Tell him we're going to trade him to Mánavargr in exchange for safe passage across the Ash-Road."* Grimnir liked the trim of her sails.

He nodded toward the ruins. "Who claimed this place before us, eh?"

"Before us?" Gífr echoed. "Well, that's a bit of a mystery, little rat. I've heard it said that these piles of rock were here when the first of us woke up with a mouthful of Nástrond's dirt and beheld the place of our eternity."

"They look . . . familiar."

Gífr stopped and stared at the moss-and-ivy-clad remains of an ancient wall standing silent sentinel along the crown of a low hill; its stones were ashlar-cut and fitted without mortar. "Skaagen," he replied quietly. "They look like the walls inside the grave mound at Skaagen."

Grimnir's eyes narrowed. "Aye, you're right." Skaagen was a rocky islet at the northern tip of Jutland, in the Danemark, inaccessible on foot save at low tide; there, unknown hands had raised a stone tower over a flat-topped grave mound. Gífr and his lads had surrounded the whole with a timber palisade. This had been Grimnir's home for more than a century, after the ruin of Orkahaugr in the Kjolen Mountains by the wyrm, Níðhöggr—sent with Odin's blessing to finally end the scourge of the *kaunar* in Miðgarðr. "What's the connection? How did it get *here*?"

"Who can say?" Gífr shrugged.

"The Lokaean Witches," Skaði said. "If you can believe those hags, all this was the Tangled God's doing. They say he stole a bit of land from here, a bit of land from there, and then bid the bog-*jötnar* stitch it all together for him with their witchery. Feh! To hear old Gjálp tell it, Father Loki meant it as a gift for *them*, as repayment for their midwifery. Those three mincing idiots proved they had spines of rotted wood when the Æsir came for Angrboða's children.

They ran like hot metal. Afterward, in his rage, Loki cursed their cowardice and denied them their prize. Instead, he gave Nástrond to his *faithful* servants, those who'd died fighting the blasted Æsir on his behalf."

"Us," Grimnir said.

Skaði made a gesture encompassing the hills and hollows, where things best left alone still dwelled. "That's how they knew where to hide, they said. They were here for the making of Nástrond. Keep in mind, though: both sisters were lying bags of pus."

"Never heard that tale, but it makes as much sense as anything else." Gífr turned away from the ruins. "Let's go, my little rats. We're almost there."

Skaði shoved yoke-bound Sægrár to get him moving. "Leg it, you filth-crusted goat's arse."

Sægrár stumbled forward. Then, quick as a snake, he dug his right foot into the soil for purchase, dipped his left shoulder, and drove that end of the yoke at Skaði with all the strength his bound physique could manage.

It missed her by a hair's breadth. Her yellow eyes flared; cursing, she leaned in and smashed her fist into the center of Sægrár's hooded face. Cartilage crunched. Black blood dribbled from under the bottom edge of the cloth.

"Don't get cute, *arsegót!*"

Sægrár's answer was a low, wet chuckle.

Before he could recover, however, Grimnir came up on his right side. He drove his iron-hard fist into his bastard brother's kidneys. Three successive punches that wrenched a gasp of pain from Sægrár, drawing him to his right to protect that side. Grimnir knotted his hand in the loose ends of Sægrár's hood and cinched it back until it was tight around his throat, throttling him.

Sægrár gurgled.

Grimnir leaned close to his cloth-covered ear. "Keep playing your games," he hissed. "I will choke the life from you and drag you the rest of the way, you milk-blooded bastard. Test me, if you think I won't."

After a moment, Sægrár relented with a nod. Grimnir loosened his grip on the cloth's edge and shoved him forward. The giant *kaunr* stayed bent over a moment. Blood and spittle drooled from beneath the hood; he drew great draughts of air through flared nostrils, coughing around the gag in his mouth as he exhaled through the scarred side of his face.

Though it was muffled, both of them heard his oath: "By Ymir, you're dead rats, the lot of you!"

Grimnir glanced over at Skaði. She winked at him; he answered with a jagged smile. Together, they hoisted Sægrár upright and shoved him after Gífr. "If I had a ducat for every time I heard that," Grimnir said, "I could beat your fool head in with a bag of coins, you whoreson. Now, move!"

Less than an hour later, Gífr led them through a narrow crevasse that threaded between two hills thick with juniper and gnarled cypress. Bracken muffled their steps. Beyond lay a strand of sand and yellowed bone brushed by the leaden waters of Lake Gjöll.

"There," Gífr said, pointing at a crumbling stone jetty protruding into the water.

Grimnir, though, did not hear him. Oblivious, the son of Bálegyr pushed past Gífr to stare at the far horizon, engrossed by what he beheld there. For despite the perpetual gloom, here, at the end of Nástrond, Grimnir was greeted by his first unobstructed view of the impossible dimensions of Yggðrasil. Wreathed in drifting shoals of vapor and fume, the upper reaches of the great Tree scintillated against the void, particolored witch-lights that flowed through the firmament like a river of stars.

"Ymir's blood," Grimnir muttered.

Through a veil of dust and mist, he could see them all—the Nine Worlds of the Tree: the gold and white of Ásgarðr, the green and yellow of Vanaheimr, the silver and gray of Álfheimr; there were the earthy shades of Miðgarðr, the browns and greens and flickers of red; the frozen hues of Jötunheimr, the shades of azure and emerald and glacial white; Grimnir winced at the harsh glimmer of Múspellsheimr, with its reds and oranges of forge-fires and ruddy blacks of bubbling lava. Under those worlds, the glittering yellows and oranges of Svartálfaheimr and Niðavellir were muted, like torches and candles carried against the utter darkness rising from the Howling Dark, the Ginnungagap. And lowest of all, cloaked in mist and bearing only the funereal lights of the dead, Grimnir beheld Helheimr, the Halls of Hel, ringed by the dark fences of Niðafjoll.

A snatch of an ancient song rose unbidden in Grimnir's mind. In a deep and unlovely voice, he sang:

THE DOOM OF ODIN

"I remember yet | these giants of yore,
Who gave me life | in the days gone by;
Nine worlds I know, | the Nine in the Tree
With mighty roots | beneath the mold."

"It's good something I taught you stuck in that sieve you call a brain, little rat," Gífr said.

Grimnir half-turned. "Don't glad-hand yourself too hard," he replied. "Everything *else* you taught me has proved useless, down here."

Scoffing, Gífr went to the shoreside edge of the jetty, where a frame made from worm-eaten wood and long bones stood to one side. Hanging from rusting chains was a concave disc of corroded bronze. Gífr drew his knife and rapped the bronze with the pommel. A deep, discordant *boom* echoed along the deserted shore. Twice more he struck the makeshift gong.

The echo rolled and slowly faded. Grimnir looked out across the water. "What now?" he said.

"Now?" Gífr sheathed his knife. He hitched at his weapons belt and found himself a seat at the landward edge of the jetty. "We wait."

13

THE BONE FERRY

A mist drifted across Lake Gjöll. A solitary shoal of fume that came on in silence, low to the water. Grimnir spied it as he tended to the edge of Hátr, his whetstone rasping down the length of the long-seax's blade. He sat under the makeshift gong, his back resting against one worm-eaten piling. His eyes narrowed as he watched the mist draw nearer to the shore; his hackles rose when he realized it did not move with the wind.

"Look lively," Grimnir muttered, jerking his chin in the direction of the mist-bank.

Gífr, who'd been drowsing in a cradle of rocks, bestirred himself. He opened one eye, following Grimnir's gesture. "Sooner than I expected," he replied. Gífr groaned as he stood, then cast a glance back at Skaði, who kept her eye on a still-struggling Sægrár. "Get him ready." Then, to Grimnir, he said: "Let me do the talking, little rat."

Grimnir clambered to his feet. Sheathing Hátr, he walked to where Skaði was prodding their captive to rise. "Up, you slag," Grimnir said, grasping one end of the yoke and hauling Sægrár to his feet. "Up! Time to see what you're worth." He glanced at Skaði. "Ready to skin out and run, yet?"

"Feh!" she replied. "You'll show your yellow belly before I will, you wretch!"

"Come on, then." Seizing each end of his yoke, they shuffled Sægrár down near the shore's edge. That strange mist shredded and curled into nothing as it neared the jetty; through it, Grimnir glimpsed the keel of an eerie longship, its hull cobbled together from bone. Yellowed bone and blackened bone, bone as white as marble; femurs, tibias, ribs, knobby vertebrae, flared hip bones, and shield-like scapulas took the place of wooden strakes, and mounted on the prow was the skeletal head of a great beast—a dragon of legend—its flaring jaws filled with knifelike teeth.

"Ymir," he heard Skaði mutter. Her yellow eyes were wide as echoes of childhood terrors came back to her. She clenched her teeth, one hand working the hilt of her sword back and forth in its sheath, loosening it in case it was needed. Between them, though blinded to what was happening, Sægrár nevertheless trembled like a newborn lamb.

Along the bulwarks, where raiders would have hung their shields, Grimnir espied a double row of bleached skulls—human, *jötunn, dvergr*—representative of every sort of people who dwelled in Yggðrasil's shadow. No oars propelled the weird craft. Neither did it possess a mast or a crew. It merely drifted from the shelter of its cloaking mist and drew abreast of the jetty. Under its keel, the waters of Lake Gjöll bubbled and frothed. A figure stood in the stern, one gnarled hand on a tiller wrought of pale, smooth bone. He was massive, nearly twice Grimnir's height and easily thrice his weight; a *jötunn*, he was, with skin the color of Northern ice and a long beard whose hue reminded Grimnir of storm clouds. Set deep in a craggy face, eyes as black as a moonless night fixed on the shore.

"Long has it been since I've answered a summons from your isle, *skrælingr*. What seek ye?"

"Passage, O Hárbarðr," Gífr replied. "Across the lake and into the mouth of the Gjöll, as far as the Hræholt Road."

"And what do ye offer?"

Gífr nodded at Grimnir. Together, he and Skaði wrestled with Sægrár, dragging him to the edge of the jetty. Once there, Grimnir kicked his half-brother's legs out from under him, dropping him to his knees despite muffled protests. Gífr reached over and stripped the hood from Sægrár's head. The giant blinked in the sudden light, dazzled by the gleam of the Nine Worlds. His nose was a blood-crusted wreck; dried blood stained his chin and the edges

THE DOOM OF ODIN

of his makeshift gag. Sægrár glanced about, seeking some ally in all this, some way out. Red eyes alight with fear implored Grimnir for succor.

Grimnir, though, merely grinned.

"We offer you blood, O Hárbarðr," said Gífr. "The blood of Bálegyr of the Eye, known from the Elder Days as Dáinn son of Thrár." At this, Grimnir squinted sidelong at Gífr but said nothing.

Brows beetled in thought, the *jötunn*, Hárbarðr, leaned over the skull-studded bulwark of the longship. One ice-hued finger touched Sægrár's chin, forcing his head up as it trailed through the blood from his broken nose. Hárbarðr raised that finger, peered close at the black stain; then, hesitantly, he touched it to his tongue. The *jötunn* scowled and spat.

"Diluted, like all the blood of your kind, *skrælingr*," Hárbarðr said. He glanced about, his eyes fixing upon Skaði. "Give me that one, as well. What say ye?"

Before Gífr could answer, before Skaði could react, Grimnir's voice cracked like an iron-barbed whip. "Touch her," he snarled, "and I will split your miserable skull before I sink that pathetic excuse for a boat!"

With a sharp gesture and a hissed warning, Gífr tried to silence him.

Hárbarðr shifted his black gaze to Grimnir. More amused than angry, the *jötunn* said, "You are high in your own esteem, little *skrælingr*. Name thyself."

Grimnir drew himself up to his full height. "Grimnir, I am called. The Hooded One and the bane of my kin! I am the last of Bálegyr's brood who plagued Miðgarðr; the last *kaunr* to prey on the sons of Adam! I have walked the branches of Yggðrasil and shaken the bones of Ymir! And if you test me, *jötunn*, I will add Ship-wrecker and Slayer of Ferrymen to my many names!"

The giant blinked. His dark eyes narrowed as he recalled something. "The Hooded One. I've heard of a *skrælingr* who calls himself such. The *sjóvættir* speak of him in whispers, afraid to say his name. From chittering Ratatoskr, who bears gossip from Yggðrasil's roots to its tip, I have heard the name, as well. The same Grimnir who killed the Lokaean Witches, cunning Gjálp and fierce Imðr?"

Grimnir's chest swelled. Something between a smile and a sneer played across his harsh features. "One and the same."

"But one of the sisters escaped you, did she not? Cruel Atla? She seeks for you, *skrælingr*. She's sworn vengeance. Does that not frighten you?"

Grimnir thrust his thumbs into his weapons belt. "Why should it? Take *this* as payment," Grimnir nudged Sægrár's shoulder, "and ferry us to the Hræholt Road. When this Atla finds me, I will give you another witch's skull for your collection! What say ye?"

At this, Hárbarðr bared sharp white teeth in a savage grin. "I accept your payment, Grimnir of Nástrond."

Even as the echo of the *jötunn*'s words died, Grimnir heard an eerie grinding, as though the ends of broken bones met and scraped together. Grimnir backpedaled with a sulfurous oath as, from the prow of the ship, two skeletal arms took shape from the tangle of bones. They flexed and stretched, long-fingered and needle-taloned. On his knees, captive Sægrár thrashed and tried to rise. He kicked out as the first one seized him, then the other. The yoke broke under the alien fingers; the chains slithered to the ground and clattered among the rocks. Suddenly free, Sægrár punched and clawed at the skeletal arms until his knuckles and fingers bled. All to no avail. Those hands of mismatched bone seized him and drew him to the keel. *Into* the keel. Sægrár's screams around the gag were high-pitched, tinged with madness, and they did not abate even as the hungry bones of the longship dug into the flesh of his back ...

Over this hideous cacophony, Hárbarðr gestured for the three of them to come aboard.

IT TOOK some time for Sægrár to die. His black and stinking blood stained the prow of the longship as it split the waters of Lake Gjöll; the *sjóvættir* cavorted under its keel like scavengers, laughing and singing at Sægrár's misfortune, eager to snap up the scraps of flesh and offal that fell from the hull as the longship consumed his bones.

Hárbarðr's ferry was not made with the comfort of its passengers in mind. The three of them crouched at the center of the ship, where the mast would have been. If he felt the least bit of consternation over his half-brother's fate, Grimnir did not show it. What was done was done, and it wasn't in his nature to second-guess himself.

THE DOOM OF ODIN

"You think this is what *Naglfar* will be like?" he said suddenly, breaking their silence.

Skaði looked confused. "*Naglfar?*"

"Aye, the Ship of Nails that comes for us after the Gjallarhorn blows."

She shrugged. "Feh! Never given it much thought." There came a long, drawn-out scream from the keel; Skaði shifted her weight. "Hel's teeth!" she said. "Just kill the *arsegót* already."

Gífr rose, suddenly. He glanced back at Hárbarðr, who manned the tiller. The world around them was cloaked in mist. They could not see more than a spear's length of water in any direction, yet somehow the taciturn *jötunn* was able to pilot them—hopefully to their destination.

Grunting, Gífr ambled back to stand next to the Ferryman.

"You think he's getting mercy for that poor wretch, up yonder?"

Grimnir gave a cruel chuckle. "That *poor wretch,* as you call him, would be all too happy to trade places with you, and have a lark at your expense, to boot. *Nár!* I think something else is on his mind." Grimnir strained to hear. Over the gurgling screams, the soft slap of water, and the voices of the *sjóvættir,* he heard a familiar name: *Raðbolg.*

"You must have heard something of him, good Hárbarðr," Gífr was saying. "He walked the Ash-Road from Kaunheimr some time ago, and with two companions he fared forth seeking news of the Tangled God, Father Loki."

"I say to thee, again, Gífr Kjallandi's son: no word has reached my ears concerning Raðbolg Kjallandi's son, or his companions . . . and my ears are long, indeed. If he walked the Ash-Road and fared among the Worlds Below, none marked his coming or his going."

Reluctantly, Gífr nodded. "My thanks, O Hárbarðr."

His brows knitted in a deep frown, Gífr returned to the center of the longship.

"What'd he say?" Grimnir asked. "Had he heard anything about Raðbolg?"

Gífr gave an absent shrug. "Nothing. It seems he has vanished."

"Feh! Is that even possible?"

Gífr glanced up at Skaði. "No. Someone will have seen or heard of him; some spirit seeking retribution will have felt his arrival and spread the word. And if they killed him, no spirit that exists in the Worlds Below could have resisted crowing about doing in a *skrælingr* son of Kjallandi. Something else is afoot, I'll warrant."

They were all silent for a moment; then Grimnir looked askance at his mother's brother. "Something you said to Hárbarðr, back at the shore. You called Bálegyr, that old sot who whelped me, by another name."

"Dáinn son of Thrár?"

"Aye, what's that business about?"

"You remember I told you that dunghill rat, Snaga, was your cousin?"

Grimnir nodded. "You said he was known in those days as Thrár the Younger, son of Thráinn."

"Well, your old da was Thráinn's brother," Gífr said. "Now, Thrár the Elder was a smith of some renown. He was high in King Dvalinn's favor, back in Niðavellir when the world was young. Well, that old bastard had three sons, all of them smiths like their father. Eldest was Thráinn, Snaga's da, who was a smith of gold. Náinn was the middle brother, and he was a smith of iron."

"It was he who forged Sárklungr," Grimnir said. "I've had . . . *dealings* with his sons, back in Miðgarðr. It was Náinn's son Náli who plotted the rebirth of that blasted wyrm, the Malice-Striker."

"Your da, Dáinn, was the youngest, and he was but a lowly smith of silver." Gífr shifted his weight. "Thráinn earned a name out from under his father's shadow by forging the ornaments of the gods. Náinn made his mark by forging the weapons of the lords of Jötunheimr. But little Dáinn . . . he earned nothing, for in his esteem silver was the metal of witches and women, and no great works could be forged alone of silver. That bitterness festered.

"After many long years of toiling in his father's and brothers' shadows, cursing his plight, Dáinn son of Thrár the Elder was visited by Loki's herald." At this, Gífr touched his open palm to his breast and sketched a mocking bow. "My master admired silver and thought it the best and noblest of metals. But there was bad blood between the House of Thrár the Elder and the House of Kjallandi, back then, and your old da would not treat with me."

"My mother was the cause, I'm told," Grimnir said to Skaði. "Náinn wanted her, but she was promised to a son of King Dvalinn—Thrár's standing with the king be damned. Old Náinn even forged Sárklungr for her, hoping to court her into breaking her promise."

THE DOOM OF ODIN

"Even back then, Skríkja was a creature who sought power," said Gífr. "When Dáinn refused to hear it from me what my master was offering, Loki went to him himself. Through honeyed words and false promises, the Tangled God lured Dáinn to the feast-hall of Mánavargr, his cupbearer. There, under the pretense of a *blót*, Loki's servants fed the nine houses of the *dvergar* he had collected from the afterbirth of his monstrous children . . . and we were changed."

"That louse who calls himself my father," Skaði said. "He was no lord. What house claimed his treacherous hide?"

"Skæfloc is one of Hrauðnir's kinsmen," replied Gífr. "A second cousin, on his mother's side. After that first night under Mánavargr's eaves, the Tangled God tasked us with bringing to him those of our kin who might prove useful. Hrauðnir brought Skæfloc on the second or third night, just as King Dvalinn was getting wind that something was amiss.

"That betrayal we owe to the House of Thrár, as well. Thráinn's brat got a taste of the meat Loki was offering, then got scared and ran home to his da. Well, Thráinn choked the life from his son, then complained to his own father, who complained to the king. Meanwhile, Dáinn reveled in his newfound power. He had become stronger, faster, and more savage than his brothers. He renounced the smithing of silver and stole ingots of iron from Náinn. With those, he turned his black-nailed hands to the forging of weapons—especially the mace he dubbed Maugrónðr, the Corpse-Hammer. Dáinn fought and feuded and murdered those who crossed him. Such were his crimes that even before our exile from Niðavellir, Thrár the Elder cursed him for a monster and cast him from their smithy. 'My son is dead!' he exclaimed. 'The Baleful One, I name you!'"

"Bálegyr," Grimnir said.

"Your old da got the last laugh, though. On the night of our flight from Niðavellir, under cloud-girt skies, he and Kjallandi made a pact. They crept into the smithy of Thrár the Elder and slew him as he slept. Then, they struck at the middle brother, Náinn. Kjallandi slew him and took Sárklungr. The last brother, Thráinn, only survived the Long Night because he was off burying his son, who calls himself Snaga, now."

"Feh!" Skaði said. "Explains why those *arsegótar* hate us, so."

"Nothing quite so savage as a war among kinsmen."

Grimnir scowled. "Been meaning to ask you ... how did your witch of a mother end up with that snake, Mánavargr?"

Gífr's eyes grew grim. "Where do you think Skríkja learned her lust for power? Not from our father. Kjallandi has no equal as a warlord, but he is no king. He only wants what he can hold in one fist. Iðuna, though ... Iðuna wants far more than that. Mánavargr's ambition is her lodestone. She—"

Gífr's words trailed off. He stared past Grimnir and Skaði, toward the prow of the longship. Slowly, he stood. "By Ymir, there's a sight you don't see every day." Grimnir glanced sidelong at Skaði, who followed Gífr's lead. She gave a low whistle. Grimnir, his back to the prow, uncoiled from his crouch and turned around.

The mist cloaking the longship was dissipating, tendrils of it curling into the aether and fading. On Grimnir's right hand, he could see the ramparts of the Niðafjoll—those jagged ice mountains that fenced in the borders of Helheimr; on his left, the cold forests of Jötunheimr, a land both mountainous and cruel. The longship moved between them, through the broad estuary of the River Gjöll. And ahead, where the river narrowed, backlit by the myriad witch-lights of Yggðrasil, Grimnir spied a gleaming bridge between the two worlds.

"So that's Gjallarbrú, eh?"

"Aye. The last bridge on the Helvegr, the shadow-road to Hel's gates," Gífr said. Wrought of wood and black iron, the bridge over the Gjöll was covered by a roof thatched in pure gold; beneath it, a sheltered roadway traversed from the worlds of the living to the realm of the dead. "The Tangled God tried to finagle his way over Gjallarbrú, back then, thinking the lands beyond would make a fine fortress for his bride, Angrboða, and their children. The Allfather outplayed him. He set a *jötunn* war-maiden to guard the bridge, and decreed that only the dead were allowed to cross. Try as he might, Father Loki could not get past her. What was her name—?"

"Móðguðr," Hárbarðr said from behind them. "Móðguðr be her name. She guards Gjallarbrú still, shepherding the dead to Helheimr's threshold and keeping all others at bay."

"Aye, Móðguðr." Gífr grunted. "The irony in all that was Hel herself. After the Æsir took Angrboða's children from the Ironwood and presented them to Odin, Hel so unnerved him that the Allfather set her up as the Queen of the Dead, in those same lands her father sought for her birthright."

The longship glided under the Gjallarbrú's arching span; pilings of ancient moss-clad stone rose from each bank; in the shadows under the bridge, unmoving but for their cold yellow eyes, Grimnir spotted a clutch of trolls. They watched the longship pass, their stony faces impassive.

Beyond the bridge, the river frothed serpentine through sheer-walled canyons. On one hand, melt-ice wept from Niðafjoll's brow, and a corpse-wind from Helheimr howled through the high passes; on the other, pine and cedar as old as Time stood sentinel over this contested boundary, swaying in the gale like immortal soldiers in a war of the living versus the dead.

Calmer water lay ahead as the longship drifted into a narrow lake—a *vatr* in the tongue of Grimnir's folk; what the Gaels would call a *loch*—where a hilltop citadel stood in ruins amid a forest of pine, ash, and elder on the Jötunheimr side. Hárbarðr guided his keel toward a strand of pebbles and sand at the foot of that ruin-crowned hill.

The three *skrælingar* gathered up their weapons and belongings. Gífr wore a hauberk of mail over a gambeson of scarlet cloth, the stag's skull that was the symbol of the House of Kjallandi gleaming on his breast. Trousers of heavy leather cased his thighs; of leather, too, were his hobnailed boots, which scraped against the bone strakes of the longship. A broad-bladed sword rode one hip, and he carried a spear and a shield.

Skaði was clad in the same war-rags Grimnir had fetched for her from the lair of the Lokaean Witches—a shirt of mail over a leather gambeson, trousers of reinforced cloth, and iron-nailed boots; her sword and knife, she carried, along with the black war-bow Gífr had given to her before Gjöll's Inlet and two sheaves of broad-headed arrows.

Grimnir, meanwhile, cinched his weapons belt tighter, hitching it around so Hátr's dragon-headed hilt was in easier reach. His long-seax and his bearded axe, his broad Roman dagger, and the stiletto in his boot were his only weapons. His gambeson and his coat of Turkish mail reached nearly to his knees, with the eerie inlaid runes of the Mohammedans in each buckle like talismans against harms that could not befall him.

All three carried cork-stoppered bottles of watered-down mead on woven straps and leather satchels stuffed with whatever rough fare they could lay their black-nailed hands upon: smoked hocks of pork, a pair of roasted squabs, half-gnawed loaves of bread, hard cheese, dried chickpeas, and onions.

The longship's hull crunched against the strand. Gífr glanced from one to the other. "Nail this to your thick skulls, my rats," he said. "This isn't like Nástrond. You take a blade to the gullet, here, and that's the long and worthless skein of your life cut like a stray thread. No more chances. You understand?"

Skaði nodded. Grimnir hawked and spat. "Then we'd best get where we're going and quick, you old sot. Can we get no closer?" Grimnir eyed the ghostly shapes of *sjóvættir* lurking in the shallows. "*Faugh!* Let me go first, then." Without waiting for Gífr or Skaði to acknowledge him, Grimnir went over the side of the longship. He splashed into waist-deep water—water reeking of salt and ash.

The moment his feet touched the bottom, the *sjóvættir* fled.

"What did you do, piss in the water?" Skaði said, dropping in beside him. "You'll have to teach me that trick."

"When I know what that trick is about, you'll be the first to know." Grimnir glanced around him, certain those blasted wights were up to something. The spirits had retreated to deeper water. "Let's go, you old sot!"

Gífr turned to the master of the Bone Ferry as Skaði splashed toward the shore, leaving Grimnir to wait by the side of the longship. "Our thanks, O Hárbarðr."

"Do not thank me, Kjallandi's son. I have done thee no service, and perhaps I have doomed the balance of the Nine Worlds by ferrying thee hence. Only the Fates know for certain."

Gífr answered with a tight smile and a nod, then followed the other two over the side. With Grimnir, he staggered through the weed-choked shallows.

"Do not forget, *skrælingr*," Hárbarðr bellowed, leaning over the skull-studded rail of his longship and poling away from the shore. "I am owed the head of a witch!"

"Hold out your hands, you *jötunn* bastard," Grimnir called over his shoulder. "Let what you are owed fill one, and let shit fill the other. See which one fills fastest!"

Hárbarðr's laughter echoed. "You amuse me, Grimnir of Nástrond! I hope death finds you last!"

"And you, Ferryman!"

Skaði reached shore first. The moment her foot touched solid earth, an earsplitting cacophony arose from the hilltop. Scores of ravens exploded from the ruined citadel. They took wing in all directions, screeching like watchmen who'd seen the enemy. "Feh!" she muttered. "That can't bode well."

"Before the hour is out, every seer, scryer, and *seiðr*-loving giantess will know *kaunar* have set foot in Jötunheimr," Gífr said as he waded ashore, watching the ravens disperse with a jaundiced eye. "It'll be a free-for-all to see who can reach us first, with our heads being the prize. We'd best leg it."

Trees ran almost to the water's edge. Gífr took the lead, then Skaði, her yellow eyes wary; Grimnir brought up the rear. As they ascended the hillside, climbing exposed roots like steps in some arboreal cathedral, Gífr gestured at the way before them. "This is the Hræholt. The Corpse-Wood. If you value your skins, cut no wood from this place."

"Why?"

"Look closer, little rat. Look at the trees."

Grimnir did. Most were gnarled elders, twisted like crones and clad in cloaks of autumnal color; in their shapes Grimnir's single eye discerned patterns: legs, torsos, arms, faces. "What devilry is this?"

"These are the slain children of Hylðemoer, the Elder Mother, the *landvættir*'s graveyard. Cut no wood from Hræholt, you louts! Not if you want to reach Mímisbrunnr in one piece."

Grimnir sniffed, a snarl twisting his lips. "Where is this blasted road we're meant to be taking?"

"We're on it," said Gífr. "Look to your feet."

Grimnir sidestepped and glanced down. Under his heel, set flush with the earth of the Hræholt, were stones of curious design. A ribbon of them climbed through root and tussock, through drifts of leaf mold and the detritus of years unnumbered.

Each stone resembled a flat, upturned face.

What's more, Grimnir could make out details: some were clearly bearded *dvergar*, others *álfar* of both light and dark; there were *jötunn* faces in the mix, and heavy-browed *troldvolk*. He even spied a handful of gimlet-eyed *kaunar*. What was striking, though, was the attitude each face presented. They were, down to the last one, open-mouthed, their features frozen in the exact shrieking instant of death.

"Ymir," Grimnir muttered.

"Cut a branch from one of the Elder Mother's trees," Gífr said, "and this is her retribution."

Grimnir dropped one long-fingered hand to the head of his bearded axe. He tapped black nails against the steel as with his solitary eye he looked askance at the limbs around him.

"Look at you!" Skaði said. "You're actually thinking about it, aren't you? Hacking a limb off just to see? Feh! We're never going to make it to Mímisbrunnr and back again with you pissing about!"

Grimnir bristled. "*Nár!* I'll be the reason you make it back, you cack-bird!"

Skaði, though, merely shook her head and closed the gap between them and Gífr.

From the gnarled boughs of an elder tree, silent as death, a massive raven marked their passage. It did not move, this beast; not a sound did it make, unlike its raucous kin. It merely watched. Watched and remembered.

Mímisbrunnr . . .

Iðuna's yellow eyes opened.

"*Mímisbrunnr*," she whispered.

Far beneath Vingameiðr, where Mánavargr met in conclave with that lout, Bálegyr, the Witch of Kaunheimr sat alone. She sat in a shadow-girt chamber hewn from the living wood of Yggðrasil, stone-flagged and lit by the amber glow of tapers. Iðuna reclined on a high-backed seat carved from sacred ash, wreathed in smoke from a golden brazier; on a low table before her, in a frame of rune-etched stone, rested a mirror made from volcanic glass. This, she studied, her citrine eyes aglow. One taloned finger tapped a tocsin of worry on the arm of her seat.

The mirror gave back no reflection. Instead, it revealed what she could not see; in its darkness, it offered illumination. It offered answers. *Mímisbrunnr.* In her mind, the landscape populated by her enemies began to take shape. That devil, Grimnir, her son, and treacherous Skæfloc's equally treacherous daughter were bound for the Well of Mímir. And, once they had whatever answers they sought, they'd return to Nástrond.

How? How will they return? Iðuna's eyes narrowed. They had no ready currency for that beast, Hárbarðr. *How, then?* "The Ash-Road?" she said. "Or . . . ?"

Her words trailed off as a niggling suspicion formed in the back of her mind. With one clawlike hand, she drew crumbs of resinous incense from a silken bag on the table. These she scattered across the coals of the brazier. A fresh gout of scented smoke arose. Iðuna leaned over the brazier and drew its fumes deep into her lungs.

She exhaled. "*Hugsjá drottningar! Sýna!* Show me Thrár the Younger, son of Thráinn. Let me hear his voice. *Sýna, hugsjá drottningar! Sýna!*" And the mirror heard. Its surface swirled, as though the immense heat of its creation still boiled within. Glass crackled and scraped. Soon, an image took shape, bas-relief figures moving across the surface, their features lacking definition.

Iðuna leaned even closer, incense caressing her raddled cheeks. She bent her will to the mirror. "*Sýna, hugsjá drottningar!*" she hissed.

And suddenly, it was as if she stood among them.

"Because *that's* our way across, long-tooth," Snaga was saying. He stood at the bottom of a deep hollow, where stone slabs were half-buried in the earth like the suggestion of steps. The *scrag* gestured to where a cave overhung with moss and thorn vanished into the hillside. Vapors coiled from within; a keening could be heard—perhaps the wind, or perhaps the fell voices of the spirits haunting this place.

Snaga was not alone. Iðuna's brow furrowed. That murder-sprite, Köttr, stood shoulder to shoulder with him, her knives bared. Arrayed against them were six *skrælingar*. She recognized her daughter's son, Hrungnir, and another of Bálegyr's brood, neck-scarred Næfr, who cradled an axe in one arm. He was as gaunt and spindle-shanked as an old hound, bits of rune-etched bone and amber entwined in his lank black hair. The other four were villains of the lowest sort, knife-biting ruffians in scavenged mail and poorly-tanned hides, as thin as starveling wolves. Skæfloc led them—Skæfloc who had the blighted majesty of a prince; a straight-limbed *kaunr*, beardless and possessed of a sinister gleam to his eyes. He watched with others with a detached, even amused air about him.

"You're an idiot if you think we're going in there!" Hrungnir snapped.

"You want to get that shit-bird or not?" Snaga said. "Me and my mates, we ain't afraid of a little darkness. We're going after that murdering sack of maggots! Bálegyr said you lot were trusty lads. Guess he was wrong—"

"Keep that name out of your filthy mouth, runt!"

"Or what, long-tooth?" Snaga spat. "Go back to your mam's skirts, if you ain't got the sand to do what needs doing! What about the rest of you?"

Skæfloc and his rogues shared glances; then, with a shrug, he said: "We'll follow your lead, *scrag*. If it means getting back in old One-Eye's good graces, then what's a bit of witchery?"

"Count me in," Næfr rasped, nailing Hrungnir with an acidic look. "He's in, too. Keep your stinking mouth closed, you pathetic arse! You talk a fine game but now's the time to put your spine on the scales. We—"

Iðuna silenced the mirror with a curt gesture and leaned back in her seat.

"Come forth," she said, directing her words to an alcove behind her. "Come forth." Suddenly, the air was heavy with menace, with the stench of cairn and barrow. A shadowy form stirred, something death-blue; something swathed in a dark cloak with a slouch hat pulled low. "You heard them? They are taking the Undiræd, the Under-Road. Can you reach them in time?"

The thing shifted its weight; it nodded once.

"Good. My gut tells me that is the way Grimnir will take to return to Nástrond—provided he survives the journey to and from Mímisbrunnr. Go after them, child. Kill Thrár the Younger, son of Thráinn, called Snaga by his people, and all you find with him. Then, hide yourself, and when the time is right kill Grimnir Bálegyr's son and his companions before they touch Nástrond's soil. Fetch me Grimnir's head. Do you understand?"

The figure bowed stiffly before it shuffled back into its alcove, its tread heavy with menace as it took its leave by unseen ways.

And far beneath Vingameiðr, where companies of war-ravens mustered under the banner of the serpent, the Witch of Kaunheimr sat alone, once more.

14
GHOSTS OF IRONWOOD

The skies over Jötunheimr were cold and leaden. Through thick clouds, Grimnir spied the watery disc of the sun. He sat heavily on a shelf of naked rock and scowled at it, wondering how it was he had not noticed it before now. A frigid wind reeking of hoarfrost moaned down from the north—*There's a north, now? Faugh!*—while over his head, leaves of orange, yellow, and umber rattled like skeletal fingers.

Grimnir uncorked his bottle of mead and took a long drink. He waited there as Gífr and Skaði climbed up to join him. The path up from the forest floor, below, was almost sheer—like the wall of a bowl. From where he sat, through a break in the trees, he got a good look at the forest ahead of them. He could discern a line of mountains in the distance, gray and snowcapped; nearer, the landscape was brutal, with rocky folds and ridges clothed in autumnal grandeur. No smoke marred the horizon. And no smoke meant no settlements.

Skaði pulled herself up, panting and cursing under her breath.

"Too much of that easy living," Grimnir said, offering her his mead bottle.

Jaundiced eyes glared at him. "*Fak þú,*" she muttered, snatching the bottle before he could draw it back. She took a long pull of the golden liquor then handed it back, wiping her lips with the back of her hand.

A moment later, Gífr clambered onto the ledge.

"Still alive, you old sot?" Grimnir offered him the bottle, too, but the old *kaunr* shook his head.

"Not as alive as I used to be, little rat."

Grimnir jerked his chin at the sky. "We get a sun, now, eh?"

Gífr followed Grimnir's gesture and looked up, shading his eyes with one sallow hand. Skaði glanced sidelong at Grimnir. "Feh! When did *that* show up?"

"This is a world like Miðgarðr." Gífr lowered his eyes. "Not some way station on the road to Ragnarök. A sun and a moon, night and day . . . it has these things, unlike Nástrond."

"Well, you might have warned us, eh?" Grimnir tucked his bottle back in his knapsack, then stood. The forest around them was preternaturally silent. Save for the wind in the leaves, nothing moved; no birds flitted from branch to bough, no beasts rooted through mast and mold. Even the shrill cry of insects grew still. It was as if the whole of Jötunheimr held its breath, waiting for the violence that was surely to come. Grimnir dropped his hand to the hilt of Hátr, daring whomever watched them to emerge from hiding. "Do you feel that?"

Gífr nodded. "Their eyes are on us."

"Whose eyes?" asked Skaði. She glanced side to side.

"Oh, *álfar, jötnar, dvergar, landvættir* . . . take your pick."

"What are they waiting for?"

Gífr stood. "An opportunity."

"Then we'd best not give them one." Grimnir thrust out a hand and helped Skaði to her feet. "Where to, now, eh?"

They'd followed the Hræholt Road until it petered out under the brow of a stony ridge; there, another trail had taken up the slack. Along the way, the elder and ash trees had thinned, the muted colors of perpetual autumn giving way to the deep evergreen of tall pines, their straight trunks scabrous and black with moss; the trail had wound among them. Now, that vestigial trail was gone, as well, and their way forward rested solely on Gífr's long memory.

"Veer off right. We go along this ridge for a league or three and that will bring us down into the Ironwood. I know a place, a few more leagues on, where we can cop a squat and maybe refill our bottles."

THE DOOM OF ODIN

"We got allies among these *jötunn*, then?"

"I wouldn't call them allies, little rat," Gífr said. "Call them *jötunn* who don't hate us quite as much."

Grimnir snorted and set off in the direction Gífr indicated.

The day waned; leagues dropped away as the three of them loped like hunting wolves through the primeval forest that was the Ironwood. In the most ancient of days, this had been the domain of Járnviðja, who was queen of the troll-women; old Halla, who had dwelled with Grimnir and Gífr in their longhouse beyond Hrafnhaugr, on the shores of Lake Vänern, had been one of her daughters.

"We crossed over from Niðavellir, not far from here," Gífr said; they paused for a moment while Grimnir dug a stone from his boot. "Halla's folk were the first we encountered. Bálegyr wanted to raze their groves and drive the troll-women off, but the rest of us shouted him down. Good thing, too. Turns out, Járnviðja and Angrboða were cousins, and violence against them would have put us on the hook with the Tangled God."

"*Nár!* Bit of a blunt chisel, my old da," Grimnir replied, straightening.

"Even a blunt chisel has its uses."

"Just not as a chisel, eh?"

Hours later, the sky turned to fire as, somewhere beyond the encircling clouds, the pale sun of Jötunheimr set in the west. A blanket of darkness was drawn across the world; through it, an eerie green fire rippled across the heavens. "I saw the same lights over Orkahaugr, before the dragon came," Skaði said, her eyes a weird shade of blue under the curtain of crackling radiance. "*Jötunn*-lights, we called them."

Gífr slowed. He stared up at the night sky. "After the battle, after our flight to Miðgarðr, we were scattered. These same witch-lights danced over the Kjolen Mountains. Those of us who remembered took it as a sign."

"Ah, the great Battle of the Ironwood you gray-hairs wouldn't stop yammering about . . . that was somewhere around here, wasn't it?"

Gífr crested a steep rise and stopped. "No, little rat. It wasn't somewhere *around* here. It was right here."

Grimnir and Skaði came up on either side of him. From the crest of that low hill—where the stone foundations of a watchtower were partially hidden by young trees and bracken—Grimnir spied the remains of a dry moat and a palisade of ancient timbers bisecting a sparsely-cobbled road running north to south. A hundred yards off there was a second hill, also crowned in overgrown stone ruins.

Grimnir snorted. "*This* was how the Tangled God meant to defend his children? A ditch and a fence? *Faugh!* No wonder the Æsir snatched them up so easily."

"Here? No, little fool. These were just the outer works." Gífr started down the hill. In places, wooden steps still existed—though mossy and treacherous. "That road, yonder ... follow it far enough north and you'll come to an ice-bridge that leads to Ásgarðr. South and you'll eventually see the fires of Múspellsheimr. But four leagues on from here," he gestured south, "and you'll come to a hilltop fortress called Jarnfjall, the Iron Mountain. That was Angrboða's hall, and that was where we made our stand.

"This ... this was where we bloodied the Æsir's nose." They followed Gífr down into the defensive works. Emerald lights danced overhead; by that thin illumination Grimnir could see that the moat was a riot of briar and nettles, with a few trees taking root in its rich soil. Some sections of the palisade bore scorch marks; others were torn from the earth by their roots. The broken gates across the road hung from rusted hinges.

"We got wind they were coming, a company of lesser Æsir," Gífr said. "Halla's people heard it from their kin, who heard it from theirs. Rumors had gone all the way up the road to that one-eyed tosspot, Odin. Loki had gotten three children on Angrboða, and to those children the Norns—those weavers of Fate—had sewn on a prophecy of doom."

"The Doom of Odin," Grimnir said.

Skaði frowned. "I thought that was meant for us ... Odin's doom upon our people?"

"The Norns appreciate murk and uncertainty like no others, so they gave the prophecy multiple meanings. Odin took it as a threat to his throne. *Nár,* to his life. Angrboða's monstrous children would spell the end of the Nine Worlds."

"Ragnarök."

"Well, that old doom-starver decided to get in front of this prophecy. He sent a handful of lesser Æsir and Vanir—led by a dolt named Bragi—to fetch Angrboða's children back to Ásgarðr. Odin would decide their fate . . . and Loki's fate, at the same time."

Gífr paused in the shattered gateway. Even now, after what must have been centuries, shards of bone still littered the roadbed; the tall weeds to either side hid *kaunar* skeletons, slumped or sprawled where they fell. "Well, once we got wind of all this, you can probably guess how it went over. This was what we were made for, what we sacrificed the bonds of family for, and we were spoiling for a fight." Gífr turned and looked back north. "And that idiot, Bragi, gave us one."

Grimnir stirred the nearest skeleton with the toe of his boot. It was clad in rusted mail with a broken-hafted axe across its knees. Idly, he wondered who this sack of bones had belonged to. "What happened?"

"Oh, I thought you'd had enough of this old gray-hair's yammerings?"

Grimnir spat. "Well, it's different when you can see it, isn't it?"

Gífr grinned at Skaði, who chuckled deep in her throat.

"Oh, toss off, the lot of you!"

Grimnir started to stalk away, but a word from Gífr brought him up short. "A slaughter. That's what happened. A hundred or so of these lesser Æsir and Vanir followed Bragi south to do Odin's bidding. *Thegns* and *húskarls*, they were, sworn men with a dram of divine blood—just enough to grant them long life and the right to dwell under the eaves of Ásgarðr's halls. I met them right here." Gífr mimicked patting the ground under his feet.

"You?"

"Who else? Was I not the Tangled God's herald? I met them, and I listened while Bragi laid out his purpose. I was to step aside, give them the road, and let my master know the will of Odin was not to be flouted. He wanted Angrboða's children, and woe-betide any who stood in his way.

"Well, I stood," Gífr said, baring yellowed teeth in a fierce grin. "I stood and I laughed in that whoreson's face. He spat and cursed at me, calling me an abomination, a nothing. You could hear the scrape of iron as his dogs drew their steel. 'Is that your answer, *níðingr*?' Bragi roared.

"'No,' I said to him. 'This is!' And that's when Kjallandi sprang our trap." Gífr raised his left hand. "He'd positioned Dreki and his archers out yonder, beyond the palisade. The half-elf Naglfari and his lads were in that direction." He gestured with his right hand. "In cover beyond that low rise, armed with slings and javelins. Here, at the gate, my kin were arrayed on either hand. Half with Raðbolg to my left, and half with Kjallandi to my right." Gífr dropped his hands. Under the curtain of green lightning, a beatific smile settled on his face. "A slaughter. Dreki's lads reaped a red harvest, their arrows sprouting like iron-tipped grain. Naglfari's dogs swept in and took the remaining Vanir, while the Æsir tried and failed to force the gate."

"And that ponce, Bragi?" asked Skaði. "What happened to him?"

Gífr turned. "Held him on the end of my spear while Sárklungr took his head. We took *all* their heads, afterward. Stitched them up in a sack and sent them back to Ásgarðr with the one Vanr we managed to capture. *Let the Tangled God's children be,* we told that red-bearded bench-rider, *and we will let the Allfather's children be. Respect the Norns!*"

Grimnir laughed. "What did they send back, eh?"

Gífr glanced sidelong at him, then nodded away to the south, down the road that led to Jarnfjall. "Keep up, and I'll show you."

Gífr sprang off the mark like an ancient runner, fueled by the heat of past glories. Skaði laughed; her hair flying, she matched Gífr's pace. And Grimnir, looking around at the overgrown defensive works, merely shrugged and set off after them.

The four leagues between the outer works and the gates of Jarnfjall sped by. Gífr led them over hills and into valleys, over creeks and across serpentine ridges. Along the way, through the trees, Grimnir glimpsed the ruins of archaic longhouses—thorn-shrouded and fire-blackened, their carved timbers canted at odd angles, and their roofs long since consumed by flames, the elements, or the slow rot of Time. The halls of his people. Ahead, a naked hill loomed from the rising night mist. Its flanks were fortifications of black stone and rusted iron; crenellated walls and peaked roofs ascended the hillside, and at its crest stood a squat tower, where a single light glimmered from an upper window.

"Jarnfjall," Gífr said. "The Iron Mountain of Angrboða." They came to a spot on the road where they could see the land at the base of the hill—land still riven by trenches and scarred by unimaginable violence, where trees refused to grow and a low mist drifted past piles of age-whitened bone. "You asked what they sent back, little rat? They sent back an army."

Grimnir gave a low whistle.

The road went through a curtain wall, threading the trenches and forged iron obstacles strewn about the inner yard, and ran to the very gates of Jarnfjall, broken and hanging from their hinges. The three of them walked side by side; a slow and measured pace, like priests approaching the holiest-of-holies.

"We abandoned the outer works, back yonder," Gífr said, his voice profaning the silence of the battlefield. Skaði's yellow eyes gleamed in the shadow; by the green and crackling curtains of light, overhead, the ancient battlefield was slowly revealed in all its glory—the mail-clad skeletons in the deep grass at the bottom of the trenches, broken spears and arrows protruding from the earth like stubble from a harvested field; the eerie ghost-glint of iron and steel, rusted blades and links of mail. "Such were their numbers that the troll-women hid themselves away. A thousand Æsir, another thousand Vanir, and their leaders were the lords of Ásgarðr. On the right of their line came Odin's son, Thor, with his blasted hammer, surrounded by the bear-shirted warriors of his hall, Bilskirnir. On the left, the wolf-warriors of Úlfvangr, led by their lord, Tyr. And the center? The center of their line was the glittering horde of Sessrúmnir, the shield-maidens of Freyja, and their golden-haired mistress led them."

In Gífr's words they could hear the echo of ancient strife, the crash and slither of blades, the screams of the dying. Shapes arose from the ground and fought anew, kindled by his imagination; Grimnir reckoned he could feel the thunderous impacts of Mjölnir, Thor's hammer, rising up through his boots as the Thunderer battered through the *kaunar* lines.

"We held them at the curtain wall ... at least, for a time. That's where Gangr and his folk died, though they took a goodly number of Thor's *berserkir* with them. Njól met Tyr in single combat, before the walls, while the wolves of Úlfvangr savaged his kin. And Naglfari's house died with him, slain to the last filthy *scrag*, even as the half-elf fell under the blade of Freyja's spear, Skjálf. The rest of us, we fell back through the trenches to the gates of Jarnfjall."

Those gates stood open, now. Broken. Grimnir stared up at them. Great portals of wrought iron, rune-carved and bound by spells of warding. Spells that snapped like kindling under the onslaught of Mjölnir. Skaði touched one, feeling the carvings with her fingertips.

Gífr exhaled. "This is where it ended. Where we ceased to be proud *kaunar* and became *skrælingar,* instead."

"Is that what you think?" Grimnir half-turned; his single piercing eye caught the look of sadness that crossed Gífr's face. "That we lost our pride?"

"We did not lose it. We sold our birthright on the cheap, little rat, just so a few of us could live. We ran. By Ymir, we turned tail and ran. While Dreki and Mánavargr and their folk held the gates, the few of us who remained legged it up that street, yonder." Gífr moved through the blasted gate and nodded to his right. "Kjallandi thought we were going to fight a running battle, but Iðuna had other plans. My cursed mother opened a gate, a door onto the Ash-Road where none should have existed. Opened it right into the side of a wall hewn from ash planks. I'd never seen the like." The old *kaunr* shook his head.

"Well, Bálegyr wasted no time; he and his sons went headfirst through that doorway with not the faintest idea where they were going. Hrauðnir and Lútr were right on his heels. None of us had many followers left—there were maybe a hundred of us, in all. The rest of them ran through without a glance back. Kjallandi meant to stay, to defend Angrboða and the Tangled God's children to the bitter end. Iðuna, though, would not allow it. This was her moment. No sniveling rat was going to steal her thunder. So, she shoved Kjallandi through the door. Raðbolg and Skríkja went after him—because to lose the path on the Ash-Road meant a death stretched across an eternity—while I stood at the threshold and glared at that blasted witch, my mother. She'd robbed my father of his choice of deaths, and for what? So she could grovel at Freyja's feet? So she could offer up the children of our Father in exchange for her useless life? Aye, I saw it! Before the doorway vanished, I saw Iðuna on her knees, begging the Æsir for mercy . . ."

Gífr turned his head and spat, as though the memory left a bad taste in his mouth. "As for us, we walked the branches of Yggðrasil, escaping Odin's wrath by slipping through a small crack that led up to Miðgarðr. We heard him pronounce his words of doom. We were to be harried, forbidden hospitality, and all men had an obligation to kill us. We were outcasts, doomed to wander, all because—"

"All because you dared defy him, herald," a soft voice said from the green-tinged shadows. Grimnir and Skaði both started, their hands going to the hilts of their blades. Gífr, though, remained still. A figure thrice as tall as the tallest of them shuffled into partial view. Grimnir had the impression of gnarled blue limbs swathed in wolf fur, of stringy red hair constrained by a circlet of iron, and of a sharply-etched face. A face dominated by scarred and empty sockets where eyes should have been.

Gífr fell to his knees. "Our defiance wasn't enough, Mother Angrboða."

SNAGA WAS the first to emerge from the cave mouth and into the emerald-shot night of Jötunheimr, the foul mists of the Undiræd clinging to him like the arms of a spurned lover. On tremulous legs he stumbled, his bones like water; he half-dragged, half-carried the whimpering bundle of knives, nerves, and hair that was Köttr. Snaga managed to make it a dozen paces from the cave mouth before he collapsed in the grass. "Shut it," he gasped to the smaller *scrag*. "Stop your whining. We made it. We're th-through."

Like a bladder losing air, Köttr's whimpers ceased.

Both were soaked to the skin by sweat and by the mists of that watery hell they'd just quit. The white skull decorating Snaga's face had sloughed away, revealing a young visage peppered with old scars, and red eyes as old as Nástrond. He pushed sodden hair off his forehead and looked around. The entrance to the Undiræd lay in a fold of a hill on the banks of the River Gjöll, where crumbling ruins watched the silent forest called Hræholt.

"We made it."

Snaga lay back and breathed. Clouds hid the lights of Yggðrasil from view. Curtains of green fire rippled across the heavens. He lay still for a moment, shoulder to shoulder with Köttr, while memories of that nightmarish journey faded with each exhalation. This time was worse than their first crossing. This time, it was as if the darkness knew them. Snaga recalled faces in the mist, screaming, hands reaching for him from the shadows; he remembered a short, stout form that reminded him of Blártunga—but it was headless and rooting around on the floor of the tunnel like a pig seeking an acorn. Snaga blinked and thrust that memory from his mind.

It was a lie, that memory. An illusion. It meant nothing. They were here;

they'd made it. They'd reached the Corpse-Wood, and soon they'd make that snake Grimnir pay ...

A litany of curses echoed from the cave mouth, behind them; Snaga sat up and twisted around. He spied Næfr emerging from the fumarole like a drunkard, that bastard Hrungnir hard on his heels. The *scrag* grinned. Both were killers fashioned on the anvil of battle, their steel quenched in the blood of countless enemies. Even so, the journey through the Undiræd left both of them pale and shaking. Terror dimmed Næfr's hot red gaze, and Hrungnir looked as though he'd pissed himself.

"By Hel's diseased tit!" Hrungnir said, falling to his knees. "What *was* that?"

Næfr leaned over with his upper body resting on the butt of his axe. "The ... The Ginnungagap," he said, panting. "The Howling Dark. Or as close to it as the likes of us can get without being snatched into oblivion."

"*A little darkness,* my lumpen arse," Hrungnir said, glaring at Snaga. "That's what you said, is it not, *scrag*? *A little darkness*? You lying sack of filth! You should have warned us!"

"You ain't dead, are you, long-tooth?" replied Snaga. Köttr shivered as she rolled onto her hands and knees and then crawled to her feet. With an out-thrust hand, she helped Snaga up. The older *scrag* gestured at the land around them.

"Have a look-see, little Cat," he said quietly. "Find any trace if they came through here, eh? I mean to sniff about that ruin, maybe get a fire going and get us dried out."

"The others?" Köttr rasped.

"Maybe they'll make it out, maybe not."

Köttr nodded; silently, she drifted into the night, bent low as she hunted with the patience of her namesake.

"What does she mean, *the others?*"

Snaga glanced at Næfr. "Skæfloc and his boys."

Hrungnir frowned. "I thought those louts were in front of us?"

"They were." Næfr eyed the cave mouth. "Bah! I'm not going in there to fetch them. You?"

Hrungnir shook his head. "Not risking my neck for the likes of them."

"You lot wait here," growled Snaga.

Both *skrælingar* stared hard at the *scrag*, as though trying to suss out if he was uncommonly brave, uncommonly stupid, or simply trying to make them out to be cowards. Even as Snaga pushed past them, poised to reenter the cave, movement in the mist brought him up short. Skæfloc staggered into view, two of his rogues at his back and leaning heavily against one another.

Skæfloc walked with the strange, leg-weaving gait of a man exhausted from battle. Like the others, he and his rogues were drenched, their red eyes cloudy and haunted by the chaotic touch of the Dark. Skæfloc had a knife drawn—a jagged and curved blade like the tooth of some prehistoric predator. He wiped his nose, lips, and chin with the wrist of his blade-hand. It shook as he extended it, pointing the knife's tip at Snaga.

"I'm going to kill you, *scrag*," he muttered. "I'm going to g-gut you like a suckling pig. You hear me? DO YOU HEAR ME?!"

It was Næfr who interceded. He stopped Skæfloc in his tracks and prodded him back with the head of his axe. "Get ahold of yourself."

"He cost us a good lad!"

"Who?"

"Old Vragi," Skæfloc said. "We lost him back there, around those glowing pools. He . . . He looked into one and—"

"And something reached up and got him?"

Skæfloc nodded. "Grabbed him by the face and pulled him under, not even a cry of warning."

Næfr spat and scrubbed his mouth with the back on one forearm. "A pale hand reached for me, too. Almost had me. We made it, though, eh?"

"We made it," echoed Skæfloc. "We made it." A measure of misplaced arrogance crept back into his spine. He scrubbed his chin with one hand, as though smoothing a beard he did not possess. "Aye. No thanks to you, *scrag*."

"Stop sniveling," Snaga replied, uncowed. "You lot are all alive, ain't ya? Here's the question, though: Think seven of us can handle Grimnir and his mates?"

Næfr chuckled. "Just as easy as eight could—though we shoulda had nine, just to make it square with old Yggðrasil. If your brat can find 'em, we'll set up a little trap for them to blunder into. Then—" Næfr mimicked the drawing of a knife across his throat. "But we're changing our deal, *scrag*. Either old

Kjallandi's son or Skæfloc's snake of a daughter we're taking alive, as payment for the Bone Ferry."

"Aye," Hrungnir said quickly, his eyes brightening at the prospect. "I'm not going back into those blasted caves!"

"Make it dear Skaði, then," said Skæfloc, the sinister gleam rekindled in his eyes. "Agreed?"

Snaga nodded. "So long as none of you ain't gonna try and poach my kill. Grimnir's mine!"

"If you can handle him," Næfr replied, "he's yours. Let's get a fire going, and get something warm in our bellies. The chill of that blasted place still lurks in my bones." He shivered and spat. "Bah! It's like that cave has eyes!"

IÐUNA'S SERVANT *heard the tramp of booted feet as its quarry walked away from the mouth of the cave. It had felt nothing as it trod the dark path of the Undiræd. Terror could gain no purchase with it, nor Fear any traction. The denizens of the Ginnungagap wanted nothing from it, for it possessed neither the life nor the blood they so craved. A shadow, Iðuna's servant was, and it had followed its quarry in silence, a wraith cloaked in gray cloth.*

The thing did not fall upon its prey as soon as their feet touched the soil of Jötunheimr, as the cat upon hapless mice. No. The force that animated its corpse-blue limbs, that fed its muscles and sinews; that clothed its moldering skeleton and gave it purpose—that grim and cold unlife that reeked of the ice-bound peaks of Niðafjoll—that force thrived on despair. It knew to bide its time. Let the terror of the Undiræd loosen its hold over their minds. Let them ease their tensions. Let them eat, drink, and jest. Let them purge their black hearts, those skrælingar, and grasp at the straws of hope. That would make what was to come tastier, more succulent; in the meantime, it would start with the smallest of them . . .

SOON, A fire of old twigs and broken branches crackled among the stones of the ruin. They sat in a semicircle, their backs to the last solid wall left standing—part of an ancient tower, eighteen feet of age-blackened stone, gnawed by Time. If an enemy came for them, they'd have to come from the path. The smell of roasting pork drifted with the smoke. The night overhead deepened, with stars winking through rips in the clouds. Snaga stared up at these.

"Ain't seen a light like that since I was a milk-lipped brat, myself."

"You're still a milk-lipped brat," Hrungnir growled. Snaga glanced sidelong at him.

"Miðgarðr-born, are you?"

Hrungnir thumped his chest. "In the Kjolen Mountains!"

Snaga chuckled. "Niðavellir-born, I was. About twenty or so years after your old da, Bálegyr. He and my da were brothers. Makes me, what? Thousand years older than you?"

"You lie!"

Hrungnir looked to Næfr, who was the eldest of his brothers, for confirmation. But Næfr nodded to the *scrag*. "He's not wrong, you rat. Old Snaga, here, was there in Mánavargr's hall, on that first night of Father Loki's *blót*. He's a *scrag* and not a *kaunr* only because his own da betrayed him."

"Choked the life out of me, that maggot," Snaga muttered. "Said I'd dishonored him by falling for the Tangled God's lies."

Hrungnir grunted. "Well, we could pay your old da a visit, over in Niðavellir. Get a bit of payback, eh? Seeing as we're family and all." Næfr raised an eyebrow and muttered his assent around the rib of pork he was gnawing.

And for the first time in a thousand deaths, Snaga flashed a genuine smile. "It's a far piece, but I know the way. And if we're calling up the Bone Ferry, anyway . . ."

Skæfloc's calculating gaze lifted from the silent observation into the heart of the fire. "Your father, he is a smith of gold, is he not? That means a fair bit of loot."

"We could go back to Nástrond and be set up like kings, lads," Hrungnir said. "Even you, *scrag*." Their laughter echoed among the ruins.

THE SERVANT'S *nostrils flared as it drank in the myriad stenches of the night— stenches it had almost forgotten: the damp stone and moss, the mud along the banks of the River Gjöll, the leaf mold under the spreading boughs of the Hræholt. It tasted the miasma of sweat and piss, garlic and meat, scorched iron and burning pine resin.*

But beneath the night's reek, almost hidden by cloth and mail and stringy flesh, the servant smelled the sweetest prize of all . . . the metallic aroma of hot, frothing gore. It surged just under the skin of its quarry, pumping through their muscular heart and given flavor by the spongelike bags of their internal organs—their liver and their lungs. It pulsed through ropes of arteries, tangled veins, and down to the tiniest of capillaries: the black wine of Miðgarðr. Skrælingr blood.

And it was coming closer.

The small one, the hunter, hove into view. She emerged from the Hræholt and bent her steps toward the path leading to the crest of the hill, to where the pale orange glare of their fire illuminated the ruins. She passed near the cave mouth, and—as quiet as Death—Iðuna's servant followed.

The thing's jaws opened, tendons creaking in the tomb-like silence of the night; its salt-dry tongue flicked out between its fangs of blackened ivory to caress the empty air. It tasted anticipation, acrid and sharp. It tasted blood, pulsing just under the *scrag's* skin. And it tasted . . . something else. It tasted hate. The thing snarled. It knew hate. It knew its shape and its texture. It knew the sundry forms it took. Hate reminded it of its lost life. It loomed over her.

A dozen more steps the little *scrag* took, before she realized something wasn't right. She stopped. A scowl on her half-hidden face, the tiny hunter tilted her head back and sniffed the night air, grimacing at the sudden stench that enveloped her. A knife slid into view. She turned, yellow eyes blazing . . . and saw what was stalking her.

The *scrag* met the servant's hypnotic gaze and went rigid, as though roots of iron anchored her to the spot. And before that scrap of a girl could open her mouth to scream, Iðuna's servant reached out with one corpse-blue hand and crushed her skull.

As THEIR laughter trailed off, Snaga stood. The *scrag* frowned. "Did you hear that?"

Næfr licked grease from his fingers and shook his head. "Probably your mate out there, having a lark."

"Köttr ain't one for larks." Snaga walked to the edge of the ruin, his gangly body backlit against the fire. "Besides, she should've been back by now."

Hrungnir stood and stretched, hitching at his belt, medallions of ivory and bronze riveted to the leather. His sword rattled in its scabbard. "I got to take a piss," he muttered. "I'll have a look around while I'm out there."

★ ★ ★

THE DOOM OF ODIN

HRUNGNIR. IT knew that one. Knew it well, from its life before. And the gaunt one with his fingers in his mouth, that was old Næfr. It knew them, but familiarity would not matter. They were its quarry, now. Its prey. And they would die like the others, like the lifeless scrag it held in one hand.

The tall, gangly one, framed by the hateful fire, cupped his hands and hollered into the night: "Ho, there! Köttr!"

"Shut that hole in your face!" Hrungnir said. "Ymir's balls! Are you trying to call every cack-handed jötunn with a grudge down on our heads?"

"Like a fire ain't gonna let them know?" snapped the gangly one, fierce beyond his years or his station.

Iðuna's servant judged now was the right time to strike, while they milled in uncertainty. With hardly any effort, it slung the dead scrag into their midst . . .

SOMETHING SMALL and heavy pinwheeled from the darkness and struck Snaga full in the chest. Bone cracked against bone, and the tall scrag catapulted backward. The blow sent him staggering through the fire. Pork fat sizzled; a cloak of embers wreathed him as he tried to keep his feet, but he collided with Næfr and the pair of them went down in a tangle of limbs.

But the howls of laughter died in the throats of the other skrælingar as they caught sight of what had hit the scrag. It was a body. The small one, the hunter, Köttr. Her head was a shapeless mass, the plates of her skull broken like the shell of an egg. Her slack face stared at them over one shoulder, her neck bones splintered, her eyes cold and dead.

A smell wafted into the ruin, an eye-watering reek of decay. It was the stench of the grave. Næfr kicked Snaga aside and clawed for his axe. He knew that smell, knew what it meant.

"*Draugr!*" he roared. "Run, you bastards!"

IT STOOD astride the only path from the ruined tower. They came in a rush of steel, a flurry of swords and axes, spears and knives, seeking a way around—or through—it. Its flesh, though, was as hard as calcified bone; no blood pumped through its withered veins, and no organs hung inside the cage of its ribs. It was a thing of corpse-dust and hate. And their steel meant nothing to it.

Hrungnir's sword slammed into its side. It was like striking an oak. The blade cracked and rebounded; lambent eyes peered from under the brim of its slouch hat. It saw a glimmer of recognition in Hrungnir's features. For a half a heartbeat, the skrælingr faltered.

"Y-You!"

Casually, the servant's fist smashed Hrungnir's chest to a pulp, sending shards of bone slashing through his heart. Hrungnir Bálegyr's son was dead before his body struck the ground. Iðuna's servant, her draugr, tore the arms from one of its prey as he tried to escape around him, then took the head off another. One whose face it had a dim memory of came for him with a long, straight sword. The servant caught the blade, snapped it, and drove the broken piece down into the top of the skrælingr's skull. Næfr lunged for it with an axe. The blade thumped into the draugr's flesh, wedging into its hip. Before Næfr could recover, before he could dart around it and make for the safety of the wood, it shattered his spine with a titanic blow, ripped the axe free of its body, and brought it down into the juncture of Næfr's neck and shoulder.

The blow split Næfr in half in a welter of blood and viscera.

Iðuna's servant straightened. Its quarry was still there, across the fire, kneeling beside the dead girl-scrag. The gangly one, the one its mistress had called Thrár the Younger, son of Thráinn, glared up at it.

"I'll have revenge, hel-blár." "Death-blue," he called it. "I'll have it for the both of us!"

The draugr nodded. And, as Thrár the Younger held the dead scrag close, the servant's corpse-blue hands reached for him . . .

STEP BY ponderous step, Angrboða—mother of monsters—shuffled from the shadows. Like Jarnfjall, its mistress was ancient and ruined, a spirit of the Elder World who lived on despite the best efforts of gods and giants. With a sigh, she settled herself on a throne-like pile of rubble a dozen yards inside the great iron gates of her fortress. In the gloom behind her, a covey of crones twittered and fussed.

"Get up, herald," she said, her head cocked to one side. "I am no more a queen now than when last I saw you. Angrboða is simply a name. And that name belongs to an old hag who has outlived her usefulness. Come, come! Get up!"

"Forgive this intrusion, Mother," Gífr said, clambering to his feet. "We come seeking news."

She waved away his apology. "We? You have brought guests, then?" Angrboða's nostrils flared. She snuffled the air. "Ah, one of them has the reek of the upper world about them, the smell of death and of hoarfrost and of ash. And the other . . . a child of bondage? I smell the stench of bitter servitude and of betrayal. Which one are you, *skrælingr*?" She shifted her sightless gaze in Grimnir's direction. "Are you the one who can tell me news of the upper world?"

At this, Grimnir leaned forward and spat into the dust at his feet. "*Faugh!* I guess I am. Grimnir, I am called, son of Bálegyr."

"Bálegyr, eh? Tell me . . . does your father still hump anything that moves?"

"Ha! That one has sown more fields than a legion of whiteskin farmers," replied Grimnir, his lips peeling back in a sneer of contempt. "And not all of them fertile."

Angrboða chuckled, a deep, burbling noise. "What of Miðgarðr, then? Is it true they have forgotten the Old Ways?"

"It's true enough, all right," he said. "A Nailed God holds sway there, now. An interloper from the East, whose followers preach peace and practice war. Made it where it's no longer safe for our kind."

The *jötunn* tsk'ed. "A shame." Her ruined face sought for Skaði. "And you? Have you come seeking an end to your thralldom?"

"Skaði is my name, Mother Angrboða. And I am a thrall no longer."

"Skaði," Angrboða repeated, as though savoring the name. "Yes. Come to me, child. The Æsir took my eyes, but there are more senses than just vision. I would touch your brow, if you would permit me."

Grimnir and Skaði exchanged glances. He shrugged, and slowly she edged closer to the mother of their people. It was her monstrous placenta, after all, that had wrought the Change, that had turned *dvergar* to *kaunar*.

Gífr stirred. "Mother, do you know what has become of the Tangled God? None have seen Loki since that final day, so long ago."

"Oh, it is news of the Tangled God you seek, is it?" she echoed, her voice dripping with scorn. "Concern for our dear Loki's well-being is what has drawn you from the safety of Nástrond's shores?" The shadowy crones behind Angrboða hissed and chittered. "Well, you have come all this way for nothing, herald. I have not seen him nor heard word of his exploits since the Elder Days." She gestured to Skaði. "Closer, child. I do not bite."

Skaði inched nearer to the massive *jötunn*. She hesitated, then reached out and touched Angrboða's hand, her fingers splayed and questing. "I am here, Mother," she said.

A grime-toothed smile cracked the scarred planes of Angrboða's face. With a gentleness that belied her size, she stroked Skaði's hair; beads of silver, bone, and amber ticked and clicked together. "Yellow-eyed and fey," Angrboða murmured, loud enough to reach Skaði's ears and no farther. "Strong and unyielding. Yes, I can see why my sisters favored you, thrall. You have it in you to take great punishment and never break. Yes." The last word came out different, a sibilant hiss.

Skaði's spine stiffened. "Sisters?"

"I had two," she hissed. "Spiteful things, like a matched pair of boils upon my arse ... until you and that thickheaded ape, yonder, went and murdered them!"

Then, quick as a snake, Angrboða snatched Skaði up, her fingers like iron bindings around the *skrælingr*'s torso. Skaði had time for a single fear-tinged curse before the *jötunn* raised her to her mouth and bit through her neck.

So quick was this slaying that even Grimnir, who was as inured to violence as any god of war, was taken aback. He hesitated for the briefest of moments, unable to give credence to what his solitary eye told him. *Skaði* ...

Blood fountained from Skaði's decapitated body; laughing, Angrboða spit her head out, upended her corpse, and let the thick ribbons of black blood fill her mouth. "For poor Gjálp," she gurgled.

Skaði's head came to rest a yard from Grimnir.

As he looked on, the amber-hued gleam of life bled from her eyes ...

"Angrboða!" Gífr's sword rasped from its sheath. "What have you done?"

"I am not Angrboða," the *jötunn* snarled. She slung Skaði's corpse aside and crooked a gnarled finger at Grimnir. "And you! You will pay for dear Imðr's death with your own!"

On that seat of piled rock, wreathed in shadow and memory, the thing posing as Angrboða stiffened. Her legs spasmed. The iron circlet slipped from her forehead, clattering on the moldering stones. The hand that had snatched Skaði up twisted inward with enough force to crack the tendons. Then, her blood-smeared mouth yawned wide, wider, until the jaw hinges broke with an audible crack. Bone splintered; convulsions wracked Angrboða's gnarled

THE DOOM OF ODIN

body as her spine and ribs tore apart. Her skull split, gushing blood and grayish brain matter.

Something white and glistening emerged. Something whose spine and skull were covered in short, bristle-like hair; something with long gangly limbs and bone-tipped talons, with eyes that gleamed like vile yellow lamps, feral and bright. It dragged itself forward, Angrboða's empty sack of a body draped over it like a grisly cloak. A bog-*jötunn* arose from the wreckage that had been the mother of monsters; when it laughed, its voice was a thick, wet gurgle.

Imðr. Gjálp. The Lokaean Witches. Hárbarðr's voice echoed from the back of Grimnir's mind: *One of the sisters escaped you, did she not?* "You're Atla," Grimnir snarled. His lone eye blazed like a beacon of raw, bleeding hate.

"Atla? How—?" Gífr did not have time to finish.

With a roar of anguish, with a primal scream of rage, Grimnir launched himself at the grotesque bog-*jötunn*.

There was a flash of gray and black, and suddenly the crones in Atla's shadow exploded from around her. There were three of them—wiry creatures with ashen skin like a shark's, great black-feathered wings sprouting from their backs. Their faces, long of nose and black of eye, were screwed up in masks of contempt. *Morðavættir,* they were, spirits of death and murder, and they wore the iron-hued sigils and runes of sorcerous thralldom around their bony necks. One slid under Gífr's sword-arm, hooked clawlike fingers into his flesh, and slung him to the ground.

The other two slammed into Grimnir. One clipped his legs, knocking his feet out from under him; the other buffeted him with its wings, dodging his ironlike fists as it shot under his guard and got its limbs around him like throttling cords. They bore him to the earth and spread their weight over him.

It was like being pinned under living statues.

"How, herald?" Atla gurgled. She plucked at the thick skin she wore. "It was easy. This worthless hag did nothing but pine for her *lost love*! Bah! That blasted Loki! I was here, in those days, though I doubt you lot laid eyes upon me. I kept to the shadows, learning what I could and biding my time. But when my idiot sisters had the bright idea to seek out Mímisbrunnr and rob the Allfather of a mere sip of his precious water ... well, need drove me to seek out a hiding place, lest I be found guilty by association." She raised the edges of Angrboða's flayed skin. "How better than to hide in plain sight?

"It was I who sent my darling sisters to Nástrond, where I could keep an eye on them. Or, I tried to. Imagine my anguish when that blasted squirrel that lurks about the limbs of Yggðrasil brought me news of their deaths... their deaths at the hands of a lowly *skrælingr*, no less! I scryed and I worked my sorcery, and I saw you, my nostalgic old fool—Loki's precious herald—and I knew if I played my hunches right, you'd bring this filthy ape right to me."

"Atla," Grimnir snarled, chewing over the name like a gobbet of rotting flesh. "I'm going to kill you like I killed your sisters! I'm going to split you open and bathe in your guts! Do you hear me, hag?"

"Are you?" she replied. "Or are you going to watch while I turn your precious Gífr into my fourth *morðavættr*, then spend the rest of your worthless life licking the shit from my heel, thrall? Bring me the herald!"

Gífr struggled, but the *morðavættr*'s arms were as tight as hemp cords. It half-walked, half-hopped with him in tow.

"Atla," Grimnir hissed. He was on a level with Skaði's head. He stared at the hard planes of her face—lifeless, now, and pale—and felt the last vestiges of control tear loose from the black corners of his soul. Hate burned bright and hot, and into that furnace poured something even greater than him. Something dark and ancient, older than Yggðrasil. He felt the ground beneath him tremble, as though some leviathan awoke from the slumber of eternity. Skaði's head vibrated; the motion caused her face to roll away, as though what spirit was left to her could not bear the thought of what was to come.

"Atla." He spat. The *morðavættr* dragging Gífr forward stopped suddenly, as though it sensed something had writhed and twisted beneath them.

"Bring him!" Atla snapped.

Grimnir's black-nailed hands clawed at the soil of Jötunheimr. He felt power surge through his limbs.

"Atla!" he bellowed, his voice the crack of thunder.

The bog-*jötunn*'s yellow eyes narrowed.

On Grimnir's back, the pair of *morðavættir* struggled to contain him. His strength had become the strength of grinding ice; it had become the strength of mountains. They writhed and punched, clawed and bit, but to no avail.

Slowly, inexorably, Grimnir got first one foot free, then the other. He staggered upright with both murder-crones screeching and flapping, hanging from his arms and back like feathered vermin.

"ATLA!"

His roar was the roar of an avalanche, and his rage no less primordial. Snarling, Grimnir reached back and seized one *morðavættr* by its wing, flinging it from him with an explosive grunt. The beast cartwheeled, righted itself in a chaotic flurry of feathers.

The other Grimnir grappled with. Ignoring its twists and its flailing, its raking claws and piercing teeth, the *skrælingr* caught it by one ankle and one wing joint; the *morðavættr* howled when Grimnir slammed it to the ground, put his foot in the center of its back, and broke both leg and wing. The eerie creature flopped and writhed, trying to escape. Grimnir's hand clawed for the hilt of Hátr.

"Kill him!" Atla bellowed. "Kill him, now! Before he draws that accursed blade!"

The murder-crone on Gífr dropped him; together, the remaining pair of *morðavættir* caught Grimnir up in their wiry arms; their wings beat a furious tempo as they pushed off the ground. Up, they bore him. Up, into the trees. Up, into the green-tinged skies over Jötunheimr. The murder-crones squalled; their wings beat faster. Twenty feet. Thirty. They worked in unison, rising with their burden into the cold night, into the clouds. They did not see Grimnir's blade hand. Over the wind and the rustle of feathers, over their screechings, they did not hear the rasp of steel on leather.

Until it was too late.

"ATLA!" Grimnir roared. Hátr thrust forward; blood fountained as the point of that blade caught the *morðavættr* on his left in the apple of its throat. Grunting, Grimnir tore the long-seax free—nearly taking the murder-crone's head with it. The unison of their wings faltered as the dying *morðavættr* released its hold on him.

Alone, the other creature could not carry him aloft. They hung there, a moment, their momentum reaching its apex before fading. And then, with a perilous cry, the three of them plummeted back toward the ground.

The living *morðavættr* struggled to free itself from Grimnir's iron grasp;

it narrowly avoided his stabbing blade by clasping Grimnir to its withered breast. The dead one fell beside them, spiraling out of control. Slivers of self-preservation crept into the furnace of wrath blazing at Grimnir's core. He looped one arm around the *morðavættr*'s neck, punched it in the face with his hilt-stiffened fist, and rolled so it was under him.

Thirty feet.

Twenty.

Grimnir saw trees flash past; he heard the bone-crunching impact of the dead *morðavættr*; the piercing shriek of the living one. A heartbeat later, he and his clinched enemy met the unyielding ground of Jötunheimr.

Leg bones snapped; pelvises shattered. Vertebrae came apart like beads on a string. Organs exploded. Black blood spewed. Skulls flattened against mossy cobbles, broke apart, and leaked their contents over the roadbed.

And there, in the shadow of the Iron Mountain, far from the soil of Nástrond, Grimnir Bálegyr's son died in the embrace of a *morðavættr*. That murder-crone heard his last breath; it heard the single word he spoke as Oblivion seized them in its cold hands.

At the moment of its death, its ear pressed to Grimnir's lips, the *morðavættr* heard him whisper, "*Skaði*."

15

THE BRIDGE OF BEGGARS

The whispered name echoed through eternity. It joined the wind; it lived on in the patter of the rain. Birds sang it as a song, and the shrill cry of insects amplified it beyond all comprehension.

Skaði.

It was written across the sky by fingers of lightning; spoken to the heavens in the rumble of thunder. It was the sound of rushing waves, of tumbling rocks. It moved the stones of the earth, and shook the bones of Ymir.

Skaði.

It was the last word upon Grimnir's lips when he met Death in the Ironwood of Jötunheimr, and it echoed across the limbs of Yggðrasil . . .

He hears that echo as he slithers through tangles of briar and thorn, his nose to the ground like a hound seeking some elusive bit of prey. He drags her headless body by one limp arm, muttering her name over and again as he roots through drifts of sodden leaves for stones that bear the ancient taint of the Stone Folk, the Cruithne. The Cruithne, who had ruled the island of the Britons and the green jewel of Ériu in the Western Sea even before the tyrant Odin arose in the North. The Cruithne, who had raised great rings of standing stones as temples to their primordial god—called the Shepherd of the Hills. He dredges through mast and muck for some sign because he knows the scratched runes of the Cruithne still ooze traces of their old potency. And if he can find something of theirs, one of their stones—just one!—then perhaps he can force a reckoning . . .

Skaði.

Her name taunts him. The memory of her voice, of her savage embrace, of her sardonic amber gaze. The memory of black blood on yellowed teeth, of the snapping of bones, of her head lying at his feet. Her last moment haunts him, that recollection of her features frozen in shock, that memory of the gleam leaving her eyes.

Skaði.

He claws and digs at the damp soil until, in that final moment of desperation, he finds what he seeks: the foundation of a ring of eight standing stones. It rests in the shadow of a gnarled oak surely as old as Miðgarðr. The elements have worn the stones down like a jötunn's teeth; thorn-draped, they barely come to his knees. Even still, he feels power massing, something welling up from deep in the earth. He treads recklessly around the perimeter of the stones.

"You'll get no blood from me, earth wight! Not this time! You've had a bellyful of it already, haven't you? Nár! You think I don't know it's you who's done this to me? You think I'm daft? What I don't know is why, or how. What do you want, you wretched tree shepherd? Is this your idea of payback for rousing you all those years ago?" He senses the movement of spirits, like a cold breeze tickling the back of his neck; he hears the creak of tree limbs, the faint clash of stone on stone, and the moaning dirge of the dead. Ravens croak in the damp dark overhead. But no answer is forthcoming.

"Faugh! Keep silent, then. But if you can meddle and connive to keep me bouncing from one death to the next, then you can do it for her!" He drags the headless body into the circle of stones, then stands expectantly over it. "I am the Corpse-maker and Life-quencher, the Bringer of Night, the Son of the Wolf and Brother of the Serpent! I am of the flesh of Ymir! Fetch her back, or I swear—by my names and by my oaths!—I will grub out every root and bole until I find you! Do you hear me, you miserable Shepherd of the Hills? Damn your black and rotting heart!"

He feels the spirits recoil from his threats. They raise a dreadful cacophony—earsplitting howls mingle with humanlike sobs and curses—like a mob that does not know whether to be angry or afraid. A breeze buffets him; oak branches clack and rattle but he stands his ground, one eye blazing with impatient fury.

Then, without warning, a voice drives him to his knees. It comes from everywhere, and from nowhere; it is a roar, and a whisper. It is the wind and the rain, the call of

birds and the trill of insects; it is the lightning and the thunder, the waves and the rocks.
It is all, and it is nothing . . .

> "Do ye forget thyself,
> Dark-cheeked child of
> Angrboða's loins?
> Dare ye beard our wrath
> For what cannot be?
> Oaths have ye sworn
> By blood and by blade;
> And now is the time
> For a reckoning."

He resists the primal urge to quail before the power in that voice. He raises his eyes to glare at the oak. "And if I say no? What then? If you cannot do this for me, then crawl back to your hills and leave me be, you blasted wight!"

For a moment, the gnarled oak at the edge of the stone circle grows larger, its spreading limbs twisting and writhing . . . and as he watches, the oak crumbles to ash, burned out from within. The stones hiss and seethe, glowing with the immense heat of something in the earth.

> "Wrong are ye, skrælingr!
> No mere wight am I;
> But master of wights,
> And skrælingar alike.
> Sworn by oath and by blood
> Are ye, but no other;
> So cease thy threats and
> Make good thy promises
> To set the balance right."

He does not move. Glaring, he remains on his knees as the ground around him smokes, as the undergrowth smolders and catches fire. His hate matches the heat erupting from the earth. Her body catches fire, wreathing him in the stench and pork-fat sizzle of *cooking flesh, and still he does not move. His knees burn; his thighs. The ground underfoot turns molten, and still he neither moves nor calls out . . . save for a single word.*

As oblivion reclaims him, he whispers . . .

"Skaði."

SKAÐI.

Her name was on Grimnir's lips as he bolted upright, gasping for breath; he clawed for Hátr's bone hilt but found the blade still sheathed at his hip. Wild-eyed, he sought the green-tinged ruins of Jarnfjall, the winged *morðavættir*, the blood-slimed bulk of that bog-witch, Atla . . .

And then, the agony in his bones hit him. The return to Miðgarðr, to the Nailed God's dominion, sent flensing wires threading through his limbs. Muscles spasmed; tendons twisted and cracked, and reek of iron boiled in brine filled his nostrils.

"Rome," he snarled.

And, true enough, his gaze picked out the anemic remains of the ancient Forum of the Romans. He spied the shattered and smoking roofs of hovels, the scorched and ruined walls, the rutted road where once Caesar had trod— and where the brittle grass of autumn crackled and smoldered. The air was cold and smoky, and stars glittered through rips in the clouds, overhead.

Skaði was dead, far from Nástrond's shores, and Gífr was left in that bog-*jötunn*'s grasp. And he? He was back on Níðhöggr's misbegotten trail, shadowing that old raven-starver, Odin, through the so-called Eternal City.

The *skrælingr* clambered to his feet, weary, empty beyond words. His mail did not flex and move with him; it felt as though whatever had struck him had fused the links, or turned them to slag. With a muttered curse, Grimnir let fall his weapons belt. He unbuckled the Turkish hauberk and shrugged out of it. The back and shoulders of the mail was a melted ruin; he felt the chill touch of air on his skin where it had burned through his gambeson, as well.

He tossed the hauberk aside but kept his gambeson. It would have to do for now.

Grimnir hawked and spat, scrubbed his mouth with the back of one grimy hand, and stared at the aftermath of the battle between the Lord of Ásgarðr and the Mother of Rome. Curiously, the fight was over. He had not come straight back, from unlife to life. Now, the Forum was silent, deserted; no one had crept in to check on their dead, or to rescue their dying. No concerned neighbors; no sign of the local militia, drawn by the clamor.

How long had he been gone?

Was this gap in time the Shepherd's doing? And was that even the Shepherd of the Hills he was dealing with, or was it something masquerading as the god of the ancient Cruithne? Grimnir shook his head. "Blasted godlings and their blasted games," he muttered. Stooping, he caught up his belt, settled it about his waist, and went looking for the victor—or the defeated. He found the latter across the Forum, fetched up against the ruins of the ancient Rostrum.

The She-Wolf of Rome had come out on the losing end of things. Grimnir heard its labored breathing as he approached. At first, he thought perhaps the *landvættr*'s fur still smoldered. But as he drew nearer, however, he realized the curls and coils of vapor he saw were its essence. It lay on its side and it was shrinking, its entire being dissolving into the night sky. Pieces of it broke off and drifted away like dying embers. One eye was sightless, half gone; the other fixed Grimnir with terrible wrath.

"Your kind leave nothing but destruction in their wake, *orcadius*," it said, weakening with each passing moment. "I curse you."

Grimnir dropped to one knee, canting sideways to meet its gaze. "This wasn't my doing, you mangy runt, so keep your curses to yourself. *Faugh!* I have enough of my own. That one—" With a jerk of his chin, he motioned out beyond the Forum in a gesture meant to follow in Odin's footsteps. "—decided to break some ancient compact among the gods. None of that's my business. I don't give a rat's arse about this world. Let it burn, I say! But what *is* my business is the blasted wyrm he's protecting. A beast drawn from the roots of Yggðrasil. The sooner I put a knife in its gullet, the sooner I can be gone from this stinking shithole. This is your little domain, you say. Then surely you can sense it? Where has Níðhöggr gone to ground at, eh?"

The She-Wolf grew thinner with each breath, smaller. It was barely larger than a mastiff, now. Curls of its being spiraled into the darkness. "I cannot," it said after a moment. "But I can sense *him*. The one you call . . . Odin. Make for the Tiber . . . broken bridge to Mons Vaticanus. Heart . . . Heart of their Nailed God's . . ."

The She-Wolf fell silent.

"What does that mean?" Grimnir said. "Heart of their Nailed God? Heart of their Nailed God's what?"

But the She-Wolf of Rome would say no more. With a sigh, the Lupa Romae, the Eternal City's guardian spirit, turned to a haze and drifted over the ruined stones of its ancient demesne. Grimnir's lips curled into a snarl. He rose to his feet and *tsk*'ed a line of spittle after the dissipating vapor.

"I'll find that maggot myself, then, you useless cur," he muttered.

Stopping to snatch a ragged and vermin-ridden blanket from the tumbled-down remains of a shack, then draping it across his shoulders and head like a beggar's cloak, Grimnir gave the Forum one last look before stalking off into the night.

The Capitoline Hill loomed over the ruined Forum; behind this natural bastion, studded with broken domes and columns and gnarled olive trees, the sky glowed like molten copper. Beyond lay the plain of Campo Marzio; this was the new beating heart of Rome, a mix of old stone and new wood, huddled together for protection with the snaking Tiber River at its back. Countless fires seared away the chill of the late autumn night. The flames came from candles and lanterns, from cressets and torches; great braziers spewed sweet-smelling smoke into the air, while bonfires blazed in palazzos across the plain. By this bright orange and yellow glow, the folk of Campo Marzio gathered in the streets.

And Grimnir prowled into their midst. He shied away from the brightest of the fires, and the moth-eaten blanket kept the curious at bay. With his off hand, he clutched it to his breast; its drape hid his gnarled frame, and the hood he'd made by drawing it over his head left only the sharp point of his chin and his thin lips visible—and the ember gleam of his eye. His blade hand never strayed far from the bone hilt of Hátr.

The Italians were a swirling, particolored mob; they capered to the music of drums, trumpets, flutes, and tambourines. Wine shops sold their wares from the backs of wagons; not to be outdone, wandering merchants hawked all manner of savory meats, breads, cheeses, and sweets. Makeshift theaters arose in the centers of broad palazzos, with mimes and bawdy shows, jugglers and dark-robed mountebanks being the order of the evening. Incense and perfume wafted on the night breeze.

From what he gathered, not even a day ago these same rats, who now caroused and humped their way through the streets like a pile of conniving drunkards—jockeying to be first among whores—had been the deadliest of enemies, locked in a brewing civil war pitting the gold-givers, the Barons Colonna and Orsini and their hirelings, against the popular Tribune of Rome, Cola di Rienzo, and his rabble—including old Signore Caetani and his rats he'd overheard out on the Via Appia, earlier in the day. The lot of them met before sundown on the east side of the city, at the Gate of San Lorenzo on the Via Tiburtina, and had their spear-shattering. When it came time to tally the price, it seemed, Colonna and Orsini had come up wanting.

"Dead," Grimnir heard some drunk proclaim as he ghosted past, keeping to the shadows surrounding an open courtyard. Wine sluiced down the man's ill-shaved chin; he waved a joint of beef toward the east. "Stefano Colonna, old Orsini, and all their lads! Dead as Christ on His cross!"

"Blasphemy!" someone else yelled from beyond the knot of rowdies surrounding the man. Knives were bared, clubs came out from under cloaks, and soon the courtyard behind Grimnir echoed with the clash of warring drunkards.

The *skrælingr's* thin lips peeled back in a derisive sneer. Beneath the color and the carnival, the arrogance and the antiquity, Rome was nothing more than a collection of armed camps, each quick to fear what it didn't understand and quicker to draw steel over it. Terrified hymn-singers, the lot of them. Afraid of hellfire, damnation, and the loss of their Nailed God's love. Grimnir gave a bark of laughter. Maggots should have been afraid of what lurked beyond their camps and their candles, their palazzos and their fires. *That* was where the real threat stalked, this night. What killed their guardian spirit now hunted them, and it bore a grudge as old as Rome; it was more real than their paltry, mincing Devil. It was a thing of the Elder World, and it reeked of ancient hoarfrost, of ash and salt-spume, of rich coppery blood and forge-hot iron. And it protected their doom.

Grimnir caught his quarry's scent early on. It left a trail of rumors, fabulous and terrifying tales that spread from palazzo to palazzo. Rumors of sickness, of La Pestilenza; rumors of a giant wolf stalking the age-haunted valleys beyond the hills, and of lightning from a cloudless sky; rumors that *something* had crept into the city from the Underworld, up through the myriad catacombs—*Leviathan,* screamed a one-eyed mendicant priest who claimed to have seen it, *the Beast has come!*

But in a city where priests are second only to God himself, those who carry the embers of unrest under their cassocks can kindle the greatest conflagrations. And that so-called mendicant, that one-eyed priest in gray robes and a slouch hat, whose breath reeked of smoke and ice . . . *he* was a master at conjuring an all-consuming flame from even the meanest of embers. It was, he declared, the night of the world's destruction, the End of Days and the beginning of Armageddon. And the folk of Campo Marzio took this madman's rantings to heart. Fights erupted and fanned out as men with grudges slashed and burned their way through rival neighborhoods; wives killed their husbands and paraded in the streets with their severed heads and mutilated genitals. Husbands killed their wives and sold their daughters to the highest bidder. All because a one-eyed stranger from the North plucked on their fears like a musician playing a lute.

And through it all, Grimnir moved unseen, like one of the countless beggars who called the Eternal City home. He dogged the Allfather's steps, and soon found himself on a high bank overlooking the silver-edged Tiber. Here, in Antiquity, a brick tower had risen from the shore—part of the temple, or of some other structure now lost. Time and the elements had gnawed at the tower's foundations, its square battlements, until only three walls and a crumbling staircase remained. From beneath the tower, an equally ancient tree thrust up from the bones of the earth. Branch and bole intertwined among the rotting bricks, until Grimnir could not say where one began and the other ended. He crouched in the lee of the tower and spied a ramshackle stone-and-timber bridge over the river.

"Broken bridge," he muttered. "And that must be Mons Vaticanus."

A hill rose from the far bank of the river. In its shadow, Grimnir could make out the walls of yet another enclave. A great basilica protected by ramparts, with gates standing open. Grimnir's eyes narrowed. The place looked as disreputable as the bridge leading to it—weed-choked and rotting, its stones crumbling and its gates hanging from rusted hinges. And like iron to a lodestone, every tramp and vagrant in Rome seemed drawn to the place.

Companies of cadgers and vagabonds thronged the bridge, setting the wood to creak and sway dangerously over the night-dark Tiber. Lepers and mendicants jostled one another for primacy, all of them drawn by the chanted words of a gray-clad priest standing atop a plinth on the far bank, a one-eyed mendicant:

> *"Come thee, children, | and cross the bridge,*
> *It is the will of the Lord thy God!*
> *Come thee, children, | and tarry not,*
> *Claim the reward that Heaven sent!"*

"Wily old bench-hugger," Grimnir murmured. He reckoned this "heaven-sent reward" Odin was flogging to these unsuspecting sheep had a lot in common with the Malice-Striker's gullet, their blood, and the hidden chains of thralldom. Yes, Grimnir could smell his prey, even over the miasma of the river—the mingled stenches of sulfur and grave-rot that tainted the air in Níðhöggr's wake. The Malice-Striker was just across the Tiber, lurking in the decayed ruin of the Nailed God's basilica. And to get to it, Grimnir first had to thread the needle under its master's nose.

> *"Come thee, children, | and cross the bridge."*

The bridge was the only way across. He could see no boats along this desolate stretch of the shore, nor any logs sturdy enough to bear his weight. That weight—from the iron in his black blood and the marrow in his bones—made him a piss-poor swimmer, to boot. And, the Tiber's current flowed *away* from the bridge, back the way he'd come. No, it had to be this bridge, and it had to be now.

> *"Come thee, children, | and cross the bridge."*

It felt wrong, but Grimnir knew it could be done. And he could do it. He could slip past that one-eyed raven-starver, creep into the enclave, yonder, and put the Malice-Striker to the knife before old Odin was any wiser. Aye, he just needed cover.

"Come thee, children, | and cross the bridge."

Not far from where he crouched, Grimnir saw a knot of stragglers emerge from behind a crumbling stone fence. They bent their steps toward the bridge, and they went without the need for secrecy or for silence. None of them took note of the gnarled, wool-shrouded figure who joined the tail of their cortege.

"What is that place? A church?" one of the younger beggars piped up, a lad barely into his fifteenth year. A toothless graybeard wrapped a fatherly arm around the young beggar's shoulder.

"Saint Peter's, that is," the oldster said, gesturing. "When I was your age, boy, that was the heart of all Christendom. Where God himself lived when he came down from Heaven to visit his flock! And he spoke to us in good Italian through his earthly emissary, the Pope. Aye, those were days of wine and finery, lad. Fat priests handing out scraps from their table, cardinals with pockets full of gold *bezants* for the poor and the needy ... and we are poor and needy, ain't we?"

"What happened to it?"

Grimnir perked up his ears.

The graybeard spat in the dirt. "The old Pope died, and those treacherous cardinals elected a buggering Frenchman to be God's emissary! A *Frenchman*! And you know what sort of liars and thieves those Gallic bastards are! Well, he refused the call to sit upon the Throne of Saint Peter, here in the blessed city. Instead, he up and moved God's entire court to France, to some pigsty called Avignon. Been there for forty years now."

The heart of all Christendom, Grimnir surmised, *must be what the She-Wolf meant ... the heart of the Nailed God's kingdom.* Aye, that made sense.

As they neared the bridgehead, the cortege of beggars fell silent. They all listened, entranced, to the lilting chant of the so-called priest across the river. The lot of them joined the throng elbowing its way across the groaning bridge—little more than boards spiked to ancient foundations. Grimnir heard yelps, and he heard the occasional scream followed by splashes as beggars at the edges of the mass slipped and fell into the Tiber.

Grimnir moved with them and kept his head down. Odin's voice droned on, never changing. He shuffled his feet, moving like one of the downtrodden.

> "Come thee, children, | and cross the bridge,
> It is the will of the Lord thy God!"

The sound of it, the cadence, set his teeth on edge. Something in the back of his mind, something not of him, screamed for him not to do this, screamed that it was wrong. But Grimnir knew in his belly that he *could* do it. That he should. Just slip across . . .

Something twisted in his guts. He felt the hot rush of bile sear the back of his throat.

> "Come thee, children, | and tarry not,
> Claim the reward that Heaven sent!"

"*Faugh!*" Grimnir snarled under his breath. Head bowed, he hawked and spat between his feet.

Behind him, a rough hand shoved him hard, sending him into the back of the leper in front of him. "Show some respect, you shit-eating pig!" a foul-breathed beggar—larger than the others—said. "You're on God's front porch, not some Suburra bawdy house!" Others laughed and jostled him; the graybeard and his young protégé turned their heads and glared.

On his best day, Grimnir Bálegyr's son had little enough patience. But this . . . this was not his best day. With the raw wound that was Skaði's death still fresh and bleeding, with the unchecked rage at the bog-witch Atla still boiling in his chest, and with the feeling of being a pawn in a game between warring gods—all coupled with his own inborn ill-humor—a harsh word spoken at the wrong moment had the potential to be the feather that tipped the scale. But a word and a blow? An insult from some gap-toothed wheedler reeking of self-importance? *Nár!* That was a step too far.

The black-nailed hand holding the blanket tight around his shoulders loosened as Grimnir whirled, his single eye fixing the beggar who had laid hands upon him with a look that could scorch iron. In that moment, with the rage in the iron pit of his belly displacing the sense of certainty, Grimnir saw the truth of the Allfather's subtle sorcery. He was isolated. Alone. Drawn to a spot over the Tiber River on a bridge fashioned from driftwood and spittle. And he was cheek by jowl with hundreds of zealous fools who had nothing left to lose in this life, but everything to gain in the promise of eternity.

Too late, Grimnir realized he'd walked right into Odin's trap.

He reckoned there was no more use in hiding. Sneering, he let the blanket slip from his shoulders; he straightened, drew himself up to his full height, and tossed his head back in a gesture of challenge. Beads of gold, silver, and bone ticked together. His single red eye blazed with wrath. The other gleamed like cold ivory, the silver runes etched into its iris glittering in the chill air. As the beggars around him recoiled from his savage appearance, Grimnir swept Hátr from its scabbard.

"Lay a hand on me again, you rat, and you'll draw back a stump!"

Anger replaced fear on the milling beggars' grimy faces. The big one was on the verge of lunging for Grimnir when a sharp voice cracked over the throng. A voice brimming with power:

> *"More lives have ye | than Freyja's cats,*
> *Dark child of Niðavellir;*
> *Thrice now, is it? | When thy portion be one?*
> *Worthy of Loki is your greed."*

"You chide me, oathbreaker?" Grimnir roared, turning to face the figure in the gray cloak and slouch hat. "Is that not what you've become? A breaker of oaths and defiler of compacts?" Grimnir's words touched a nerve. Across the river, the Allfather struck his staff against the plinth in a fit of pique. The sound carried like thunder.

> *"My business is none | of thine, skrælingr,*
> *So keep thy nose from it!"*

THE DOOM OF ODIN

Grimnir bared his teeth. "I want nothing to do with your business, lord of maggots! What I want is your blasted pet! The one you hide, yonder. Fetch out that wretch, Malice-Striker, and I will put an end to this!"

Their eyes met; a stare as cold as Northern ice met one as hot as a smelting fire. Neither looked away; neither ceded an inch of ground. After a moment, Odin *tsk*'ed.

> *"What thou wish for, | thou cannot have,*
> *Bastard of Angrboða!*
> *And no compromise | can exist between*
> *The Wolf and the Serpent."*

"As you will," replied Grimnir with a shrug. He walked toward the far end of the bridge, toward Odin; with the edge and the point of Hátr, he moved beggars from his path. Soon, they parted of their own accord to let him pass. Their rheumy eyes glared at him as he strode on. "What is another death to me, eh? My mother's sire told me, not long past, that we *kaunar* are like the steel in this blade. Age and neglect dulls our edge, it weakens us. But slaughter is our anvil. Slaughter forges us into deadlier fighters. It hammers us, folds us, and gives us strength. And death? Death is but the quench. *Nár!* When all is said and done, you bench-hugging raven-starver, another death will make me stronger, but what will it make you?"

Odin chuckled. Using his staff for support, he stepped off the plinth. His cloak swirled around his legs as he started to turn away, then stopped. From beneath the brim of his hat, that singular eye—the other a gaping socket—pierced Grimnir with its hard-edged gleam.

> *"Death comes never for me, | wretched* skrælingr,
> *But only for thee;*
> *And this time, I shall not | let thee from my sight.*
> *Bring him, my children!"*

And like a pack of dogs suddenly let off their leashes, the collective of beggars surrounding Grimnir came for him in a writhing, howling mass. In the split second before their grasping hands reached him, the *skrælingr* heard once more the voice of Kjallandi, deep and as heavy as the weight of his years: *Killing is in our nature. It is our nature, what we were bred for—the wrack and ruin of war; it is the purpose given to us by the Tangled God. What does it matter if we kill over the least slight or the greatest insult?*

To Grimnir, in this moment, it mattered not at all. As that first grimy hand reached him, as the first droplets of rage-blown spittle touched his cheek, he poured out every last dram of wrath, rancor, and choler left in the cauldron of his being. Thus, when the first beggar seized him by the ragged breast of his gambeson, what he seized in truth was not a creature of the Elder World but a hate-fueled machine of slaughter.

That beggar died with a foot of steel in his gullet. With a howl of laughter, Grimnir whirled and sidestepped; he ducked and wove, and Hátr left freshets of spilled blood in its wake. Fingers and hands flew from the stumps of arms. An unshaven throat met the honed edge of Grimnir's long-seax. Eyes were slashed, bellies ripped, and groins pierced. A fey-haired woman hurled herself at Grimnir, missed, and took two other snarling curs with her when she pitched over the edge of the bridge. Another beggar tripped over his own entrails. Gore-slick boards grew treacherous, and the patter of blood from the bridge to the breast of the Tiber sounded like a winter's rain.

The son of Bálegyr could not endure. The bridge was too narrow, the press of bodies too numerous; their eagerness to die in the service of the Lord was too ardent. It was only a matter of time. It began when a dying blighter locked his stringy arms around Grimnir's knees. The *skrælingr* tottered a moment; he slashed down at the beggar even as another pair seized his off hand and arm. Their legs gave way, and their added weight pulled Grimnir even more off-balance.

Suddenly, a rush of stinking and leprous beggars overwhelmed him. Filth-crusted nails scratched at his face; rotting teeth bit his hand. Fists flailed and punched, and shuffling feet kicked him as he tried to rise, to break free of their myriad grasps. Quilted cotton ripped as they shredded the gambeson from his shoulders. Fingers knotted in his hair, wrenching his neck this way and that. A thumb went for his eyes, missed, and retreated with a yelp when Grimnir bit the tip of it off and spat it into a beggar's face.

THE DOOM OF ODIN

And so, shackled by chains of human flesh, Grimnir felt himself hoisted into the air; he felt himself borne along, across the bridge, and through the open gate in the crumbling walls surrounding the ruined Basilica of Saint Peter...

THE LIGHT of a bonfire painted the atrium of Saint Peter's the color of blood. Rough hands had carried Grimnir up the cracked and broken steps of the basilica and through the ramshackle gatehouse—its wooden doors long since gone into the belly of some squatters' fire. They carried him across the portico and into the weed-choked atrium, where colonnades of scavenged marble were cloaked in autumnal ivy; the broken fountain at the atrium's center played host to the spreading boughs of a young and vigorous oak tree.

Though he struggled and kicked and head-butted any idiot who strayed too close, the beggars nevertheless wrestled Grimnir's weapons belt from around his waist and used the thick leather to bind his hands. His feet were secured with strips of his torn gambeson, and around his neck the chief of the beggars—a tall man with a patriarch's beard and small, vicious teeth—tightened a hempen noose. The other end of the rope went over an oak branch. And, by increments, the beggars hoisted Grimnir up onto the tips of his toes. Air whistled between his clenched teeth as he spun slowly.

"Behold, my lord!" the beggar-chief said, over the din of the throng and the crackle of the bonfire. Others brandished makeshift torches. "What shall we do with him?"

Sitting on the steps leading from the atrium to the shadowed heart of the basilica, the Allfather sat alone. His staff rested in the crook of his shoulder, and in his gnarled hands he cradled Grimnir's long-seax, Hátr. Behind him, emerging from the gloom, the *skrælingr* beheld a long and sinuous neck rising over the Lord of Ásgarðr's shoulder. Patches of leprous fungus grew between age-blackened plates of bone; a single, baleful green eye blazed with bloodlust as its forked tongue darted between long fangs.

"*Níðingr,*" the Malice-Striker whispered, and the exhalation from its jaws bore the jaundiced tinge of pestilence.

Odin glanced sidelong at the wyrm.

"Long have ye suffered | for this filth's blood-thirst,
So upon ye word I hang his doom;
If the Norns manage not | his fate's warp and weft,
Then their knife Yggðrasil's wyrm must wield.
"What say ye?"

Níðhöggr's reply was long and drawn-out, a sibilant hiss wreathed in disease: "*Death.*"

With a nod, Odin tossed the long-seax at the feet of the beggar-chief. That one stooped and retrieved it; around him, his folk cheered, their shadows cavorting against the atrium's walls. And hanging there by his neck, his toes barely touching the ground and his face blackened from congested blood, Grimnir saw his doom written in the beggars' scabbed and dirty faces, in their dull and hate-filled eyes.

And he heard it in Odin's command:

"Come thee, children, and | send him to the Lord."

As the torture began, as the knives came out and the strangling rope tightened, as black blood from a thousand cuts pattered on the weed-edged flagstones of the atrium, Grimnir's jaws became like clamps of iron. Nothing but ragged breath escaped them, even when the knives ripped deeper and deeper ...

Overhead, a shoal of fumes from some great burning in Múspellsheimr drifts over the face of Yggðrasil, dimming its lights and bringing a hint of true night to Nástrond's shores. Still, even by the thin radiance that filters through the boiling clouds—like starlight on a clear night—Grimnir is able to find his way.

He spies the glimmer of light at the heart of a small grove, oak and willow rustling in the warm breeze; his keen ears catch the soft rasp of steel on stone. Around him, he sees familiar ruins, ivy-clad walls of pitted stone and columns broken off like rotted teeth.

There, he finds Skaði sitting beside a small fire. She'd gone back to his camp, next to a spring that trickled from the rocks; there, she tends to the edge of his long-seax with a whetstone.

"You're dead," he mutters, by way of greeting.

Her yellow eyes glitter with mischief. "Feh! So are you, you yammering ape. Or near to it."

"So, what now, eh?" Grimnir sits beside her. "Is this what happens when we kick off somewhere besides Nástrond? We live on in a memory until the maggots finish off what's left of our blasted corpse?"

"Hel's tits!" she says, squinting down Hátr's length. Black blood drips from the blade. "How should I know? This is your memory, idiot. As far as I know, you're still out there, wasting time while you wait for one of those conniving bench-huggers to finally grow a pair of balls and do you in, once and for all."

Grimnir chuckles. "So, while those blasted kneelers torture me for old One-Eye and his wyrm's enjoyment, I'm going to torture myself with the memory of the first furrow I plowed in a thousand years. By Ymir, those hymn-singers must have truly rubbed off on me."

She glances from the blood-smeared blade. Quietly, she says: "Aye, I was fond of you, too, you arrogant arsegót."

Grimnir lapses into silence, his brows knitted into a frown. "There is no word for it in our tongue," he says, after a long moment. "No word for what the whiteskins call love. Old Gífr always thought that was a strange one. Lust, aye. We have a dozen words for that. Fucking and fighting, we have hundreds of words for both—some the same blasted thing. Faugh! We have scores of words, alone, for slaughter. But unless it's a love of slaughter . . ." He trails off. "I would have slaughtered all of them, for you."

"I know," she whispers.

"I have to go," he says, wincing. Blood pours from the blade in her hands. Thick ropes of it. His heart's blood.

"What happens now?"

Grimnir rises. "Wisdom tells me this is the end of the road. It tells me I died beyond Nástrond's shores, so the jig is up. But my gut . . . my gut tells me there's more for me yet to do. Whatever's been pulling my strings and making me dance to its tune isn't quite done with me, I think."

"So you'll go back?" Skaði's yellow eyes watch him as he retraces his steps.

"I will."

"And when you get there?"

Grimnir stops. He looks back at her, his single burning eye narrowing. "Oh, when I get back, I mean to take the blood-price for your life out of that bog-jötunn's hide.

And then, I mean to find this Mímir and beat the answers out of him. By Ymir, you have my oath on it."

"I'll hold you to it," she says, her voice fading. "Sing a song over my cairn, Grimnir Kin-slayer . . ."

Grimnir shivered. He pried his eye open. Dawn was not far off. The eastern sky lightened, star-flecked velvet giving way to a thin ribbon of fire. Through sheeting blood, through gut-twisting agony, Grimnir had uttered not a sound—until just this moment, when a single word spilled unbidden from his lips:

"Skaði."

Inches from him, he saw the bearded visage of the beggar-chief, his cheeks spackled with black droplets. "What did you say, child of Satan?"

Grimnir's lacerated face writhed into a horrific smile. Quick as a snake, he lunged forward and caught the chief's bulbous nose between broken teeth. Like a man tearing flesh from a joint of beef, he wrenched his head from one side to the other and sawed through the tough cartilage. Rich, coppery blood filled his mouth. The beggar-chief howled as the *skrælingr* ripped the nose from his face and spat it out with a flint-hard chuckle.

Enraged, the mutilated chief plunged Hátr's blood-slimed blade deep into Grimnir's chest, piercing his heart . . .

16
MÍMISBRUNNR

There was a moment between deaths, the barest sliver of an instant, where the worlds were wreathed in utter silence. A moment between the pain of the Nailed God's Miðgarðr retreating and the return of the murderous rage that sustained him. In that singular slice of Time, Grimnir understood the breadth and majesty of Yggðrasil; he saw the weavings of Fate that connected all things, and apprehended his people's place in the tapestry of the Nine Worlds. But this Golconda of Northern wisdom could not last. It was wrought of tissue and dust, and when the nature of the *skrælingr* reasserted itself, when the forge of hatred in his breast rekindled, this fragile skelf of profundity was its first victim.

Grimnir opened his eyes. He lay in the broth of slaughter, cradled by broken wings and shattered limbs, with the cold iron spike that was Hátr still clutched in his hand. The sky of Jötunheimr crackled with eerie green radiance; the primordial trees of the Ironwood rustled in the biting wind. He remembered the trap set by that bog-witch, Atla. He remembered Skaði's death—sudden and with no chance to fight back; he remembered the *morðavættir,* the winged murder-crones, whose broken bodies lay under him on the road leading to the gates of Jarnfjall. And he remembered meeting Skaði one last time, in the respite of a memory. *"Sing a song over my cairn, Grimnir Kin-slayer . . ."*

Each remembrance was like a shovel of coke added to the bed of a blacksmith's fire; each memory, the *shuff* of a bellows. And from that white-hot flame, from that unquenchable rage, Grimnir would fashion bloody-minded vengeance. His single eye narrowed; the gleam in its depths turned a deeper red, and the knuckles of his blade hand cracked around the bone hilt of his long-seax.

He heard the echo of Gífr's howl of rage and pain at seeing his sister's son fall to his death, so far from the sheltering soil of Nástrond. Whatever spirit or god pulled Grimnir's strings also lent him life eternal—the gift of death and rebirth no matter the circumstance. This, he would use ...

"What is wrong, little herald?" he heard Atla snigger. "Come, you cannot imagine it would have ended in a different way? That one spilled the blood of my kin! He—"

"And you just spilled the blood of mine, witch," Gífr snarled. Steel scraped against the brazen mouth of a scabbard as he drew his sword—a bone-hilted gladius, honed to a diamond point. "So now, it is between you and I."

Atla laughed. "That is no contest, herald."

He heard the grunt of effort, the whistle of a blade through the air as Gífr lunged for her. And then, a bone-wrenching word of command; a word he'd heard before:

"*Stoðva!*"

What followed was cold crackling silence.

"Poor little herald," Atla crooned, her voice grating on Grimnir's nerves. "What is wrong, son of Kjallandi? Did the cat steal your tongue? Your meddlesome kin has left me without servants. My poor *morðavættir*! Look at what he did to them. Go on, herald. Look. See what that one has cost me? Do you—"

Out beyond the gates of Jarnfjall, surrounded by broken wings and shattered limbs, by blood and viscera, Grimnir rose to his feet. The glare of his one eye was like a corpse-lantern, leading the unwitting to slaughter.

He saw Gífr frozen in place, his body locked in the act of striking at the witch. Her sorcery had twisted his head around, so he might see the place of Grimnir's death. Atla herself still sat on her makeshift throne, bloody and fey. Angrboða's loose blue skin and red hair draped from her shoulders like a queen's mantle.

The bog-*jötunn*'s piss-yellow eyes had gone wide with shock.

"What's wrong, poor little witch?" Grimnir said, stalking through the rusting iron gates. "Cat got your tongue?"

Atla recoiled; she raised one white and gnarled hand, intent on hexing the revenant *skrælingr* before he could close on her, before he could use that cold iron blade in his hand. She opened her mouth to shout a word of power ...

But Grimnir was faster. With a titanic stamp of his foot, he roared: "*Stoðva!*"

Atla went rigid; the stones she was perched upon cracked under the force of Grimnir's command. At the same time, her hold over Gífr failed. He stumbled forward, caught himself, and whirled to face Grimnir.

"By Ymir, little rat! I thought you were done for!"

Grimnir did not shift his gaze from Atla. "Whatever's got its blasted hooks in me isn't finished, yet," he said.

"And Skaði? Maybe—"

"I tried." Grimnir's jaw clamped shut as he bit back his rage.

Gífr stared at him a moment, then nodded. He turned his attention to the bog-*jötunn*. Her neck muscles strained, standing out like cords as she struggled to break free of Grimnir's will. "Say the word, little rat ... I'll cut out her tongue and lop off her hands. After that, you can take your time with her. Skaði deserves every drop of that maggot's blood."

"I've got something else in mind," Grimnir replied, eyes narrowing.

Using short, terse commands, he forced Atla to her feet. He made her gather up Skaði's body, reuniting it with her head. Under Grimnir's guidance, Atla arranged Skaði on that makeshift throne, still in her mail, her naked sword across her knee and her black war-bow at her back. When it was right, Grimnir nodded. Then, stone by stone, he willed Atla into constructing a cairn around Skaði's seated corpse.

The night lengthened, fading as Atla worked. Grimnir sat to one side, the whole of his attention focused on the bog-witch. Sweat beaded his forehead; his teeth ground together as he guided her actions. And Grimnir gave the milk-colored witch no respite, working her until her breath came in short, sharp gasps, her hands broken-nailed and lacerated. He drove her on until handprints of blood stained each rock she placed in the cairn.

"Can you hold her?" Gífr said, glancing sidelong at Grimnir.

"I can hold her."

As dawn stained the eastern horizon, touching the clouds over Jarnfjall with pale yellow fire, Atla laid the last stone atop the cairn—a beehive shape even with her height. She looked near to death herself. Her limbs quivered; blood dripped from her cramping fingers, and her hateful yellow gaze found Grimnir's lone, merciless eye.

"Kneel."

Unable to resist, Atla dropped to her knees. Then, without preamble, without warning, and without mercy, Grimnir stepped up behind her, wrenched her head back, and ripped Hátr across the tough sinew of her neck and through the gristle of her throat.

"If there's a world beyond these Nine, you wretch," Grimnir growled, "then may Skaði's shade find yours and harry you until the death of Time itself."

Atla's foul black blood sprayed the stones of the cairn as she fought for breath. To no avail. She clawed at the rocks, slowly sinking beside the cairn as her life's blood pumped through the severed arteries of her neck. And as the witch died, Grimnir did the thing Skaði's memory had asked of him.

He sang a song over her cairn.

> "Daughter of Wolves and Serpent-kin,
> Fallen far from Nástrond's shore;
> Mount now the wolf-ship's prow and ride
> To lands of iron and gold.

> "Doom you found under jötunn skies,
> From cold Death you did not quail;
> Now mount the wolf-ship's prow and ride
> To lands of mutton and ale.

> "By iron blade and jötunn blood,
> Do we mark your death-debt paid;

THE DOOM OF ODIN

So mount the wolf-ship's prow and ride
To the worlds beyond the Nine . . ."

As the echo of his harsh and flinty voice faded, Grimnir turned from the cairn and walked away from Jarnfjall.

FOR DAYS, Grimnir and Gífr traveled in near silence. Hardly a word passed between them, and even curses fell rarely from Grimnir's lips. Like wolves, they loped through primordial forest, under leaden skies glazed silver by the pale light of a hidden sun, or else under a moonless night sky that gleamed with green witch-lights; they moved in single file, with Grimnir following in Gífr's wake, his brow furrowed as he turned something over in his thoughts. Gífr held his tongue and did not pry.

Moving ever northward, toward a looming shadow that could only be mighty Yggðrasil, they left the Ironwood behind and ascended into the hill country abutting the eaves of the vast and deadly Myrkviðr—the Murk-Wood, where things better left to their own devices lurked in perpetual darkness. They skirted stinking fens and crossed a mist-wreathed moor, where trilithons of mossy stone stood like giant gateways.

"Never go through one, little rat," Gífr warned, glancing over his shoulder. "Always go around."

At this, Grimnir stirred. He frowned at a trio of stones ahead of them—two upright and one across the top like a lintel. "*Nár*, why's that?"

Gífr slowed, then stopped a few feet from the trilithon. Bending, he snatched up a rock the size of his thumb and shied it at the center of the three stones.

It struck, vanished, and left ripples in the fabric of existence at the heart of the trilithon.

"*Fak mir*," Grimnir muttered.

"They're snares," Gífr said. "The Howling Dark, the Ginnungagap, lies just beyond. Something from *there* set them up *here*, hoping to get a bite of flesh from the unwary."

"What lives in that blasted Void, eh?"

Gífr glanced sidelong at him. "Things better left alone." They stared at the placid-seeming trilithon for a moment. Finally, Gífr stirred. "Listen, little rat," he began, his words uncertain. "If I had known that that blasted bog-witch had killed Mother Angrboða and taken her skin..."

"You think I blame you? For Skaði?" Grimnir moved away from the trilithon.

"Do you not?"

"Look who's all full of themselves, now, eh?" Grimnir chuckled. "*Nár!* If anyone's to blame, it's me. I led her out here to her death, and for what?"

Gífr followed him; side by side, they set off north, again, this time at a walk. "You're forgetting one thing, little rat: seeking answers in Mímisbrunnr was *her* idea. You didn't force her to come."

"But I didn't try to stop her, either. Or you. *Faugh!* I practically dragged you with us! No, I should have left the both of you on Nástrond and come on this fool's errand alone."

"It's a fool's errand, now, is it?"

"And I'm the fool," Grimnir replied. He stopped. "Here's what I think: I think I'm being played like a lute here, as revenge for something I did a couple hundred years ago, back when I was on Bjarki Half-Dane's trail."

"What did you do?"

Both of them crouched; they shared their last bottle of mead, and Grimnir handed Gífr a piece of hard bread and a strip of jerky. As they munched this thin repast, Grimnir told him how he'd caught himself a hymn-singer in the Danemark, and how they'd wound up in England—and how his captive, Étaín, managed to get herself in a worse fix by falling prey to "some cack-handed English lordling," as Grimnir put it.

"Thing is, though... that little lordling was a revenant," Grimnir said. "Went and got himself killed a few years before, and was possessed by a willow-spirit ere he died. Well, that wayward *landvættr* went and got religion, of all things. Became a dyed-in-the-wool cross-kisser... but a cross-kisser with a fortress and an army. I needed that little kneeler, Étaín, back, so I recalled some of the things you used to say. Some of the Old Ways."

At this, Gífr groaned. "I knew something I said or did would come back around and take a bite from my arse."

"Ha! Then you should have been more careful with what you said, you sot. Anyway, I remembered your tales of the Cruithne, the Stone Folk who dwelled there before the coming of the Romans. Even before the rise of the Britons, you said."

"I did, blast my eyes."

"Well, I found one of their stone circles and called up their old, sleeping god—"

"The Shepherd of the Hills," Gífr interjected, giving Grimnir a strange look. "Ymir's beard, little rat! You don't lack for sand in your belly, do you?"

"No half-measures, you always said. Anyway, I struck a deal with the Shepherd—it broke open the walls of Badon and I went and fetched back its wayward *landvættr* . . . and my stolen hymn-singer, to boot."

"And you think the Shepherd of the Hills is the one pulling your strings, now?"

"Who else?" Grimnir stood; he wiped his hands on the thighs of his trousers. "I've wracked my useless brain for some hint, some memory that might explain it. And the Shepherd is the only thing that makes sense. Even the glimpses of a tree, of eight stones . . . that was the ring of rocks I found in the valley of the Avon River, back then. I'm sure of it."

Gífr seemed skeptical. "Seems like a lot of water to carry for a sleepy old Cruithne spirit."

"It's the only thing that makes sense," Grimnir repeated. He looked off in the distance, at the suggestion of Yggðrasil's branches gleaming through the ever-present clouds. It was like looking at the dark heart of a universe. "And I should have figured it out sooner. *Faugh!* Maybe if I had, Skaði might still be—"

"Don't go traipsing down that path, little rat," Gífr interjected. "Take it from me. No good can come of it."

"You got regrets?"

Gífr rose to his feet, uncoiling like an ancient spring. "Raðbolg. Something felt off, down in my gut, when he told us all he meant to fare forth from Nástrond and find the Tangled God. I should have stopped him."

"How long's he been missing?"

"No way to tell, down here," Gífr replied. "But if we were topside, I'd say at least a hundred years."

Grimnir shrugged. "Maybe Mímir can tell you something, eh? Kill two crows with one arrow. How much of this stinking moor is left? *Nár!* Those standing stones give me the willies."

Gífr glanced at the sky. "We should reach Mímisbrunnr by sunset, if we pick up the pace."

"Well, let's quit all this jawing, then, you old sot."

"Just try to keep up, you fat little laggard!"

With barks of laughter and rude jests, with the clash of mail and the rattle of harness, the wolves resumed their hunt.

A ROOT of Yggðrasil sheltered Mímisbrunnr, and it was visible long before Grimnir spied the path down to the Well. In the faint light of the setting sun, he saw what appeared to be a range of mountains hewn from rough, scabrous wood. Moss grew like a forest along its flanks, and its peaks glittered with a rime of frost.

As night fell, they descended a weed-edged trail into a hollow eroded from the soil of Jötunheimr by Time and the elements—a trail that led to a cavernous hole bordered by hanging moss and ancient stalactites of splintered wood. Vapors issued from it; a moist exhalation that reeked of mustiness, old wood, and the sweet stench of incense.

"This is it, eh?" Grimnir muttered. "No guards?"

Gífr hitched at his scabbard, resettling his weapons belt on his hips. "None I've ever heard of."

"Guess they'll just let any old rat meander in." Grimnir loosened Hátr in its sheath. "Who is this Mímir, anyway? Skaði'd said he was a fierce lout, who defended his well like a rabid dog."

Gífr grinned. "Let me guess . . . she told you a tale about Mímir and Odin becoming fast friends, and all it took was the Allfather plucking out his own eye?"

"Aye," Grimnir nodded. "That sounds about right. Why?"

"Well, it's only partly true. All of that happened, after a fashion, but they never became fast friends. Odin was Lord of Ásgarðr and Mímir was just another blasted *jötunn*, though one who schemed far above his station. But he had something old One-Eye wanted." Gífr indicated the way ahead. "He contrived to send Mímir on an embassy to the chief of the Vanir, to broker a

THE DOOM OF ODIN

peace between the two clans—a Vanr and an Æs would brawl over the color of the sky, given half a chance. Now, some say the Vanr chief did Odin a favor; others say Mímir overstayed his welcome ... whatever the truth of it, Mímir ended up shortened by a head, and that head was sent back to Ásgarðr in a sack. In the end, the Allfather got what he wanted—ownership of the Well. Odin, though, took pity on him."

"How?"

Gífr nodded. "You'll see. Let's go."

The pair of them crossed the threshold into Mímisbrunnr. Past the fanged maw of the entrance, the cave became a broad and winding throat into the belly of some leviathan of legend. Uneven steps carved from Yggðrasil's rootwood carried them deeper into the earth. Bones and detritus crunched under Grimnir's hobnailed heel; cobwebs brushed his face, sending tingles of apprehension down his gnarled spine. The hiss he made as he brushed them away echoed in the ponderous silence.

With each step, the darkness around them paled. Silver, first, like the glow of moonlight; then, the fading dark became edged in amber and gold. And as they crept around the last curving stair, they laid eyes on the wondrous heart of Mímisbrunnr.

At first blush, it reminded Grimnir of the tree-garth on Sjælland, in the Danemark, where more than three hundred years ago he'd coerced the dwarf Náli son of Náinn to open the Ash-Road; this, too, had the air of a temple, a fane to forgotten gods. Lamps wrought in fantastic shapes, from copper and silver to glass and gold, sent jags of light across a floor thick with a labyrinth of rootlets. Smoke from censers and braziers hazed the air. It smelled faintly of spring, of wildflowers and of cedar boughs.

Mímir's Well had its genesis far over Grimnir's head, where a spring of cold sweet water flowed from Yggðrasil's heartwood; it gathered in mossy pools, spilled down exposed roots, and dripped from curling tendrils stripped of bark—mingling with the sap-blood of the Old Ash as it did so. At the end of its journey, the water of the Well splashed into the center of a round stonekerbed pond among the tangle of rootlets in the floor.

And on a stone shelf jutting from the wall behind the pool, a *jötunn*'s severed head glared back at them. It was the size of a boulder; pale and bloodless, its features looked as though a sculptor had molded them from old wax. Its eyes were open, opaque, and over a rune-etched brow its once-red hair had long since faded into a colorless thatch. The head's beard draped like moss over the shelf's edge, its ragged ends dipping into the water.

"Behold, the Allfather's pity," Gífr whispered. "Dead, but alive. Trapped till the Gjallarhorn blows . . ."

"Fie, fire, and fume!" the severed head roared, its voice deep, like the tolling of a bell. "I smell the stench of *skrælingar*! You dare profane this sacred place? Fie! Abominations, you are! Begone, ere I catch you and grind your bones for my bread!"

"Mímir, I presume," Grimnir muttered.

"You presume much, little *skrælingr*! You presume to trespass into my halls! You presume, no doubt, to steal for yourselves a draught of Yggðrasil's precious fluid, these waters of my well! And you presume no one will stop you! You presume wrong—"

"We're not here for your water," Grimnir said. He exchanged glances with Gífr, who nodded him forward. "Ymir's beard! What would one such as I do with the sap-water of the Old Ash, eh? Grow wisdom? *Nár!* We've come seeking answers *now*, beardling. Not however long it takes that blasted water to work. We've come for *your* wisdom, Mímir of the Well."

Mímir frowned. "Long has it been since someone has sought *my* counsel." Grimnir was certain the severed head would have shrugged if only it still possessed the shoulders to do it. "Fair enough. My wisdom does not come without a price, though, *skrælingr*. Fetch me a drink."

"A drink?"

"If a perplexity of questions have caused you to seek answers far beyond Nástrond's shore, then a draught from the Well that bears my name is not too much to ask."

Gífr scowled. "Won't that draw Ásgarðr's notice?"

"Not if you use the silver vessel, yonder," replied Mímir. Following the disembodied *jötunn*'s gaze, Grimnir spied a horn wrought of silver, as long as his forearm, cradled in a structure of roots.

"Smells like mischief in the making." Nevertheless, Grimnir shrugged. He walked to where the horn rested, hesitated, then snatched it up. "So, just ... scoop out a draught? *Faugh!* Sounds easy enough."

"Indeed, it is," Mímir said. "Hearken to this, *skrælingr:* touch the surface of the water with anything but the horn—or spill even a drop outside the confines of the pool—and the Allfather will bring the wrath of the Æsir down upon you."

"Will he, now?" Grimnir hefted the horn. "I'd best be careful, then."

Drawing a draught of water from the stone-walled pond was not as simple as it looked. Though his arms were apish and long, Grimnir still could reach neither the center, where water spilled from the roots far above, nor the surface of Mímir's Well. "*Fak,*" he snarled under his breath. Mail scraped stone as he clambered atop the waist-high kerb. Lying on his belly, he let his long arm hang down as far as he could and held the horn by its narrow end ... and it was still inches from the pool's surface.

"*Arsegót!*" He leaned farther over, anchoring himself with one hand. He reached, stretching, grimacing ...

And lost his grip when an eye the size of a shield boss floated up from the black depths, still trailing its fibrous roots. It surfaced under his hand—a massive eye whose twin he'd seen before, plucked from its socket and sacrificed for a taste of Yggðrasil's wisdom—floated a moment, then sank back into darkness. Unbalanced, Grimnir flailed; steel links rasped as he went over the kerb's edge. Only quick-thinking Gífr kept him from plunging headfirst into the water, lacing his fingers in Grimnir's belt and hauling him back from the brink.

"Careful, little rat," Gífr said through clenched teeth. "Careful."

From his shelf, Mímir gave a chuckle.

"Hold there," Grimnir said. "Ready?" And with a grunt, he reached for the water's surface. He dipped the mouth of the horn into it, letting a good-sized draught swirl into the silver vessel. Then, with a nod, he motioned for Gífr to draw him back. With the horn clutched in his hand, and his arm at full extension over the Well to make sure no droplets escaped its stone-edged confines, Grimnir crawled from his belly to his knees, and thence to his feet. In this manner, he moved around to the shelf and offered Mímir the horn, tilting it to his lips and pouring its contents down his black maw.

And though the disembodied head swallowed and smacked its lips like a man savoring a fine wine, the water escaped through the stump of its neck. It pooled under his beard and trickled down the shelf, returning to whence it came.

"Curious," Mímir said, flaring its nostrils. "There is a familiar stench about you, *skrælingr*. No matter. The price is paid. What is it you wish to know?"

Grimnir tossed the horn to Gífr, then crouched on the Well's edge, meeting Mímir's white-eyed stare. "I want to know who's got their blasted hooks in me! Which god has me in their clutches?"

The bodiless *jötunn's* eyes narrowed. "What is the nature of these 'hooks,' as you call them?"

"Our lot here in the Worlds Below is to dwell on Nástrond," Gífr said, returning the silver horn to its cradle of roots. "There we fight and make ready for the time when the Gjallarhorn calls us to the field of Vígríðr, where we will face Odin's precious chosen few, his Einherjar, in the Last Battle."

"I am familiar," Mímir said.

"We die and resurrect within hours. But when *he* dies—"

"When I die, beardling, I return to Miðgarðr, to live and die, again!" Grimnir snarled. "And when some toad puts the steel to me in Miðgarðr, I return to Nástrond and return to what passes for life, there, a heartbeat after my last death. Back and forth seven times, now! By Ymir! I want to get to the bottom of it! Who is doing this, and why? Is it that blasted god-spirit of the Cruithne, the Shepherd of the Hills? I had dealings with it in the past . . ."

"No *vættr*, not even one as ancient as the patron of the Stone Folk, could exercise such power over the Sisters of Fate, the Norns. No. But . . ." Mímir's voice lapsed into a confused mumble. "Could it be as simple as that? It would explain the stench about him, *a child of Miðgarðr*, after a fashion. But *he* is more than just Miðgarðr . . . he is . . . would he meddle in *their* affairs? Not for vengeance, I think . . . but what if he's grown weary? Perhaps . . . and oaths . . . oaths are the way . . ."

"What are you muttering about?" Grimnir said.

"Your oaths, *skrælingr*."

"What about them?"

"They guide you, do they not? And do not those to whom you pledge your oath hold you accountable?"

THE DOOM OF ODIN

Grimnir looked askance at Gífr. "They . . . do. Or, they should. It has seemed to me that our oaths aren't hollow like those of the hymn-singers."

The severed head's waxen features grew animated. "Because they're not. Not hollow. Good. You are not totally blind, then. No, when one of the Elder Folk makes an oath, it has power, and it has accountability. And you have made many oaths, have you not?"

Grimnir shrugged. "I've made a few."

"And to whom do you aim your oaths?"

"The Tangled God—"

"Is a captive of the Æsir, bound with his son's entrails to a rock deep under the earth, where none can reach him until the Gjallarhorn blows, calling us to the Last Battle. A serpent the gods perched over his face, its fangs dripping the venom that tortures him. No, it is not your Tangled God who hears your oaths."

"*Faugh!* That answers *that* question, then, eh? Where the Tangled God's gotten off to? But if not Father Loki, then who?"

"Ymir," Gífr replied. "Ymir hears our oaths."

"Yes. The primordial giant," Mímir said. "Slain by Odin and his brothers, and slaughtered like a sacrificial bull. He *is* Miðgarðr, but he is more than that. A part of Ymir exists in all the worlds under the Tree."

Grimnir dropped off the kerb of the pool and paced in a tight circle, like a wolf chafing against captivity. "Ymir, eh? Why? What does he want with—" Grimnir's question faltered. He already knew what the Lord of Frosts wanted. He pulled the words from his memory:

> "*No rest will there be,*
> *For thee and thine,*
> *Until the Tree is put right.*"

"That's what he told me. He wants the Tree put right, the balance restored," Grimnir said, staring up at the root-wood that soared above his head. "Ymir wants that blasted Níðhöggr put back in its place. Why, though?"

"Ragnarök," Gífr said. "All things must be in order before the Twilight of the Gods can fall, is that not so?"

"That is so," Mímir replied.

Grimnir's eyes narrowed. "And Odin, he knows this?"

"He knows."

"All this time," Grimnir said, rubbing the sharp point of his chin. "All this time, we've told ourselves that that one-eyed bench-rider was just pissing about, trying to protect his *hamingja*, the luck he lent that idiot, Náli son of Náinn, so that he might work mischief in the Allfather's stead. But he's been playing a different game, all along, hasn't he? He's been playing the long game—picked a piece to be his king, then moved it off the board, eh? Moved it so there can be no victory, no Ragnarök. And no Ragnarök means Odin never falls in battle against the Wolf, does he?"

"Ymir's breath," Gífr muttered, realizing the scope of what Grimnir was saying. "That means he laid the foundations of this back before Mag Tuiredh."

"Two dooms for the price of one—unchain the Malice-Striker to delay *his* doom, then send it to settle the doom he pronounced on *our* folk once and for all. And when all is said and done, he doesn't fetch it back to the roots of Yggðrasil, does he? *Nár!* He lets it wander about Miðgarðr."

Gífr shook his head. "That's why he changed the rules. Raðbolg put his plan in peril when he shoved Sárklungr through the wyrm's skull."

Grimnir chuckled. "Had to hotfoot it back here, I'll warrant! Lest his wyrm find itself back in chains, gnawing on the Old Ash's roots. Sárklungr's iron blade was his saving grace . . . it kept Níðhöggr's spirit nailed to its corpse long enough for Odin to mutter that ridiculous prophecy and sink the cave where Raðbolg did him in under the waves of Lake Vänern, hiding it away for nigh upon eight hundred years."

Grimnir turned his ruddy eye on Mímir. "We weren't wrong. Fimbulvetr came and went during Níðhöggr's long sleep, didn't it? And no call to battle. No Ragnarök."

"Only the spreading malice of the Nailed God and the destruction of the Old Ways," Mímir replied. "And Ymir bore witness to it all."

> "*Out of Ymir's flesh | was fashioned the earth,*
> *And the mountains | made of his bones;*
> *The sky from the frost-cold | giant's skull,*
> *And the ocean | from his blood.*"

THE DOOM OF ODIN

Grimnir said: "So he heard my oath, and ... what? Had the idea to snatch the last of us up as his ice pick? His chosen weapon? Then just send us back and forth, from death to death, until we rid Miðgarðr of Odin's precious little pet?" He *tsk*'ed, clicking his teeth. "Well, seven times or a dozen, I reckon I can get it done ere the world breaks."

"Ymir's gift has its limits, *skrælingr*," Mímir said.

Grimnir shot the disembodied head a scathing look. "What do you mean, *limits*?"

"Nine is the number of worlds in the Tree, it is the number of days Odin hung by his heels in his quest for the runes. Nine is the number of years that pass between great sacrifices at Uppsala, in Sweden ... and nine is the number of lives you have between Miðgarðr and Nástrond."

Grimnir spat. "And, fancy that ... I've already used seven of them. Hel take you maggots and your rules! I have one death here, and one death there ... and after that?"

"After that, Odin tastes triumph. The Tangled God will remain forever imprisoned. The Gjallarhorn forever silenced. The Wolf forever chained. The threat of Ragnarök will cease to be, for there will be none left among the world of Men with the knowledge to defeat Níðhöggr—or the gifts by which its master's power can be removed from play."

"Well, if that's the case ..." Grimnir gave Gífr a malicious grin, then leapt back atop the kerb. Legs braced wide, he freed his member from his trousers and loosed a stream of piss into the waters of Mímisbrunnr. He spelled out his name, splashed urine in the floating eye. Gífr roared with mirth; Grimnir's own harsh laughter echoed about the chamber. "Here's a taste of *my* wisdom, you one-eyed rider of benches!"

"You are a fool, Grimnir Bálegyr's son," Mímir said.

"I might be," Grimnir replied, tucking himself away and dropping back down to the floor. He leaned closer and wiped his hands in the severed head's mossy beard. "But I'm also Ymir's champion, it seems, and I suspect the Lord of Frosts would not have chosen me if I trembled before the so-called might of Odin Allfather." Grimnir glanced Gífr's way. The older *kaunr* nodded. "One last thing, then we'll take our leave of you: Raðbolg Kjallandi's son, have you seen him?"

"He and a pair of mates left Nástrond nigh a century ago," Gífr added. "Gone into the Worlds Below to find word of the Tangled God."

"The Ash-Road brought him to me," Mímir said. "Alone. His companions, he had said, were lost on the road. He, too, met my price. I told him of Loki's whereabouts, of the futility of thinking a mere *skrælingr* might attempt a rescue. These answers did not satisfy him, and he left by the Ash-Road, shortly after. I have heard nothing of his travails since."

Gífr scowled. "My thanks, good Mímir," he muttered.

"What is it?" Grimnir sketched a lazy bow toward the disembodied head and turned his back on it without another word.

"A feeling in my gut. Something's amiss."

"*Faugh!*" Grimnir clapped him on the shoulder. "The Ash-Road almost had me, once. Maybe he's lost up there, among the branches. Or, maybe he's just mad enough to try and bend it to his will, to use it to reach the Tangled God. That would explain his long absence."

"Perhaps." Grimnir could tell his mother's brother was not convinced. In silence, they retraced their steps from the heart of Mímisbrunnr.

17

THE HOWLING DARK

The journey back to the Hræholt Road passed quickly, with the days and nights blending into one. Their supplies had dwindled to nothing; when they had a thirst, they drank from icy streams. When hunger dug at their bellies, they caught squirrels or small birds and ate them raw. They lived as wolves because wolves they were—fierce and predatory, masters of their autumnal domain. They neared Jarnfjall, and Grimnir's mood darkened. He muttered under his breath, and cursed every branch, bole, blade, and boulder between Jötunheimr and that burning ice-bridge, the Ásbrú, that led to the fields of Ásgarðr. Here, Gífr left him, for a time. When the old *kaunr* returned, he carried something in a sack over one shoulder.

Grimnir raised an eyebrow.

"Our fee for passage across back to Nástrond," Gífr replied. "The witch's head. With this and what we know, Hárbarðr should be amenable."

Grimnir grunted. "There's also a cave somewhere near the Hræholt Road, or so that rat, Blártunga, told me ere he died. Goes *under* the lake and comes out in a hollow near Lútr's territory. He said he and his mates had gone through it, once."

"The Undiræd? Ymir! That *scrag* had some massive low-hanging fruit if he and his mates ventured along the Under-Road."

"What is it, this Undiræd, and *where* is it?"

"Remember the hill with the ruins, there by the banks of the Gjöll?" replied Gífr; Grimnir nodded. "The entrance is under that hill. As for what it is, it's like those trilithons back on the moors. A shortcut through the Howling Dark, the Ginnungagap. You wade *through* the broth of Chaos, little rat." Gífr shivered. "You could offer me Odin's spear, Thor's hammer, and Ymir's blessing and I'd still think twice before I set foot on that accursed path."

"I'd do it for less," said Grimnir, his manner growing once more sullen as he retreated back into his thoughts.

His black mood did not last, however. As Jarnfjall dwindled behind them, Grimnir's rage-spiced melancholy faded by increments.

"How long have we been away?" he asked a couple of days later, as they crossed from the Ironwood into the Hræholt. Gífr's sense of direction was uncanny; he guided them to the first stones of the Hræholt Road before night fell. A few hours later, under curtains of crackling green radiance, they drew near to the River Gjöll.

"About a fortnight, I think," Gífr replied, shifting his burden from one shoulder to the other. Atla's head was ripe; even through the heavy canvas, the juices of corruption dripped.

"That long?"

"Time has a strange way of passing without notice, down here, little rat. A fortnight is a good guess." Gífr regarded the younger *skrælingr*. "How do you mean to handle our return?"

"I figure we got time," Grimnir replied.

"Time? For what?"

"If Skríkja's distraction has worked, then I reckon they're all squared off against each other. I'd go so far as to bet my eyeteeth that Bálegyr's managed to finagle Mánavargr and his louts into the fray."

"So?"

"So," Grimnir said, "that gives us as good an opportunity as any to slip into Kaunheimr, open the Ash-Road, and see if we can't fish Raðbolg from its depths."

"You've got Ymir's business to attend to, or have you forgotten?"

"Ymir's business can wait! *Nár!* I thought you'd jump at the chance to get that brother of yours back?"

Gífr stopped. He dropped the bag, which landed with a rank *squelch*. "We can't just go larking off along the Ash-Road, little rat! Not now. Not with the stakes being what they are. You got two deaths left. Two! If you don't seal the deal on your next trip back to Rome ..." He trailed off. Grimnir fumed in silence. Gífr said nothing for a long moment, then: "Look, I like the idea of just the pair of us, faring forth along the Old Ash's branches, rescuing that lout of a brother of mine from himself. Then, maybe the three of us go plundering in the Worlds Below. I like that idea down to the soles of my boots, lad. But we're tinkering on borrowed time, here. We've got to get back to Nástrond, put our house in order, and then send you on your way to do the deed Ymir's tasked you to do. Raðbolg or no Raðbolg. You understand, little rat?"

"Hel's teeth," Grimnir muttered. "I can die anywhere and still put half a yard of steel through that blasted wyrm's skull once I'm back in Rome. How many chances do we have to pluck Raðbolg's fat from the fire, eh?"

"You're serious about this, are you?" Gífr chuckled; he reached down, adjusted his grip on the mouth of the bag, and hoisted it to one shoulder. "Like I said, you got sand for days, little rat. Only you would tell Ymir to bide his blasted time while you traipse off to drag a lost mate off the Ash-Road. We'll see what those louts are up to when we get back, and—"

Grimnir's arm shot out, stopping Gífr before he could set off in the direction of the river. The younger *skrælingr* tilted his head back; his nostrils flared. "You smell that?"

"All I smell is this blasted head."

"No, there's another stench." Grimnir snuffled the air. "Salt and ash ... river mud ... the Gjöll. But there's something else ... black blood ... rotting flesh. *Faugh!* Something's not right, you old git. Death's lurking about."

"Well, let's tease the bastard out into the open," Gífr said. He dropped the sack; steel rasped as he eased his sword from its scabbard. Grimnir drew Hátr. The reforged shards of Sárklungr reflected the eerie green lights of Jötunheimr.

LIKE A wolf stalking its prey, Grimnir crept from hiding at the edge of the Hræholt. He moved in absolute silence, each footfall planned in advance; he kept Hátr low and in a reverse grip, the blade angled against his forearm. Gífr followed a short distance behind and to Grimnir's left. He, too, moved like a wraith.

Both of them could feel it—that sense of malice, of sinister scrutiny; something watched them, and it meant them ill. Grimnir led them up the path to the ruin crowning the hill. Once, it had been a mighty watchtower, the work of some *jötunn* warlord, perhaps, or a sorcerer seeking solitude. Whatever its antecedents, the inexorable march of Time had worn it down like an infected tooth. Now, all that remained was a semicircular wall of lichen-encrusted stone rising thrice Grimnir's height, scattered rubble, and the stumps of carved and fluted columns. The path, with its switchbacks and grassy steps, showed signs of recent use; a multitude of footprints, small and large, spoke to the passage of only a few. What Grimnir found curious, though, was that all the footprints led *to* the ruin. None led away . . .

For days on end, Iðuna's servant had stood in the same place. As still as a statue hewn of whalebone and gristle. It had no need for rest, no need for food. It did not grow thirsty as the days stretched on. Nor did it grow restless or bored. It simply stood there, perfectly still, in an alcove between a pair of columns, hidden by a well of darkness so absolute that not even the eerie green glow of Jötunheimr's night sky could touch it. It had baited its trap, reckoning on the inborn curiosity of its quarry to bring him into reach.

Now, it watched its prey emerge from the accursed wood, the gleam of its eyes muffled by the brim of its slouch hat. It watched as the pair of skrælingar *skulked nearer. The servant's telltale stench was masked by the rising reek of rotting flesh. Gray cloth swathed its desiccated frame. Næfr's axe was cradled in its arms. Though it had no need for it, the axe was nevertheless a good weapon. A fearsome weapon. It would use the axe to dismember its prey, to remove his head and ferry it back to its mistress.*

All it needed was an opportunity.

Grimnir edged up the last few steps to the level of the ruin. The place smelled like an abattoir, and as his solitary eye swept the emerald-shot gloom, he could see why. That was precisely what it was. A gesture from his off hand brought Gífr to his side. The older *kaunr* came abreast; he followed the nod of Grimnir's head, then gave a low whistle. There'd been a fire in the center of the ruin—now a cold bed of ash; bodies and parts of bodies were scattered around it. Flies buzzed over dried lakes of black blood. The nearest corpse lay on its side, its chest caved in by some titanic blow, likely a mace or a maul. Grimnir shoved it onto its back with the toe of his boot. He grimaced as he recognized the rotting and worm-gnawed features.

"Hrungnir," he said.

Gífr squatted on his haunches. "This pile of offal," he said, stirring a slurry of rotting entrails from a body cut in half at the shoulder. "This was Næfr."

"Three more, here. Don't recognize any of them."

Old Gífr rose and crossed to where Grimnir stood. The first corpse had had its arm ripped off; the second, its head. The third had died from a broken sword blade being rammed into the crown of its skull. Gífr grunted in surprise. "That," he motioned to the last corpse, "is Skæfloc, Skaði's bastard father."

"I think someone had a surprise in store for us, once our business with Mímir was done," Grimnir said. He stepped across the fire and knelt. "And I think I know who."

Gífr followed and saw the final two bodies—a pair of *scrags*, the larger cradling the smaller. "Snaga," Gífr said. Both had died from having their skulls crushed.

"And his precious Cat." Grimnir nodded at the smaller *scrag*. "Köttr. Seems Thrár the Younger, son of Thráinn, got in over his head. I'd bet my last ducat that this idiot planned whatever they had in mind, here. An ambush, I'd warrant, and a bit of retribution."

"Something got to them first, though."

"Could they have cut a bit of wood from the Hræholt?" Grimnir said, eyeing the remains of their fire. "Woken that Elder Mother you told us about?"

Iðuna's servant did not move. Even though its prey was right there, within easy reach of its purloined axe, it did not reach out to snuff the life from him. Instead, it felt a strange sense of reticence. The draugr *had no conscience; it had no will of its own. What the Witch of Kaunheimr commanded, it made a reality. If she wanted blood, it brought her the still-beating hearts of her enemies. It could not refuse.*

But as it watched this pair, its corpse-blue limbs were weighted down by chains of indecision. It could not disobey. Its mistress had commanded their deaths. And yet . . . and yet, something stayed its hand. Was it the power emanating from its prey? A dark and primordial force that made even one of the restless dead pause? Perhaps. But there was something else. Something it could not define. Something that banked the fires of hatred, which was all that was left burning in its hollowed-out soul. All that sustained it. Without that . . .

The servant's jaws opened in a silent scream of bewilderment, tendons creaking. It could not refuse. Its mistress had spoken. A will not its own drove it forward. It had to kill Grimnir Bálegyr's son and all who were with him. It could not disobey . . .

Gífr shook his head. "If this was Hyldemoer's handiwork, there'd be nothing left to find. *Nár!* Look there. This was done with edged iron and steel. We—"

"Listen." Grimnir's head shot up. He cocked his head slightly, his burning red eye drawn to a well of shadow between two tall columns—an alcove, of sorts. He heard the creak of dried tendons, the rustle of cerecloth. A pair of lambent flames kindled there, in the darkness, as something shuffled into view. Something as tall as Gífr; something swathed in a cloak of tattered gray, with a slouch hat pulled low over its features. Something that reeked of the grave, of cairn and barrow. Gífr backed away. Slowly, Grimnir rose to his feet.

A *draugr* loomed over him, and in its death-blue hands it cradled Næfr's blood-encrusted axe. For half a heartbeat that tableau held; then, with a speed that belied its shuffling gait, the revenant lunged for Grimnir. The only sounds were the explosive *whuff* of breath as the *skrælingr* danced aside, and the solid *thock* of the axe-blade burying itself in the soil where he'd been standing.

Nor did Grimnir give the thing any respite. Even as it wrenched the axe free, clods of dirt dripping from it like a *landvættr's* blood, Grimnir lashed out. His long-seax, Hátr, carved a furrow across the *draugr's* brow. Any living thing would have reeled away, bellowing and clutching its bloody face; it would have been blinded by that strike when Hátr's razored edge cut across its eyes. To the *draugr,* it was nothing. Hátr skittered across its desiccated skull, knocking its slouch hat askew but little else.

Grimnir leapt back as its axe sought the source of his life, once more.

Gífr gasped sharply; he bellowed something, a warning that left Grimnir wrong-footed as he retreated from that whistling axe.

"What?" Grimnir risked a sidelong glance at his mother's brother.

THE DOOM OF ODIN

"Look at it, I said!"

Grimnir turned and met the thing's dead-eyed stare ... and recognized the immobile features, so akin to his own, and to Gífr's. Its skin was corpse-blue, and marked in places by old tattoos. Its hair was colorless thatch, with beads of tarnished silver, yellowed ivory, and filth-crusted amber clinging to clumps and strands like memories; its nose was sharp, its face long and pointed. A salt-dry tongue lolled from between blackened teeth. Around its neck, the rope scars and ligature marks of its death were still in evidence—as were the runes of power carved into its bloodless flesh. A conjurer's runes. A witch's runes.

"Is that—?"

Gífr's answer sent a shiver of despair down Grimnir's spine. "Raðbolg, my brother. What happened? Who did this to you?"

There was no recognition in its eyes. Only burning hate for all things living. It tilted its head, glancing at Gífr as though seeing him for the first time. The old *skrælingr* held up one hand. "Raðbolg," he said, his voice cracking. "Look at me. Remember. Who—"

But the *draugr*, Iðuna's servant, who was once Raðbolg Kjallandi's son, backhanded Gífr with the flat of its axe. The blow catapulted him off his feet. Grimnir watched as he cartwheeled across the ruin, landing badly amid the broken stone and toppled columns; he heard the sick crunch of splintering bone, a wheezed curse, then nothing.

"Gífr!" he called out. No answer.

And as the *draugr* came for him, Grimnir gave his rage free rein.

Their fight was a clash of elements—the cold fury of a dead thing against the hot rage of the living; where the two met, lightning sparked from the thunderous crash of steel. Grimnir dodged and wove, never still; always, he gave ground. As the thing that had been Raðbolg's tireless axe sought to cut the thread of his life, Grimnir answered with quick, surgical strikes. Hit and fall back. Hit and fall back. But not even his rage-fueled limbs could maintain the punishing pace of his foe—a thing that never tired, never felt pain, never faltered.

Grimnir was at the foot of the hill, being driven back one blow at a time toward the eaves of the Hræholt, when he made his first misstep. His heel caught on a tussock of grass. The *skrælingr* fell onto his back, the breath exploding from his lungs.

The *draugr* that wore Raðbolg's form did not gloat. It did not taunt him, nor did it show any emotion beyond cold deathless rage. It raised its axe like a woodsman and brought it down, aiming for the center of Grimnir's mailed torso ...

And hacked into the ground, once again.

All that saved Grimnir was an ignominious backward crab-scuttle-and-roll. A move that left Hátr lying on the ground at the *draugr*'s feet.

"Ymir's teeth," Grimnir muttered. He scrambled to his feet and sprinted the short distance to the looming elder trees at the Hræholt's edge. The implacable *draugr* followed. A part of Grimnir thought: Why not just let the bastard put that axe into his skull? He could handle his business in Rome, then maybe return to get the drop on the thing. Or, could he? And he worried what the dead thing might do to Gífr if his absence dragged on. The old sot did not have Ymir's blessing, and he'd lived too long both above and below for it all to end at the hands of his brother, so ignominiously betrayed.

Panting, Grimnir put his back to the trunk of an elder tree. The *draugr* marched inexorably toward him, its face impassive. His mind raced, seeking a way out. Something dug into his shoulders where he rested his weight on the tree to shore up his flagging strength. Grimnir half-turned, saw the graceful outlines of a dead *landvættr* in the bark of the elder, and recognized the shape of his savior.

He turned back to face the *draugr*. It was less than a dozen feet from him, now, and it showed no sign of recognition; it did not suspect a trap, nor did it take subterfuge into account. Its lambent gaze was bent solely on Grimnir.

The son of Bálegyr grinned at it. He nodded. A bit of doggerel rose unbidden to his lips as that dirt-and-gore-crusted axe drew back for the killing blow:

> "*Hyldemoer, Hyldemoer,* | *mother of all,*
> *Protect your children,* | *lest the axes fall;*
> *Hyldemoer, Hyldemoer,* | *mother of all,*
> *Protect your children,* | *come fire and maul.*"

The *draugr*'s axe fell. It smashed through a branch of the elder tree as Grimnir sidestepped, sinking into the trunk with a titanic *thock*. Grimnir stumbled back. A strange sap leaked from under the axe blade as the *draugr* struggled to withdraw it. It did not take note of the eerie moaning that emerged from deep within the forest. It ignored the rustle of autumnal leaves, the tremor of the earth. It was solely focused on reclaiming its axe and using it to strike down its prey.

And when the axe refused to budge, the *draugr* let go of the haft and turned toward Grimnir. It managed but a single step in his direction before something ancient and equally implacable loomed from the forest.

The Elder Mother had come.

Grimnir had the impression of a great tree, scarred and careworn, but as strong as the foundations of the Nine Worlds. Its limbs were pliant, like bark-clad tentacles, and it snagged them around the interloper who had dared desecrate the grave of its child. Grimnir backpedaled, moving farther away from the eaves of the Hræholt as the Elder Mother ripped the *draugr* asunder. Piece by piece, the thing that had been Raðbolg Kjallandi's son vanished into the canopy of leaves. It made not a sound as the Elder Mother wrenched its head from its body. The last sight of it Grimnir had was of that impassive face—corpse-blue and still bearing the marks of strangulation and sacrifice—staring back at him with lambent eyes.

"By Ymir," Grimnir muttered, retrieving Hátr from where it had fallen. He stropped the blade clean on his thigh, then slid it back in its sheath. "By Ymir, you will be avenged, Raðbolg Kjallandi's son."

Grimnir staggered back to the ruin. He found Gífr where he'd fallen, still unconscious. Black blood oozed from the corner of his mouth, and his breath made a crackling sound as he wheezed.

"Come on, you old sot," Grimnir said, crouching at his side. "*Nár!* Shake it off. We're just a short ferry ride from home."

Gífr's eyes fluttered. "R-Raðbolg?"

"Raðbolg died a long time ago," Grimnir replied. "That thing, that *draugr* . . . that wasn't Raðbolg. *Faugh!* I let Hylðemoer deal with it. And we'll deal with the one who made it. You and me, you old git."

Gífr flashed a weak smile. "Go on, then," he muttered, bubbles of blood breaking upon his lips. "Go t-take care of your . . . of your b-business. I'm j-just going . . . going to r-rest."

"The *fak* you are! No one's resting on this side of the Gjöll. Get up. We'll leg it back to Nástrond." Grimnir got an arm under him and lifted Gífr to his feet. His limbs were undamaged, but his chest and abdomen ... even that lackadaisical blow from the *draugr's* axe had shattered Gífr's ribs and filled his chest with shards of iron. One lung was gone, and by the sound of it the other was filling with blood.

"There's no time for Hárbarðr," Grimnir muttered, eyes narrowing.

Gífr looked up, his gaze unfocused. "Undiræd," he said. "The ... The Under-Road ... through th-the ... Howling Dark."

"You're game for that, eh?" Grimnir nodded. "*Nár!* Might as well. If a handful of pissant *scrags* can cross it, so can we."

THERE WAS nothing ominous to the mouth of the Undiræd, on the far side of the hill from where the Bone Ferry had dropped them. From where Grimnir stood, nothing set it apart from any other weed-choked cave entrance. Just a hole in the earth, rock-strewn and overhung with brambles, a mist drifting from the darkness within; Grimnir could smell damp salt and ash, corruption and decay.

"Can you walk?" he said.

Gífr nodded. And though his legs would bear his weight, he nevertheless shuffled with an odd, stiff-backed gait—as if the iron of his spine was all that kept him from collapsing. Sweat beaded his pale brow, and he clenched his teeth against waves of pain and nausea.

"All right, then. You got any words of wisdom, left?"

Gífr managed to speak, forcing the words between clamped jaws in a harsh and grating whisper. "Nothing you c-can fight, down there. Re-Remember that, little r-rat. Ignore it and keep ... keep moving."

"Keep moving, aye." Grimnir hawked and spat. Overhead, the skies of Jötunheimr lightened with the approach of a new day. The green glow faded, and the clouds grew as dark as blackened iron. It smelled like rain ...

With Gífr leaning on him, they ducked under the curtain of brambles and set foot on the Undiræd. The antechamber of the Under-Road was as nondescript as the opening. Just a cave, sloping back and down. Runes scratched by diverse hands marred the walls, providing a recollection of the lost souls who entered this place, never to be seen again, and the ones who emerged unscathed on the other side.

At the rear of the cave, a crevice led deeper into the earth. With a last look at the outside world, they squeezed through that rift with Grimnir in the lead. The way forward was steep; they eased down shelves like steps, down ramps that curled around columns of living rock. Farther on, always around the next bend, there came a cold teasing gleam like moonlight rippling on water. It was faint, but it was enough light for Grimnir to guide their path.

This was no labyrinth, with offshoots and side passages that dead-ended in the darkness. No, this was a road in truth—a single passage of varying size, from a narrow tunnel between damp walls to soaring chambers filled with shafts of rock rising from the floor or descending from the ceiling; chambers with pools fed by silken curtains of wet stone. But always, that eerie glow preceded them.

"Don't see what all the fuss was about," Grimnir muttered.

"This," Gífr panted. "This is . . . s-still Jötunheimr."

"You make a piss-poor traveling mate, you old rat."

As though to prove Gífr's point, from up ahead the *skrælingr* heard spectral noises, sound echoing back upon itself; voices, there were, and snatches of song, garbled but oddly familiar. Faint screams, moans, the dull scrape of iron on bone . . . all of these things Grimnir's sharp ears picked out. And as they squeezed through a crack in the walls and entered the next chamber, the source of the silvery light revealed itself.

It was a shimmering wall of water. Stretching from floor to ceiling, it resembled the placid surface of a lake turned on its end—a milky veil that glowed with a filthy gray-white light. Inside, Grimnir could discern shapes, movement.

"The d-door to the Undiræd," Gífr said. "On the threshold of the Ginnungagap, the Howling Dark."

Grimnir's lips curled into a snarl of defiance; he bared yellowed fangs. "Ready?"

"Just k-keep moving."

"Hold on to me, then, and don't let go. You hear me?"

Nodding to each other, they plunged through the veil . . .

And emerged into an eerie world of opalescent stone and diffused mists, of skin-drenching dampness and disjointed sounds. They moved as though they were underwater, slow and jerky; Grimnir's hair floated around his face, creating a halo of darkness shot through with bone, silver, and gold. His mail weighed him down, its links and the gambeson beneath sodden. He could breathe, though he almost choked on the stink of ash and corruption.

"Move," Gífr said, the sound lagging a moment behind the movement of his lips.

The floor was riddled by holes, pools of radiance where the stuff of Chaos had eaten through the brittle veneer of reality. Grimnir skirted these, moving as fast as he could. Even so, something sensed their passage. Pale arms reached out from these fistulas, talons grasping, elongating like boneless tentacles. Grimnir kicked them aside, or else let their fingers skitter off his mail. Gífr was not so lucky. Like lashing whips, those pale arms snapped out, catching him in his already shattered rib cage.

He staggered; his hand turned loose from Grimnir's shoulder as he fell to one knee, his face screwed up in a rictus of agony. Blood drifted from his lips, staining the stuff of Chaos seething around them with a black haze.

Blue-veined, questing hands came for him. Grimnir, though, got to him first. He snatched Gífr from their grasp and put himself between the old *kaunr* and those clawing fingers. When they touched *him,* what they got in return was the razored edge of Hátr. Their tainted flesh burst like bladders of air; something screamed, deep under their feet, and the air around them rippled like water.

Grimnir turned, snagged Gífr by the arm, and half-carried him away from the glowing pools. He ran with a slow, loping gait, his singular eye ablaze in the mist-shrouded gloom of the Undiræd. His nostrils flared as he drew deep, racking breaths.

"Keep . . . Keep going," Gífr gasped. "Don't look b-back."

"Why?" Grimnir snarled.

"D-Don't—"

And that's when he heard it. The low, sultry laugh that ended in a scream of rage. A familiar voice emerged from the pearlescent mists around them, from the stuff of the Ginnungagap that bubbled like a cauldron under their feet. "Feh! You left me behind, you swine!"

Grimnir skidded to a stop. "Skaði?"

"Not her," Gífr said, holding on to Grimnir and dragging him forward. "K-Keep...just keep m-moving!"

The voice shrieked. "Did you hear me? You left me! YOU LEFT ME!"

Grimnir half-turned, despair warring with rage across his broad forehead. Gífr's grip tightened. He staggered, trying to drag Grimnir with him, but the old *kaunr*'s strength was failing. "No! That's what it wants."

The voice screamed. "Look at me! LOOK AT ME!"

And Grimnir did.

Something emerged from the mist, a figure wearing Skaði's lean and hard-muscled form. Naked, it drifted toward them, arms spread wide; its sallow skin bore familiar tattoos and runelike scars. Dark hair writhed like snakes around its head.

"You left me," it said, speaking in Skaði's voice—though with a wet gurgling at the end of its words.

"You're dead," Grimnir snapped, as rage won the war. Shoving despair aside, he drew himself up to his full height and leveled Hátr at the floating spirit. "Go back to whatever hole you crawled from, wight! You'll get nothing from me!"

"Nor will the Frost Giant," it burbled. "Oh, we know you, son of Bálegyr. We've been waiting for you."

"*Faugh!* You think you're Ymir's equal?"

A chuckle escaped the spirit's throat. It moved slowly, looking at Grimnir with eyes that wept tears of black blood. Tremors ran through its naked limbs. "The Frost Giant is but one, spawn of Angrboða," it said, clots of flesh drooling from its chin. "We are Ginnungagap, and we are legion!" The Skaði-thing opened its mouth to scream. Wide. Wider... until its jaw hinges cracked...

"We...We c-can't fight it! Move!" Gífr staggered away from the creature, toward the far end of the chamber. Grimnir, however, stood his ground. He stared in contempt as the transformation wracking Skaði's frame reached its gory and inevitable culmination. A shiver of revulsion coursed down his spine at the sight of her head splitting open, at the multifaceted yellow eyes gleaming through the black gore and gray curds of brain matter, and at the sound of splintering ribs and vertebrae—like the crack of green twigs—as hairy jointed legs burst through Skaði's back. He tamped down his rising gorge; he pushed every scrap of fear into the back of his mind and willed himself to move.

This was the moment the thing was at its most vulnerable, before it could shed the husk of flesh it sprang from. Even so, the fiend was far from defenseless. Grimnir lunged forward, intent on ramming Hátr through the thing's body; its chitinous fangs clacked in outrage. It spat a gobbet of greenish bile. The viscous spittle missed him, but a few droplets spattered his thigh. Mail links disintegrated; the fabric underneath smoked, and Grimnir cut loose with a string of salty oaths as he arrested his lunge and backpedaled.

Suddenly, he planted his back foot, snatched his bearded axe from the frog at his belt, and hurled it with every ounce of power he could muster. The blade flashed end over end . . . and *spang*ed off a bony claw the thing raised to protect its vile yellow eyes. Nevertheless, the thing fell backward from the force of impact. While it flailed, tearing the husk of its host apart in a flurry of blood and lacerated flesh, Grimnir sprang after Gífr.

"Leg it, you old rat!" Grimnir caught his mother's brother by the arm and hoisted half his weight. A sound rose behind them—a sinister chittering like the march of a thousand flesh-eating insects. "This is not a place for dying, eh?"

"Or fighting. Ymir's beard!" Gífr snarled through gritted teeth. Even with Grimnir's aid, his stride faltered. He wheezed blood. "I'm spent, little rat!"

Grimnir, though, caught him by the neck of his mail and hauled him close. "You're not dying here, I said!"

"Not your decision, lad." Gífr sagged, weary beyond his years. His words were nearly drowned out by the scrabble of bone claws on stone.

"*Nár!* Today it is!"

With a speed and grace his gnarled frame belied, Grimnir exploded into a sidewise leap that carried him clear of the scuttling thing's path. But not old Gífr. He had enough time to bellow a curse before the eight-legged thing rammed into him, its eyes gleaming with a jaundiced light, its jaws clicking and drooling acidic venom. Gífr went down in a welter of limbs. The impact ground the ends of broken ribs into his organs, and the thing dragged him half a dozen feet over naked rock, wrenching a scream from him.

Before the thing could recover, before it could pierce its prey with chittering fangs, Grimnir leapt onto its blood-slimed back. Hátr was clutched in one scarred fist, and a jagged yellow snarl twisted his features. The long-seax flashed in the pearlescent gloom. Its keen edge crunched into the spider-thing's head, splitting it open like a rotten melon; Hátr bisected its yellow jewel-faceted eyes, splintered its chitinous mouth-parts, and sank into the soft neck where it joined the brutish body. Blood and slime erupted from the hideous wound.

And like lamps in a windstorm, the spider's eyes flickered and died.

Its hairy legs twitched and curled as Gífr crawled clear of it, profanity dripping from his lips like venom. "Just like your old da," Gífr snapped. "Give me a warning, next time, you lout!"

"Where's the fun in that?" Grimnir grinned. He dropped down off the spider's back, wrenched Hátr free of the wreckage of its nightmarish head, and slung ichor from the blade. "Can you stand? We're not out of the fire yet."

"There's no need," Gífr replied. He looked past Grimnir, back the way they'd come. Shapes scuttled in the mist as a horde of creatures bore down on them—from the smallest of spiders to eight-legged titans born of nightmares with eyes like burning lanterns. Above their insane chittering, above the clicking and clacking of teeth and talons, Grimnir heard an obscene laugh, wet and congested.

"We are Ginnungagap, and we are legion!"

"End me," Gífr said, looking up at him. "End me, and go finish your business in Miðgarðr."

"It's not my business," Grimnir replied. "It's *his*!" He strode forward, arms outstretched. His voice rose in volume, in power, echoing with the fury of chained lightning. "Hear me, O Ymir! Bear witness, Father of Giants and Lord of Frosts! Corpse-maker and Life-quencher, I am called; the Bringer of Night, the Son of the Wolf and Brother of the Serpent. The Hooded One, I am; the Kin-slayer and the Slaughterer of Witches! The Butcher of the *Morðavættir*! I am Grimnir Bálegyr's son, and this is my oath: If Gífr Kjallandi's son dies here, there will be no balance! There will be no peace! There will be no Ragnarök! Help us—both of us—or we are quits! Do you hear me?"

For a moment, there was silence. Even the chittering laughter of the Ginnungagap faded. From somewhere beyond his reckoning, Grimnir imagined a great scale tilting, creaking, one pan weighted with the concerns of the Nine Worlds; the other, the feather of Grimnir's need.

And he felt the balance shift. It was a nigh-imperceptible rumbling, a tremor that ran along the roots of Yggðrasil. Grimnir took a step back. The creatures spawned by the Howling Dark stopped; their hellish eyes sought the source of the movement underfoot and found nothing.

The rumbling stopped.

Gífr snorted. "There's your answer."

Grimnir's lips peeled back in a snarl of contempt. He reached for the dagger at the small of his back . . .

And was thrown from his feet as the Undiræd exploded around them. Something slammed into the cavern, cracking the stone and causing avalanches of debris. Cursing, Grimnir scrambled back to where Gífr lay. Both of them stared open-mouthed as a fist wrought from countless tree roots punched through the roof of the Under-Road. Behind it, the bitter waters of Lake Gjöll poured into this abscess beneath the earth. And wrapped in that milky flood came a harrowing horde of *sjóvættir*.

Grimnir got Gífr to his feet. Arm in arm, they backed away from the rapidly filling rift between Chaos and its creation. The spider-things were unmade by the *sjóvættir,* who fed upon their warped essence, even as questing roots ripped those pale and sinuous arms from their pools like a gardener plucking weeds.

"Not something you see every day," Gífr muttered.

"*Faugh!* Now we've seen it, it's time to hotfoot it out of here before this place floods. Let's go, you old sot."

But as they turned to leave, they found their way out blocked by a creature unlike any they'd seen—a *jötunn*-shaped thing made from tree roots and stone, with chips of obsidian for eyes and a beard of curling grass. It was taller than either of them, and twice as broad. It regarded them for a moment.

Grimnir screwed up his courage. "Are you just going to stare, or has your master sent you to aid us?"

The earth-spirit's answer came from everywhere, and from nowhere; it was a roar, and a whisper. It was the wind and the rain, the call of birds and the trill of insects; it was the lightning and the thunder, the waves and the rocks. It was all, and it was nothing . . .

"*Wrong are ye, again!*
No mere servant am I;

But master of sjóvættir,
And landvættir alike.
Thy oaths I have heard,
And I answer ye in kind;
Cease thy foot-dragging!
Return ye to Miðgarðr
And set the balance right."

Before Grimnir could open his mouth to protest, however, this thing of root and stone erupted into its constituent parts. The roots swept them up in their embrace even as the acrid floodwaters lapped around their calves. He heard a muffled cry from Gífr, felt the sensation of rapid movement, and then ... nothing.

Grimnir's world went black.

THE SON of Bálegyr awoke on his back. He lay on a shelf of rock surrounded by a reedy marsh, at the bottom of a tree-girt hollow. Overhead, fumes and smoke hid the lamps of Yggðrasil. Nearby, stone rumbled and soil ripped; he sat up, glancing about in time to see an army of roots withdrawing into the earth, destroying every last vestige of the Undiræd as they retreated. That way was closed to them, now, and for whatever was left of Time.

"*Faugh!*" Grimnir snarled and stretched his aching back. He smelled the air of Nástrond. At his elbow, he heard Gífr's labored breathing.

"L-Little rat."

"Aye, you old git," Grimnir said, leaning toward him.

"We ... We're b-back? N-Nástrond?"

"Told you you weren't dying in that wretched hole, didn't I?"

Gífr spat blood. "S-Send me ... send me on m-my way, then."

Grimnir reached down, drawing the stiletto from his boot. "I'm going to have a look around," he said, placing the tip of the blade against the links of Gífr's mail, in the hollow of his left armpit. "When you get back, we'll deal with the one who murdered Raðbolg."

Gífr's lips writhed. "Iðuna."

"That's my reckoning on it, too. I'll find out where she is."

"Do nothing," Gífr gasped. "Do nothing until I get back."

"My oath, you old sot." And without further ado, Grimnir rammed his thin-bladed stiletto through the mail links and into Gífr's ragged heart. "My oath."

18
WOLVES AND SERPENTS

Smoke stained the skies over Úlfsstaðir.
Grimnir spied it from a distance: a pall of fume flung up by camp fires, burn pits, and tar-soaked incendiaries. A war was unfolding in that direction, and it drew him in like a jackal to carrion. By Gífr's reckoning, they'd been away from Nástrond for more than a fortnight; in that time, in this place, entire dynasties could rise and fall.

He'd left the hollow where the Undiræd was—now just a bog between the folds of a hill—and headed toward the Tree. Yggðrasil's cloud-wreathed lights guided him along knife-edged trails and across the forested ridges that formed the spine of Nástrond. He had a full day to gather what information he could, to see how Skríkja's diversion was unfolding, and to find Iðuna.

That last bit was foremost on his mind. The witch would pay ere he left for Miðgarðr; by his blade or Gífr's, it did not matter. At the same time, he'd have to rein in these warmongering maggots and clue them in on Ymir's plans—both for him and for them. Nástrond was part of the balance, he reckoned, and too long had things been left to drift. This was meant as a proving ground for the Last Battle, not as a place where some overly ambitious *arsegót* might carve out a kingdom and impose his notion of peace.

Once, through the trees, he caught sight of what must have been Lútr's fortress of Skrælingsalr. From what he could see, it was a thatch-roofed stave hall on a walled island in the middle of a shallow river. Fields and orchards surrounded it, worked by *scrags* and thralls. Grimnir scoffed. Right *there* was all the proof he needed that the eldest of their folk had lost their way. While the *skrælingar,* at least, still scrapped and fought among themselves, the *kaunar* sought to domesticate the killing fields, to grow beans and turnips in furrows that should have been fertilized by blood for the harvest of iron to come.

Peace was meant to be anathema to his people; up in Miðgarðr, peace—and the inactivity that came with it—could kill them. But here, you had a rat like Mánavargr. A useless bastard who had done nothing of note except fetch Father Loki's wine in the before-times and die at the gates to Jarnfjall, with this *dvergar* notion of bringing the other Nine Fathers to heel and turning Nástrond into a prosperous little fief. To what end, though? And for whom? Who among them demanded peace?

Grimnir left those questions to dangle as he emerged from the trees and onto a shelf of rock, where he got his first good look at siege-bound Úlfsstaðir. The sight of it warmed the cockles of his black heart. Grimnir crouched and read the field like a scholar reading a text.

The plan of the siege looked solid. Mánavargr, perhaps under Bálegyr's influence, had thrown a cordon of soldiers around the Wolves' Abode; four companies, each bearing the colors of one of the allied Fathers, were ostensibly divided along its perimeter, with the largest concentrations being at the main gate and the back porch. The *plan* was solid, but its execution was slipshod. Most of the lads in those four companies had deserted their posts along the flanks, leaving a weak chain of fire pits manned by *scrags*. None of the *kaunar*—and precious few *skrælingar*—wanted anything to do with the tedium of standing watch. No, that sort of make-work they left to servants and thralls. They had bigger fish to land.

The choke points drew them in. Grimnir observed a near-riot of soldiery milling and elbowing their way to the main gate, eager to be in on the breaking of Úlfsstaðir. Others headed to the back porch, choking the narrow winding path that led to that heavy single gate. There was precious little discipline among the besiegers, and the besieged would make them pay.

Conversely, Úlfsstaðir's defenders were machines of war, driven by a fell-handed queen and guided by a lord of war. From his vantage, Grimnir could see Skríkja stalking along the parapets above the main gate, the crown upon her brow blazing in the muted lights of Yggðrasil. She brandished her spear, and all around her even the most die-hard supporters of Bálegyr left inside the Wolves' Abode roared in adoration. Here was the ruler they'd waited so long to follow—a cruel and feral goddess who loved them and sheltered them and kept them replete with ale, meat, and blood. And in answer to whatever she'd asked of them, the defenders turned toward the looming tide of attackers and poured forth a torrent of spears, javelins, arrows, rocks, and crocks of flaming pitch. The angled ramp leading to the gates became a snarled sea of pierced and burning corpses.

Above the back porch, cunning Kjallandi took a different tack. Among the punishing hail of arrows and javelins, rawhide ropes snaked and looped from the battlements, snaring necks and arms. His lads hauled them up like fishermen dredging up their nets. Those simply ensnared were pulled to the top, their throats slit, and tossed back—chum for the sharks. Those caught by the neck were hoisted up halfway and left to kick and writhe as they were slowly strangled. The attackers recoiled and trod each other underfoot in their haste to get away.

Grimnir shook his head, chuckling.

And where were their great lords in all of this? By Grimnir's reckoning, there were only eight Fathers of the *kaunar* left—he'd disposed of Gangr at Gjöll's Inlet; Kjallandi led the defense of Úlfsstaðir, and two others, Lútr and Hrauðnir, had not yet thrown in their lot with Mánavargr. That left five Fathers, including Mánavargr. Grimnir had counted only four companies, each bearing the sigil of their house. One must have been left behind, to guard Kaunheimr. He spied Bálegyr in the throng trying to take the main gate, his bastard brothers serving as an honor guard and the balance of his soldiery drawn from the now-leaderless ranks of Gangr's folk. He picked out two others by their finery—Dreki in the debacle by the back porch, and Njól, who was farthest from the fray, trying to hammer some semblance of order from the chaos. Where was Mánavargr, though? And, more to the point, where was Iðuna?

Grimnir surveyed their camp, looking for clues. The same lack of discipline extended to their encampment, which was on the road from Gjöll's Inlet. It was an unfortified mess, a collection of tents and pavilions strewn across both sides of the road, clustered around the war-totems of their leaders without any thought for defense. Even here, they'd left the security of the perimeter to the *scrags*—knots of squabbling rats huddled uselessly around their fires, likely fomenting fantasies of rebellion and conquest among their ranks.

Mánavargr's pavilion was a gaudy complex of red cloth at the center of the camp. It looked largely deserted but for a pair of red-cloaked guards. Grimnir's narrowed gaze roved over the camp, from edge to edge and end to end . . . and that's where he found an odd sight that piqued his curiosity.

At the tail-end of the camp, he picked out a much smaller pavilion the same hue as the cloaks of the True Sons of Loki. It faced *away* from the others, in the direction of the marshes bordering Gjöll's Inlet, and someone was trying their damndest to make it look unobtrusive and common, with washing lined out to dry and a cooking fire to one side surrounded by a trio of dark-cloaked shapes—*kaunar* seemingly uninterested in the blood and thunder of the siege. If that wasn't something tied to Mánavargr's scheming, he'd eat his bone eye.

"Found you, you sneak," Grimnir muttered. "But what are you up to, eh?"

On impulse, Grimnir left his perch and threaded his way down the wooded flanks of the hills. The camp's edges were as open as a sieve. Still, it paid to be cautious. He'd wandered into camp near the place where they toss the dead, when they could, to await their return. Here, he snatched a cloak with a hood; there, a heavy black bow. From a pole nearby, he stole a brace of hares tied together by a leather thong. And in a twinkling, he was just another footsore hunter, heading back to his tent with a bit of meat to share with his mates.

He reached the rear of that odd pavilion without anyone batting an eye. Ridding himself of his purloined props, the bow and the hares, he sidled through a slit in the fabric . . . and found himself less than a foot from the red-cloaked-and-mailed back of a *kaunr*. For a split second, Grimnir took in the fellow's garb—his sword in its scabbard, the great brazen horn hanging by a baldric, the beast-faced helm tied to his belt—and realized this was Bölthorn, Mánavargr's herald.

Bölthorn frowned at the intrusion, and started to turn toward the sound.

Grimnir did not give him time to react. In a single smooth motion, he tangled the fingers of his off hand in Bölthorn's hair even as he bared the edge of

Hátr and struck, ripping the long-seax across the back of the herald's neck. It was a swift and brutal blow that parted the *kaunr*'s skull from his spine while leaving the cartilage, muscles, and arteries of his neck intact.

Without uttering a sound, the herald went limp. Grimnir eased him to the ground by the hair of his head and left him there to die. A curtain divided the pavilion. Grimnir stepped up to it and peered out from between the folds of fabric.

"Secret meetings, now, Cupbearer?" he heard a harsh voice croak. "What will the other Fathers think, you cavorting with the likes of us?"

"As is usual, Hrauðnir, they will think what I tell them to think."

Grimnir saw Mánavargr's back. The slender *kaunr* was sitting in one of his throne-like seats, while a mismatched pair of *skrælingar* stood near the entrance to the pavilion, wary and unwilling to enter further. The one that must have been Hrauðnir laughed. He was sallow-skinned and pale, with a slit-like mouth full of broken teeth. He wore no mail, but rather green cloth and mud-colored leather, and he carried a curved and jagged blade; the finger bones woven into his snaky locks clicked as he turned his head to regard his companion. "*Garn!* You hear that, Lútr?"

Lútr was as brown as dead leaves, with a hairless scalp tattooed in a dizzying array of runes and sigils. His eyes were small and fierce, his frame gaunt and rawboned. The wolf-fur cloak hanging from his shoulders rustled as he leaned forward and spat. "Is that what you want from us, *níðingr*? Our silence and our obedience?"

"Nothing so dramatic." Grimnir saw Mánavargr's head turn as he regarded these two rebellious Fathers—his equals under Father Loki's dominion. "A brief truce is all I seek. Your oaths that you will not aid Kjallandi, nor thwart me. Simply let us do what must be done, without interference."

"You think you can defeat Kjallandi, eh?" Lútr flashed a nasty smile.

"He is outnumbered and cornered. What's more, my witch is at Kaunheimr as we speak, devising a way to crack Úlfsstaðir's walls. Their time is short. Kjallandi's defeat is a foregone conclusion."

"That's rich!" Hrauðnir laughed, a sound akin to diseased wheezing. "You know what, Cupbearer? I accept your truce. Because I want a ringside seat when old Kjallandi teaches you a lesson in warfare."

"And you, Lútr?"

The rawboned lord of Skrælingsalr shrugged. "Why not?"

"Then our meeting is at an end. I expect—"

"Not so fast," interrupted Lútr. "Now it's our turn. What about this Outsider we keep hearing about, eh? How does he figure into these plans of yours?"

"That's right," Hrauðnir replied, snapping his fingers. "I hear he defeated Gangr, Njól, *and* the cream of your True Sons almost single-handedly. And, I hear the only reason he didn't get you, Cupbearer, is because that witch of yours pulled your fat from the fire."

Grimnir could not see Mánavargr's face, but he heard a distinct tightness in his voice, the sound of barely-checked ire. "You are misinformed, brothers. This Outsider, as you call it, was a beast of the Howling Dark who wore the form of a son of Bálegyr, called forth by your little compatriot, Lútr—that insolent maggot, Snaga. Iðuna has taken care of both problems."

Lútr spat at Mánavargr's feet. "Bully for your witch, then. Pity she can't pour the awesome power she commands into the problem of Father Loki's whereabouts."

If it were possible to hear a slow and gloating smile, Grimnir imagined it would sound much like Mánavargr's voice, just then. "Perhaps she has, and I simply choose to keep that bit to myself. Perhaps she's discovered all those tales of Ragnarök and the Twilight of the Gods were just lies. Stories told to keep us at each other's throats. Perhaps Nástrond is our eternity, and it's on us to make of it what we will."

"You paint a bleak picture, Cupbearer," Hrauðnir said, shaking his head. "What is our purpose if not to prepare for the Last Battle?"

"Your purpose is to serve, you lout," Mánavargr snarled. "You're just too stupid to realize it. As for my purpose . . . my purpose is to ru—"

Grimnir had heard enough. His arm snaked out from behind the curtain, Hátr clutched in his fist. And as quick as the serpent that was Kaunheimr's emblem, that blade curled around the throne and pressed hard against Mánavargr's neck—hard enough to shave the apple of his throat, if he tried to swallow.

Feral-eyed, Grimnir stepped into view.

There was a moment of apprehension, a moment of indecision as Lútr and

THE DOOM OF ODIN

Hrauðnir tried to work out the meaning of this interruption. For his part, wide-eyed Mánavargr pressed himself as far back in his seat as he was able, trying to relieve the razor-edged pressure on his throat. Grimnir cocked his head and stared from one to the other. His single eye glowed like a forge-coal. "You seem like trusty lads," he said, "and I got no quarrel with you. *This* lying wretch, though ..." Mánavargr opened his mouth to protest, but Grimnir silenced him with enough pressure to draw a thin ribbon of blood from his throat. "*Nár!* If I want any bile from the likes of you, Cupbearer, I'll rip out your liver and squeeze it dry myself. And if you think your precious Bölthorn can help you, think again."

It was Hrauðnir who broke the impasse, lifting his hand from the hilt of his blade and holding both up in a gesture of peace. "You must be the Outsider. The one he said his blasted witch had taken care of." He glared at Mánavargr.

"Give the old girl some credit," Grimnir said. "She did manage to murder poor Snaga, his little Köttr, my idiot brothers, Hrungnir and Næfr." Grimnir nodded at Hrauðnir. "And that treacherous cousin of yours, called Skæfloc, along with a pair of his lads, and her own son, Raðbolg. And she did it in Jötunheimr, so none of them are coming back."

Hrauðnir gave a low whistle. "A regular slaughter-maven, that one."

"What does any of this have to do with us?" replied Lútr.

Grimnir's eye burned in the gloom. "You're the last two not to have bent the knee to this idiot. Mánavargr, here, thinks like a dwarf, with all his talk of kingdoms and dynasties and peace. Peace? *Faugh!* We are *kaunar*! We were bred for war, and Nástrond is meant to be the anvil upon which our steel is tempered for the Last Battle! Ragnarök is coming, lads. And Father Loki with it. Only one piece of the puzzle is left to put in its place, and then the Horn will call us all to Vígríðr."

"Liar!" Mánavargr managed around the edge of Hátr. "Loki's done for! The Æsir have him imprisoned—"

"You know this? And you've kept it from us?" Hrauðnir's hand found the hilt of his sword, once more. "How?"

Grimnir glanced sidelong at Mánavargr. "He got it from his precious witch, who had it from Raðbolg, who put the question to Mímir. I wondered if this worm was in on that bit of murder ... and what was done after."

Mánavargr turned pale, but said nothing.

Lútr raised an eyebrow at Grimnir. "After?"

"Aye." Grimnir's voice turned hard, like rocks scraping iron. "After she murdered him, Iðuna made a *draugr* of her own son. Kjallandi's son." The air of the pavilion turned frigid. Lútr and Hrauðnir both stared at Mánavargr as though the cupbearer were something they'd stepped in. Mánavargr started to speak again, but Grimnir silenced him with pressure from the blade across his throat. "You've been judged, wretch. All that's left is to find a fitting end for you."

"My gut tells me you have a plan, Outsider," Hrauðnir said.

Grimnir said nothing for a long moment, then: "It's time to set the balance right, lads. Gather your warriors. All of them, down to the last *scrag* and thrall you've got squirreled away. Wait for my signal, then march on Kaunheimr."

"And him?"

"The cupbearer is my gift to you. Do with him what you will—use him as bait, as fodder, or as insurance. It's no skin off my teeth. But if I were in your shoes, lads, I'd hold him safe for Kjallandi."

Mánavargr spluttered; for the first time, fear replaced indignation in his voice. "My True Sons will hunt you down, *scrag*! They will hunt you down and slaughter you, and all who are with you!"

"Bring them, Cupbearer." Grimnir leaned close to the lord of Kaunheimr. "Bring them, and I will show those useless louts the true meaning of slaughter." Grimnir handed him to Lútr and Hrauðnir. "Bind him, gag him. Parade him like an ass in front of his people before you carve the blood-eagle in his *argr*-loving back. I don't care what you do with him. But make certain the lot of you come running when you see my signal."

Lútr's long-fingered hand choked off the hue and cry rising in Mánavargr's throat. "What's the signal?"

A slow grin twisted Grimnir's lips. "You'll know it when you see it."

And with a nod, he vanished back the way he'd come.

By the time he returned to the hollow of the Undiræd, Gífr was already up and about. The older *kaunr* had moved away from the marshy verge and built a small fire to dry out his gear, the smoke from it lost in the haze and fumes of

Nástrond. When Grimnir came bounding down the path, Gífr was sitting on a rock with his naked sword across his knee, tending its edges with a whetstone. He looked up.

"I was beginning to wonder if I should push on without you, little rat," he said by way of greeting.

"*Nár!* I had to kick over the hornet's nest to find what we needed."

"But you did find it, eh? You found *her*?"

Grimnir sneered. "They left her all warm and dry back in Kaunheimr, where she's supposed to be working on a weapon to end their little war and make Mánavargr lord of Nástrond, to boot."

Gífr wiped his blade, stood, and sheathed it. "Pity she won't live to see it done."

"Neither will Mánavargr," replied Grimnir, relating what he'd done to the chief of the True Sons, and the strife he'd sown among the Fathers, thanks to Lútr and Hrauðnir.

Gífr replied with a smile that was hard and merciless. "As it should be. Mánavargr won't have left his precious city undefended."

"Do you think me some green-handed war-virgin? One banner was missing from the siege, so at most there's one company watching over Kaunheimr. Near as I could tell, it's the half-elf, Naglfari. The rest were accounted for, one way or another."

"And the witch will have *her* minions."

Grimnir scoffed. "You take the witch. Leave the rest to me."

Gífr started to say something, to frame a rebuke to Grimnir's arrogance, but thought the better of it. He'd witnessed the slaughter at Gjöll's Inlet, the Kin-slaying at Úlfsstaðir, and the harrowing of the *morðavættir*. What threat would a mere company of *kaunar* pose to the Champion of Ymir? In the end, he simply nodded. "Let's see this done, then."

The journey to the end of Nástrond where Kaunheimr lay took them a couple of hours. A mist lay heavy on the ground as they left the forested heights and descended into settled lands. Farmlands. They crossed fallow fields and cut through orchards, passing even a farm where thralls tended—and bred—captive hogs. "Look at this," Grimnir snarled. "It's shameful. And this lot sees nothing wrong with it."

"Most of them have spent more time down here than they ever did up top, in Jötunheimr or even Miðgarðr," Gífr said. "This is all they know."

"That's no excuse!"

"Stay here a thousand years, little rat, and see if you still have that fire in your belly. There comes a time when you've had your fill of blood and all you want is a warm fire, a flagon of ale, and a bite of sup. Let the young slags scrap it out."

"Aye, let others do the fighting while you warm your useless arse," Grimnir said. He shook his head. "Peace isn't for the likes of us!"

Gífr spat. "Keep telling yourself that."

Through the thinning mists, Grimnir got his first good look at Kaunheimr. It was a city with a single street that crawled up the landward face of the Root, the gnarled tendril of Yggðrasil that thrust up from the soil to form ridges and peaks of moss-hung wood. A maggot-city, bored into the flesh of the Old Ash and infected with the blight of order. This was no fortress; it was a place of *commerce*. Grimnir could smell it. The air here tasted as rotten as the air of Old Miklagarðr, the great Stone City of Constantinople—the stink of gold as the weapon of choice, rather than iron. This was a place where slaves were made, where warriors bartered the tools of their trade for plowshares, then grew fat and indolent arguing over the price of grain. It would not have surprised him to see a hymn-singers' cross rising from the hall at the crown of Kaunheimr.

And after the fashion of the Nailed God's folk, a shantytown clung like a beggar to the foot of the root; striations where poverty gave way to plenty were demarcated along the single rising street. "You don't even see it, do you?" Grimnir said.

"See what?"

"This is a nest of hymn-singers in all but name, you old sot. Look at it! From dirt to gold. From heaven—" Grimnir gestured to the heights of Kaunheimr, where Mánavargr's hall, windswept Vingameiðr, stood . . . then down to the muddy streets and ramshackle hovels of *scrag*-town. "—to hell. It's as plain as the nose on your face."

"Bollocks!" Gífr replied. "You're just—" His defense of Mánavargr's city faltered when what was blatant to Grimnir became obvious to him, as well.

"Well, damn my eyes," he said, barely above a whisper. "But surely there are no kneelers among us?"

"There doesn't have to be. All it needs for a rot like that to take hold is some fool who thinks his way is the truth and all others are lies. Someone like that blasted cupbearer, who thinks beyond his station, and then uses that to convince the rest of you louts he has the right to rule. You were Loki's herald. By that measure, you stand above Mánavargr. But you don't put on airs and prattle on about creating a kingdom."

"No," Gífr said. "No, because I believe what my sister said to you, back at Úlfsstaðir. That everything here belongs to the Tangled God. Everything here is meant to serve him, every *kaunr, skrælingr,* and *scrag*, their blood and station be damned. Herald though I may have been, and privy to his counsel, I would not dare put myself above Father Loki."

"You understand our purpose, then. We are here to make War, not to learn the pleasures of Peace."

Gífr nodded, silent.

The path they followed became a road, and that road became a muddy street cutting through the heart of *scrag*-town. It was largely deserted, its folk having been drafted into the war with Úlfsstaðir, but Grimnir spied a few grimy faces glaring back at them. Angry faces. And as they neared the bridge that led to the foot of the Thousand Stairs, a single *scrag* blocked their way.

He was as tall as Grimnir, though painfully thin, with a shock of mud-stiffened hair. A tattered mail shirt hung from his sparse frame, and he held a short spear before him in both hands, parallel with the ground. "Oy! You lot ain't welcome here!"

"We're going up top," Grimnir replied, his stride unchanged. "You can move, or you can eat that spear, you spindle-shanked maggot."

"Hey," the *scrag* said, backpedaling. "Ain't you the ape Snaga and the Cat went after? Where are they? You kill 'em?"

Grimnir paused. He looked askance at the spiky-haired *scrag*, his single eye alight with rage. "The witch got to them first. In Jötunheimr. Your mates ain't coming back."

"You lie!"

"No," Gífr said. "He speaks the truth. She killed your mates, *his* brothers," he jabbed a thumb at Grimnir, "and my brother. And we've come to bring a reckoning. There's blood to be paid, and plenty to go around. Come with us, if you fancy a bit of vengeance."

"The witch?" The *scrag*'s voice grew as hard as iron. He glanced up at the heights of Kaunheimr. "Aye, I'll bring a few of my lads. 'Ware the red-cloaks, long-tooth. They won't be so keen to let you pass."

"They won't have a choice," Grimnir snarled.

Shrouded in the armor of purpose, Grimnir and Gífr crossed the bridge and began their ascent of the Thousand Stairs.

"There are intruders on the Stairs." Naglfari's eerie green eyes glanced sidelong at the pale Witch of Kaunheimr, who had appeared from the shadows and moved to join him at the heavy inner doors to the great hall of Vingameiðr.

She sighed, leaning on her staff. "I told Mánavargr not to trust Hrauðnir, much less Lútr. Both will parley with one hand and stab you with the other. Can you hold them with what forces you have?"

"A strange assumption you make, witch," the half-elf said. He had the fine, sharp features of his father's *álfr* blood with the black locks and sallow complexion of his *dvergr* mother. From Father Loki he'd received the wiry strength of the wolf and the poisonous cunning of the serpent. He wore a hauberk of tightly-woven silver mesh, blackened with age, under a robe of emerald silk and black linen. About his lean waist, he carried the sword of his forefathers: an elf-blade, curved like a saber, thin and graceful, but as strong as steel from a giant's forge. Vargfœðir, he called it. The Wolf-Feeder.

"Well?" Iðuna said, her tone snappish. "Can you hold them or not?"

"There are only two of them," Naglfari replied with a shrug. "But they are neither Hrauðnir's dogs, nor Lútr's. One you know well, the Tangled God's herald, Gífr Kjallandi's son. The other is the Outsider. And no, I cannot hold them. Those of my lads who were at Gjöll's Inlet have already skipped out rather than face *him* again. The others merely stand aside. They offer no violence and receive none in return."

"The Outsider," Iðuna hissed, her brow furrowed. "The Outsider ... how is this possible?" Robes of smoke and silver rustled as she turned abruptly; the heel of her staff cracked on the cold stone floor as she returned whence she came, to the shadows at the rear of the hall, where steps coiled down a shaft driven into the flesh of Yggðrasil.

Naglfari turned to watch her go. "They come for you, witch. What would you have me do?"

She waved him off, impatience fueling her gesture. "Run or die, half-elf. It is all the same. Let them come. I will deal with them."

At the end of those curling steps lay Iðuna's sanctum, a crypt hewn from the ancient heart of the Old Ash. Its walls were smooth, light sapwood mingling with dark heartwood; underfoot, precisely laid flagstones, each one etched with runes, sigils, and wards, made a solid floor. The glow of candles gave the incense-laden air a rich amber hue.

Iðuna retired to a solitary high-backed seat before a low table. Before her, framed in rune-carved stone, rested the Eye of Freyja, a mirror crafted from volcanic glass. "How could it be?" she muttered, pondering the mirror. Her citrine eyes narrowed. Minutes ticked away. Suddenly, she leaned forward.

"*Hugsjá drottningar! Sýna!* Show me Raðbolg Kjallandi's son. Let him hear my voice. *Sýna, hugsjá drottningar! Sýna!*" In answer to her command, the mirror's surface swirled; it glowed with the radiance of its creation, born from the molten blood of the earth itself. An image formed in its depths, but it lacked definition. It lacked focus. Iðuna could not fathom what the Eye was seeing. "*Sýna, hugsjá drottningar!*" she hissed.

To no avail.

"You cannot see him," a familiar voice at her back said, "because he has gone back to the earth where he belongs."

Iðuna passed her hand before the Eye of Freyja; the mirror cooled, becoming a simple tool of black glass. In its reflection, she could see the figure of her eldest son, Gífr. He stood a short distance off, wary, a naked sword gripped in his fist.

"You must think me a monster, to do such a thing to my own flesh and blood," she said.

A sneer curled his thin lips. "*Nár!* I've always known you were a monster. What I never knew was how deep your hatred for us ran, for your children."

"Oh, *my* children?" Iðuna stood and faced him. They were of a similar height, and they shared the same long jaw; the same piercing stare. "My children? You were never mine! Always, you were *his*! His little sorceress, his little jarl, his little captain! Bah!"

"Perhaps because Kjallandi treated us less like tools and more like the fruit of his affection." She gestured, as though a wave of her long-fingered hand could banish that idea. Gífr snarled. "Did you ambush Raðbolg when he came through the Ash-Road?"

"He was already wounded," she replied. "Stung by an *álfr* arrow. He'd fallen afoul of a hunting party on the branches of Yggðrasil. I merely helped along the inevitable, then made him useful to me."

Gífr took a step toward her, his rage barely leashed. "He told you what he discovered, didn't he?"

Iðuna looked past him, her eyes becoming slits of yellow balefire. "Where is your precious Outsider?"

"Answer me!"

"Oh, I already knew, you fool!" she spat. "I've known what became of that despicable godling, Loki, since the Elder Days! Lady Freyja took mercy upon me, and I was with her the day they chained that *flyte*-tongued bastard to the rock with the entrails of his son! And I would be at her side, still, if you deluded fools had but shown the good grace to die when you were meant to!"

"Us?" Gífr bellowed. "You're the one who saved us!"

Iðuna laughed, a sound like ice tinkling against a stone cairn. "I was trying to save myself, you idiot. I conjured that doorway to get Lady Freyja's attention, to pique her curiosity. For is she not the goddess of magic? I did not give a fig if the lot of you lived or died. But you had the gall to live, to escape into Miðgarðr, where the compact between gods kept Odin at bay. In his anger, the Allfather pronounced the Doom of our people, and in doing so he signed the warrant for my death. Lady Freyja had no choice. And that sent me here." She raised her hands, gesturing at the crypt, but encompassing not only the city, but the island around them. "To Nástrond. To suffer the indignity of serving either my viciously stupid husband, or that wine-dribbling moron, Mánavargr. The cupbearer, at least, was easier to control."

"You could have told us what you knew. About Father Loki."

Iðuna smiled, a cat toying with its prey. "Perhaps. But I would not have had the pleasure of stealing one of Kjallandi's little playthings from him, would I? His precious little captain. Now, where is the Outsider?"

Gífr's visage hardened; his voice became a deadly rasp. "Oh, Grimnir is the least of your worries, witch."

Even as Gífr took a menacing step toward her, Iðuna exploded into action. With a speed her age belied, the witch snatched up her staff and threw it at her eldest son like a spear. As it left her fingertips, she spat a word of power: "*Støkkva!*" In answer, the staff came apart in midflight, becoming a cloud of razor-pointed darts—slivers of wood that could slide between mail links, pierce organs, and leave their victim to choke on his own blood.

Gífr, though, was not without his wiles. That step became an ironshod stamp of his foot, and he answered with a word of power of his own: "*Stoðva!*" he roared.

The darts hung between them, their forward momentum shattered. Then, with a sharp gesture, Gífr sent them into the wall, where they snapped and skittered along the tough heartwood of Yggðrasil.

Iðuna raised an eyebrow. "Kjallandi's little jarl has learned a thing or two, it seems." She reached into her robes and withdrew something. Near as Gífr could tell, it was a small glass phial; it glowed in her hand like a banked fire. "Good. Now, let's see how you fare against *this*."

With a snap of her wrist, Iðuna flung the phial at the wall behind her. It shattered; mingled with the tinkle of broken glass, Gífr heard a faint crackling, like a skin of ice expanding over the surface of a lake. Along the floor near the wall, the flagstones with their carved runes and sigils shimmered as a rime of frost crept across them. Where the phial struck, he saw an oval of darkness emerge, black as night; it writhed and roiled like a living thing. Sounds came from it, distant and phantasmal: the clash of steel, the roar of voices, music, harsh laughter, the cries of the dying, howling and monstrous grunting and tearing—the din of the Nine Worlds, he knew. The Ash-Road.

"*Vakna*, Yggðrasil!" she screamed, and suddenly a great inhalation of air rushed past her. It reached out for Gífr like a monstrous unseen hand, tugging at his hair, at the sleeves of his mail, his gambeson. He sank lower as it threatened to tear his legs out from under him. The inhalation became a roar, and the oval spun like a whirlpool. There was no branch of the Old Ash beyond that portal, Gífr was certain. She'd opened a doorway to the void *between* worlds. A doorway to an agonizing death.

"*Vakna!*"

Gífr felt his feet begin to slide. As his body started to topple forward, he did the only thing he could think of...

He hurled his sword.

Caught off guard, the Witch of Kaunheimr could not avoid that missile. It struck the left side of her chest, its force multiplied by the howling rush of air into the aether; it pierced her flesh, tore through her lung, and wedged in the outer wall of her black heart. She staggered under the force of the blow, yellow eyes wide with shock. A spray of blood misted the air—and was sucked into that rip between worlds.

Iðuna fell sideways, into the vortex of her own creation. It snatched her up in an instant. Flickering with instability, as though shackled to the force of her life, the outrush of air spun her through the oval; abruptly, it snapped shut.

Gífr stumbled and fell to his knees. He gasped for breath. There before him, half-hidden by the frost-born mist rising from the stones, he saw the last remaining piece of his mother, Iðuna. Lying there on the floor, gently rocking, was the upper half of her head—severed bloodlessly at the hinge of her jaw.

Those dead yellow eyes stared, forever frozen in horror, as Gífr Kjallandi's son reached for that grisly token.

GRIMNIR SPRAWLED on Mánavargr's throne, sullen and cross. His enemies had faded before him, driven off by the news of his coming. None wanted to face the Beast of Gjöll's Inlet. Not even the half-elf, Naglfari. That green-eyed bastard had simply bowed, told them where the witch was, and left Mánavargr's hall, Vingameiðr, without a fight.

"So much for loyalty," he grumbled.

His ears pricked up when he heard Gífr's heavy tread on the steps, returning from the witch's bolt-hole. He looked disheveled and an empty scabbard hung at his side, but he was whole and hale and he carried an odd trophy in his knotted fist.

"It's done," he said, tossing the head of his mother on the floor between them before dropping into one of the lesser thrones. "Raðbolg is avenged." He glanced about. "Is there no wine?"

"All the servants hightailed it out of here when Naglfari made his oh-so-graceful exit," Grimnir replied. With a groan, he put both feet on the floor and heaved himself up. "Besides, it's time to finish this. Time to bring all the wayward children back home and let them know what's expected of them, from here on out."

"Have you decided *how* to get them all together?"

Grimnir glanced up at the fluted columns and the fine wooden beams holding up Vingameiðr's peaked roof, at the dwarf-wrought lanterns and the candles burning in their gilded copper trees; he looked at the rich tapestries lining the walls, and the carpets on the floors. A malicious gleam curled in his single eye, like a tongue of flame. "I have," he replied. "Oh, I have."

19
OATHS OF BLOOD

Vingameiðr burned.

Through the perpetual gloaming, through the haze and the mist and the endless roiling smoke of the Nine Worlds, the light from that hall-burning shone like a beacon. Wind whipped the flames into a towering column that could be seen surely as far away as the mouth of the River Gjöll.

That ferocious blaze of light from the far end of Nástrond brought an ignominious end to the Siege of Úlfsstaðir. Skríkja paced the parapet above the main gates, her spear-butt thumping in time with her measured steps. Back and forth, she marched; shrewd yellow eyes tried to make sense of what she was witnessing.

The enemy were withdrawing. Not in any unified manner, but piecemeal—ten or twelve at a time—without waiting for orders from their chiefs. Nor were they breaking down their camp. Lads snatched what they needed, stole what they wanted, and hightailed it down the road, making for the boats at Gjöll's Inlet, or for the swamp-path that would take them into Hrauðnir's territory. She had no doubt they were headed for the burning brand that was Mánavargr's hall.

She heard her father's heavy tread. "Rumor is, Mánavargr's missing," he said. "My spies seem to think he was taken by either Lútr or Hrauðnir, or both. That leaves only Dreki or Njól to command this rabble, but they do not trust one another. Or Bálegyr, whom no one trusts."

"Could this be a ruse to draw us out?"

Kjallandi pursed his lips. "But for the fire, that would be my thought. It seems like a ham-handed attempt at subterfuge—the very thing Bálegyr would devise—but that burning..."

Skríkja raised her eyes to the horizon, to the column of fire. "The burning changes things?"

"It does. Destroying Vingameiðr in such a grand fashion smacks of rebellion or of misjudgment. Naglfari could have turned on his master. Or..." Kjallandi half-turned toward his daughter. "The witch has somehow immolated herself."

"This isn't Iðuna." Skríkja shook her head. "This is something else. It feels..."

Kjallandi waited for her to finish her thought. When she did not, he pressed her. "What does this feel like, daughter?"

The pale queen of Úlfsstaðir's brow furrowed. "A message."

"From whom?"

"Grimnir. I think he's trying to get our attention. All of us. Instinct tells me we are meant to gather at Kaunheimr."

Kjallandi looked sidelong at her, the fiery gleam in eyes banked. "That's a giant leap of faith to place on your instinct."

Skríkja bared her teeth. "I've never been wrong and you know it! Oh, look there." She gestured to the base of the road leading to the gates of Úlfsstaðir. A figure emerged from the gloom carrying a banner of parley; a handful of others were clustered at his back, waiting. "We have a visitor."

It was Bálegyr. He was unarmed; he walked slowly, both hands clutching a broken spear-haft to which they'd tied a scrap of once-white cloth.

"Look at him, crawling back on his belly," Skríkja snarled. When he reached the halfway point, she bellowed: "That's far enough, swine! One more step and I'll have you skewered like a fat bog-chicken!" She raised one hand, and a half a dozen archers leaned over the parapet—archers who had once been among Bálegyr's staunchest followers. Now, they hung on Skríkja's every word.

She could tell he longed to rage and rail, but he bit that back and instead raised the banner a little higher. Skríkja licked her fangs and smiled. Oh, how that must have stung his overweening pride.

"Will you parley?"

"No," she said. "But I will accept your surrender. Your army flees, your allies have left you. Why would I parley with twenty-one fools and their idiot father? I have the upper hand! I have Úlfsstaðir! What do you have?"

"I have news," Bálegyr replied. "News of our son."

"So-ho! He's *our* son now, is he?"

Kjallandi placed a conciliatory hand on her arm. "Curb your bile, daughter."

"Bah!" Skríkja slapped that hand away. "Listen to this lying tub of suet! He lost, and now he thinks he can weasel his way back by using Grimnir as bait! In a moment, he will say something meant to tickle your nostalgia. Mark my words!"

"Perhaps," Kjallandi said, and then to Bálegyr he added: "Is it true? Does your son summon us to Kaunheimr?"

Bálegyr nodded. "That's the tale those louts, Hrauðnir and Lútr, tell. They say this was prearranged, and that it was Grimnir who took Mánavargr captive and bundled him over to them for safekeeping. They're marching back on the double-quick, and the others follow."

"Do you propose a truce?" Kjallandi said.

"*Truce?*" Skríkja spat. "We've won! There will be no *truce!*"

"There's something stirring in the air," Bálegyr replied, looking over his shoulder at the burning brand that was Vingameiðr. "Can you feel it? It reminds me of the days leading up to the Ironwood."

Skríkja nudged her father's elbow. "What did I tell you? He appeals now to your nostalgia. My instinct is never wrong."

"Then we must go, if your instinct never fails you."

She lapsed into snarling, spitting silence.

"We accept your truce for the moment," Kjallandi said. "We make ready to march out. Your sons will march in front of us, and you will march at my side, One-Eye. If I get even the slightest inkling that you're up to something, then I will do to you what I stopped Grimnir from doing in the first place—I will cut the head from your useless body and feed you to the *sjóvættir*. Do we have an agreement?"

Bálegyr's eye twitched; a shudder ran through him and a bit of color leached from his face as he realized how near he'd come to a traitor's death. And at the hands of his youngest son, no less. "We have an agreement. Bring everyone, down to the most measly *scrag*. That's what Grimnir told Hrauðnir and Lútr. Leave no one behind."

Skríkja screamed in frustration. "This crown is mine! Úlfsstaðir is mine! I'll not go back into your fat shadow, you maggot! Do you hear me?"

Before he turned away, Bálegyr flashed her a malicious smile. "We'll see."

Kjallandi motioned for old Elðr, who had been with him since the Elder Days. "Make ready to march. Everyone goes. No stragglers, and no one left behind. Even the dead come with us."

Skríkja watched Bálegyr descend into the knot of his sons; she felt their hot looks, their rage. "Do you believe he will keep his word?"

Kjallandi followed her gaze. "No," he said. "But I do not think it will matter. Whatever you think of One-Eye, he is right: there is something in the air, and *my* instinct tells me it is the beginning of the end . . ."

As Vingameiðr smoldered and turned to ash, the folk of Nástrond gathered in the shadow of its destruction. They came in waves, without any sense of order; a profane rabble who laughed and jeered at the misfortunes of others while bemoaning their own. They came with the rattle of harness and the stamp of booted feet. Horns blared; nakerers hammered on their hide-covered drums, and pipers skirled a discordant tune.

They tramped across fields and through orchards, stamping and hewing as they came. They filled the valley of Kaunheimr with their numbers. Dozens became hundreds, and hundreds became thousands. And as they neared the bridge that led to the Thousand Stairs, they found their way blocked.

A solitary figure awaited them, facing them from the apex of the bridge. He stood under a banner. The wind caught it, unfurling it in a ripple of white cloth. But it wasn't a banner of parley, nor one of surrender. As they neared, the horde saw an ancient emblem woven into it—one they had not rallied around since the Elder Days. It was the war-banner of Jarnfjall: a wolf and a serpent entwined over a grinning skull. And all knew it as the sigil of their master, Father Loki. An excited clamor ran among them at the sight of it.

Grimnir held that banner aloft. He glared at every *kaunr, skrælingr,* and *scrag.* Nearly five thousand faces stared back at him, red and yellow eyes glittering in the smoke-thickened air.

"You think you deserve to stand here, under the Tangled God's banner?" Grimnir roared. The ironshod butt of the banner's pole crashed against the bridge, creating a thunderous reverberation. Five thousand snarling and growling voices answered him.

"*Yes!*"

"Do you?"

"*YES!*"

"Even you louts who go slouching after peace?" The pole crashed, again; in the echo of the reverberation, the voices faltered.

"Even you swine who bend the knee to one rat over any other? Does this make you worthy? DOES IT?"

A third crash. Silence greeted the rolling echo of iron against wood. Grimnir's blazing eye swept the throng. He spied Hrauðnir and Lútr to his right, amid their mingled warriors; they nodded in unison. The True Sons of Loki gathered in the center, directly across from the bridge—Dreki, Njól, and Naglfari standing in an aggrieved knot; their folk muttered and cursed, fingering knife hilts and sword pommels. To his left, his gaze met the towering figure of Kjallandi, who stood with Skríkja and—surprisingly—Bálegyr. The latter had a sullen glower plastered across his face. His brothers and half-brothers would not meet that ferocious stare.

"*Faugh!* What would Father Loki say, if he were here?" Grimnir bellowed, his voice carrying. "What would he think of this lust for peace you've contracted?"

"The Tangled God's not here!" someone yelled. Another added: "*Garn!* He's forsaken us! We had to do something!"

"Aye!" a third added. This one stepped from the ranks of the True Sons—a tall mailed *kaunr* with a tangled topknot, his red cloak swirling. "Where is he?

Where has he been these past centuries? Why has he not come among us and set us right, if he disapproves?"

"He is a captive of the Æsir!" Grimnir replied. And an abashed silence followed. "A captive! Taken in the days after the defeat at Jarnfjall. The bastards hauled him to a cave deep under the earth, chained him to a rock with the entrails of his son!" A susurration arose, the cumulative sound of five thousand snarling throats, punctuated by hissed curses and angered mutterings. "They placed above his head a serpent! It drips venom onto the Tangled God's flesh as a torture! And there he remains until the Horn calls us to Ragnarök! This, Mímir told us!

"But we weren't the first he'd told this to! He told it to Raðbolg Kjallandi's son!" Grimnir pointed to the tall and taciturn *kaunr*, Kjallandi, who had been the warlord of Jarnfjall in the Elder Days, second only to Father Loki himself. "And Raðbolg told it to the Witch of Kaunheimr, his own mother . . . right before she killed him." Silence fell like a shroud across the valley of Kaunheimr. Kjallandi's eyes blazed, a glare matched only by that of his daughter, Skríkja. "But what is death to the likes of us, eh? We shrug off bolt and blow and come roaring back for a second helping! But what she did . . . what Iðuna did to her own son . . ." Grimnir's voice trailed off. He shook his head.

"What did she do?" Kjallandi snarled. "Tell me!"

Grimnir glanced up at him. He started to speak, but another voice cut him off.

"It is not his tale to tell!"

As Kjallandi glowered at this interruption, Gífr appeared from over the bridge, mailed and girded for war. He walked solemnly under the white-daubed staff of a herald, its crown a knot of ravens' feathers. In his off hand, he carried a sack. Behind him came two other figures: the spiky-haired *scrag* Ratbone, and—on the end of a rope the *scrag* carried—the bound and disheveled figure of Mánavargr. At the sight of their bruised and bloodied lord, the True Sons of Loki exploded in fury. Steel rasped and rang; voices howled as though stung. As one, they began to surge forward.

Grimnir met them with the rage of Ymir. "BE SILENT!" he roared. "AND STAND WHERE YOU ARE!" The ground under their feet shifted and cracked, and the power that bled from Grimnir's solitary eye was enough to cow the lot of them. They stumbled back; not even their leaders dared to move.

Gífr strode past Grimnir and went to stand before his father. Skríkja came up beside them, her eyes like molten amber.

"Speak, my son," Kjallandi said.

"On his return from Mímisbrunnr," Gífr began, "Raðbolg was ambushed along the Ash-Road, where he was pierced by an elf-arrow. He made his exit into Iðuna's sanctum. He must have told her what he had discovered about the Tangled God's whereabouts. Instead of patching him up, though, the witch carried him far from Nástrond's shore, strangled him, and buried him in a barrow. Then, by her arts, she made a *draugr* from his corpse. A revenant who existed only to serve her."

Skríkja raged; she stalked back and forth, her spear like a living thing in her hands. "By Ymir! Where is she?" Kjallandi, though, silenced her with a gesture.

"You say 'existed,'" he said. "Does it no longer exist, this *draugr*?"

"No. It ambushed us upon the banks of River Gjöll, near the head of the Hræholt Road. It dealt me a mortal wound, and before it could finish me off, Grimnir lured it away. They fought from the old ruins near the entrance to the Undiræd to the eaves of the Hræholt. That's where . . . it had an axe, and it took a limb off one of those accursed trees in its haste to kill Bálegyr's son. The Elder Mother, Hylðemoer . . . her retribution was swift."

Kjallandi winced; he grew visibly pale, though his eyes never lost their murderous light. "And Iðuna?"

"Around her neck must also be hung the true-deaths of my brothers, Hrungnir and Næfr," Grimnir said. "Also, Hrauðnir's kinsman, Skæfloc, and two of his lads, and the *scrags* known as Snaga and Köttr. The ones *he* sent to kill us—me, Gífr, and Skaði." His black-nailed finger pointed out Bálegyr, who suddenly looked as though he'd taken a bite of rancid flesh.

"Bah! It was all Snaga's idea! That wretched *scrag*—"

"Got what was coming to him, and then some," Grimnir said. "*Nár!* So did the others. And good riddance to them! Not a saint to be found among *that* lot. But you—"

"Iðuna," Kjallandi growled. He was fast losing patience. "Where is she?"

From the sack he carried, Gífr drew out the remains of his mother—half a head, severed at the hinge of the jaw. He held it by its lank white hair. "I confronted her. We fought. She conjured a doorway to the emptiness between Yggðrasil's branches, but I managed to get the upper hand. *This* is all that is left of her."

There was nothing but silence around them.

Kjallandi stared into those dead yellow eyes. His lip curled in disdain. "Give it to the *sjóvættir*, my son. Let that offal rest on the bottom of Lake Gjöll until the Nine Worlds burn! And *never* mention her name in my presence again!"

Gífr nodded. "So be it." With little effort, he shied that grisly trophy at the base of Kaunheimr. It struck the wood, bounced, and vanished into the seething waters of the cavern under the Root. "Ere she died, the witch told an interesting tale. She was witness to the chaining of Loki, there as Freyja's little pet. All this time, she had known!" Gífr turned slowly toward the mass of *kaunar, skrælingar,* and *scrags* pressing in around them. "And that is why *this* scoundrel is bound!" He jabbed a finger at Mánavargr. "Was he not her master? Was he not her protector? Were they not in league together?"

"Upon my oath, I did not know!" Mánavargr said. "Upon my oath!"

"Your oath to whom, maggot?" Grimnir said. "Not Father Loki, for he cannot hear our oaths. So, to whom will you swear?"

"Ymir! I will swear by the Lord of Frosts!"

"And you will abide by Ymir's decision?" Grimnir walked back toward the head of the bridge. Gífr joined his father and sister; even Rat-bone dropped the rope he held and faded into the throng, leaving Mánavargr alone before Grimnir. "If Ymir hears your oath, will you hold true to what you swear? Upon pain of death?"

"I . . . I will."

"Then swear it!" Grimnir growled. "Swear by Ymir, Lord of Frosts, that you had nothing to do with the death of Raðbolg Kjallandi's son! Swear by the Father of Giants that you had no knowledge of the Tangled God's whereabouts! But know this: if you're lying, Ymir's wrath will be swift!"

Mánavargr drew himself up to his full height. He stood straight as a rod, shoulders squared and unbowed. He nodded. "Witness my oath, O Ymir! Hear me, Lord of Frosts! I swear by the blood in my veins that I had no foreknowledge of Father Loki's plight! I swear by the heart beating in my breast that I had nothing to do with the death of Raðbolg Kjallandi's son! If I lie, may you take the heart from me, and the blood!"

Grimnir stood with his head cocked to one side, listening. His hand rested on the pommel of Hátr; one long finger tapped reflexively on the ivory dragon's head. He heard no crash of thunder, no distant reverberations. He heard nothing . . .

Grimnir raised his thin lips, baring his teeth in a sneer of certainty. He approached the lord of Kaunheimr; the rasp of steel punctuated every step as he drew the long-seax at his waist.

Mánavargr shrank away from him.

"I—I swear it! I do not lie!" he muttered.

Hátr flashed out.

And the bonds that had secured Mánavargr's wrists fluttered to the ground.

"Rejoin your people," Grimnir said. He raised his voice. "Ymir accepts his oath, and finds no lie in his words. The cupbearer is a fool who dreams of an empire, but he is innocent of these monstrous deeds. He may remain chief of his house."

Mánavargr started to turn away, but stopped. He stared at Grimnir with a hatred that transcended all reason. "Oh, I *may* remain chief of *my* house, eh? By what right do you decide such things? Who are you, Grimnir Bálegyr's son, but a vagabond *skrælingr* born too late to witness the Golden Age of our people? You deride me as a mere 'cupbearer,' but what role did Father Loki assign you? You tell me *I* am a fool who dreams of an empire, and yet here you stand, spouting orders like some self-crowned monarch of Nástrond! I *may* remain chief of *my* house? You are a dog and son of dogs! I am Mánavargr, who stands at the Tangled God's elbow! I am the lord of Kaunheimr! I am the master of the True Sons of Loki! And if I must answer for my so-called crimes, then you must answer for yours! You must answer for the murder of Skollvaldr, for the slaying of Gangr, and—for all we know—for the killing of your brothers and their companions in Jötunheimr! And, I am owed for the burning of my hall, you piss-blooded *skrælingr* maggot!"

Howls erupted from among the red-cloaked True Sons, with curses and derisive laughter. Grimnir took it all in stride. He glanced at the cheering faces, then back to Mánavargr, an odd sneer on his thin lips.

As the clamor died down, he said: "You are chief of the House of Mánavargr, and that is *all* Ymir grants you. And as for my crimes—" Grimnir paused; when he spoke again, his voice deepened to a sorrow-tinged growl. "As for my crimes, I have answered for them already."

Mánavargr's indignation rose. He strutted in a tight circle. "So-ho! You presume to speak for the Lord of Frosts, now?"

"Yes." And suddenly, Grimnir loomed over him. Red of eye and dark of visage, he seemed to swell with unseen power. His voice became the grinding of ice; his gaze like molten rock. Lightning crackled along his frame, from his mountainous shoulders to the boulders of his clenched fists. "I am Ymir's champion," he thundered, "and through me, the Lord of Frosts makes his will known. Do you doubt me, you preening rat?"

Mánavargr's tongue clove to the roof of his mouth, and for once in his long unlife, he had nothing to say. He merely shook his head and withdrew into the ranks of his cowed followers.

"Then pay heed, the lot of you!" Grimnir said, and in his voice was the crashing of waves and the howling of winds. "The days of Ragnarök are upon us! But Odin of the Æsir, that wretched bench-rider, has discovered a way by which he can forestall his own death—and cheat the Fates of their ending! I have one last chance to intervene, one last chance to set the Nine Worlds back on the path to the Twilight of the Gods! First, though, the balance of Nástrond must be restored!

"This is not meant to be a place of peace and prosperity! Nástrond is meant to be a place of war. Endless war! Nine is the number sacred to Ymir, so there must be nine halls, nine war-camps! Nine Fathers intent on killing each other rather than trying to forge an empire! If one of you seeks to grasp more than his due, it's on the heads of the others to tear down the walls of his dream and throw him back in the muck! If one of you bends the knee, it's upon the heads of those who follow to knife that traitor in the back as many times as it takes! This is the balance of Nástrond! This is who we're meant to be!"

The roar of five thousand voices was deafening. Swords clashed on shields; spears were thrust aloft, and horns blared like the war-cries of ancient beasts. How long it went on, none could say, but as the tumult faded, a grin split Grimnir's features. "But we're a Father short, it seems," he said.

THE DOOM OF ODIN

"Thanks to you, *arsegót!*" someone shouted.

Grimnir sneered at this remark. "Sons of Gangr, you are free to gather under the banner of your choice—and any of you feckless lords would be wise to take them in and treat them like your own sons! Choose now!"

And slowly, the House of Gangr was consumed by their neighbors. Some went with Bálegyr; others joined the House of Kjallandi. Most, however, chose to close ranks with the red-cloaked sons of Mánavargr. When this was done, Grimnir nodded. "The ninth House of Nástrond, then, will be a tribe of yellow-eyed harridans! The crows of war! And their chief shall be Skríkja Kjallandi's daughter!"

Grimnir went to stand before his mother, whose face was an unreadable mask. "What say you?" he said. "Will you give up a crown forged by someone else and forge one of your own making?"

It was Bálegyr who answered. "Impossible! She is already queen of Úlfsstaðir! Choose another, you lout!"

Mother and son regarded each other for a long moment.

Then, Skríkja reached up. She tugged the iron crown of Úlfsstaðir from her brow; sparing him but a withering glance, she dropped that bauble at Bálegyr's feet. "Impossible?" she hissed. "Why, you sad sack of offal. I'm going to take Úlfsstaðir from you and use the fat from your haunches to caulk her walls!" Skríkja glanced at her father, who nodded, then stepped away from the Houses of Kjallandi and of Bálegyr. "Where are my daughters?" she roared.

And in answer, a chorus of fierce cries arose. From the ranks of every House came yellow-eyed fighters, shield-maidens, brawlers, and dagger-witches. The daughters of her blood joined her, and the daughters of every last Father. If their mates or sires sought to stop them, they did not voice their disapproval. Grimnir's fiery gaze kept them in line.

Soon, the space where Gangr's lads had stood was brimming with an army of war-crows, piss-eyed and angry. Skríkja looked over their ranks and nodded, growling in contentment. "We may not have long until the Horn calls us to the fields of Vígríðr and the Last Battle, but we will take what time we have! Sing these louts their death-songs, my ferocious Daughters of Hel!" The keening cry that arose from their throats froze the blood of those who heard it.

Grimnir nodded. "Then, let us seal this compact," he said. "And we seal it in blood! My blood!" He stripped off his Turkish mail, his gambeson. He kept only Hátr, the blade naked in his grasp. This, he raised to the cloud-girt heavens, where the lights of Yggðrasil gleamed. "Hear me, O Ymir! Bear witness, Father of Giants and Lord of Frosts! Corpse-maker and Life-quencher, I am called; the Bringer of Night, the Son of the Wolf and Brother of the Serpent. The Hooded One, I am; the Kin-slayer and the Slaughterer of Witches! The Butcher of the *Morðavættir*! The Beast of Gjöll's Inlet and the Outsider! I am Grimnir, your champion! Let the lords of Nástrond make their oaths, and let my blood bind them to it! Let them send me back to Miðgarðr one last time!"

Kjallandi approached him first. He drew a knife. "I am Kjallandi of the Stag-Skull, son of Hjalti of the Axe, and by this blood I make my oath." He embraced Grimnir . . . and sank his knife into the *skrælingr's* side. Grimnir hissed, but said nothing.

Mánavargr came next, and he did not try to suppress the gleam of malice in his eyes. His knife was curved and jagged. "Mánavargr, I am; lord of Kaunheimr and cupbearer to Father Loki, and by this blood I make my oath." His embrace was fleeting, but the knife plunged into Grimnir's opposite side. His single eye flared with rage, but he said nothing.

Dreki came next, then Naglfari and Njól, their knives sharp and hungry; Hrauðnir followed Lútr, and both stabbed him with the utmost respect. Blood oozed from Grimnir's clamped jaws, but he said nothing. Bálegyr sauntered up to him, making a great show of drawing a short punch-dagger from his belted sash. He moved to embrace his son, stabbing him up under the right armpit. Air bled from his pierced lung. Bálegyr twisted the blade and withdrew it. "I am Bálegyr of the Eye, *rightful* lord of Úlfsstaðir, and by this blood I make my oath."

Grimnir spat at his feet, but said nothing.

Last came Skríkja. Her knife was long and thin, and as she took her youngest son in her arms, she held that knife between them, burying it in the corded muscle of his belly. Grimnir hissed. "I am Skríkja daughter of Kjallandi," she said, "and this blood is my blood, the blood of my womb. On this, I make my oath." Yellow eyes met red, and Grimnir nodded. Still, he said nothing.

He staggered, blood pouring from his torso. The monstrous vitality that fueled him was as yet undiminished, even after nine grievous wounds. He cast a glance at Gífr; a subtle question, a favor passed between them. The son of Kjallandi, who was like a father to him, handed his herald's staff to another. He drew a dagger from the small of his back.

Grimnir walked to him, and heedless of the blood they embraced. "Go on, little rat," Gífr said, his voice barely rising above a whisper. "Take Odin's doom to him, and send that blasted wyrm back to where it belongs."

They broke apart. There was a set to Grimnir's jaw, a vicious cast to his face, as though it were a mask chiseled from whalebone and flint. One eye was cold ivory, ringed in delicate silver runes that caught Yggðrasil's light; the other was a forge-glede of hate. Grimnir nodded.

And without another word, Gífr Kjallandi's son stabbed him through the heart . . .

20
THE DOOM OF ODIN

Overhead, a shoal of fumes from Múspellsheimr drifts over the face of Yggðrasil, shrouding its lights and bringing a hint of true night to Nástrond's shores. Still, even by the thin radiance that filters through this seething wrack—like starlight on a clear night—Grimnir is able to find his way.

He spies the small grove at the foot of the hill where Úlfsstaðir perches like an uneasy crown. Leaves of oak and willow rustle in the warm breeze; his keen ears catch not even the slightest sound beyond that. Around him, he sees familiar ruins: walls of pitted stone clad in black ivy, columns like jagged and broken teeth.

There, he finds the remains of a small fire, its ashes cold and dead. Water trickles from a spring among the rocks. He stands there a moment, looking around as his expectations bleed away. What did he come here for? What did he hope to find?

"Skaði?" he mutters, his voice profaning the silence.

There is no answer.

Crestfallen, he turns away and retraces his steps.

Beyond the grove, a light pours from the open gates of Úlfsstaðir. Harsh and white, it causes him to raise one hand, to shade his solitary eye from the glare. He is supposed to go there. Part of him does not want to. Part of him wants to return to the grove, rekindle that fire, and hope its soft glow might draw her restless spirit back to him. Deep down, though, he knows better. There is no going back. Only forward. With a sigh that is part *frustration and part regret*, he bends his steps forward. He ascends along the road until he is even with the open gates.

The Wolves' Abode. It is empty now. None of his kin walk its parapets. Not here. Through the open gate, he sees the short and murderous tunnel any intruder would need to traverse to gain the inner courtyard. This is meant to be a fish trap—two portcullises to trap the enemy inside, loops and murder holes for archers to rip them to shreds; a secret door where heavily armored kaunar might issue forth, using spear and shield to gaff the dregs.

The light streams past him. It comes from beyond the gates. From the stave hall at the center of Úlfsstaðir. He approaches it, as wary as its namesake. Vargholl. The Wolf's Hall. He takes the steps to the open doors slowly. The light is no longer entirely harsh and white. Not here. Here, upon the threshold, it is suffused with vile yellows and dirty reds, the colors of suppuration, of infection.

And he is not alone.

He threads among shadows; strange silhouettes move around him like figures wrought of smoke. They move slowly. So slowly. And at the heart of each one is a tiny candle-flicker of light. It is a reflection of their souls, he reckons. They are weak, ephemeral; they will die in a score of years, give or take. These shadow-figures seem oblivious to their fate. Like cold sap, they roll toward whatever Doom lies beyond those doors, their frail soul-candles dancing with sadistic glee.

He follows, crossing the threshold, weaving among them. He recognizes the place. It's not the hall of his people, but rather the atrium of a hymn-singers' basilica. What was it called? Saint Peter's? This is Rome, on the far side of the Tiber River, on the hill called Mons Vaticanus. And these shadow-forms are beggars, lepers, and thieves. Even so, the lamps of Yggðrasil burn overhead, like a field of jewels strewn against the black velvet of heaven.

The light, here, is white and pure, but also filthy with red and yellow, the colors of diseased blood and bile. They war against one another. There is a throng of shadows at the center of the atrium. Their soul-lights are stronger, fueled by anger and giddy with the promise of violence. They mob around a solitary oak tree. It is the source of the white, of the pure. Its light is the radiance of the sun, reflecting off the ice fields of the uttermost North, white and blinding and as cold as death. Its purity carries the astringence of the sea, the bite of salt water against lacerated skin.

It is waiting, this Tree.

THE DOOM OF ODIN

It is waiting for him.

Through the sea of drifting shadows, he apprehends the source of the diseased light, the jaundiced yellows and sickly reds: it comes from a large shadow sitting on the steps leading to the cathedral proper. He looks upon that source and feels the hatred surging within. It is a well of darkness, and its soul is a raging bonfire of disease, where angry red weals of light spread from that infectious heart to corrupt those lesser shadows. It feeds upon them, snuffs their measly light and leaves them hollow. The perfect vessels for its corruption.

A second, smaller shadow sits alongside it—like a hound to its master. It is a part of the whole, but separate. And he realizes with clarity how closely the two are intertwined. That is his enemy. That is his quarry.

The shadows are most densely packed near the Tree, their flickering souls lost amid the blinding radiance. He threads among them. They dance and cavort like frozen motes of dust, each movement an eternity. One is caught in the act of reeling away. He grins. That shadow will be missing half his blasted nose. He moves to the Tree. There is an absence of light, a void bearing his shape, hanging from one limb, and he knows instinctively that is where he must be.

Through the glare, he can just barely make out the face of a titan—bearded, its planes and angles composed of all of nature—ice and frost, green growing things, water, clouds. It is not a kind face. It is the face of thunderous storms, the face of lighting; it is the face of boiling seas and the steam arising from vents in the earth. It is the face of earthquakes and red-hot magma, the face of crushing glaciers and flesh-freezing cold. It is brutal. It is implacable. And it is angry.

But it is patient. The Tree waits. Its patience is the patience of the earth. His patience, though, is the patience of fire. He knows what he must do. And so he does it. He cracks the tendons in his neck, rolls the tension from his shoulders, and moves his body into the void that is shaped like him . . .

And finds there is a long-seax buried in his chest. It is an annoyance, nothing more. With bound hands, he reaches up and starts to pull that blade free.

The diseased shadow, the well of darkness, takes note. It sits up straighter. It realizes something is amiss. The lesser shadow recoils from its master, sensing its rising choler. Clouds boil and seethe overhead, hiding the glorious lights of Yggðrasil.

The blade scrapes through pierced bone. The path of the wound heals as the long-seax is removed. The edges of his myriad lesser injuries glow with white light and knit together, leaving new scars behind. He feels a strangling noose around his neck, rough and abrasive rope; the muscles sheathing his neck and protecting his throat flex like iron cables, and they resist the bite of the noose.

He feels the touch of the Tree, feather light, like the caress of a stray leaf. They exchange no words. None are needed. Both of them know what's at stake, and they both know what is expected of them.

The last bit of the long-seax's blade slides free of his body . . .

When Grimnir's bound hands finished drawing Hátr from his chest, the radiance of the spirit world vanished. What replaced it was the feculent light of a bonfire. Its crackling flames ran the gamut of greasy and unclean hues— from blood red to bilious orange to purulent yellow. Those drifting shadows lit from within by their meager soul-candles resolved into a horde of grimy and diseased beggars, many of them already showing signs of the wyrm's pestilence. Around him, the landscape came into sharp, if smoke-hazed, focus: this was the atrium of Saint Peter's basilica, weed-choked, its broken columns draped in fiery-hued ivy. And Grimnir was hanging by his neck from the branches of an oak tree that grew in the ruined and broken basin of a fountain at the center of the atrium.

Time was a frozen sliver, a single thread from a larger tapestry teased out and examined. The nearest beggars were jeering and hooting at their chief's misfortune; their chief reeled away from Grimnir, half his nose missing and blood spraying from the ragged hole with each curse. None of them appeared to notice Grimnir, who stood on the tips of his toes with his long-seax clutched in his bound hands—the long-seax that had only moments before been buried to the hilt in his heart. They did not notice the rising wind, the roiling clouds overhead, or the tremble of the earth as the hill of Mons Vaticanus swelled with tectonic fury.

But Odin took note. The Allfather bolted to his feet, wrath blazing from his single eye. In his shadow, Níðhöggr hissed and arched its back.

Grimnir knew he had only a score of heartbeats to act. With a singular clarity of purpose, he reached up with his bound hands and sawed through the rope holding him up; those tough fibers parted like cobwebs under the edge of Hátr. The rope broke with a snap. Landing on his feet, he bent and slashed the scraps of his gambeson that the beggars had used to bind his ankles. These, too, the blade cut like they were nothing. Finally, with his teeth, he ripped the leather straps—taken from his weapons belt—from about his wrists, and straightened.

Only then did the mass of beggars realize something was amiss. Shouts and curses erupted from the mob; their chief whirled back around, blood sheeting down his face and a murderous light dancing in his eyes. He lunged for Grimnir.

And Grimnir put Hátr's diamond-hard point through the beggar-chief's open mouth, punching it through the back of his throat and into the base of his brain. The man dropped like a sack of oats.

"Níðhöggr!" Grimnir roared, flicking blood from his blade as he leveled it at the wyrm. Deafening crashes of thunder accompanied his flint-hard voice; the earth trembled. The oak tree burst into light—not fire, but the actinic white light of chained lightning. All around, the beggars and the lepers blenched and cowered. Those nearest the gatehouse stampeded for the doors leading away from the atrium, screaming and yammering with fright.

Amid this chaotic spectacle, mighty Odin stood alone, a towering titan. He slung his slouch hat aside, revealing fey locks of gray hair—hung with feathers of raven, hawk, and eagle—and a tangled beard. His solitary eye was the blue of the Northern skies. He flung back his cloak, revealing silvered mail, his weapons belt festooned with the scalps and heads of his enemies. His staff sloughed off its glamour, becoming the iron-headed spear, Gungnir.

The ground shook as he trod into Grimnir's path.

Behind the war-girded Allfather, Níðhöggr slunk away, dragging itself along by its powerful forelegs. Its wedge-shaped head turned a moment, glaring at the *skrælingr* with unvarnished hate. And then it was gone, vanished into the gloom of the ruined basilica.

Odin's voice throbbed with the whir of kettledrums and the brazen call of horns. He matched Grimnir's stance, leveling Gungnir at him.

"*I am done with thee, | filth-born skrælingr!*
Thy sorcery is at an end!
Go back—"

Odin had no chance to finish. He was mid-threat when a blast of harsh white light erupted from the ground *under* his feet. A blinding, branching tree of lightning engulfed him, reeking of frost and salt-spume.

Grimnir knew his call to action when he saw it. As the giant lord of the Æsir reeled, he was off his blocks, sprinting and shouldering his way through the throng. He trampled beggars underfoot; their hands clutched at him, but slid off his sweat-slick hide. Grimnir was naked to the waist; they'd even taken his boots, leaving him clad in naught but ragged trousers. The only bit of iron he carried was Hátr, the blade inverted as he powered through their fleeing ranks.

He gained the steps to the interior of the basilica. For an instant, he sensed Odin's presence looming over him, reaching for him. He imagined Gungnir speeding for his heart. But that blow never fell. Those otherworldly hands never touched him. He heard a roar—and heard it choked off as a lance of oak pierced the Allfather's mailed side. From the corner of his eye, Grimnir saw the titanic Lord of Ásgarðr fall; he saw sinuous branches loop about one arm and his legs. Only Gungnir was left free, and it turned from Grimnir and lashed out at the now-colossal oak, its roots and bole engorged with the power of the earth itself.

Gungnir's dwarf-forged blade skittered from the iron-hard bark of the tree.

"*Ymir!*" the Allfather bellowed, thunder in his voice. Chains of lightning rippled from the heavens; lashing rain fell, and hail stung and pierced like sling-stones of ice. That slumbering god of the earth—made by Odin's own perfidy at the dawn of the ages—did not relent. Its endurance was the endurance of mountains. Their struggle was a clash of titans, earth versus air, and here, in this place, Ymir was the master of both . . .

Without a second glance, Grimnir cleared the last few steps and passed into the shadow-haunted gloom of the ruined basilica. He skidded to a stop, his body hunched, nostrils flaring. The place was cavernous. Its walls were brick, and its wooden rafters and beams were upheld by hundreds of mismatched marble columns; its floor was a patchwork of mosaics and scavenged tile. But four decades of neglect had left its mark. Its structure was crumbling, its wood rotting and worm-eaten. In the years since its abandonment, lightning had charred a hole through the clerestory; tremors of the earth had toppled columns and collapsed underground crypts, ruptured tiles and scattered mosaics. This damage and decay allowed nature to regain a foothold.

Ivy wound serpentine up columns, while weeds grew among the dislodged tiles. Algae-scummed water pooled in the low places, made worse by the torrential rains summoned by the strife and struggle of ancient gods, outside. It sluiced through the gaps in the roof. Mold bloomed across once-grand frescoes. The air was dim and murky; it smelled of bird droppings and old incense, and the leavings of wild dogs.

Grimnir moved cautiously down the long nave leading to the altar. He was wound tight, like a spring. The *crack* and *thrum* of hail against the roof of the basilica was deafening, its echo amplified by the vast open spaces. He skirted the edges of the hole in the roof. He spared a glance at the lightning-scarred rafters, his raking gaze seething with hate. He wanted Níðhöggr, that wretched Malice-Striker; he knew his prey was close . . .

That stench of it, the reek of sulfur and grave-rot, was the only warning the *skrælingr* had. Níðhöggr lunged for him through a curtain of rainwater. For all the speed his reflexes could conjure from corded muscles and iron-laced tendons, Grimnir could not avoid the wyrm's striking maw. In that fraction of a heartbeat between recognition and impact, Grimnir had his first good look at the Malice-Striker since their confrontation on the wooden bridge at Holmgarðr, on the Volkhov River in the land of the Kievan Rus, some seventy years before.

A great, wedge-shaped head thrust into view, bristling with bony spines, its mouth yawning to reveal long ivory fangs. One eye socket was merely an empty hole, black and menacing. The other gleamed with an unclean emerald light. Rivulets of water ran from the age-blackened scales sheathing its neck—two meters long and sinuous, scarred from countless battles. The body that followed had once been the size of a Viking longship; at Holmgarðr, it had been the size of an ox with a spiked tail. Now, it was barely as large as a draft horse and its tail was smooth, like a snake's. What hadn't changed, however, was the overlapping plates of bone armoring its body. The thing half-slithered, half-pulled itself along on two powerful forelegs, both tipped with iron-hard talons.

It struck from his left side, his blind side; the impact was like a battering ram. Níðhöggr's fangs pierced the flesh of Grimnir's chest and back, at the juncture of his neck and left shoulder. Driven by powerful jaws, those curved ivory daggers knifed through muscle and bone. Air whistled from Grimnir's punctured lung; dark black arterial blood splattered the mosaics underfoot. Anyone else but a scion of the Elder World would have died, then, their life's blood pumping down the greedy maw of Odin's wyrm. But the son of Bálegyr was hewn from sterner stuff, from whalebone and gristle. The agony inflicted by those knifelike fangs was but fuel for the forge of his hate. And his was a hate that burned bright. It reflected in his solitary eye: a murderous gleam like a beacon, drawing Death in with the promise of slaughter.

And with a gurgled roar, Grimnir staggered in the beast's jaws, tearing those punctures even further as he twisted and brought the cold iron blade of Hátr to bear. The long-seax punched into the side of Níðhöggr's head; it crunched through scale and bone to pierce the jelly-filled sack of the wyrm's remaining eye. Green ichor gushed from it, and that sickly emerald glow was forever extinguished. The beast bellowed and brayed.

But before Grimnir could lean on the blade, to drive it deeper into the wyrm's skull and pierce the gray curds of its brain, Níðhöggr slung him aside. He cartwheeled through the murky air; bone crunched as he slammed into a column and slid to the floor. Grimnir lay there like a dead thing, blood leaking from the wreckage of his body. Even so, he was alive—his chest rose and fell, though with effort, and his singular eye burned with a hatred for all life. Somehow, he'd managed to keep a tight grip on the hilt of his long-seax. He looked down at it.

Hátr glittered like an iron spike, eager to taste the life of its ancestral enemy.

He raised his gaze and saw his foe, that blasted wyrm. The thing lashed its head from side to side, raised one taloned foot to rake at the blood-dripping socket. Outside, the world had fallen silent; thunder ceased its reverberations, and the rain and hail slacked off. He did not see the mailed form of Odin striding through the wreckage of the basilica, so Ymir must have triumphed. Now, it was his turn.

"How's it feel, *arsegót?*" Grimnir gasped, coughing blood. His wounds were mortal. This, he knew. But through the blinding agony of ripped organs and broken bones, the *skrælingr* managed to stagger to his feet. He swayed, his left arm hanging useless, Hátr clutched in his right; black blood stained the floor under him, wreathing him in the stench of wet iron. "You get to meet your end here, you wretch. In the Nailed God's house," he said. "And for what? What did that one-eyed raven-starver offer you?"

Níðhöggr's head shot up. Its forked tongue flicked between those blood-slimed fangs, tasting the stale air of the basilica. Dampness misted from the wyrm's broad nostrils as it exhaled. "*Blood,*" it hissed. It half-crawled, half-slithered in Grimnir's direction, letting its tongue guide it. "*I can smell yours, níðingr. I can smell your fear.*"

"That taste is all you're going to get, wyrm," Grimnir said. The column he'd struck was already partially dislodged, sitting half off its pedestal thanks to some tremor of the earth. The individual drums of marble were also askew, each weighing as much as the stones of a siege machine. With a malicious grin, Grimnir wiped his hand across his torso, then slathered that blood on the marble. Again and again. When it ran so thick as to obscure the flutings of the column, Grimnir faded into the shadow alongside it.

Unseen, he coughed and spat, cursing and wheezing. Níðhöggr heard. Níðhöggr tasted his distress. And the wyrm sped up, its talons digging at the tiles of the basilica. "*There will be no Ragnarök for you, níðingr,*" it whispered. A drawn breath later, the blinded beast struck, aiming for the site where it smelled the most blood.

Its fangs splintered against Egyptian marble even as its momentum rammed it through part of the teetering column's shaft. In an explosion of dust, drums of fluted marble crashed down on the wyrm's back, compressing it against the pedestal. From above, vertebrae snapped; from below, ribs caved in like kindling. The thing's wounded roar echoed through the cavernous heart of the basilica. Before those powerful legs could drag it free, however, the *skrælingr* emerged from the shadows and struck.

Hátr pierced the wyrm's throat from below, near the base of its skull. That blade, forged from the ancient shards of Sárklungr, the Wound-Thorn, carved through Níðhöggr's flesh, half-severing the beast's wedge-shaped head. Black and stinking blood pulsed from the wound. Grimnir's bare heel stomped Malice-Striker's neck down, pinning it against a fallen drum of marble.

Twice more, Hátr rose and fell before the wyrm's head came free of its neck. Though pinned by the parts of the fallen column, Níðhöggr's lower body thrashed and writhed in its death throes. Grimnir, though, wasn't done. He put Hátr between his teeth, oblivious of the wyrm's blood, and cast about for a spot upon which to finish this.

The capital of the fallen column lay upside down, half a yard away, its carved acanthus leaves once painted realistic shades of green, now caked in dust and grime. It would do; onto this, Grimnir wrestled Níðhöggr's severed head, its drippings staining the marble shades of black.

Grimnir took the blade from between his teeth. To the heavens, he roared: "Hear me, O Ymir! Bear witness, Father of Giants and Lord of Frosts! Corpse-maker and Life-quencher, I am called; the Bringer of Night, the Son of the Wolf and Brother of the Serpent. The Hooded One, I am; the Kin-slayer and the Slaughterer of Witches! The Butcher of the *Morðavættir*! I am Grimnir Bálegyr's son, and this is my oath fulfilled!" And with a titanic stroke, he drove Hátr down between the wyrm's eyes, burying it to the hilt in Níðhöggr's misshapen skull. An eerie gray mist drifted from the wyrm's gaping eye sockets. For a moment, it looked like the pale silhouette of a man—a figure in a slouch hat and a voluminous cloak—and then it was gone, shredded apart by a stray breath of air.

Silence. Grimnir drew a racking breath. And then . . .

He heard the bellow of a brazen horn, deep and reverberating. It came from the earth and from the sky. In its drawn-out notes he heard the roar of voices, and the whirr of kettledrums. Its echo was the rasp of unnumbered swords being drawn from their scabbards, and the creak of countless bows being made ready to loose; the clash of axes on shield bosses, the rattle of spears, the jangle of harness, and the howl of wolves. It was the Gjallarhorn, and it called the Nine Worlds to war . . .

Grimnir sank down, his back against the makeshift altar. He could barely breathe. One lung was gone; the other was filling with blood. What was left in his veins leaked from the ragged holes in his chest and back. His left shoulder and arm, his left hip, all were broken, and their jagged ends grated with each movement.

Through holes torn in the clerestory, he saw the sky lighten, a harbinger of the dawn. At the edge of his blurring vision, he could just make out the dead husk of the oak tree. Part of its trunk, now, was a desiccated cadaver. *Faugh!*

THE DOOM OF ODIN

The balance was put right. The call of the Gjallarhorn was proof of that. Ragnarök was coming . . .

And with a final cough of laughter, Grimnir—the last of Bálegyr's brood to plague Miðgarðr, last to prey on the sons of Adam—toppled onto his side and died.

EPILOGUE

The sound of his own voice woke him. Not a shout, nor a roar... but a whisper. "*Skaði*," he'd said, and in its faint echo was the melancholic reflection of unhealed pain. And though he awoke, he did not bolt upright, or even bother to move. He simply lay there, rough boards beneath his naked shoulders, and listened to the sounds of hammers ringing on anvils and the *slish* of stone wheels honing blades. It was the music of war, and the players were getting their instruments in tune.

Grimnir opened his eyes. He recognized the rafters of Varghǫll, smoke-stained and black with age. He did not wonder how he'd gotten from the bridge at the foot of Kaunheimr to here, across Nástrond. He presumed it was Gífr's doing and left it at that. He lay on one of the long trestle tables, a mass of aching muscles and bruised flesh. He'd died his last death upon Miðgarðr; now, all that was left was the shield-breaking at Vígríðr. Grimnir exhaled.

The light filtering through the clerestory overhead was gray and smoky, even though the fires of the hall were cold. He coughed, rolled to one side, and spat on the rush-strewn floor. Though he felt as though a team of *scrags* had dragged him through the arse-end of a dead goat, at least he was whole, reasonably hale, and where he was supposed to be. What was on his mind, now, was getting a horn of mead, some meat and bread, and finding out the news from Gífr. He sat up, looked around . . .

And saw a dark-visaged figure staring back at him from the dais, from the now-singular throne of Úlfsstaðir. This newcomer sat with one leg thrown over the arm of the chair. A giant in truth, it was. A *jötunn,* with skin the color of deep glacial ice, a well-trimmed beard, and hair like flames. Scabbed wounds healed upon his face, and something as malicious as it was angry lurked in his glittering eyes. He met Grimnir's gaze, and the *skrælingr* knew instinctively whose presence he was in.

This was the Tangled God.

"You said something, just now," Loki rumbled, as though they were the oldest of friends in the midst of a conversation. "A name, I believe. Whose was it?"

Grimnir's good eye narrowed. "Skaði."

"Ah, Skaði." Loki nodded, as though the name meant something to him. "She was Skæfloc's daughter?"

"She was, though she disowned the wretch."

"And she was your mate?"

Grimnir looked away. "No," he replied, after a moment.

"A pity," the Tangled God said, removing his leg from the arm of the chair and hunching forward. "I'm told I have you to thank for my freedom."

Grimnir shrugged. "Ymir was the one behind it, and that bastard knows his iron from his slag."

The Tangled God chuckled. "Well, I'll not owe that one a boon, so it must be you. Ask of me what you will, Grimnir Kin-slayer. Though . . ." He paused, his sharp black eyes narrowing as he apprehended Grimnir's heart. "Not even *I* can bring back the dead who walk beyond the Nine Worlds."

Grimnir's heavy brow furrowed. "Then, give me mail and weapons, my lord. Give me enemies and space to slaughter them. If this be the end, then let me make such an end as to shake the very bones of Yggðrasil!"

Loki's luminous eyes grew distant, as though he could see what awaited them on the loom of Fate. "Mail and weapons you shall have, and a place of honor. For soon we sail for the killing fields of Vígríðr and the Twilight of the Gods. The Elder World must pass away, son of Bálegyr. It must die as it was born, in fire and in blood and in the doing of fell deeds. And we must pass with it." The Tangled God gestured for Grimnir to follow, and the two of them walked to the doors of Varghǫll. They stood in silhouette against the burning lights of Yggðrasil. "Our blood will fertilize a New World—a world where we will be nothing but legends, myths told to children, nursery rhymes, and dark memories." Loki sighed. "But that is fine. A few will remember us, Grimnir Kin-slayer. They will remember the songs written by blade and by axe, and they will tell of our deeds around their fires. And in the telling, in those death-songs, we will live forever . . ."

**Here Ends
the Saga of
Grimnir**

Acknowledgments

The journey of a thousand pages often begins with a single word. For me, that word was *Grimnir*. His name was my lamp in the dark—a burning, hateful lamp, but a lamp, nonetheless. That old wretch kept me going, chiding me from the shadows about finishing his blasted Saga. Even when he realized what the English word *ending* really meant, he kept at me. This is his book, and may it sing of his deeds for many years to come.

And though it's not quite a thousand pages long, it has been a journey. Along the way, I've had the most amazing support system. This book quite simply would not have existed without my editor at St. Martin's, Pete Wolverton. During the Dark Years, he and my wonderful agent, Bob Mecoy, kept the fires burning while my mind wandered far afield, missing deadline after deadline. They felt the end result was worth the headache of dealing with a *skrælingr*-obsessed ball of neuroses, and I thank them for that.

This is also my wife, Shannon's, book. She's part cheerleader, part brawler,

ACKNOWLEDGMENTS

and she'll throw hands at anyone who gets in the way of me and my words. Though not quite a yellow-eyed harridan of war, she would definitely raise the mead horn with Skaði and Skríkja, if she could. This is for her—for her steadfast love, her support, and her uppercuts when my foot-dragging gets in between her and her dream of a Hobbit-hole.

A special thanks goes out to Christian Cameron, who answered a spear-versus-long-seax question with a video of how it might happen.

My readers have kept me going. From my excellent crew of first readers to you, Gentle Reader, who nabbed this in a bookstore and made it this far. To Rusty Burke, Josh Olive, Vincent Darlage, Tom Doolan, Stan Wagenaar, Darrell Grizzle, Matt "Alpha" John, Logan Whitney; to Jeff Bryant, Scott Hall, James Allen, David Doyle, Joseph Crow, Tony Dallape, and Gregory Amato . . . you guys rock. Thank you for your insights and your enthusiasm.

This book is for all of you, my friends.

SCOTT ODEN
31 JANUARY 2023

GLOSSARY

Æsir (EYE-sur)
The Norse gods; inhabitants of Ásgarðr.

Álfar (ALE-far)
Norse elves; singular, *álfr*.

Álfheimr (ALE-fame-ur)
Realm of the Elves; one of the Nine Worlds.

Angrboða (AHN-ger-bo-tha)
A giantess; mother of Fenrir, Jörmungandr, and Hel.

Arsegót (ARE-se-goot)
Profanity; plural, *arsegótar*. Means *asshole*.

Ásgarðr (ASS-gar-thur)
Home of the Æsir; one of the Nine Worlds.

Atla (AT-la)
Giantess; one of the Lokaean Witches.

Bálegyr (BAAL-uh-gear)
"The Baleful One." One of the Nine Fathers of the *kaunar*; Grimnir's father.

Blártunga (BLAAR-toon-guh)
A *scrag*.

Bölthorn (BUL-thorn)
Kaunr; Mánavargr's herald.

GLOSSARY

Dáinn (DAYN)
Dwarf, a smith of silver; Bálegyr's birth-name. Youngest of the three sons of Thrár.

Dreki (DRECK-ee)
Kaunr; one of the Nine Fathers. Called "Dreki of the Nine Fingers."

Dvergar (DWAIR-gar)
Norse dwarves; singular, *dvergr.*

Elðr (EL-thur)
Kaunr; one of Kjallandi's lads.

***Fak þú* (FAK THUU)**
Expletive; sassier version of "screw you."

Fenrir (FEN-rear)
The Wolf of Ragnarök; one of Angrboða's monstrous children. Fated to slay Odin.

Frægr (FRAY-gur)
A *scrag;* one of Grimnir's brothers.

Gífr (GHEE-fur)
Kaunr; Kjallandi's eldest son and Grimnir's maternal uncle. Herald of Loki.

Ginnungagap (GIN-noon-ga-gap)
The Howling Dark; the chaos that existed before Creation.

Gjallarbrú (GYALL-are-brew)
Bridge over the River Gjöll leading to Helheimr; guarded by the giantess Móðguðr.

Gjallarhorn (GYALL-are-horn)
The horn that calls the Nine Worlds to Ragnarök.

Gjálp (GYAALP)
Giantess; one of the Lokaean Witches.

Gjöll (GYULE)
The lake surrounding Nástrond; also, the river it feeds into, separating Helheimr and Jötunheimr.

Grimnir (GRIM-near)
Skrælingr; our hero.

Hárbarðr (HAIR-bar-thur)
Giant; master of the Bone Ferry.

Hátr (HAY-tur)
"Hate." Grimnir's long-seax; forged from the shards of Sárklungr.

GLOSSARY

Hel (HELL)
Mistress of the Dead and queen of Helheimr; one of Angrboða's monstrous children.

Helheimr (HELL-haim-ur)
Realm of the Dead; one of the Nine Worlds.

Hólmganga (HOLM-gang-uh)
Ritualized trial by combat.

Hræholt (HRAY-holt)
The Corpse-Wood; graveyard of the *landvættir*, under Hylðemoer's protection.

Hrauðnir (HROTH-near)
Kaunr; one of the Nine Fathers.

Hrungnir (HRUNG-near)
Skrælingr; Grimnir's brother closest in age.

Hylðemoer (HILL-the-mow-er)
The Elder Mother; guardian of the Hræholt.

Iðuna (ITH-oon-uh)
Kaunr; the Witch of Kaunheimr. Grimnir's maternal grandmother.

Imðr (IM-thur)
Giantess; one of the Lokaean Witches.

Jarðvegur (YARTH-vee-gur)
Hrauðnir's hall on Nástrond, located in the sunken fens inland from Gjöll's Inlet.

Jarnfjall (YARN-fee-yall)
The Iron Mountain; Angrboða's hilltop fortress in the Ironwood, a forest of Jötunheimr.

Járnviðja (YAARN-veeth-ya)
Troll; mother of the troll-women of the Ironwood.

Jörmungandr (YOUR-moon-gan-dur)
The Serpent of Miðgarðr; one of Angrboða's monstrous children. Fated to slay Thor.

Jórsalahaf (YOUR-sal-uh-haf)
"Jerusalem Sea"; the Mediterranean Sea according to the Vikings.

Jötunheimr (YO-tun-haim-ur)
Land of the Frost Giants; one of the Nine Worlds.

Jötunn (YO-tunn)
Giants; plural, *jötnar*.

GLOSSARY

Kaunar (KAWN-are)
The Plague Folk; Grimnir's people. Singular, *kaunr*. On Nástrond, *kaunar* are those who died in the Battle of the Ironwood, in and around Jarnfjall; the highest caste.

Kaunheimr (KAWN-haim-ur)
Mánavargr's fortress-city on Nástrond.

Kjallandi (KYAL-lan-dee)
Kaunr; Grimnir's maternal grandfather. One of the Nine Fathers.

Köttr (KOTTUR)
A *scrag*.

Landvættir (LAND-vite-tur)
Spirits of the land, large and small; singular, *landvættr*.

Langbarðaland (LANG-bartha-land)
Italy, according to the Vikings.

Loki (LOW-kee)
Trickster god of the Norse; creator of the *kaunar*. Called "Father Loki" or "the Tangled God."

Lútr (LEWT-ur)
Kaunr; one of the Nine Fathers.

Mánavargr (MAAN-ah-var-gur)
Kaunr; former cupbearer to Father Loki. One of the Nine Fathers.

Maugrónðr (MAW-groon-thur)
"The Corpse-Hammer." Bálegyr's mace.

Miðgarðr (MYTH-gar-thur)
The realm of Men; one of the Nine Worlds.

Miklagarðr (MICK-la-gar-thur)
The Stone City; Viking name for Constantinople.

Mímir (MEEM-ur)
Giant; a severed head who guards the font of all wisdom.

Mímisbrunnr (MEEM-is-brew-nur)
The Well of Mímir; the font of all wisdom.

Móðguðr (MOOTH-goo-thur)
Giantess who guards the bridge Gjallarbrú.

Morðavættir (MOR-tha-vie-tur)
Spirits of murdered travelers; Atla's guardians. Singular, *morðavættr*.

Múspellsheimr (MOOSE-pell-shay-mer)
Realm of the Fire Giants; one of the Nine Worlds.

Næfr (NAYF-ur)
Kaunr; Grimnir's eldest brother.

Naglfar (NAGEL-far)
The Ship of Nails (meaning human fingernails, harvested from the dead) that will launch at Ragnarök.

Naglfari (NAGEL-far-ee)
Kaunr; originally of mixed *dvergar* and *álfar* blood. One of the Nine Fathers.

Náinn (NAYN)
Dwarf, a smith of iron; Grimnir's paternal uncle. One of the three sons of Thrár.

Náli (NAHL-ee)
Dwarf; Náinn's son.

Nár (NAR)
Expletive in Grimnir's native language; meaning varies according to usage.

Nástrond (NAS-trond)
Island in the middle of Lake Gjöll; site of the *kaunar* afterlife. Grimnir's folk can return to life only if they die on the soil of Nástrond.

Niðafjoll (NEE-tha-fee-yall)
Range of mountains bordering Helheimr.

Niðavellir (NEE-tha-vell-ur)
Realm of the dwarves; one of the Nine Worlds.

Níðhöggr (NEETH-hoag-gur)
The Malice-Striker; dragon who lurks at the roots of Yggðrasil.

Níðingr (NEETH-eng-ur)
Deadly Norse insult; using it means violence.

Njól (NYAWL)
Kaunr; one of the Nine Fathers.

Odin (OH-den)
The Allfather, Lord of Ásgarðr; chief of the Norse Gods.

Raðbolg (WRATH-bolg)
Kaunr; son of Kjallandi. Grimnir's maternal uncle.

Ragnarök (RAG-nah-rock)
The Twilight of the Gods, heralded by the Gjallarhorn; Armageddon.

Ratatoskr (RAT-uh-toe-skur)
The chattering squirrel who foments trouble along the branches of Yggðrasil; a bit of a gossip.

Reðr (RETH-ur)
A *scrag*.

Rúmaborg (ROOM-ah-borg)
Viking name for the city of Rome.

Sægrár (SIGH-graar)
Kaunr; bastard brother of Grimnir.

Salfangi (SAL-fang-ee)
Kaunr; called "the Eunuch." Grimnir's brother.

Sárklungr (SARK-lung-ur)
"The Wound-Thorn"; sword forged by the dwarf Náinn. Was taken by Kjallandi, then passed to Grimnir through Raðbolg. It was reforged into Hátr.

Scrag (SKRAG)
A *kaunr* who died before reaching maturity; lowest caste on Nástrond. The equivalent of a goblin.

Seiðr (SEE-thur)
Sorcery.

Sjóvættir (SHOW-vite-tur)
Spirits of the water, great and small; they lurk off the shores of Nástrond.

Skaði (SKA-thee)
Skrælingr; Skæfloc's daughter. Died when Grimnir was a child.

Skæfloc (SKEF-lock)
Kaunr; one of Hrauðnir's folk.

Skrælingar (SKRA-lin-gar)
Norse name for *kaunar*; singular, *skrælingr*. On Nástrond, those *kaunar* who escaped the Battle of the Ironwood to hide on Miðgarðr. Considered lower caste than "true" *kaunar*.

Skrælingsalr (SKRA-ling-sal-ur)
Lútr's hall on Nástrond; located in the mountains in the center of the island.

Skríkja (SKREEK-sha)
Kaunr; Grimnir's mother.

GLOSSARY

Snaga (SNA-guh)
A *scrag*; his name means "Snag-axe."

Stoðva (STOTH-va)
"Stop." A word of power; will paralyze an opponent.

Støkkva (STOOK-kva)
"Splinter." A word of power; will shatter wood.

Svartálfaheimr (SVART-ale-fame-ur)
Realm of the Dark Elves; one of the Nine Worlds.

Svartálfar (SVART-ale-far)
Dark elves.

Thráinn (THRAIN)
Dwarf, a smith of gold; Grimnir's paternal uncle. Eldest of the three sons of Thrár.

Thrár (THRAAR)
Dwarf, master-smith; Thrár the Elder is Grimnir's paternal grandfather. Thrár the Younger is the birth-name of the *scrag* Snaga.

Úlfsstaðir (OOLF-stath-ear)
"The Wolves' Abode." Kjallandi and Bálegyr's fortress in the hills near the coast on Nástrond.

Undiræd (UN-die-ride)
"The Under-Road"; an eerie rift between worlds that takes the form of a tunnel between Nástrond and Jötunheimr.

Vanaheimr (VAN-uh-haim-ur)
Realm of the Vanir; one of the Nine Worlds.

Vanir (VAN-ear)
Older Norse gods, subservient to the Æsir; inhabitants of Vanaheimr.

Vargfœðir (VARG-foeth-ear)
"The Wolf-Feeder"; Naglfari's elf-forged sword.

Varghǫll (VARG-haul)
"The Wolf's Hall"; a stave hall where Kjallandi and Bálegyr jointly rule Úlfsstaðir.

Veðrfölnir (VETH-ur-fyol-near)
The giant hawk who perches atop Yggðrasil; Ratatoskr's ancestral enemy.

Vígríðr (VIG-rith-ur)
The site of Ragnarök and the final battle between gods, giants, heroes, and villains.

Vingameiðr (VING-ah-my-thir)
"Wind-swept"; Mánavargr's hall atop Kaunheimr.

Yggðrasil (YIGG-thra-sill)
The Old Ash; the spine of Norse cosmology. Its branches uphold the Nine Worlds.

Ymir (EE-mer)
The primordial frost giant; slain by Odin and dismembered, his body parts being used to create Miðgarðr and the other Nine Worlds.